"A tale that's sure to keep fans at the edge of their seats . . . a must read." —Darque Reviews

"[Caine] in_____ ____ ___ ____sting ways to ramp up the tension an_____ _____ _____try in a series that's beer___ ____ _____ ____ _____ Man Review

"Exhilara___ _____ _____ and filled with plenty of ____ _____ ____ ____ovides another terrific tale in one of the str____ _____ _____ntasies on the market today." —Midwest Book Review

"Powerful. . . . From the first page to the last, the pulse-pounding action is nonstop. Caine delivers one terrific high-seas adventure." —Romantic Times

"Like every other book in this series, *Cape Storm* is the equivalent of a 300-page adrenaline rush. . . . Caine writes with her trademark flair for action and plot contortions. . . . [An] impeccably written thriller, imaginative and well paced . . . I loved *Cape Storm* from beginning to end. It's another win by Rachel Caine—with the only drawback? Waiting another year for book nine." —The Book Smugglers

Gale Force

"Rachel Caine is still going strong, throwing one curveball after another as she continues to shake up the status quo. She successfully maintains a sense of impending doom and escalating tension as the stakes get ever higher. . . . I really like this series, because it's urban fantasy that . . . tell[s] something exciting and original and ever changing." —SF Site

continued . . .

Books by Rachel Caine

TOTAL ECLIPSE

A WEATHER WARDEN NOVEL

Rachel Caine

A ROC BOOK

ROC

Published by New American Library, a division of
Penguin Group (USA) Inc., 375 Hudson Street,
New York, New York 10014, USA
Penguin Group (Canada), 90 Eglinton Avenue East, Suite 700, Toronto,
Ontario M4P 2Y3, Canada (a division of Pearson Penguin Canada Inc.)
Penguin Books Ltd., 80 Strand, London WC2R 0RL, England
Penguin Ireland, 25 St. Stephen's Green, Dublin 2,
Ireland (a division of Penguin Books Ltd.)
Penguin Group (Australia), 250 Camberwell Road, Camberwell, Victoria 3124,
Australia (a division of Pearson Australia Group Pty. Ltd.)
Penguin Books India Pvt. Ltd., 11 Community Centre, Panchsheel Park,
New Delhi - 110 017, India
Penguin Group (NZ), 67 Apollo Drive, Rosedale, North Shore 0632,
New Zealand (a division of Pearson New Zealand Ltd.)
Penguin Books (South Africa) (Pty.) Ltd., 24 Sturdee Avenue,
Rosebank, Johannesburg 2196, South Africa

Penguin Books Ltd., Registered Offices:
80 Strand, London WC2R 0RL, England

First published by Roc, an imprint of New American Library,
a division of Penguin Group (USA) Inc.

First Printing, August 2010
10 9 8 7 6 5 4 3 2 1

To all the wonderful people who've supported Joanne's adventures through this series—THANK YOU. You all rock.

But I'll single out one, because she was the first to tell me that the idea for Ill Wind *was a good one.*

Thank you, Sharon.

Okay, I lied; I will single out two, because about the time I was going to give up on this whole writing gig, I talked with fantastic writer Joe R. Lansdale, and he gave me the encouragement I needed to keep on defying gravity. Thank you, Joe. And hey, thanks for Bubba Ho-tep, too, while I'm at it.

ACKNOWLEDGMENTS

Joe Bonamassa
Lucienne Diver
Sheila Hanahan Taylor
Felicia Day
P. N. Elrod
Jackie Leaf
Heidi Berthiaume
Charles Armitage
Jackie Kessler
Richelle Mead
Patricia Anthony
R. Cat Conrad—always

What Has Come Before

My name is Joanne Baldwin, and I used to control the weather as a Weather Warden. These days, I can also control the forces of the earth, such as volcanoes and earthquakes, and the forces of fire. Don't ask—it's a long story. Just go with it, okay?

Controlling all those awesome forces sounds like fun, eh? No. Not when it makes you a target for every psycho world-killing danger that comes along.

Good thing I've got my friends at my back—Lewis Orwell, the most powerful Warden on the planet; Cherise, my best (and not supernatural) friend; a wide cast of sometimes dangerous allies who've got their own missions and agendas that don't always match up with mine.

And I've got David, my true love. He's also a supernatural Djinn, the fairy-tale-three-wishes kind, and he's now coruler of the Djinn on Earth.

But not even the most powerful friends in the world can help when real devastation hits. And it hit me and

David, dead center, in our final battle with my old mentor and enemy . . . and it took our power away.

For me, that's an inconvenience.

For David, it's fatal.

I have to find a way to fix this before it's too late to save my beloved—and maybe even humanity, because Mother Nature is waking up . . . and she's *pissed*.

Chapter One

Black corner.

It was the name Wardens—and Djinn—gave to a section of the world that had been scorched by something unnatural; a place where the basic energy that coursed through the world, the pulsebeat of the Earth, no longer existed.

A black corner *looked* fine, but to anyone with sensitivity to power, it was desolate and sterile. Wardens—those who controlled the basic powers of nature—suffered when they were trapped inside one of these dead zones. Still, we got off better than the Djinn.

Djinn died.

We'd been trapped in the massive black corner, sailing hard for the horizon, for days, and it was taking its toll at an increasingly horrible rate.

It was so hard, watching them suffer. It was slow, and painful, and terrifying to watch, and as our cruise ship sailed ever so slowly through the dark, empty seas, trying to get outside the supernatural blast radius, I began to wonder whether we would make it at all. The New Djinn—the Djinn who'd been born human and had become Djinn during some large-scale disasters—were in a lot of pain, and slipping away.

Still, they fared better than the Old Djinn. Original, eternal, with no real ties to humanity at all—they declined far faster. In a very real sense, they couldn't exist on their own, without a direct connection to power—a connection that was nowhere to be found now, even though we were many miles out from the site of the disastrous ending to our fight with my old enemy. He'd opened a gateway to another dimension, and what had come through had almost destroyed me and David; it had definitely blasted the entire area for hundreds of miles in all directions.

I couldn't imagine what the consequences of that were going to be. It was a terrible disaster, and I felt responsible. Hell, who was I kidding? I *was* responsible, beyond any shadow of a doubt. I was recovering from the after-effects of the long battle and the injuries I'd gathered along the way, but that was secondary to the guilt I felt about how I'd handled things.

I should have been *better*. If I'd been better, none of this would have happened. I wouldn't be watching my friends and allies suffer. I wouldn't be watching helplessly as the best of them, the ones who'd given the most, lost pieces of themselves.

Dying in slow motion.

Lewis Orwell, the head of the Wardens, my old friend, the strongest human being I'd ever met . . . Lewis had developed a perpetual, deep-chested cough that sounded wet and thick. Pneumonia, maybe. He looked as if he hadn't rested in weeks, and he probably hadn't. His reserves were used up, his body beginning to shut down in protest.

And still he was up in the middle of the night, sitting with the Djinn. Offering them what little comfort he could. There weren't so many of them . . . not now. We'd seen three of them die in the past twenty-four hours. The ones who were left were sinking fast.

Djinn were exotic and beautiful and unbelievably powerful. Seeing them laid so low was heart-wrenching. I didn't know how Lewis could stand it, really. The misery hit me in a thick, sticky wave as I limped into the small infirmary, and I had to stop in the doorway and breathe in and out slowly to calm myself. No sense in going overwrought into this mess. It wouldn't help anyone.

Lewis was sitting in a chair next to a bed that held a small, still human form the size of a child. Venna—who'd always borne an uncanny resemblance to the famous Alice, of Lewis Carroll renown—was still a pretty thing, with fine blond hair and big blue eyes. The supernatural shine that usually seemed a few shades too vivid for human eyes was missing now. She looked sick and afraid, and it hurt me deeply.

I sank down on the other side of her bed and took her hand. Her gaze, which had been fixed on the ceiling, slowly moved to rest on me. She felt cold. Her fingers flexed just a little on mine, and I felt rather than saw the faintest ghost of a smile.

"Hey, kid," I said, and smoothed her hair back from her face. "How are you?"

It was self-evident how she was doing, but I didn't know what else to say. Nothing I could do was going to help. Like Lewis, I was utterly helpless. Useless.

"Okay," she whispered. It seemed to be a great effort for her to form the word, and I saw a shudder go through her small body. I tucked the blanket closer around her, although I knew it wasn't going to help. The chill that had sunk into her couldn't be banished by warm covers and hugs and hot toddies.

We'd tried putting the Djinn on the deck of the ship,

hoping the sunlight would help revive them, but it had seemed to make things worse. Venna—who had been alive as long as the Earth, as far as I could tell—had *cried* from the sheer, desperate agony of being in the sun and not being able to absorb its energy.

It had been awful, and here, inside, she didn't seem as distressed. That was something, at least.

We were no longer trying to save them. We were just managing their decline.

Venna's china blue eyes drifted shut, though it wasn't exactly a natural sleep; she was conserving what energy remained to her. The Old Djinn burned it faster than the New Djinn, it seemed. We'd already lost the only other Old Djinn on board—a closemouthed sort I'd never gotten to know by name.

And, in truth, I loved Venna. I cared about her deeply—in the way you'd care for a beautiful, exotic, very dangerous animal who'd allowed you to become its friend. I'd never thought of her as fragile; I'd seen her slam tanker trucks aside with a wave, and fight monsters without getting so much as a hangnail.

It was hard to see her look so helpless.

Lewis looked almost as bad—worn down and fighting to keep himself together. I met his eyes, which were bloodshot and fever bright. "Go to bed," I told him. "I'll stay with them for a while."

"And do what?" he snapped, which hurt; I saw the flare of panic in his face, quickly tamped down. He hadn't meant to say it, though of course he'd been thinking it. They were all thinking it. "Sorry, Jo. I mean—"

"I know what you mean," I said softly. "But the fact is that you're just as handicapped as I am right now, and you're punishing yourself by wearing yourself down to nothing. Lewis, you can't. You *can't*. When we get out of this, the Wardens will need you more than ever. You can't be running on fumes when the rest of them need you. This is going to get a lot worse. We both know it."

I could see that he wanted to tell me not to preach to him, but he bit his tongue this time. He knew I was right (not that it would stop him from arguing), and on some level, he was aware that he was hurting himself as punishment. Like me, he felt that he deserved it.

He looked down at Venna. I saw it in his face, all that weariness, that guilt, and a fair amount of bitter self-loathing.

"Lewis." I drew his gaze and held it again. "Go to bed. Go."

He finally nodded, rose—had to steady himself against the wall—and left. I looked around the room, with its sterile high-tech beds and medical facilities that could do nothing about the problem we were facing. Every bed was filled by a Djinn.

And every Djinn was, to a greater or lesser extent, dying.

The Djinn Rahel—a New Djinn, and one of the oldest friends I had among their kind—turned her head slightly to look toward me. Rahel had always seemed invincible, like Venna—polished, wildly beautiful, with her elaborately cornrowed ebony hair and lustrous dark skin, and eyes that glowed as if backlit by amber.

Now she seemed so diminished. So fragile. Her eyes were still amber, but pale, faded, and ... frightened. She didn't speak. She didn't have to. I patted Venna's hand, then got up and went to Rahel's side. I put the back of my hand against her forehead. She felt hot and dry, consumed by some bonfire inside.

"Well," she whispered with a shadow of her old, cocky charm, "isn't this peculiar? The lamb caring for the wolf."

"You've never been the wolf, Rahel."

"Ah, sistah, you don't know me at all." She heaved a

slow, whispering sigh. "I have played at being a friend to you, but I'm nothing *but* a wolf. We all are, even your sweet David. Djinn are born because we are too ruthless to accept our own deaths as humans do. It suits us ill to face such an end as this."

"It's not the end."

"I think it could be," she said, and closed her eyes. "I think it will be. And so I will tell you something I've never told you, Joanne Baldwin."

I swallowed hard. "What?"

Her lips took on the ghost of a smile. "I am glad that we have been friends. You remind me of someone I knew long ago. My cousin, in breathing days. You have her soul. And I am glad to have looked on that bright-ness again."

"Stop it," I said, my voice unsteady. "Just stop it. You're not going to die, Rahel. You can't."

"All things can. All things should, in the end." She didn't sound angry about it, or sad, or afraid. She just sounded resigned. "The world is changing. That is not a bad thing, you know. Just different."

Maybe she had the perspective of millennia, but I didn't, and I was sick and tired of things being changed. I wanted it all to go back to the way it was.

I wanted *peace.*

But I didn't say anything else to her, and she lapsed into a quiet, waiting stillness, conserving her energy. The room was eerily silent, all those immortal creatures counting the minutes until they ceased.

And it was my fault.

I put my head down on the crisp, clean sheets next to Rahel's hand, and silently wept.

I felt a hand touch my hair, and thought at first that it was Rahel. But no; her hand was still exactly where it had been, limp and unmoving on the covers. I took in a deep breath and sat up, swiping at my eyes and sniffling.

David looked down at me, and for a moment we didn't say anything at all. He looked almost as bad as the Djinn lying in the beds, although he'd been spared that particular fate; his decline was slower, more insidious.

There was still a connection between us despite the hit we'd taken when Bad Bob had done his worst at the end. Our powers were gone, and David was trapped in mortal flesh, but on some level he was able to bleed off just a little power from me. Enough to survive, at least temporarily.

The difference was that when we sailed out of the black corner, the Djinn would get better. David wouldn't get his powers back that way. Neither of us would. And if he couldn't reconnect to the aetheric, he would get weaker.

I read the misery and concern in his eyes, and took his hand in mine. Touching flesh would have to do; we couldn't touch in all those familiar supernatural ways. It felt oddly remote and clumsy.

"You okay?" he asked me.

I nodded. "As long as you're here. You?"

That won me a faint smile from him, and a widening of those honey brown eyes. He was still beautiful, even contained in human form. He'd lost that glowing, powerful edge, but what was left was pure David. As time went on, I had the sense that I was seeing the David he'd once been—a friend, a lover, a warrior in days that had come and gone well before any history we knew.

Not a good Djinn, but a good *man*.

Still, he hadn't been just a man in so, so long. And I wondered whether he could go back to being just that, just human, without dying inside of regrets.

David's smile faded as he looked at Rahel, replaced by that intense focus I knew so well. He didn't speak, but I knew how deeply he was feeling his own helplessness. I was feeling exactly the same thing. I leaned my cheek against his warm, strong hand, and his thumb gently stroked my cheekbone.

Small comforts.

"Lewis left you alone here?"

Yeah, there was no part of that that didn't sound accusatory toward Lewis. "I made him leave. He was exhausted," I said. "And there's nothing he can do except what I'm doing. What you're doing."

"Stand here and watch my brothers and sisters die?" He paused, shut his eyes for a second, and then said, "That sounded bitter, didn't it?" I measured off an inch of air between my thumb and forefinger. He sighed. "I feel that there ought to be something. Something we can think of, do, *try*."

"We have, we did, and we will. But we're not exactly at the top of our game, honey."

"I don't know what this game is," David said softly. "I don't like the rules. And I don't like the stakes."

"Well, at least you have a good partner," I said. "Later, we can kick ass at table tennis, too."

He bent and kissed me—not a long kiss, not a passionate one, but one of those sweet and lingering sorts of promises that comes from deep, deep down. Passion we had, but we also had something else. Something more.

Something that mattered to me more than my own life. *I'm not going to lose him, too*, I told myself. I wondered whether that panic and determination showed in my face. I hoped not.

Just as David was pulling up a chair next to me at Rahel's bedside, the door to the ship's hospital opened, and Cherise staggered in, burdened by a tray so huge that it should have come with wheels and its own parade clowns. She was a tiny little thing, drop-dead gorgeous even under the ridiculously stressful conditions. Somehow she'd found the time to shower, make her hair shampoo-commercial shiny and full of body, and scrounge up clean, attractive sexy-girl clothes, which today included shorts and a striped shirt—a look I was sure I couldn't have pulled off without looking like a very sad Old Navy reject. She had no makeup on, but then again, Cherise didn't really need any. She had that kind of skin.

I got to my feet to help, but David was already there, taking the tray and setting it on a side table. Cherise let out a long sigh and shook her hands and arms to release the stress. "Man," she said. "I forgot how hard it is to be a waitress. Remind me not to work for tips again, unless it involves a pole." She looked up at David and flashed him an infectious smile. "You get what that means, right?"

"Do pole vaulters get tips?" he asked innocently, and lifted the silver cover on one of the large platters on the tray. He reached in and snagged a piece of bacon, which made my mouth water suddenly; I couldn't remember the last time I'd eaten. Ever.

Cherise stared at him with a wounded expression. "That's a joke, right? Please tell me you are joking, because if you're not joking, that is just tragic, and I'm going to have to stage an intervention."

David munched bacon and explored the rest of the buffet she'd delivered as I got up from my chair. "Strippers. Poles. I understand."

"Thank God. Because if a hottie like you had never seen a stripper, my faith in God was going to . . ." Cherise suddenly clammed up, which wasn't like her at all. She looked down, then around at the silent, still Djinn. "Yeah," she finished very quietly. "Guess that ship has sailed. And, oh look, we're on it."

It wasn't like Cherise to fail to find the sunny side of the cloud, but then again, we'd been under clouds for what seemed like years at this point. I guessed that even the eternal optimist had to reevaluate, given the circumstances.

"How is everyone else?" David asked. I reached over him to take a slice of bacon as he poured coffee from the small thermal pot.

"The Wardens are all freaking out because they're Joe Normals," Cherise said. "For me, it's just another sunny day in paradise, really. Not that I'm in the mood to tan or anything."

She really *was* depressed. Well, I could see why. . . . She was probably the only person on the entire ship, other than the hired crew, who couldn't feel anything odd about the area through which we sailed. The Wardens were reduced to shakes and panic, feeling suffocated by their isolation, and they probably resented her for her lack of suffering.

I was starting to actually get used to it. A little.

The food helped steady me, and I could see David's body language easing a little as well. He hadn't needed to pay careful attention to his metabolism in, oh, about five thousand years or so, and since he'd originally been killed and reborn as a Djinn at the tender age of what was probably his early twenties, if that, it wasn't too likely he'd ever experienced the kind of human trials I was already starting to put up with.

My mother used to say that getting old isn't for sissies. Neither is being human, for that matter. And the fact that David had managed to pull himself together so fast, and so gracefully, was humbling. I hadn't functioned *nearly* so well when I'd, in turn, been pulled over to the Djinn side. That should have been a lot more fun than it turned out to be.

The ship's motion had increased a little—difficult to tell, in a ship this big, but I could feel the pitch and yaw deep in my guts. If I'd still been a Weather Warden, I'd have been able to tell a whole lot more—how the air was moving, the tides, the deep and complex breathing between the water and the air above. Two kinds of fluids, moving as one. Symbiotic.

Now all I could tell was that my stomach was rolling with the motion. Great.

"The captain says we should be able to dock in a couple of days," Cherise said. "I don't know about you guys, but I could dig my toes in some sand. I'm starting to feel like I'm lost on *Gilligan's Island*. And I can't even be Ginger, because I don't have any evening gowns."

David stopped in the act of lifting a grape to his mouth. Just . . . froze. And I thought maybe he was confused about the pop culture reference, but that wasn't like him, and anyway, he didn't usually just . . .

Every Djinn lying in the beds suddenly sat straight up and *screamed*.

It was an eerie, tormented, unearthly wailing sound, and shockingly loud. I staggered, dropping my glass, pressing both hands to my ears, and setting my back against the wall for primal protection. There was something *wrong* with that sound, deeply and horribly *wrong*. Cherise crouched, covering her head; if she was screaming I couldn't hear her over the incredible, deafening sound of raw pain coming from every one of the Djinn.

Every one of them but David, who was pale, standing frozen in place, and unable to make a sound or movement. His eyes, though—his *eyes* were screaming.

It seemed to go on forever, the needle-sharp sound piercing the fragile barrier of skin and bone I'd put over my ears. It shattered into my brain, filling it with a horror I'd never experienced and wasn't sure I could survive. I felt my heart racing, thudding in panic against my ribs, and my knees failed me. I slid down the bulkhead wall.

I was weeping hysterically, struggling to catch any hint of a breath. It felt as if the sound itself were a weight on me, driving the air from my body. . . .

And then, as suddenly as it had started, it cut off. Not because the Djinn stopped screaming.

Because the Djinn, every single one of them except David, had vanished in a flicker of cold blue light.

Gone.

David fell hard, eyes still wide and locked in a terrible, panicked stare. I peeled my hands away from my ears, gathered strength, and managed to crawl on shaking hands to where he lay. I sat and pulled his head and shoulders into my lap as I stroked his hair and face. His skin felt ice-cold and clammy. His color was awful.

I couldn't hear anything, just the ringing echo of that awful, eternal scream. I wondered whether I'd gone deaf. I thought I'd hear that sound for the rest of my life, or until I went mad, but I realized it was slowly fading. I could hear Cherise gasping and crying a few feet away. She'd collapsed on her side, curled into a ball. Her hands were still pressed to her ears.

"Baby," I whispered to David. "Baby, talk to me. Talk to me."

He tried. His lips parted. Nothing came out, or if it did my damaged ears couldn't separate it from the still-ringing echoes of the screams.

He was shuddering. As I watched, he curled himself on his side, like Cherise, and pulled his knees up.

What just happened?

In seconds the sick bay door slammed open, and at least a dozen Wardens pelted into the room, with Lewis in the lead. He looked as shell-shocked as I felt, but at least he was on his feet and moving. He took it in at a single glance—Cherise, me, David, the empty beds where the Djinn had been.

The breath went out of him, and he went pale. Lewis

took a slow, deliberate second, then turned to face the other Wardens. "Kevin, see to Cherise," he said. "Bree, Xavier—get David into a bed. Warm blankets." He crouched down to put our eyes level, and whatever he was seeing in my face, it obviously didn't comfort him. "Jo?"

I tried to speak, then wetted my lips and tried again. The two Wardens he'd delegated were taking hold of David's arms and helping him rise. He wasn't able to offer much in the way of assistance. "I don't know," I finally managed to say. "Something—happened."

"Where did the Djinn go?"

I just shook my head. My eyes blurred with tears. I felt lost, alone, cut off, horribly frightened. Lewis reached out and gripped my hands in his.

"Jo," he said. "Jo, listen to me. I need you to focus. You need to tell me what you saw. Tell me what you heard."

I tried to remember, but the instant I did, that *sound* filled my head again, as fresh and hot and painful as before. Shatteringly loud. I clapped my hands over my ears again, and dimly heard myself screaming, begging him to make it stop.

The next thing I knew, I felt a small, hot pain in my arm, and then the sound was fading, drifting away along with the light and the pain and everything in the world.

Darkness.

Silence.

Chapter Two

The first thing I heard when I woke up was a distant, soft echo of screaming. With it came a jolt of adrenaline, a feeling of drowning, of being consumed by something . . . massive.

Then it receded, like a tide, and I was left shaking and cold despite the piles of warm blankets on top of me. Lewis was asleep in a chair next to my bed, leaning forward with his head resting on the covers next to me. One long-fingered hand was touching mine, very lightly.

He was snoring.

I smiled wearily and ruffled his hair. "Hey," I said. "How can anybody sleep with that noise?"

Lewis sat up, blinking, wiping his mouth, and looking so cutely rumpled and abashed that I felt something in me wobble off its axis. *Don't look like that. Oh, and please don't look at me like that while you're doing it.* He was tough enough to resist when he wasn't being adorable.

"Sorry," he mumbled, and scrubbed his stubbly face

with both hands. "Bad night." Some focus came back into his eyes, and I was able to get that wobbling part of me back in balance. "How are your ears?"

"I could hear you snoring like a chain saw. I must be healed."

That got a grin from him, brief as it was. "Then I guess they're intact."

I looked around. David was lying in the next bed over, still asleep. He looked pale and tired and anxious, even resting.

Cherise was curled in on herself in the next bed after David.

"How are they?" I asked. I was afraid of the answer, but he just nodded briskly, and relief flooded in on me in a warm wave. "No lasting damage?"

"Worn-out," he said. "David was able to talk a little before he drifted off. Cherise just needs sleep."

"He told you—" My brain flashed back to the screaming Djinn, that *sound*, and I felt the panic race back, slamming into my body and jolting me into a sudden sitting position. It wasn't as loud this time. Or I was getting used to hearing that awful, awful noise. I swallowed several times and concentrated hard, and the screaming died away.

I was holding Lewis's hand in a death grip. I eased off, remembering to breathe, and saw the worry and fear in his face. "I'm okay," I said. If I said it enough, maybe it would even be true. "David told you—"

"About the Djinn disappearing," Lewis said. "We heard the—the sound out there, everywhere in the ship. According to radio communications, we weren't the only ship that heard it. It blew out speakers on a tanker ten miles out. It came from the Djinn? You're sure?"

I nodded, not sure I could trust my voice just then. I was controlling the effects of the experience, but my body was still reacting in flight-or-fight mode. Finally, I said, "They just screamed and vanished. I don't know what happened."

"I do," Lewis said. "We reached the edge of the black corner."

I stared at him. I hadn't felt . . . *anything*. No change in my perception of the world. No connections snapping back in place.

I was still cut off.

That shouldn't have surprised me, but it did. It felt as if all the props had just been knocked out from under me, as if some joker had pulled the handle on a trap-door and I was going to fall forever. I'd *said* I understood what had happened to me, but deep down inside, I'd believed—I'd believed that I was better than that. That my power would come snapping back, and once we were beyond the borders of the black corner, I'd be . . . myself.

Lewis could tell. I hated to see the pity in his face, so I looked away, fighting back the tears. I couldn't do much about the trembling, though. "So," I said, and forced my voice to be something like normal. "The Wardens are back in business?"

"More or less," he said, and broke up into a fit of wet coughing. Once he'd gotten that out of the way, he smiled ruefully. "Some are feeling better than others. Jo—"

"We knew this was going to happen," I interrupted him. "David and I. We knew our powers were . . . gone. We just have to figure out how to get them back."

"It's possible that they'll come back on their own, over time. That your body will be able to repair the damage."

"Don't bullshit me, Lewis. I'm not a child, and I don't want false hope."

"I'm not offering any," he said. "Look, we just don't know. Things are—nothing makes sense right now. The Djinn . . . the way things feel—"

"What about the way things feel?" I thought he was talking about the two of us, and that was dangerous, uncertain territory. But he wasn't, as it turned out.

"The world isn't right," Lewis said. "Things are wrong out there. Badly wrong. Bad enough that it blew the Djinn out like candles once they came out into the storm."

My breath caught in my throat, and I grabbed his hand again. "They're not—"

"I don't think they're dead," he said. "But they're not visible to us, not anymore. I can't reach any of them, even on the aetheric. It's like they've been—taken."

"But what if they're more than gone? What if they're—"

"They're not dead," he repeated. "I'd know if they were. Hell, the whole world would know, I think."

I shuddered, trying hard not to think about that. If the Djinn were gone, one of the key support structures in the delicate architecture of the planet had disappeared, sending us screaming off balance into the dark. We wouldn't survive that. Any of us, including Mother Earth herself. The Djinn were like antibodies in her bloodstream, designed to attack and defend her against dangerous infections. She needed them.

"So what now?" I asked. Lewis yawned, tried to cover it up, and failed miserably. "Besides about a month of bed rest for you, and inhalation therapy, and a boatload of antibiotics?"

"Yeah, like that's going to happen. We both know the reward for a good job is more work, only done faster and more difficult."

He wasn't wrong about that, but I didn't know how much more Lewis could take. He'd been through as much as I had—more, maybe, depending on how you count such things. And he didn't have a loved one's strength to rely on. Lewis only had himself.

And whose fault is that? a little voice whispered nastily in my head. *Who shoved him away? Who ran off and fell in love with somebody else?*

It didn't matter, I told that little voice as firmly as possible. Things were what they were. Lewis knew I cared for him, but David was my love, my lover, my husband. We all had come to accept that.

I thought.

Lewis was watching me, and I couldn't fathom what was going on in his head. I hoped he couldn't guess the argument going on inside mine, either.

"We're two days from port," he said. "Once we get there, we need to hit the ground running. There are reports of all kinds of problems breaking out."

I shook my head. "Not exactly new."

"Not exactly," he agreed. "But we're the mechanics of the world, Jo. And things need to be fixed. So most of the Wardens will get back to doing what they do best."

"Most," I repeated. "Meaning?"

"Meaning that I'm going to pull the top three Earth Wardens, and we're going to do our best to analyze what happened to you and David, and make it right if we can. I've been on the phone to Marion Bearheart. She thinks that, in theory, it should be possible to open up the energy conduits within you again, if that's what's gone wrong."

That sounded hopeful. It also, at second breath, sounded painful. I winced a little, and saw sympathy flash across Lewis's face. "Yeah," he said. "It's going to hurt."

"Used to that."

"And David?"

Signing myself up for painful psychic surgery was one thing, but David . . .

"David can speak for himself," said a voice from the next bed, and Lewis turned in that direction. Behind him, I saw that David had pulled himself up to a sitting position, chest bare, sheets wrapped tight around his waist. He looked tired and vulnerable, but the sight of him up and alert made my heart take a mad leap of joy. "What do humans take for headaches these days?"

"Depends on how bad it is," Lewis said, already moving in the direction of the locked medicine cabinets. "On a scale of one to ten?"

David thought about it, then sighed and rubbed a distracted hand over his short brown hair. "Twenty-five."

Luis didn't seem surprised. He retrieved a preloaded syringe, came back, and unceremoniously delivered a jab to David's biceps. David flinched, lips parting in shock, and said, incredulously, "*Ow!*" He sounded horribly betrayed by the pain. I wondered how long it had been since he'd really been subject to a human nervous system—one he couldn't control, anyway. "What *was* that?"

"Wait for it," Lewis said, as he disposed of the hypo in a medical waste container. "Should be about—now."

David suddenly relaxed—not quite enough to collapse, but I saw the tension just bleed out of him. His eyes widened and went a little unfocused. "Oh," he said. "Well, that's better."

"Welcome to modern medicine."

"It's nice," David said, and raised his eyebrows. "It's *really* nice." He slid off the bed, landed on his bare feet, and padded over to claim the chair Lewis had been using. Before he sat, he bent over and kissed me, long and sweet and slow, and I savored every bit of it.

Lewis cleared his throat.

"Oh, bite me, big man," I said, too full of relief to care. "You're okay, honey?" David's skin felt warm against my hand—human warm, not the banked fire of a Djinn. He gave me a small, reassuring smile. "Really?"

"I'll be fine," he said, and sat down. "As long as you are." He turned his head toward Lewis, and his body language altered itself, just a little. Although I couldn't get the subtleties, it seemed to me that he was making an effort to be friendly, but he wanted Lewis to be anywhere but here. "Lewis. What do you know?"

"About what happened to the Djinn? Nothing. We came out of the black corner, they screamed, they disappeared."

David's eyes went briefly blank, and I knew that, like me, he was struggling not to relive that awful sound. There was something about it that just wouldn't die; it was like an endless recorded loop, playing in the back of my mind. The best you could do was keep the sound turned low. "No," he said. "That's not what happened. Jo understands."

I did? I didn't. I shook my head.

"You saw it before," he said. "At the coast. You saw it take me."

I had no idea what he meant, and I was about to say so. . . . And then it came to me, like a physical slap. I sat up, staring at him. "No."

"Yes," he said. "Exactly that."

"But—the Wardens would know."

"Not if she didn't wish them to."

"Excuse me," Lewis said, a little too loudly. "Somebody want to clue me in?"

David was the one to say it, which was good, because I wasn't sure I had it in me. "It's the Mother," he said. "It was her scream, echoing through the Djinn. She's been hurt, and she's angry. She gathered the Djinn to her. They're in her power now."

I watched Lewis's face go very quickly pale. He put out a hand to steady himself. "You're saying—"

"I'm saying that the Earth is awake," David said. "At least, I believe she is coming awake. The Djinn serve her, and when she calls, they must come."

This was, beyond any doubt, the worst thing that

could happen. The Earth slept. We *liked* it that way. Even in sleep she was difficult, but once that vast, slow consciousness was roused . . . we had no idea what she would do, except that it almost certainly would end in extinction for a great many species, and the end of human civilization, at the very least. The Earth could not be reasoned with, or even directly *communicated* with. Not even the Djinn could do that. The only ones that had a chance, even a whisper of a chance, were the three Djinn Oracles.

Thinking of the Oracles made me think about my daughter, Imara, and I felt a leap of terrible fear. Had she screamed, like the others? Had she lost herself, too?

"No," David said, and his fingers tightened on mine. "She's all right, Imara is all right. We'd know—" His voice trailed off, and I saw a flash of panic in his eyes. We *wouldn't* know. We were only human now, and our daughter, our child who'd been born half Djinn and raised to become an Oracle . . . she was beyond our grasp now. David normally would have been able to reach out to her, over any distance, but now he was just as trapped in flesh and as clueless as I felt.

We both turned immediately to Lewis.

"I don't know about the Oracles. I haven't heard anything," he said. He knew immediately what we were thinking about, and the frown on his face said that he was worried about it, too. "I'll get somebody on it. David, do you know *why* she summoned the Djinn?"

"Pain," David said softly. "You heard the scream. That was her pain."

It rolled over me in a fresh, overwhelming wave of memory, and I had to concentrate hard to keep myself from shaking with the intensity of the experience. "The black corner," I said. "She's been hurt. That's why she's waking up. *We* did this."

David visibly swallowed, then nodded. Our hands

tightened together, the only real comfort we could offer each other. It had been bad enough when we'd been responsible for the pain and death of Djinn. Now we might be responsible for a whole lot more.

"We'll find a way to get back to ourselves," he said. "We have to find a way."

I wished I could believe him. Lewis wasn't looking at me, and I could tell that he was trying not to reveal his own doubts. He pushed away from the bulkhead wall and said, "You asked what we were going to do. I don't see that there's any reason to change the plan. We hit land, the Wardens scatter to handle crisis events. I'd like you two at Warden HQ for the time being. It'll be easier to work with you there, and you can help us with coordination."

Coordination.

If the Earth was really waking up, really angry, really hurt—we'd be coordinating firefighting during a nuclear war. And it was a waste. He was sidelining us, and I didn't like it.

"We have something more important to do, Lewis. I know you're trying to keep us out of the way, but we have to try to find a way to get our powers back," I said. "David can't live like this. You know that. We have to see the Oracles. If anybody knows, they do."

"I can't give you help."

"We don't need any," David said. "This will work, or it won't. But isn't it worth a shot?"

Lewis thought about it for a moment, then nodded. "Yes," he said. "It's worth a shot. But if it doesn't work, I need you at Warden HQ. Understand?"

"Understood," I said.

No way in hell.

I got used to feeling sealed inside myself over the next two days; if David didn't, he hid it well. We didn't need confinement in hospital beds, so we checked ourselves out while Lewis wasn't looking. It wasn't really our fault, though. Cherise instigated it.

"No way am I sleeping in *this* horrible bed the rest of the trip," she declared within a couple of hours of waking up. For Cherise, she looked ragged. For anyone else, she looked magazine-cover ready, but I could spot the subtleties—a smudge under her eyes, a slight pallor under her tan, hair that wasn't quite as bouncy as usual. "And the shower in here *sucks*. What is this shampoo stuff, anyway? Medical soap? Ugh. No. I am not doing without product. There's a limit."

With that, and without anybody giving her permission to vacate the bed, she was up and moving, wrapped in a sheet and searching for her clothes. David helped—more afraid that she'd end up dropping the sheet and he'd see more of Cherise than he intended, I think—and once she'd laid her hands on her shorts, shirt, and shoes, there was no stopping her.

Which was all fine with me, actually. I was heartily sick of this room. I dressed quickly. David was hilariously slow; I wondered how often he'd actually had to pull on his own pants in the last few thousand years. Probably zero times.

"Sunshine," Cherise declared as we followed her out of the medical area and into the more spacious public area of the ship. The utilitarian carpet and walls were replaced by lusher stuff the higher we went, and by the time we could see daylight streaming through windows, we were in posh territory, with fancy sitting rooms and dark wood paneling. And bars. A lot of bars. A few were even serving.

Cherise stopped at one and ordered us all margaritas.

"I don't think this is the time—," I said, but she pressed the glass into my hands firmly.

"Sweetie, this is *exactly* the time to drink," she said. "We survived, right? We're heading home? Definitely happy hour, from now until, oh, ever after." She clinked glasses with me, then David, and led us out a side door onto the deck of the ship. We didn't much feel like celebrating, but it was tough to resist Cher when she was in a mood like this.

And she was right about taking us outside. It was *beautiful.*

Hard to believe that we'd spent the last few weeks—no, months? years?—under such strain, facing such dire circumstances. When we'd sailed out of Miami, we'd done it in the teeth of a monstrous storm.

Today the sun was warm and kind, the sky a rich, clean-scrubbed blue. The breeze that blew in off the waves was gentle as it glided over my bare arms. The sea was calm; it glittered in diamond-bright swells, a sparkling fabric unrolled as far as the eye could see.

So beautiful.

David put his arm around me, and we stood there for a moment in silence, staring out at the vista. Cherise leaned on her forearms on the rail, smiling, turning her face up to the sun with an expression of pure delight.

"Cher?"

She turned at the sound of her name, and I glanced back to see Kevin coming at a run from a lower deck, taking the stairs two at a time. My relationship with Kevin—the youngest Warden we had, I believed—was complicated. *He* was complicated, more than most people I knew: damaged, and dangerous, and unpredictable, but still struggling to find and hold on to that core of goodness that against all odds survived within him. He'd been through a lot, in his—what was it now, nineteen years? He was three years younger than Cherise, which seemed like a lot at their ages. But that didn't stop him from being head over heels in love with her.

"Hey, Kev," she said, turning from the rail as he jumped to the top of the steps and lunged to grab her in a hug. She was a very small girl, and he was tall and lanky, putting on more muscle all the time. An odd couple, but also oddly appropriate for each other. Cherise's unending optimism was something Kevin needed in his life, which had seen way too much darkness. She was laughing in bright, silvery peals as he spun her around in his arms. "Whoa, whoa, easy, don't make me yak!"

He stopped and let her go, but she didn't go far—just far enough to kiss him, with authority. David raised his eyebrows a little but said nothing. I wondered what he thought about it. I suspected he was just as wary as I was of Kevin, generally.

"You're okay?" Kevin asked. "Lewis said—"

"Yeah, look, the Djinn kind of freaked out and there was a thing, but I'm all good now. See?" Cherise did a runway twirl for him. "I'm fine."

"Yes, you are."

She made a purring sound low in her throat and arched against him like a cat. "Don't tease unless you mean it."

"Oh, I—" Kevin suddenly stopped in midflirt, blinked, and looked at her with a baffled expression. David and I both turned to look at him. Cherise was just as baffled as Kevin, it seemed.

"What?" I asked, because it didn't seem like Cherise could even remember the word.

Kevin closed his eyes for a second, rubbed them, and opened them again. Relief spread across his face, and he shook his head. "Nothing," he said. "Jesus, I'm tired. I thought—it's nothing. I'm okay."

Cherise stepped forward and put her hand against his cheek, one of those loving gestures that I find myself doing to David so often. Kevin relaxed and bent toward her, covering her hand with his. "Well," I said to David, "they've gotten cozy. Not really sure how I feel about that."

He acknowledged it with a nod, but I could tell his mind was elsewhere. Shadows in his eyes, weariness in his face. For the first time, it struck me that every minute he spent in a human body—a *real* human body, cut off from the Djinn—he was growing older, just as I was. I tried to imagine how it felt for him to have lost so much, to be so alone. I knew how *I* felt. Surely for him it was millions times worse.

"David." I put a hand on his arm, and got his full focus. "Are you okay? Do you need Lewis to—"

No mistaking the weary twist of his mouth. He hated being dependent on anyone, but he'd have to face facts— he couldn't draw enough power from me to fuel his life well, and Lewis was the best bet. But David didn't like being beholden to the first man I'd ever loved. At all. "I'm fine," he said, voice unnervingly soft and even. "If I have to see him for help, I will."

I didn't believe him, but he wasn't asking me to, in so many words. It was the big lie, and he was asking me not to push it. David wasn't the kind to be reasonable about his limits; after spending millennia without many at all, he was going to crash into human borders pretty hard, and it was going to hurt.

It wasn't the kind of thing he'd thank me for pointing out, either.

"Coordinating," I said, bringing us back to the dark center of things around which our lives revolved now. "He really wanted to stick us with coordinating at headquarters."

That got a smile from him, if a brief one. "It's not going to suit you if we have to do it."

"Speak for yourself, Master of"—I was about to say *Djinn* but caught myself in time . . . ouch—"the obvious.

I'm not giving up yet. We'll find a way to get our mojo back. See if we don't."

David drained the rest of his glass and dangled it from his fingers, staring down now into the sparkling waves. "You sure you want it back?"

"Are you *kidding* me?"

"No," he said, and his voice had that odd, flat, soft inflection again, as if he were pressing all the emotion out of it with great care. "Jo, think about it. We both want to be together, but we've always been of two worlds. I tried to make you part of mine, but that didn't work. This— this is a chance to make me part of yours."

I forgot all about the drink in my hand, the beautiful day, the laughter of Cherise and Kevin standing a few feet away, and fixed him with a disbelieving stare. "David, you're *dying.*"

"Everyone's dying," he said. "Mortal life is short to someone like me even in the best case. If I don't— resume my life as a Djinn, I can be a true husband to you. Living a human life." His eyes finally moved to meet mine. "Giving you human children."

We didn't talk about Imara very often; our Djinn child was a beautiful, complicated gift, but she had never been a baby, never rested in my arms, never taken her first steps. The mothering instinct in me craved more, and he knew that. I'd never said it, but of course he knew.

"David—"

"It's not a good time," he finished for me, and he was right on, even though we no longer shared that deep supernatural bond that had made it so easy for him to read me. "I know. But there's so little good about all this, Jo. We should take what we can, when we can, for as long as we can."

"I'm not having children just to watch them die, if this turns bad," I said, and somehow managed not to add, *again.* Imara's death, before she'd been made an Oracle, was something that would haunt me forever. "We're in trouble. Don't think I haven't noticed."

"You know what I've learned from thousands of years of watching humanity? It's always a bad time." He put his arms around me and held me, and the simple warmth of it made me want to weep. I didn't. It wouldn't do for me to get all girly and soft on him now. "But all the bad times end, too."

"Thus sayeth the dude with a long view."

"Dude?"

"Sorry, it was my bad eighties teen years coming back to haunt me."

He kissed me, as if he couldn't think of any more words. That was okay. It got the point across just fine.

It was very strange to be on the outskirts of the whirl-wind of activity inside the Wardens—a bystander, like Cherise. Someone included me in some of the meetings, out of courtesy, but being outside of the direct flow of crisis information made me feel like I was just holding down a chair at the table. It was, in fact, a literal table, the biggest one on the ship, and it seated about twenty; I supposed they used it for swank corporate meetings on the high seas. Or really large families, with equally large checkbooks. Lewis sat at one end, looking down the long expanse of wood; around it, every chair was filled with some powerful Warden or other.

Except mine and David's, of course. We were just keeping the cushions warm.

We were an hour into the meeting, and what had started out as a grim list of problems had only gotten worse.

"Reports coming in from South America," said Kyril Valotte, an exotic-looking young man who missed being handsome by the narrow set of his eyes. "Earthquakes and lava flows in Venezuela. We've got teams heading there now, but we've also got reports of odd animal attacks in Panama, some kind of disease outbreak in Guatemala. . . . It's a lot for the Earth team to handle at once."

"I can send four Wardens out of Texas," said the head of the Southwest U.S. region, and made some notes on his map. "Earth Wardens I got. Weather Wardens I need."

"I'll send as many as I can," Kyril said with a nod. "We'll need ground transportation."

I held up my hand. "I'll take it. I can still make phone calls."

They looked up, and I saw the frank confusion in their faces for a second before memory caught up. Then they both just looked uncomfortable. Kyril nodded and murmured something meaninglessly kind. The U.S. Warden—Jerry something?—didn't bother. He just went back to his maps.

There was a lot of that going on. Lower-ranked Wardens came in and out, delivering notes and whispered messages to their bosses, and with each note, the deployments ended up revised. Thankfully, Cherise had come to my rescue with a genuine computer and network uplink, so I was dispatching travel authorizations and setting up rental cars at the speed of—well, not light, but at the speed of whatever satellite I was bouncing my signal from. It was something useful to do, at least.

I was glad, because listening to the trouble was somehow worse than not knowing about it at all.

Lewis looked at his watch and said, "Hour update," which was the trigger for us to go around the table, one by one, and list off the emerging issues, the ones being handled, and estimated numbers of casualties. I tallied it up in a spreadsheet. Nice and clean and neat.

By the time silence fell again, and my fingers stopped

typing, I was shaking. The pause was deep and profound. I stared at the list of things I'd recorded.

"Jo?" Lewis's voice was gentle. He already knew.

I cleared my throat. "We're up to more than a thousand reported anomalies and severe issues," I said. "Estimated casualties worldwide are climbing steadily. Right now, from what we have reported, the worst case scenario puts human lives lost at about half a million people."

People who were bad at math took in sharp breaths around the table.

"It's going to get worse," David said, in the silence. "The Djinn aren't intervening. I believe they could be causing some of these events."

"Why? Why would they do that?" It was an emotional question, not a rational one, and it came from Kelley, down near the end of the table. She was upset, clearly.

"Because they don't have a choice," David said. "The Djinn aren't operating under their own control anymore. At least, I don't believe they are. Otherwise, at least one of them would be here now. You can't count on any assistance from the Djinn, and where you meet them, you have to consider them as hostile."

We all knew what that meant; hostile Djinn were pretty much worst-case scenario all by themselves, and they were now only a part of our problems. I felt sick and light-headed, and I was pretty sure from the faces around the table that I wasn't the only one.

"Focus on what we can control," Lewis said. "We're dispatching Wardens to cover the hot spots, but that's reacting. We need to get ahead of this."

Someone let out a hollow laugh. "How?"

"We need to get to the source of the problem," Lewis said. "We need to get to the Mother herself."

This time, I felt *David* take a breath. A sharp one,

which he let out slowly before saying, "I don't think that's a good idea."

"I realize that we're just humans," Lewis said, "but sooner or later, she needs to understand what she's killing."

"You think she doesn't?" David asked, very mildly. That brought another few seconds of silence around the table. "Humanity has done stupid things in the name of its own blind survival, worse in the name of its own comfort. She's not concerned with individuals, Lewis. She's concerned with balance. If you put all of humanity on one side of the scales, and all of the other life on Earth on the other side ..."

"You know what? I'm not here to debate humanity's crappy conservation record," Lewis snapped, and then he rubbed his face and sat back in his chair. "Sorry. I get your point, but this has been brewing for a long time. If we can't establish direct contact with the Mother, we have to rely on the Djinn to influence her. Frankly, I'm not feeling good about that plan, since the Djinn are already on her side. Are you?"

"Not at all," David said. "But then, I'm not feeling good about putting a human face to face with a being so vast and powerful that the Djinn themselves won't go there."

"Oracles do," I said. "Imara does."

"And Imara's done all she can to make humanity's case. She's young, she's new, and the Mother may not listen."

"I could do it."

"No, Jo, you can't. You had a lot of advantages the last time you tried something like this; you were a Warden, you had access through Imara and through me. It's not a good idea."

"Because mere humans shouldn't be front and center?" I shot back to David. "Come on, this is *about* mere humans. Not Wardens. Not Djinn. It's about millions of regular people who are going to die, and their voice needs to be heard. They're not invisible. They're *real.*"

"I know they're real," he said. "But they have no voice—not that she can hear and understand. *You* have no voice, Jo. Not as you are."

"Bullshit!"

He smiled. "Yelling isn't going to solve the problem, you know."

"But it makes me feel *tons* better, sweetie." I wasn't about to let his charm veer me off course. Well, not *far* off course, anyway. "We needed to go to the Oracles anyway. They're our one real hope of getting our powers back, fast. I'm the logical one to do it. Lewis, if I get burned out, you're not losing much at this point."

He was looking at me, and I saw the expression that flickered over his face. We both knew that in personal terms, that absolutely was a lie, but on pure, coldly logical ground I was correct. I was human. Not a triple-powered Warden any longer. Not consort to the leader of half of the Djinn anymore.

Just Joanne Baldwin, snappy dresser and fast-car fan, mother and daughter and sister. Just another human being spending my short time on the face of the Earth, unnoticed.

And Lewis nodded, face gone utterly still and controlled. "Yeah," he agreed. "It makes sense. You've got the technical knowledge, we can help you get where you need to be, and if it doesn't work—then we haven't lost a vital Warden."

David stood up. "Are you insane? You can't encourage her. You know how she is."

"I know exactly how she is, and who she is, and what she can do if I give her the chance. Don't underestimate her just because you love her and you want to protect her." Lewis's eyes were bleak and full of things that I didn't want to see, didn't want to know. "Jo, we're fourteen hours out from port. Get ready. Once we make landfall we're going to be very busy."

"You know me, I love a good crisis," I said. "I'll be ready."

Lewis nodded, and the meeting broke up for the next four hours so most could get some much-needed downtime. Not that they *would* get it, considering the pace at which things were happening.

I felt oddly . . . disconnected. Again. I kept waiting for some sense of the world around me to return, but all I had to work with now were what my limited human senses chose to give me. Not much, and not enough.

Then again, I'd made the case that being just plain human was an asset. Inconsistency, thy name is Joanne.

I saved the spreadsheet and left everything up and running for the next shift of Wardens, who were already shuffling into the room, yawning and gulping coffee and looking as shell-shocked as I felt. David waited silently for me. He took my hand as we exited the room, and waited for a whole three steps before he said, "Are you insane?"

"Clinically, or in general? I'm pretty sure there's a 'yes' in there somewhere no matter what I do."

"Jo." He pulled me to a halt and turned me to face him. "I'm not kidding." His hand was tight around my arm, and his face was drawn and very serious. "You can't do this. I can't let you do this. I'm not going to lose you, and there's no part of this plan—if you want to call it that—that doesn't end up with you dead. It's bad enough you want to go to the Oracles. Going to the Mother is suicide."

"We're all dying," I said, and saw him flinch as I threw his words back at him. There wasn't any satisfaction in it. "I have to try. You know I have to try. You'd do the same, in my place."

He let go of my arm and put his hands on my face, and for a breathtaking minute we stared into each other's eyes, all barriers swept away. Two people poised on the edge of something awful, afraid and alone even with each other for comfort.

He hugged me close, stroking his fingers through my hair. When he'd been Djinn, he'd straightened my curls—a private sort of joke between us, a memory of a time when I hadn't battled that problem. Now, he couldn't wield that power, but it didn't matter. It soothed me in deep, primal ways, and I relaxed against him, feeling the deep rush of his breath in his chest, his heartbeat, his strength and love and commitment.

"Then we go together," he murmured in my ear. "The two of us. Together."

Tears suddenly welled up in my eyes. I'd been prepared to go it alone, resigned to it; and yet, knowing he was with me . . . it made all the difference. I didn't know how to feel; relief and horror struggled for dominance. The horror was because I was dragging him with me into the mouth of the lion.

But I wasn't alone. And that mattered, in this moment, more than I could say.

"We have fourteen hours," I said, and pulled back to wipe my eyes with the heel of one hand. "Let's spend them doing something productive."

That put him back on firmer emotional ground. "I'm trying to think what that is, in your world. Shopping?"

"Jerk. No. Although not a bad idea—I could use a couple of outfits."

"Interesting." His arms tightened around me, and the heat between us changed from comfort to something else. Something with its roots in a wilder place. "So what would you consider productive?"

"I need to do laundry."

"And?"

"That means I should take my clothes off. You know, to be sure I have everything clean."

I loved the smile he gave me, slow and sweet and hot. It wasn't a Djinn smile, not with the kind of hidden power that it had just a few days ago, but it was more purely *him*. The core of David that I loved so very much.

"I can help with that," he said.

"You mean, with the laundry."

"Absolutely."

We walked back to the cabin with our arms around each other, savoring the hours, minutes, seconds together. If other people spoke to us, I'm not sure either of us really paid attention.

As he was locking the cabin door behind us, David said, "Be gentle, it's my first time." I laughed, and then I understood. It *was* his first time with me—and my first with him, in a very deep-seated way. We'd been together as Djinn and Warden, both of us bringing power into the relationship even if that hadn't been a deliberate plan.

This was different. Very different. This was just skin, and human emotion, and the kind of love shared by so many others. Which made it oddly precious and special, I realized.

We came together slowly, in a long and leisurely kiss. After the first few seconds I stopped thinking about what this wouldn't be, and began thinking of what it *was*. It felt sweet and intimate and passionate, and his mouth tasted different now. Human. Hard as it had been to see it, even his best imitation of mortality hadn't quite been completely honest. He'd unconsciously skewed it toward making it perfect.

And this was honest, and imperfect, and wonderful.

He broke the kiss and pulled in a deep breath, looking shaken. I had to laugh a little. "What?"

"It's been a long time since I had reactions I couldn't fully control," he admitted.

"Yeah? Scared?"

"A little."

I took pity on him, and kissed him lightly again on the lips. "Me, too. You're doing fine."

He was, indeed, doing fine already, gently undoing the buttons on my shirt and moving it aside, brushing his fingers over my bared skin, trailing them down to the waistband of my jeans in a suggestively delicious manner. "I usually can tell if I'm doing this right," he said in my ear. His warm breath made me shiver. "Am I? Doing this right?"

"Oh yes." I caught my breath and arched against him as he slipped his fingers beneath the waistband. "*Hell* yes."

He seemed completely fascinated from that moment on, forgetting his own odd awkwardness. Every action had a reaction, and for the first time, he was engaging every sense to understand me, read me, *feel* me. For two people who'd been so closely, inextricably linked by our nerves, this was like making love blind—deliciously different, sweetly erotic, utterly human in ways that neither of us had anticipated. Mapping each other's imperfect bodies, communicating in whispers and sighs and moans and thrusts that built to something brilliant and explosive for us both.

David collapsed against me, gasping for breath, shaking. "It's the aetheric," he finally managed to say. "That's what it is. That's what you feel. You touch the aetheric. I never knew. . . ." He gulped in more air, eyes blind and bright, and then looked at me. "Let's do that again."

"Easy, tiger," I said, and cuddled up next to him. "Take a breath. It'll still be there."

He put his arms around me, and I listened to the frenzied pounding of his heart slow down, his respiration subside. I felt warm and complete and deliciously relaxed. "You'll still be here," he said, and kissed my forehead, my eyelids, my nose. Silly, sweet little kisses. He was just as giddy as I felt. "That's all that matters."

I was trying not to think about it, but the thought darkened my mind, just for a second: *Tell that to the half a million people about to die.*

But I'd face that soon enough, and more.

And for now, I just wanted to be this, here, with him.

Sometime, hours later, I murmured sleepily, "Oh crap, I forgot to do the laundry."

And he laughed.

And somehow, it was all okay, just for now.

Chapter Three

The Port of Miami looked weather-beaten but under repairs, and as far as I could tell, life was going on just fine. That seemed . . . odd. I stood at the rail and watched people strolling the boardwalks, coming in and out of shops with hands full of bright-colored bags, eating at outdoor cafes. It seemed so *normal.*

It didn't seem like the end of the world as we knew it. In the movies, everybody's looking up at the skies (conveniently, all at the same daylight hour, everywhere in the world, all at once) when the big disaster is coming. But in real life, people just carry on until the disaster's in their face, and sometimes even after. I've lost count of the number of people I've personally fished out of flooded homes and businesses during hurricanes, for instance—and the ones that the Wardens couldn't save. All because they denied the ability of the world around them to destroy them.

There were potentially big losses of life brewing everywhere around the world, but so far they were just breaking news stories happening (for most people) somewhere else. Interesting and tragic, not personal and panic-bringing. Nothing to interrupt dinner at Pascal's on Ponce over, for sure.

That would change, very soon. I knew it, even though I couldn't sense the aetheric disturbances anymore. Wardens were talking about it, and I could sense the suppressed anxiety in their voices.

This lovely day in Miami was the last we might ever see. I had a sudden, crazy impulse to start yelling like some wild-haired, sandwich-board-wearing street preacher, but I held my breath until it passed. Doomsaying wouldn't make anybody's day better. Or postpone the inevitable.

The ship was maneuvering up to the docks, and I could see, in the distance, a massive presence of cars, vans, and trucks. I nudged Lewis, who was standing next to me at the railing. "What is that?"

"The transportation you arranged," he said. "Cars and vans to shuttle people where they need to go."

"*All* of that?"

"Plus the press."

My palms immediately got damp, and I scrubbed them against my blue jeans. "What's our plan to handle them?"

"Benign neglect. We're going to be neck-deep in Apocalypse tomorrow. I can't see how issuing a press release is going to make a damn bit of difference, so we're not talking."

Worked for me. "David's going with me. To the Oracles."

Lewis didn't take his eyes off the docking process. "Good. I didn't like sending you alone." He paused, and then said, very quietly, "I don't like sending you at all. You know that." Yeah, and I knew why. So did David. Uncomfortably personal territory, so I skipped it.

"It's a dirty job, but that's why you picked me to do it," I said cheerfully. "Besides, if I can pick up some of my powers along the way, this might not be the rush to martyrdom you think."

"It's a big *if*, Jo."

"It's a gi-normous *if*. Not to mention an embarrassingly large *how*. So let's not dwell on it. Besides, you're the one going up against Djinn and insane planets with a grudge. I've got the easy job."

He shrugged, because I wasn't wrong. Nobody was guaranteed to come out of this thing with a whole skin—Lewis, the most powerful Warden in several hundred years, least of all. The more powerful you were, the more the bad things tended to want you dead. At least, in my experience.

Which meant I was practically bulletproof right now, ironically. I literally wasn't worth noticing. Was that a comfort? I really wasn't sure.

"You've been taking the hits for a long time," Lewis said. He hadn't even glanced at me, but he could read me just fine. "Let the rest of us get the battle scars for a change. We're big kids."

"Did I ever say you weren't?"

"No, but your hero complex scares the crap out of me," Lewis said, and straightened up. "Here we go."

I thought he meant that we were ready to disembark, but he turned toward me, and before I even knew he was intending to do it, he kissed me. Not one of the desperate kind of kisses he'd given me in the past, none of that longing or anguish or pure lust I knew was still locked up inside of him. This was surprisingly . . . pure. Chaste.

It was a good-bye kiss.

I didn't fight it.

He didn't say another word, and it wasn't necessary. I watched him stride away, already calling orders to the Wardens who flocked around him like birds, swooping in to get instructions and then breaking off on their own.

That left me alone at the rail, until I sensed a warm presence next to me, and looked over to see that David had joined me. He had no particular expression on his face. It was just—studiously neutral.

"You saw," I said.

"Yes. I know what it was," he said. "And he's right. We might never see him again. I'd kiss him myself, but he might kill me."

Which made me laugh, as he intended. Though, knowing how ancient David was, I wasn't entirely putting that kind of flexibility past him, either. "You're a good man," I said.

"Am I?" He frowned down at the docks, as if it was a difficult question. "Maybe I was, once. Maybe I can be. But I've done a lot of things that wouldn't qualify as good. I think—I think this is a chance to remember what that means."

"Bullshit," I said crisply. "We're not in the navel-gazing business, my love; we're in the world-saving business. Don't you forget it."

That surprised a smile out of him, a spark that reminded me of the fire he'd had before . . . before the island, and that black corner. "I won't."

Cherise arrived, out of breath, rolling two suitcases. She had on a Miami-length sundress (as in, just too long to qualify as a shirt, and illegal in forty-nine other states), clunky platform shoes, an enormous sun hat, and designer sunglasses. Very Cher. "Well?" she snapped as she breezed on past us, leaving a smell of crisp lemony perfume in her wake. "Hustle it up; what do you think—the world isn't ending or something? I am *not* holding a cab for you slackers!" Kevin trailed her, looking as slouchy as ever but somehow a little less unkempt—maybe Cherise had been after him with a comb—dragging two *more* suitcases. Considering we'd come on this journey with almost nothing, that was quite an accomplishment. Only Cherise could pump up her wardrobe while evading death. I generally just ruined mine.

David offered me his arm. "She's right," he said. "So are you. Fight first; introspection later."

"We're going to make it," I said. "You believe that, right?"

He looked around—at the seemingly normal seafront, at the Wardens disembarking from the ship, at the world all around us. And he said, softly, "Not all of us."

I shivered.

Four in a cab was a stretch, but we voted Kevin to sit up front, much to the displeasure of the driver, who groused about rules and such until I tossed money at him. The money had been issued to all of us out of the ship's treasury—another thing that was going on the Wardens' already staggering tab for saving the world again. It wasn't going to be enough, but it was enough to get us moving, and that was all that mattered.

I had the driver drop us at a car rental place—not Avis and Budget, which were already swarming with Weather Wardens attempting to secure their own preferred methods of transpo, not liking what I'd booked for them—but a luxury place, where I plunked down the gold American Express Warden card to the clerk behind the counter. She was a professionally lovely girl, the way a lot of South Beach ladies are, and she had a practiced, customer-service-approved smile. "What kind of vehicle are you—"

"What's the fastest car you have?" I asked.

"Um . . ." She glanced down, and I'm pretty sure she would have frowned except that the Botox no longer allowed that particular expression. Not that I wasn't in favor of Botox; I was starting to develop some disturbing furrows in my own brow. "We have a Porsche Carrera. . . ."

"Something that seats four," I said.

"Comfortably," added Cherise.

"Okay, well, we have a classic Mustang that I understand is really fast. . . ."

I couldn't believe my ears. "What kind of classic Mustang?" Because with my luck it would be a 1974, which was the start of the Mustang Dark Ages.

"It's a Boss 429," she said, reading from a card with the air of someone who really didn't speak the language and was sounding it out phonetically. "From 1970."

She hadn't even *thought* about being born when Ford had rolled that racing car off the assembly line, but my heart was starting to pound. "Seriously? You're *sure* it's a Boss 429?"

"We just got it in," she said. "It has about sixty thousand miles on it."

I swallowed hard and tried not to get my hopes up. "Can I see it?"

She gave me another professional smile—not quite as polished as the last one—and then brightened the wattage considerably at David. "Sure," she said, and nodded to another woman, identically lovely (only with dark hair), who came from the back to take her place at the counter. Out we went—although Cherise left the mountain of suitcases sitting in the lobby, thankfully—into the parking lot behind the reception building.

It was like a candy store for car addicts. Seriously. There were a lot of very rich people in Florida, and a lot who visited, and this was their toy box. Classic red Lamborghini? Choose from dozens of identical clones. Want a high-end Porsche? A Jag XJ220? No problem. Even I slowed down and stared as we passed the sleek, rounded chassis of what surely couldn't be . . . "Hey," I said, and pointed. "Bugatti Veyron?"

"Reserved," our guide said. "And you'd need more than a gold Amex, I can tell you that."

No doubt, because the last time I'd seen a price tag attached to one of those monsters, it was soaring up into the $1.5 million range. I felt I should genuflect or something, because that was definitely one of the Gods of Cars.

Then we cleared a giant, gleaming, black row of tricked-out Hummers, and found . . . *my car*.

There was just no doubt about it, really. This was *mine*. The thick, hot pleasure that spread through me at the sight of it couldn't have felt better if accompanied by a shot of heroin, administered by a male stripper.

Yes, cars are my drug of choice.

She wasn't wrong. It *was* a Boss 429, absolutely cherry, painted in Intimidator Black. No stripes, no frills. It looked *dangerous*. Oh, and it was.

Rental Car Girl was holding a set of keys. She handed them to me and opened the driver's-side door. It smelled faintly of cigar smoke inside, but the interior was beautifully maintained. The seat was comfortably broken in, and even the leg length was almost right. One minor adjustment, and I fired it up.

A low, deep-throated throb of an engine, hot with power and hungry for speed. *Yes*.

I realized I was obsessively running my hands over the steering wheel, with a lust that was making David look at me funny. I cleared my throat, shut the engine off, and got out of the car. "Fine," I said, trying to sound normal. "I'll take it."

"Day rate?"

"For the month," I said.

She didn't even blink; I supposed the rich did rent things on that scale on a regular basis. Probably for longer. "You'll have to pay the deposit plus two weeks," she said. "The car has LoJack, of course. We maintain our own insurance, which we will require you to carry if you can't provide valid coverage that would include—"

"Fine," I said. "Whatever. Charge it. We're in a hurry."

Surprisingly, that phrase did not inspire confidence. We waited through ID checks, credit checks, whispered conversations, and finally a massive set of paperwork, including a clause that I was fairly sure included forced organ harvesting in the event of nonpayment.

I just signed it, scribbling as fast as I could anywhere her well-manicured finger pointed. She wished us a pleasant stay in Miami. I didn't correct her, just stood tapping my foot impatiently until the uniformed valet had brought the Boss around to the front.

Cherise opened the trunk and looked inside. "You're kidding, right? My luggage will never—"

"Downsize," I said. "You're not packing for a photo shoot, you know."

"How do *you* know? There's always time to book a good gig before the end of the world. . . . Okay, fine." She crammed two of the suitcases in, and rolled two more back inside. She came out empty-handed, and I raised my eyes. She scooted her big round sunglasses down to roll hers. "They're shipping them to Warden HQ," she said. "What, you really thought I'd just leave them? Girlfriend. There is *Elie Saab* in there. Ready-to-wear, but still. Respect."

"Hey, you've got your drug. I've got mine." I made sure the trunk was closed, and opened up the door for her as I flipped the driver's seat forward. She got in with care. I was glad, because I really didn't want to see any tabloid flashing. Kevin piled in next to her, and I smirked a little as I slammed the passenger seat back into place. With those long legs, he was not going to be overly comfortable . . . but then again, he wouldn't have been comfortable in much except a stretch limo.

David and I slid into the front seats, and I turned

the key. The vibration of the engine came straight up my spine, doing interesting things in all kinds of key pleasure points, and I hit the clutch and shifted into first gear.

The Boss scratched right out of the box, leaving a thin mist of smoke behind us as it roared off. Zero to thirty, way too fast, and I had to back off dramatically on the fuel mix. He was temperamental, this beast. I liked that. It took a few experimental shifts to find the sweet spot in the clutch and get the feel of the pedals, but not more than a minute. The rental company had added a plug-in GPS, which showed me the route to the nearest freeway, and by the time I hit the on-ramp me and the Boss were good friends.

Oh *God*, it felt good to be behind the wheel again, in control, heading somewhere with a purpose. No more Bad Bob. No more old ghosts haunting me. Just me, the car, my lover, and . . . okay, Cherise and Kevin. And a trunkload of couture. But still. I felt . . . light.

And oh *Lord*, the Boss had power. I had to watch to keep it hovering at reasonable speed, and it was still blowing the doors off Italian sports cars in the other lanes. I was glad it wasn't a convertible. We might have died of the wind buffeting.

"Storm coming in," Cherise said, after we'd put about twenty miles under the fast-turning wheels. I glanced in the rearview. She was facing west, out the window, with an odd expression on her face. I looked, and saw a smear of clouds on the horizon. I automatically tried to reach out and grab information from the aetheric, but I had that phantom limb syndrome that amputees sometimes have. Nothing there. Just a sensation that there had once been.

"Doesn't look like much," I said.

"It's bad," she said. "I think it's bad."

I gave her a sharper look. "What?"

She shook her head and slipped her sunglasses on, leaning her head back. "I'm going to take a nap. Wake me if we pass a hot male strip bar."

Kevin growled, and she smiled and tucked her small hand in his. "Could we at least have some tunes?" he said. "Or is this car too sacred for a radio?"

"No car is too sacred for a radio," I said. Sure enough, there was one—not factory original, apparently an upgrade from the rental agency. Satellite radio. I fiddled until I found a classic rock station. Billy Preston, "Will It Go Round in Circles." Sweet. I cranked it up, opened the throttle a little more, headed for trouble.

Feeling better than I had in months.

I drove like the devil was after me.

As it was, because Cherise had been right about the storm. Even I could tell now that it was going to be a bad one; the clouds were massing up, boiling in black towers as warm and cool air collided. A huge anvil formation, spreading out over the entire western horizon. It hadn't been moving fast, but it had been moving, the last I could see of it before it blocked out the sunset and sent us into premature darkness. I shifted stations from rock to weather, and caught reports of massive winds, fleets of tornados, flooding. The Weather Wardens were having one hell of a bad time, though so far they'd kept the tornados from touching down in any heavily populated areas. That was the best maintenance strategy— let the storm vent its energy where it wouldn't do as much damage and injury. But just from the news reports I could tell how much power was stored in that storm. Massive. And even the best Weather Wardens weren't going to be able to get to everything.

The rain hit us viciously about two hours later, right about the time that my body began urgently waving the yellow caution flag. I checked the clock; it was after midnight, and I'd been driving for far too long. I found a halfway decent roadside motel—a bland chain thing, but I wasn't concerned about originality right now so much as availability of pillows and mattresses. Cherise and Kevin had both fallen asleep some time back, and I had to wake them to check in. I hated leaving the Boss unescorted—*somebody* was going to recognize its value—but the best I could do was park it outside the two rooms I rented, under a strong light, and hope for the best. I couldn't keep my eyes open any longer.

One hot shower later, I crawled into bed next to David, who was flipping channels on the television. Looking for a twenty-four-hour news channel, apparently, because that was where he stopped. I sat there rubbing my wet hair to get it as dry as possible while I read the screen crawl at the bottom. The news airing at the moment was about the very storm we were in—not just us, but most of the eastern seaboard. Nasty. Easily as nasty as anything I had ever handled as a Weather Warden. There was a lot of damage. The death toll was already well into the hundreds and still rising.

What caught me, though, was the screen crawl, because it was *all* about disasters. Not just the storm, or its attendant deadly little brother, flooding . . . earthquakes along the New Madrid fault line, a whopping 7.5 on the Richter scale—more than twice as powerful as the biggest thermonuclear weapon ever exploded. It could have been worse; the scale went all the way up to 10, though the worst humans had ever lived through had measured a 9.5. Past that, it wasn't really going to be our problem anymore.

The quake had shaken pictures off of walls in South Carolina, and rung church bells as far away as Boston. At the epicenter of the shift, in Portageville, it was going to be much, much worse. There'd be nothing much left standing.

The Portageville quake was far from the only thing going on, aside from the storm. The screen crawl tallied up unexplained increases in animal attacks, particularly by bears and mountain lions, and an unexpected increase in poisonous snakebites in the Western states. Wildfires had started up in the deep forests, in total defiance of wet conditions, and seemed to be getting the better of fire teams and—presumably—Fire Wardens.

And that was just the U.S. The devastation wasn't confined to our shores. Virtually every continent was under attack. End-of-the-world prophets were out in force already, and they'd only get loonier and louder as things got worse.

The thing was, the end-of-the-world prophets probably weren't wrong on this one.

I found myself holding David for comfort. He shut off the TV, and we sat in silence, watching the afterimage burn for a few seconds before we collapsed together back to the mattress and pillows I had, just a little while ago, so greatly lusted after. Now I wasn't sure I could—or should—sleep. My body was still exhausted, aching, and needing to find some oblivion, but my mind was playing the Blame Game. *We did this. We started this. And we have to do something to stop it. People are dying.*

"Shhh," David whispered, and kissed my temple. His arms were warm and strong around me, even though I knew instinctively he was right now despairing of how much power he'd had, and lost. How frustrated and grief-stricken he was, too. How helpless in the face of the inevitable. "Let it go, Jo. You have to let it go, just for now. Rest. Please."

I didn't want to, but he seduced me into it, with the comforting heat of his body curled around mine, the steady calm rhythm of his heartbeat, his love obvious even to all my blinded senses in every touch and caress. He was being strong for me. Maybe he needed to be.

Maybe I needed him to be, too.

I fell asleep finally, wrapped in his arms, and we woke up hours later to a clap of thunder so loud it rattled pictures bolted to the wall, and set off car alarms in the parking lot. I felt blinded, instinctively terrified, and cringed against David. Clinging for comfort. How long since I'd been afraid of a storm?

I got hold of myself and crawled out of bed to look out the motel room window. It was like looking into a strobe flasher; the lightning was bright, constant, and *close*. Thunder followed, so loud that I could see the glass vibrate under the pressure of the sound waves. The lights were out in the parking lot, and, I realized, in the room as well; even the low-level night-light glow from the bathroom had gone dark. We'd been busted back to the primitive days, hiding in a cave, cowering from the storm.

It kind of pissed me off. So instead of retreating back into the dark and hugging David, I stood there in front of the glass window, practically daring the storm to do its worst. If I'd still been a Warden, it probably would have taken me up on it, too—but a normal human? It didn't even know I was there. That wouldn't keep it from killing me, just as it would ants, birds, cats, or anything else that got in its way, but it wasn't personal.

I would officially be collateral damage. Which *really* pissed me off.

Another eye-searing flash of lightning, and this time I saw the blue pop of a transformer blowing on a pole not far away. The pole caught fire, blazing like a creosote-smeared torch even through the driving rain. It gave the whole thing a hellish glow that was really, really unsettling.

"I think we need to get out of here," I said. David was already out of bed and dressing in the dark—cursing softly in a language I didn't recognize, mainly because he probably hadn't had to dress himself in the dark for, oh, about five thousand years, and in those days, there weren't quite as many challenges to the process anyway. "Is the phone working?"

His cursing got louder as he knocked the receiver off, but paused when he checked the line. "Yes," he said, and handed it to me to continue his fight with pants. I dialed Cherise's room number by touch. She picked up on the first ring.

"Holy crap, we need to go!" she said breathlessly. "That's what you were going to say, right?"

"That's what I was going to say."

"*So* glad I didn't unpack the luggage from the trunk. Let's do it. But you go first and unlock the doors, okay? Because I am not standing out in that."

She hung up before I could tell her that the castle had called and wanted its princess back. She was right, actually. I had the keys. I was the point person for this little expedition.

"Stay here until I get everything open," I told David, and tossed a towel over my head as I opened up the door. The wind promptly blew the wood back against the wall with a crash, and knocked me back two steps by sheer force before I got control and leaned into it.

Then I stepped outside, into the teeth of the monster.

I didn't dare look up, or around, or anywhere but at the Boss, sitting there with its chrome blazing in the flashes of lightning. Water was running off it in silver strings, and I lunged for the driver's-side door, got in, and manually unlocked the passenger side before diving out again, honking the horn. Cherise's door opened, and Kevin ran out, heading for the other side of the car.

Cherise followed him, staggering in the buffeting wind like a post-happy-hour drunk on her clunky platform shoes. The wind definitely made that flirty little

South Beach dress not safe for anywhere, but in seconds rain had flattened it securely down against her body. It was the next best thing to a swimsuit, really. Not that my shirt and jeans weren't waterlogged and streaming.

I didn't feel it coming the way I would have as a Warden. I felt the hairs rise on my arms, as if trying to escape my body, and for a blank second I wondered, *What the heck is that?*

And then a pure white bolt of power hit Cherise.

The force of it blew me over, and if it made a sound I don't remember hearing it. The shock lasted for at least three heartbeats, and then the cold rain brought me back around and I realized that *Cherise had just been struck by lightning.*

I staggered up. Cherise was still standing there, exactly as she had been. Wisps of steam curled off her bare arms and legs, up from her hair, and I screamed and closed the distance fast, waiting for her to collapse into my arms.

Instead, she opened her eyes, looked at me with a drugged, blissful expression, and said, "Wow. That felt . . . great."

I stopped, fighting for balance in more ways than one. She looked utterly relaxed. Unafraid. Maybe it was some weird side effect . . . ?

No, I realized. No, it wasn't, because over the two of us, the rain had stopped falling. It was running off a clear shield that enclosed us in a warm, still cone of air.

I knew what that was. I'd done it myself, many times.

Not Cherise. Cherise doesn't have Warden powers. . . . She can't . . . She never . . .

The shock was slowing me down, obviously, because I should have known already. David did, as he threw open the door of the Mustang and got out again. I saw the sudden, rigid set to his body, and the way he went completely still, even pounded by the rain.

Kevin got out, too, and in the next lightning flash his face looked ghostly and haunted, his eyes gone huge as he stared at Cherise. He looked empty. No, he *was* empty, I realized; he had gone up into the aetheric, and for a few seconds his body was just a waiting shell. Then he flinched and shook his head. "It can't be," he said. "She's—she's—"

"She's got Warden powers," I said flatly. "What are the odds that they came from someone else but me?"

Cherise smiled, warm and sweet and lovely, and said, "And it is *awesome*, by the way. Just so you know. It feels so—big! Like I'm part of everything, everywhere in the world—there's all this energy, and—"

"Cher!" I grabbed her by the shoulders, hard, and shook her until the bliss faded from her eyes. "Cherise, listen to me. You're not trained. You have no idea what you're doing. Don't—"

Electric shocks zapped through my hands, straight up my arms, and knocked me back with a stunning blow all the way to the Mustang. I found myself on the ground, skin tingling and aching, shaking all over. My muscles were buzzing.

David no longer moved at Djinn speed, but he was just as fast as any man seeing a threat to someone he loved, and as I tried to shake off the shock he did a classic cop roll over the hood of the car and went for her.

Kevin summoned up a fireball and dropped it neatly between David and Cherise, sending my husband stumbling back. "Don't try it, man," Kevin said. "It's not her fault."

I wasn't the only one in shock. Cherise hadn't moved since she'd given me the zap, but now, as the fire flamed unnaturally high between her and David, she let out a sharp, horrified cry and dropped to her knees next to me in the filthy water. "Oh my God, Jo, I didn't mean—I just—I just wanted you to let go of me, I—"

She reached out to touch me, then hesitated, staring at her hands.

I coughed and sat up. My ribs ached. I could feel residual trembles in all of my long muscles, but my heart seemed to be ticking along, if rapidly, and I was in control enough to be able to push dripping hair back out of my eyes. Even if it felt like a lot of effort to do so. "I think that proves my point," I said, and then had to pause for a racking round of coughing.

David tried to get to me. Kevin moved the fire in front of him, and I saw David really get angry—angry enough to do *anything.* He was only human now, but that kind of anger was nothing to fool around with. There was still a trace of Djinn in there somewhere; I could just feel it—even if it was only a memory of power. It made him fearless, and a little bit crazy.

He plunged through the fire.

Kevin yelped, surprised, and damped the flames down quickly—including the ones that had taken hold of David's clothes even in that brief instant of contact. David ignored the burns. He grabbed Kevin and slammed him back against the car with a hand around his throat, and I saw his muscles tighten. Kevin's eyes widened, and he clawed at David's hand, wheezing.

"David, don't," I managed to gasp, and got my coughing under control. There was something unpleasant in my mouth. I spat it out and tasted blood, but not a lot. That was good, right? Not a lot? Some part of my brain was grasping desperately for good news. "We don't have time for this."

"Don't," David said, attention still locked on Kevin's face, "*ever* do that again. Do you understand me?"

Kevin managed to nod. David let go, shoved him away, and knelt down to gather me in his arms. The look he turned on Cherise was black with fury.

"It's not her fault," I told him. "Kevin's right. She got

slammed with a ton of power, and she has no idea how to use it. She's like a baby with a nuclear bomb and a big shiny red button."

"Hey!" Cherise said, in almost her old tones. "I'm right here! Have a heart."

"No offense," I said, "but Wardens get trained. They get trained a lot. And even then, we make massive mistakes, and people die. You don't have that luxury, Cher. You're too powerful, all at once. Your learning curve means death tolls. Now take down the shield."

"What?" Cherise seemed blank. I pointed up at the invisible umbrella she was holding over us. Rain was pouring off of it in silver sheets. "I'm not—oh. I guess I am, huh?"

"Instinct. It'll kill you. Or actually, other people," I said. "Drop it. I'll show you how to build it right."

"I—don't think I know how to drop it. I mean, I didn't know how to put it up in the first place."

"Talk later, flee now," Kevin said, rubbing his throat and glaring at David. "Seeing as how we're going to *die* if we hang around here in Lightning Central."

I looked up at David, and saw his fierce love and anger and desire to lash out. And protect me. He was taking this being human thing harder than I was, after all. "Kevin has a point," I said. "Let's work it out in motion."

He didn't like it; I could see that, but he nodded and helped me to my feet. I was shaky but serviceable. Wetter than a sponge on the bottom of the ocean, but maybe I could get Cherise to dry me off as a training exercise. Then again, she'd probably desiccate me completely and leave me a dry, dead husk, so maybe not such a great plan after all.

"Maybe you shouldn't drive," David said.

"Ha! The day I can't drive the Boss is the day that you need to wrap me in plastic and leave me by the side of the road for the buzzards."

"Jo, I'm serious."

"So am I," I said. "Nobody drives it but me. Those are the rules. Now *get in the car*. Please. I don't need to argue, I just need to drive."

He didn't like it, but he nodded and helped me in. Cherise was maintaining the rain shield above the car, which was convenient even though it worried me in a Warden sense. There were all kinds of ways to power that kind of defensive capability, but the best ways, the ones that would ultimately have the least impact on the world around us, were the most difficult to learn. Cherise was, without a doubt, just grabbing raw power and slamming it into a form without regard for how out of balance the equations fell.

The storm had already noticed her. And it was going to get very interested now.

Everybody piled into the car, and I found the keys and started up the Boss. His engine caught with a fierce grumble, and I threw it into reverse as another lightning bolt slammed home, this one torching a tree near the corner of the parking lot. Combined with the still-burning telephone pole, the place was starting to look like it needed to be renamed the Disaster Drive-In.

"Sorry," I whispered, and peeled out of the parking lot. Once I hit road speed, I began to really start liking Cherise's shield, even if it was an energy suck monster. It was like driving under a mobile bridge, and it kept the rain from hammering the windshield, which was excellent. I opened up the Boss as we gained the access road for the freeway. When we reached the top of the ramp, I glanced over and saw three stabs of white-hot light smash down from the boiling clouds into the roof of the motel.

The trees weren't the only thing on fire anymore, and now there were innocent lives at risk—not just ours. The roof was burning, and it was possible that even with the rain, it would spread. The tree and telephone pole weren't showing any signs of going out.

"Kevin," I said. "Get that fire out."

"The rain will take care of it. I don't need to—"

"Did you hear me ask? Because I'm pretty sure I put it as an order, not a request for your opinion. Just do it. Now, Kevin!"

Kevin shut up and looked toward the burning roof. Seconds later, it snuffed itself out. He ended the blazes on the telephone pole and tree for good measure. Show-off. "Anything else, *boss*?"

"Yeah. Be quiet."

He shot me the finger, which did not shock me, and slumped back in his seat with a mutinous, pouty expression. Still not out of his teen angst, I saw. Or maybe he'd just grow up to be a pouty, petulant man. Yeah, that was going to be attractive.

I took a deep breath and looked over at David. "Are you okay? Not burned?"

"I'm fine," he said. "He put it out before it did any damage."

I made sure I had the Boss aimed straight and steady on the nearly empty rain-slick highway, and focused on the blurring lane markers for a while. Finally, I said, "Cherise, I need you to think how it felt when you put up the shield. What made you do it?"

"Um . . . I guess . . . I was getting wet. I didn't like it."

"Okay. Are you getting wet now?"

"Obviously not . . . Oh. Right. Okay. But I'm still wet. And kind of cold."

I turned up the heater and directed the blast toward the back, although I was cold and shivering, too. "Once your body is convinced you don't need it, you'll be able to let go," I said. "Your instincts are controlling your power, and that's a very bad thing, Cher." The other bad thing, although I didn't dare say it, was that in my experience, regular people weren't Wardens for a reason. There were changes in body chemistry in Wardens: different nerve conduction times, subtle differences that allowed us to handle and channel the kinds of power that would destroy—sooner or later—non-Wardens who tried to handle the same forces.

I didn't know whether the transfer of powers from me to Cherise—if that was what had happened—had also given her an upgrade on the physical side. If it hadn't, it was like putting jet fuel in a car's gas tank. It would run for only a short time before it exploded under the stress.

I needed her to back off from using them until a specialist, an Earth Warden with real knowledge, could get a look at what was happening inside of her. But if she allowed instinct to dictate how those powers were used, we were all in serious trouble, and there was no way she'd be able to control any of it. I didn't feel much like Yoda, but I'd have to do as a mentor.

"There is no 'try,' " I said, and then swallowed a laugh. "Okay, how is it now?"

"Better," Cherise said. "I feel better. Not as cold."

And sure enough, overhead, the shield holding the rain off us cut in and out for a few seconds, then collapsed completely. Instant white noise, from the rain pounding on the Boss's metal, and I engaged the wipers on full. No trouble seeing the road ahead, even with the torrential downpour. . . . Lightning was a constant event, strobing everything into horror-movie shadows and glares. "Good," I said, and put warm approval into my voice, even though I was freezing, still. "Good work, Cher. Did you feel it when it let go?"

"Yeah, I think so."

"All right, here's your first test. Try putting the shield back up again."

It took about thirty seconds, but she reestablished a

flickering, uncertain rain shield above the car, then, at my direction, let it go. We did that three times, until she could put up and take down the shield on command. "Good," I said. "Now you're controlling it; it's not controlling you. You feel that pulse of power that comes when you call? If you feel it coming when you *didn't* mean to call it, stop it. You know how. It's the same way you dropped the shield."

As teaching went, this was desperately inadequate. She ought to be sitting safely in a secured facility, hooked up to biofeedback equipment, getting instruction from a qualified Earth Warden who could walk her through things properly. But this was the Warden equivalent of first aid to the injured. . . . I just needed to get her stable for now. That meant teaching her whatever I could, as quickly as I could, while limiting her use of powers to the smallest expenditures possible.

It also meant outrunning this storm.

I opened up the Mustang and let him fly, and oh man, could he *fly*. The road vibration that was noticeable at lower speeds vanished as he hit his stride, and then it settled into a power glide so smooth it was like levitating as the speed needle hit a hundred.

This was dangerous. It wasn't that I hadn't driven this fast, under these conditions, before; I'd even done it while splitting my attention between controlling external supernatural forces and the road. But now I felt acutely human, powerless, and exposed. David couldn't cover me. Cherise was now as much of a hindrance as a help, and Kevin—God only knew what Kevin could do, other than blow things up. Which he would do with great enthusiasm, of course. That wasn't always a downside. . . .

"Something's happening," Cherise said suddenly. There was suppressed panic in her voice, and when I looked in the rearview mirror I saw that her eyes had gone wide, her face tight with fear. "I feel—it's like a spike, in my head, this feeling—something's *looking at me.* ..."

I knew that feeling. It was the storm, and it had found her. We were about to be targeted.

"Easy," I said, in my most calm and soothing voice. I gripped the steering wheel tightly to keep my hands from shaking. "That's okay, that's normal, all right? Take a deep breath. I need you to close your eyes now, and tell me what you see."

"What I see? With my *eyes closed*?" She laughed wildly. "I can tell you that right now. Black!"

"Just do it, Cher."

"Bitch, you are on my last nerve right now."

"I know. Just do it."

She shut her feverish, terrified eyes, and said, "Okay, happy now? It's dark. And—" Her words fell away into a sudden silence, and then she said, "Oh," in an entirely different voice. "What the hell is *that*?"

"Oversight," I said. "It's sort of the heads-up display version of going up into the aetheric, the energy realm. In the beginning you have to close your eyes to see it so you can concentrate. What do you see?"

"Uh . . . colors? Lots of colors. It's a trippy lava-lamp groove thing up in here. Which is cool, I guess." She was back on firmer ground now, and I could hear the relief in her voice. "What am I looking at?"

"Remember those Doppler radar maps we used back at the TV station?" I asked, and that helped steady her, too: the reference to our time together working at that low-rent local station as your stereotypical weather girls. Not that we hadn't gotten our own back on that one. "The neon-colored ones?"

"Oh yeah. Those things. So this is the storm I'm seeing."

"You're seeing the energy flows. I need you to tell me where it looks worst."

"Worst how, exactly?"

"You'll feel it." I couldn't explain it any better than that; I wasn't sure that how I'd perceive it would be a guide to how she would be able to process the information.

After a few seconds, she said, "That spot looks radioactive."

"Where?"

Without opening her eyes, she lifted a hand, and pointed.

Straight through the front window.

Ahead of our speeding car.

I jerked my attention away from her and took my foot off the gas exactly one second before the next lightning flash revealed what Cherise had seen in Oversight. . . .

A person.

Standing in the road.

Waiting for us.

"That's a Djinn!" Kevin yelled.

Like I didn't know that already, even without powers.

Chapter Four

"Hold on!" I screamed, and tried to change lanes. It was deadly at this speed, on wet roads, but I didn't have much choice; I had the distinct impression that hitting this particular Djinn would be like slamming full speed into the side of a mountain. Car versus mountain: never a good thing.

Unfortunately, physics was not my friend on either side of the choice just now, and as soon as I changed direction, the seal broke between the tires and the road, and we began to hydroplane. No antilock brakes on a vintage Mustang—it was all up to me, and it was happening in hypertime, speeded by adrenaline and sheer, massive momentum. I acted on ingrained training, turning the wheel gently into the skid, letting off the gas, staying off the brake. I kept us out of a spin and managed to keep us on the road, but we'd gone into a Tokyo drift sideways, sliding past the motionless Djinn at better than eighty miles per hour.

It turned, tracking to follow us.

"David!" I yelled.

"Old Djinn!" he said back. "Not one of mine!" Not good news under the best of circumstances, and these were far from the best.

The Djinn suddenly turned as we slid along, leaving it behind, and ran after us. In only three long strides it had hold of the bumper of the car, and I felt the slamming jerk of it stopping our skid. We were all thrown forward, hard enough to make my head feel a little fuzzy. Before I could blink, my driver's-side door was open, and the Djinn was leaning over me, close enough to bite my throat out. Which they had been known to do.

I yelped and flailed, but the Djinn put a hand flat on my chest and shoved me firmly against the seat. I thought for sure he was going to lean in and smash me like a bug, but the pressure seemed just enough to keep me still, not enough to shatter bone.

He unhooked my seat belt, picked me up like I weighed no more than a bulky bag of feathers, and came around to David's side of the Mustang. David was fumbling for the door latch, just about as out of it as I felt. The Djinn got there first, dumping me unceremoniously on my husband's lap. I pulled my legs in as he started to close the door again, and put my arms around David's neck.

"What the hell is going on?" David asked. I shook my head, mystified, as the unknown Djinn got in on the driver's side, ignored seat belt laws, and slammed the car into gear.

Whoever he was, he could drive like the proverbial devil. The Boss roared like a lion as he opened the engine up, and no matter how fast I'd gone, this was faster, wet roads be damned. I tried not to look. It was way too scary.

"Hey," Cherise said, in an out-of-it kind of voice that gained strength as she went along. "Who's driving this thing?" By the end, she sounded positively paranoid, which was a very bad thing. A scared Cherise was a dangerous one right now. I shook away my lingering bleariness and looked at her over the seat.

"It's okay," I said. "Everything's fine. We're in good hands." I dropped back down on David's lap and looked him in the eyes as I moderated my tone to a whisper. "We are, right?"

David cleared his throat and addressed himself to our new driver. "I don't know you." That was a neutral opening gambit, neither aggressive nor friendly. Considering the dude had just supernaturally carjacked us, I thought it was quite thoughtful. It was also quite useless, though. The Djinn didn't even glance at us. He just drove like a machine—like some extension of the car itself. He didn't even blink. His eyes were glowing, an unsettling color that hovered somewhere between green and gold, and—like most Djinn—he was striking in features. His were prominent and blunt, not handsome as most chose to be. A face of strength and immovable power, and a body to match. Greek sculptors would have adored him.

"Chatty," I said. "So what do we do?"

David shrugged very slightly. "He's taking us in the direction we were going anyway," he said. "He's better protection than we could ask against whatever might want to get in our way, including bad drivers. I suppose we wait and see just what he wants." He shifted a little, settling my weight better on his lap.

"Sorry," I said. "I know I'm not that light."

"You're fine," he said, and dropped his voice to an intimate whisper by my ear. "This is going to be a *very* enjoyable ride for me, you know. But frustrating."

I smiled and touched my lips gently to the pulse point below his jaw, where I knew he was especially sensitive, and felt him shiver. His hands tightened around me.

"Well," I whispered back, "we'll just have to see about that once we have some privacy."

"Time was I could make our privacy."

I didn't say anything to that, just put my hand flat on his cheek and looked into his eyes. He was tired, and still, on some level, quite sick. Lewis had done his best, but David's nature had been Djinn for a long, long time, and being human wasn't something he was good at dealing with long term. Some essential core of him *couldn't* deal with it. I could no longer feel the slow, inevitable drain of energy inside of him, but I knew very well that it was there.

Nice as it was to pretend that everything was going to be fine, we needed to get David's powers back where they belonged. That was much more important than recovering mine, at the moment. I could live without them for now. Not well. But . . . live.

"I'm okay," he said, and kissed my palm. I rested my head against his shoulder, content for the moment to be cuddled in his warmth as we hurtled at Djinn-inspired speed toward . . . what?

I couldn't begin to guess.

And somehow, with him, that was okay.

I fell asleep, and when I woke up the sun was blazing in the window like the fiery wrath of God. I winced and groaned, shifted my weight, and felt uncomfortably locked muscles protest. David woke up, too, and must have felt identically horrible, because he winced and tried to stretch out his legs.

The Djinn at the wheel hadn't blinked, moved, or otherwise communicated, as far as I could tell. I looked over David's shoulder. Cherise and Kevin were tangled together on the backseat. Kevin was snoring. Cherise was drooling on the knee of his blue jeans.

"Where are we?" I mumbled, and swiped hair out

of my eyes. How the hell did my hair get messed up when I had nowhere to move? Mystery of the universe. I didn't seriously expect anyone to answer—Kevin and Cherise were obviously in La-La Land, and David wouldn't have any more of a clue than me—but I got a response.

The Djinn who was driving opened his mouth, and said, "I'm taking you to the Oracle." He had a very odd voice—almost a chorus of voices, as if some group was speaking through him. Chilling, in fact. "We'll arrive in a few moments."

I felt a bolt of pure adrenaline that sent my heart racing at uncomfortable speeds. "Which Oracle?" There were three to choose from, and only one of them could be said to be on our side, even a little. The Earth Oracle was my daughter, Imara. . . . But we hadn't magically sped across half the country overnight, either. This still looked like eastern seaboard, to me, not the desert around Sedona. Which meant one of the other two Oracles, most likely . . . Air, or Fire.

God, I hoped it was Fire. Please.

David was looking . . . odd. I guessed he didn't know how to feel, considering that he used to have every right to talk to the Oracles, and now—being busted back to human—he wasn't sure whether he'd even be allowed to enter their presence. Or survive the experience.

"Relax," I said. "If whichever one it is hired us a driver, I'm guessing they're not going to just kill us on sight."

But it was a guess, pure and simple, and he knew it. I turned to Cherise and Kevin, who were waking up, yawning, stretching, and groaning just like David and I had done. "Before you ask," I said, "we're almost there. Wherever that is. And when we get there, the two of you are going to stay in the car. I don't want you anywhere near this."

"This what?" Cherise mumbled around a jaw-cracking yawn. "Ow."

"You don't need to know," I said. "And you don't need to do anything stupid, like try to rescue us, no matter what happens. Understand?"

Kevin nodded, not looking overly concerned one way or the other. Comforting. Cherise, at least, frowned and looked cutely annoyed, but she finally agreed.

Me, I was just hoping that wherever our newfound chauffeur was taking us had a bathroom, because I was in need. Badly. And my throat was parched, too.

It only took another five minutes or so after that for our driver to pull off the freeway, expertly whip in and out of traffic (which he could do with impunity, being Djinn and therefore beyond the reach of human law enforcement), and pull to a stop in front of a . . .

A mall.

He shut off the engine and sat there like a marble statue. David and I exchanged looks. I finally said, "Uh, hello? Instructions? Are we supposed to go shopping?"

His head turned. Well, it was more of an *Exorcist* twist, really—like it was on a swivel, not connected to the rest of his body. *Creepy.* Also creepy were his eyes, which continued to blaze an unearthly fire in a color that defied description.

"Out," he said. Just that. And the passenger-side door flung itself open, David's seat belt snapped back, and I felt a supernatural shove that sent me stumbling out onto the pavement. David collided with me a second later, and we steadied ourselves as the Mustang's door slammed shut again.

Cherise and Kevin goggled at us from the backseat. Cherise tried the door. Locked. She held up her hands in defeat and mouthed, *Sorry!*

That was fine. The last thing I wanted was for Cherise to try her hand at slinging some power around. It wouldn't end well for anyone concerned. She was so far overmatched right now that the Djinn in that car wouldn't even have left a smoke trail in destroying her. Not that she didn't have the potential inside of her—she did, in spades—but she had zero ability to channel and control it. She'd be more likely to blow herself, the mall, and whatever major metropolitan area we were in off the face of the Earth instead.

"Right," I said, and steadied myself on my cramping legs. "I guess we go in?"

"Seems like it," David said, and took my hand. He smiled. "Remember the first time you took me to a mall?"

"Yeah, that ended well. I almost got suffocated."

"And you drove off and left me behind," he said. "Don't try it again."

"Not a chance."

We looked at the glass doors of the entrance like it was the gates of Hell, and after a second to gather our composure—well, I was gathering mine, at least—we moved forward and into the mall.

I don't know what I expected to happen—maybe that we'd be transported to some other, intimidating supernatural place?—but on the other side of the doors was a busy food court, full of cheap tables and flashing neon and the smells of a dozen different kinds of food. Families with crying kids in tow. Teens traveling in packs, for whom nothing existed outside of their own insulated circle of friends. Seniors in walking shoes making the rounds. It was a bustling indoor community, with snacks and shopping bags and a life of its own.

"I love a good mall," I said to David, "but I really have no idea what we're supposed to do here. I mean, I could use a pair of shoes. . . ."

"If you're going to shop, you'd better get Cherise, or

she'll kill you," he pointed out. "But I think we're supposed to do something else."

"Well, it'd be nice if someone gave us a *sign*. . . ."

· At the far end of the food court was the neon-lit entrance to a multiplex theater. The NOW SHOWING signs were giant TV screens, which I supposed was easier than the old stick-up letters.

One of them was flashing text in the biggest possible letters. It said ENTER HERE.

I cleared my throat and pointed. "Would you call that a sign?"

The letters immediately changed to read ENTER NOW OR DIE.

"I'd say so," David said. "And not a welcome-to-the-neighborhood sign, either."

Didn't seem so. I tried to control the twisting of my stomach as we moved off toward the theater, threading past baby strollers and people just standing in the way. When we were still twenty feet away, the lettering changed again.

It said, in red flashing letters, FASTER.

"Crap," I said, and dropped David's hand to race him to the entrance. That drew stares. I wondered why nobody could see the sign, but then decided that the Oracle wanted it that way. It was meant for us. And it was meant to scare us.

It was working.

I plunged through the door under the flashing sign, just a step ahead of David, and stumbled into . . . fog. White, featureless fog, cool and damp and cloying on my skin. It felt thick and heavy and *alive*, pressing down on me as I stumbled to a stop, unable to see anything in the thick white mist.

I reached back and flailed for David's hand.

He wasn't there.

I spun around and scissored my arms wildly, trying to find him, sure he had to be *right there* . . . but he wasn't. He was nowhere within reach. "David!" I shouted. "David, can you hear me?"

Nothing. It felt as if my words were swallowed up, as if the fog around me was so thick and heavy it was suffocating sound. It was like drowning in a cloud, and my breath came faster as the feeling of claustrophobia intensified. I held out my hands and took a step, hoping for something—anything—to tell me where I was. This was worse than being blind, somehow. It felt like I *should* be able to see, and my eyes constantly strained, trying to focus on nothing.

"Hey!" I yelled. "Oracle? You wanted me, here I am!"

The mist around me suddenly thickened, choking me, trapping me in a gelatinous blanket, and I struggled to get a breath that didn't feel like a ball was being shoved down my throat.

A shape appeared out of the mist—but only a shape. A shadow, like glass filled with the same mist that surrounded me. No features, no face, nothing but a chilly kind of menace. It was terrifying, and I realized that I was seconds away from dying if I couldn't get the Air Oracle to stop tormenting me.

I did the only thing I could.

I gave up.

I stopped struggling, stopped trying to choke in a breath, and relaxed. The mist supported me, flowing like syrup through my clothes, along my skin, caressing me in intimate and cold ways that felt repulsively invasive.

I let it happen.

The pressure of mist inside my lungs let up, and I whooped in a breath of air just as the edge of my vision started to go dark and sparkly from oxygen deprivation.

Human.

It wasn't a voice, exactly, or a thought either. It was more of a vibration that didn't register in my ears, but in my flesh. As if the Oracle was speaking through my bones.

It hurt.

I gasped, and suddenly the mist holding me up let go, dropping me to my hands and knees on the featureless white floor—except that it still felt like more insubstantial fog. I had the dizzying sensation that I was standing on a cloud, that only the Oracle's whim kept me from hurtling through the vapor tens of thousands of feet down to my death. . . .

Weak, the thought vibration came, this time rich with overtones of contempt. *Useless. As I thought.*

I coughed and wiped my mouth with the back of my hand. I tasted blood, but it seemed to be confined to my throat. "The Mother's waking up," I said. "Isn't she?"

No answer. The ghostly form of the Air Oracle wavered, changing in fluid, subtle ways.

"*You* don't want her to wake up," I said, filling in the blanks. "It will take away all your power. All your individuality." The Oracles weren't necessary if Mother Earth, the consciousness of the planet itself, took direct command of her Djinn. They'd be blown out of existence, burned away—or reduced to Djinn, no more or less. The Air Oracle, of all three that I'd met, was by far the most haughty and power-mad. No wonder it had taken action. "Look, it's not in the interest of the Wardens or humanity for her to wake up, either. Or even the Djinn. They lose their individuality to her, their ability to think for themselves. They don't want that. Not even the Old Djinn."

No answer. The Air Oracle just hovered.

"David and I both lost our powers," I said. "If you help us get them back I may be able to stop this. I can try, at least. The Wardens need every bit of help they can get."

You ask a favor, came the reply, in slow, measured throbs through my body.

"No. I'm asking you to act in your own interests," I said. "It's in your interest to put back what I lost, and restore David's powers."

That was risky. The Air Oracle had *never* been on the side of humanity. If anything, it was on its own side, only paying lip service to the other Oracles. There were a few times when it had intervened, but not many, and never from altruistic motives.

Mercenary little sexless bastard.

The Air Oracle was silent. I hated dealing with eternal beings. No sense of urgency. "At least restore David's powers," I said. "He is a Conduit. He can reach the Mother. Maybe he can stop her."

No, the Oracle said immediately, and the single word, the *concept*, was rich with contempt. *He cannot. It is a waste of energy.*

Great. David hadn't made a fan out of this Oracle, any more than I had.

Once humans are gone, the Mother will release us, the Oracle continued, with cold and inexorable logic. *The world will be ours. As it should be.*

I swallowed hard. "If you really believed that, why bring us here?"

There were no features on that misty face, but I had the impression of a shark's smile, something hungry and merciless. *To be sure you don't stop it.*

The mist closed in, and this time, it wasn't just suffocating, it was *crushing*. I had time to gasp in one inadequate breath before the weight slammed into me from back and front, squeezing. When I opened my mouth, the mist jammed itself in, choking me.

No! I'm a Weather Warden*! This can't happen!* But it

was happening, no matter how much I wanted to deny it. I had no power to fight an Oracle, no tricks, nothing but the sheer panicked will to live.

And that wasn't enough. Not here.

I felt hot sparks of pain through my body as muscles strained, joints began to fail, bones bent. It was going to smash me flat and leave me a leaking carcass, and there was nothing I could do to stop it. . . .

All of a sudden, a hurricane wind whipped through the mist, cold and clear and edged with ice. It tattered the forces holding me, revealing the Air Oracle looming over me in its faceless, sexless menace. Suddenly, I could breathe. I dropped to my hands and knees, gasping in ragged gulps, and looked around to see what the hell had just happened.

Oh crap.

Cherise stood there, tiny and cute in her flirty dress and perfect tan. She was showing teeth. It wasn't a smile. Maybe it had started out being a confident grin, but as the Air Oracle focused its attention on her instead of me, it became more of a demented, if terrified, snarl. Her blond hair was streaming in the wind, and as I watched, she extended a hand out toward the Air Oracle and pushed force at it.

"No!" I yelled, and dropped flat on the white, slightly spongy floor, pressing myself as low as I could go. Cherise's attack rolled over me, and even as small a target as I'd made, I felt it freeze my back as it glanced over me.

Cold air is heavy, and Cherise wielded it like a bat, slamming it into the fragile Air Oracle and scoring a home run. The Air Oracle broke apart into streams of white-hot energy, and its scream echoed through my bones with such force I actually thought something would break inside me.

"Cher, *stop*!" I screamed. "You can't win this! Stop!"

"Shut up," she said, and grabbed me by the ankle with both small hands as she backpedaled through featureless white space. "What the hell did you get me into this time? Stop kicking!"

"Stop pulling me like a toy pony!" She let go, and I rolled up to my knees and bounced to my feet, driven by adrenaline and sheer terror. "We have to leave. Right now."

"Yeah, about that, how?"

I made a helpless flailing motion with my hands, frustrated beyond any measure. "Just—I don't know—*do it!* Gah! This is not the time for on-the-job training, because that Oracle is going to be—"

Really pissed, I was going to say, but honestly, that fell far short of what was happening about fifteen feet away, where the Air Oracle was reforming in a black, roiling cloud that glittered with icy edges. It was lit from within by flashes like swallowed lightning, and even as paranormally blind as I was right now to subtle forces, I could feel the menace in the air. It was going to kill us really, really dead, and it wasn't going to screw around doing it.

"Out!" I yelled, and grabbed Cherise's hand. "Think about the mall!"

Cherise said, in a plaintive little voice, "But I don't know what's *in* this mall. . . ."

Oh *fuck*, we were going to die.

The Air Oracle roared toward us, and the mist closed in, and hope vanished with the open space. I felt Cherise's hand in mine but I could no longer see her, couldn't see anything but white, as if the mist had entered my eyeballs and filled them up.

Cherise let out a shriek of pure, full-throated terror, and suddenly we were falling *through* the floor, as if those imagined white clouds had given way. Ten thousand feet to the killing ground . . .

... but we landed on carpet in about six inches, just enough to jolt and send us both staggering a couple of steps. Mist curled off of both of us in thick, milky wisps, and as Cherise dropped my hands and frantically batted at her clothes, it leaked out in streams, sliding down her legs to pool on the carpet and disappear.

"Oh my *God*, that is creepy!" she said. "Is it in my hair? Tell me it's not in my hair!"

I couldn't, because it was rolling down in waves down her back. From her hair. She was right; it was creepy and it felt wrong, like some kind of ectoplasmic slime instead of just an innocent water vapor. Ugh. I shook my hands and arms and watched it fly off me to melt in the air.

Then I took a look around. We were in a store. A shoe store, to be precise, and it was empty except for one store clerk who'd apparently been in the back, and now came around the counter, having missed the whole appearing-out-of-nowhere-dripping-with-ectoplasm floor show. "Hi, can I help you?"

"Sorry," I said, recovering whatever remained of my composure. "Give us a second."

He looked doubtful, but nodded and backed off. I turned to Cherise and dragged her off to admire a rack of shoes neither one of us wanted, at least right at the moment. "I have to find David!" I hissed. "We were together, but we got separated!"

"Oh my God, he's not still in there . . . ?"

If he was, I'd just lost him forever. The enormity of it slammed in on me so hard that I literally lost my balance, and Cherise had to grab my arm to keep me from toppling into the size sevens. *If you hurt him*, I thought to the Air Oracle, *if you kill him, I will destroy you. I don't know how, but I will.*

"It couldn't," I said aloud, and tried to make myself believe it. "David's not just anybody. It can't just kill him. Even Ashan wouldn't ignore that."

Presuming anything made sense anymore. Presuming Ashan, the leader of the Old Djinn, had an identity of his own, still, and was capable of making his own decisions. If the Mother was waking up, the Djinn were lost to us as individuals, and while she might notice and care about the Djinn David, the human David might not even be noticed.

"I'll go back," Cherise said.

"Are you *mental*? You're not going anywhere!"

"Well, *you'd* go back. And I'm kind of you, now."

"No, Cher, you're not! Just—I told you to stay in the car!"

"You'd be dead if I had!"

Well, she did have a point there. "I have to find David," I said.

"Yeah, what's your plan for that? Mall intercom?"

"No," I said. "Movies."

We headed out of the shoe store, which was inexplicably halfway across the mall, and made the best possible time back to the multiplex cinema outside the food court. The sign was no longer flashing ENTER HERE, or making dire threats. It was advertising a Disney film.

I turned a slow circle, taking in the standard mall view—tiled floors, towering indoor plants, escalators, elevators, stores, shoppers, food vendors with all their flashing neon. Crying children and harassed clerks.

Someone in a black windbreaker and cheap uniform pants moved past us, walking fast. Mall security, talking on a brick of a walkie-talkie. She sounded tense, although she was keeping her voice down.

I zeroed in on her and followed.

"Where are we going?" Cherise asked. I didn't answer. "Because we really need to get out of here. This Oracle person wasn't fooling around, you know."

"The Air Oracle has no set space," I said. "It can go anywhere it wants. If it wants to get to us, it will."

"Oh, *that's* comforting. You could have told me that before I pissed it off."

Despite everything, I smiled. "Yeah," I said. "I could have. But it wouldn't have been as much fun."

"Bitch." Cherise fell silent, because the mall security lady was hurrying even more now, heading for a figure slumped on a bench with two more security guards around it. One pale hand was resting on the tiled floor, and I could see blood dripping.

As the security guards turned to look at the newcomer, I saw a glimpse of auburn hair.

"David!" I shrieked it, couldn't stop myself, and plunged for the knot of people without any regard for my own safety, or theirs. They sensibly got out of my way, and oh God, I was right. It was him.

David was lying on the bench, curled on his side, breathing shallowly. His face was shockingly pale, and he looked . . . fragile. Terribly . . . human. There was blood, but I couldn't tell where it was coming from.

He opened his eyes when I touched his face, and it took a few seconds for him to focus on me. When he did, relief flooded through him, and he tried to sit up. "No!" I said, and made him stop. "What *happened*?"

"I was right behind you," he said. "But you were gone. You were gone, and I was running—"

"You know this man?" one of the officers said. "Miss?"

"He's my husband," I said. My voice was shaking. "David, are you okay?"

"He ran into a plate glass window," the guard said. "He's got a nasty cut on his side. Paramedics are on the way. Sir, have you been drinking?"

"What?" I sat back on my heels, staring up at him. I

couldn't honestly understand what he was talking about. "Drinking?"

"He came out of nowhere and ran face-first into the glass," the guard said. "Usually that means alcohol or drugs. Maybe both."

"No. No, he just—he was looking for me." I looked down at David's pale face, at the red, human blood soaking his shirt. "He was afraid for me."

"Guess I had no reason to be," he said, and tried to smile, but it turned into a wince. "What happened?"

"Nothing."

"Liar," he whispered. His eyes closed for a few seconds, then opened again. "Cherise? I thought we told you to stay in the car."

She shrugged, back to her old self. "It's the *mall*," she pointed out, blankly mystified. "I thought you were kidding. Hey, and I saved your girl, so there."

He looked at me a little doubtfully, so I smiled. "She did," I said. "Although to be fair she almost got us both smashed, too."

"Sounds right. Help me up."

"Nope. You're staying down."

The security guards didn't quite know what to make of us now. . . . They'd pegged us as drunken troublemakers, but we weren't acting that way. A little giddy with relief, maybe but not intoxicated—though I admit, if somebody had passed me a bottle, I'd have taken a generous swig right about then.

All three of the guards' radios suddenly crackled, and a voice on the other end brayed, "Get over here, guys, right now! South entrance, in front of the—"

It broke up into static. The three security guards exchanged a *what now?* look, and then the most senior of them looked down at me. "Miss, you stay right here. Paramedics will be here in a couple of minutes."

I nodded, and the three windbreakers hustled off into

the milling crowd, heading for whatever trouble was brewing. I started to return my attention to David, but I heard something.

Screaming.

Coming from the south entrance, which was all the way at the other end of the mall. The screaming was dopplering our way, and as I stood up to look, I saw that at the long straight end of the hall, people had rounded the corner and were stampeding in full flight in our direction. Some were still carrying shopping bags, but I had the impression that it was only because it hadn't occurred to them to drop everything. They certainly weren't slowing down as they ran, and I wondered exactly what could have put a full hundred dedicated shoppers to flight. Terrorism? Fire? Ebola?

I felt a tremor through the floor, and felt a sick twisting in my stomach. "Change of plans," I said. "David, up. We'll help you get back to the car. "Cher—where's Kevin?"

"In the car."

"He let you go by yourself?"

"I told him I had to use the bathroom."

Well, that wouldn't hold him for long, if I knew Kevin. As I looked around, I saw that most of the mall crowd had taken alarm and was streaming for the exits—not yet running at this end, but certainly moving with purpose.

One tall, lanky, skinny figure was pushing through upstream, heading for us. "Jesus," he said, taking us in as he arrived. "When you chicks go to the mall, you really tear the place up."

He was looking toward the south, where the screaming crowd originated, and I said, "What do you see?" I felt frustratingly handicapped, as I helped David to sit up and got his hand firmly placed over the wound in his side. "Kev?"

"No idea," he admitted. "It's just a mass of—

something. I can't see what it is, except it's heading this way, and I think all these people running might have a real good idea."

He grabbed David's arm and hoisted him to his feet, taking most of David's weight, and we blended with the general exodus.

Behind us, something exploded. Kevin turned, staring back, and extended a hand to snuff out a ball of fire that was rolling through the broad tiled hall in a hellish, orange-black rush. He stopped it before it did more than singe the lagging runners. Before he could turn around again, another explosion rocked the building, prompting more screams and a mob of panicked, running people through the food court, sending tables and chairs flying.

"Let go," David said. "Go do what you need to do."

Kevin glanced at him, nodded, and spun away to plunge toward the danger. I quickly braced David as he wavered, and Cherise bit her lip and looked indecisive. "Should I . . . ?"

"No," I said firmly. "Cher, if you want to help, look out for people who can't get out on their own." There were plenty of them—people in wheelchairs struggling to make headway through the sudden minefield of debris, people on walkers shuffling along at their best speed, a few who'd tripped and were trying to get up but kept getting knocked down. Situations like this, people would get trampled.

I took a deep breath. "David, can you stay up?"

"Go," he said, nodding. His face was ghostly, but his eyes burned with determination. "I'll make it. You two help."

I headed for a grandmotherly type in a power scooter, who was stranded by a drift of fallen chairs, and kicked them out of the way as I offered a bracing arm to an older gentleman with a cane who'd been knocked off his feet. "Here," I said, and put them together. "Buddy system. Make sure you both get out, okay?"

They nodded, too scared to do anything but obey whatever order sounded official at the moment. It was a good partnership. The old guy shoved things out of the way, and kept one hand on her scooter for stability as they moved along.

I grabbed up a couple of screaming kids who were missing their parents and flagged down a lady with a stroller, who took the toddlers on. There was a teenage girl down near the Subway counter—out cold, with a swelling bruise on her head from where she'd fallen and knocked herself out on the tile. I dragged two teen boys to a stop and put them in charge of her. They looked shocked. It was probably the first time anybody had asked them to be in charge of anything. They grabbed her and towed her out.

By the time I'd made it close to the north exit, most of those able-bodied shoppers had cleared out, leaving a few injured, and one asthma sufferer who needed her inhaler, dropped somewhere back in the panic. Nothing I could do for her but send her on her way, and appoint yet another unwilling Samaritan to make sure she got to emergency help.

"Jo!" Cherise yelled from the other side of the food court. "Get out!"

I wasn't about to, because not only was Cherise still inside, so was David. He'd stopped moving, in fact, and turned to face the south entrance. The food court was unnaturally empty and full of discarded bags, purses, coats, and spilled food and drink. Neon buzzed and blinked. I smelled acrid smoke and burning food on a grill somewhere.

Then there was a sound like nothing I'd ever heard, and Kevin came flying from around the corner, driven back like a limp rag doll. He hit the ground unconscious, or dead, and rolled to a flopping, boneless stop against the far wall. Cherise screamed and did some broken-field running through the maze of debris, heading for him.

I headed for David. He was very still, tense, gasping in shallow breaths that told me he probably had cracked ribs. Or, God forbid, internal injuries. Blood was a thick, dark stain spilling down the side of his pants, dripping over his shoes, and spreading on the floor.

"Djinn," he said. "It's the Djinn."

"That's not possible."

Except it was.

A Djinn walked out of the smoke and darkness, and where she walked, flames broke out, concrete shattered, glass powdered, water gushed. She was the touch of destruction, neatly packed in an almost human form.

Tall, strong, dark-skinned, with a multitude of thick black cornrows that shifted like snakes on her head. She was wearing bright blood red, and her eyes had taken on a pure white shine.

Rahel.

But she was no friend of mine. Not anymore.

Cherise made it to Kevin's side and tried to drag him out of the way. A fireball blasted out of Rahel's hand, heading straight for them. Cherise screamed and shook Kevin to try to wake him, but he was out completely. . . .

Sheer instinct guided her, and desperation, and—I strongly suspected—love. She flung out her hand, and the fireball smashed down on them—and flared around them in a white-hot glowing blast, diverted to gouge steaming chunks out of the wall on either side.

Rahel stopped, cocked her head, and considered Cherise for a second before renewing the attack. Again, Cherise blocked it. Barely. When Rahel ended the fire stream, I saw Cherise collapse back against the wall, weeping, shaking, unable to summon up the energy to even put a brave face on it.

Rahel raised both hands.

"No!" I screamed, and flung myself forward, swinging my arms over my head and jumping up and down. "Over here! Fresh meat!"

"What the *hell* do you think you're doing?" David hissed. Rahel turned her head and locked on us with those white, blind, shimmering eyes, and I felt panic well up in my throat, strong enough to choke me.

I had no *idea* what I was doing. Except buying time for my friends to live another moment. And maybe that was enough. Right now, in this one instant, I had a kind of shining clarity of purpose that I didn't understand, and really couldn't have said was sane, exactly.

David took my hand in his, and Rahel turned to face us. Pieces of the mall were falling apart behind her, smashing and shattering. Choking dust and smoke flooded the hall, and the neon lights—no, *all* the lights— went out.

We were going to die in the dark.

I could still see Rahel's eyes in the dim glow of the distant skylights overhead—unblinking and predatory, the eyes of something with no purpose but destruction.

She'd lost herself to the madness of Mother Earth, who was lashing out against what had hurt her, with no rational thought. There was nothing David or I could do to reach her. I thought about Rahel lying in the hospital bunk on board the ship, and I felt tears burn in my eyes that weren't due to the smoke and dust. I'd thought we'd lose her then, but at least she would have died as herself.

I wished I was dying as myself. My *old* self. That would have been . . . better.

Rahel's lambent eyes blinked.

She didn't fry us.

"David?" I whispered. "Is that her, or—?"

"I don't know," he whispered back.

Whatever internal battle went on, Rahel lost it. She raised her hand, palm out, and I knew we were going out not in a blaze of glory, but just in a blaze.

Fire streaked at her from her left and slammed into her with overwhelming force, knocking her sideways and to the floor. In the sudden lurid light, I saw that Kevin was turned on his stomach, still flat on the floor, but holding up a hand and burning the holy hell out of the Djinn. She flailed, trying to get up; he kept up the attack, not letting her get her balance or counterattack.

"He can't," David said. "He can't do that!"

"What, act like a flipping idiot? He does it all the time!" I yanked on David's arm, trying to get him to move with me. "We need cover—come on!"

"No, he can't *do that*," David said, and I watched as Kevin continued to pour more and more power through his body, crushing Rahel down. "Jo—"

I knew, in a blinding flash, what he meant. Oh *crap*. No freaking *way*. It made a weird kind of sense, but . . .

Kevin surged to his feet, and his eyes flared into colors that shouldn't have been possible in a human. Hot, fluorescent green. He bared his teeth and walked *toward* Rahel, pummeling her now with massive pieces of concrete he levitated up from the wreckage.

"You think you can take me, bitch?" he said, and laughed. It rolled through the devastation like thunder. "You think you can hurt *us*? Think again!"

Something in Kevin had woken up. Something terrible and powerful and raw.

And it wasn't just Warden powers, no matter how powerful; there was something else inside him.

Djinn powers. *David's* powers.

"Can he kill her?" I asked. David was shuddering

slightly now, taking in the full extent of what had happened. "David! Can he?"

"Yes," he said, in a faint, distant voice. "If he doesn't stop."

I let go of David's hand and lunged forward, vaulting over the debris, ignoring the resulting scrapes and bruises and cuts as I scrambled toward Kevin.

And when I got there, I slapped him across the face. Hard.

Kevin blinked, shocked, and turned those eerie Djinn-green eyes on me.

Then he backhanded me ten feet across the floor.

"Hey!" Cherise yelped, and stepped in front of him as he tried to come after me. "Enough! What are you doing?"

Cherise brought him back to himself, enough that he dropped his attack against me and looked back at Rahel, who was buried under a mess of rubble, motionless. When he blinked this time, his eyes faded back to their normal color, and he staggered and almost fell. I rolled slowly to my feet, feeling every twinge myself. I'd been lucky he hadn't shattered bones. If there had been a wall in the way, I'd be drowning in blood.

David was picking his way slowly toward me. I motioned for him to stop, and looked at Kevin and Cherise. "We have to go," I said. "Now."

They both nodded, clearly not sure what the hell was going on anyway.

We left Rahel where she lay—alive, I presumed, though she wasn't stirring—and our bruised little band of heroes limped out into the parking lot of the mall.

Which no longer looked like a parking lot.

Cars were twisted and smashed, rolled over on their sides and tops, some torn into scrap. People wandered helplessly, looking shell-shocked and confused. One woman, clearly not thinking at all, kept pointing her key-chain remote at one wreck after another, trying to identify her own car, as if it would matter.

Shivering clumps of people were huddling for comfort. Nobody was screaming now. It was too overwhelming, and there was nowhere to go. The woods beyond us were on fire, and smoke darkened the sky. So did roiling black clouds, streaming in from the south.

"My God," Kevin breathed. It sounded like a prayer—which was new, coming from him. "It's really happening, isn't it?"

The Mustang was sitting right where we'd left it. The Djinn was sitting motionless behind the wheel, like some crash test dummy. His head swiveled to regard us as we got near. "Get in," he said.

I didn't. I didn't trust the Djinn anymore, after what I'd seen of the Air Oracle, not to mention Rahel. Still ... his eyes weren't that tell-tale shining white, and he'd managed to keep the car safe in the middle of a truly world-class disaster scene.

"Get in," he repeated, and I heard that odd chorusing effect in his voice again, as if more than one person was speaking through him. "Lord, you people are so hard to save."

The voice had shifted again, one taking prominence—a honey-dark voice with a Southern accent. Female. I knew it, but I couldn't exactly place it. "Who—who am I talking to?"

"Who did you think you'd be talking to, sugar?" the Djinn mouthpiece said, and all of the doors blew open on the car, inviting us inside. "Who's still locked up like that damn genie in a bottle that all the stories talk about?"

David smiled in pure, wild relief. "Whitney," he said. "It's Whitney."

Kevin and Cherise looked at us both like we'd gone

insane. "That guy is talking like a girl," Kevin pointed out. "Like a *Southern belle*."

"More like down-South trailer—"

"Hey," the Djinn said, annoyance curdling the honey in her voice. "This is *my* long-distance call, children. Don't waste my minutes. Now get in the car, please."

"She's okay," David said. "Get in."

And we did, although none of us except David felt a hundred percent good about it, I thought. As soon as we were strapped in, the Djinn's out-of-character voice said, "Y'all hold on now. This is going to get real interesting." She said it with all the vowels. *Int-er-est-ing.*

I gulped as I felt the car lurch, and then it rocketed straight up, twenty feet in the air, and zoomed like a jet over the wrecks in the parking lot. Well, more like a sustained, long jump, maybe, because as we reached the road the trajectory sharpened, and we thumped down on the pavement in the first open space available.

The Djinn hit the gas and started his Jeff Gordon impersonation again.

"Whitney is the Djinn I left behind as insurance when we sailed out," David said. "Sealed up in a pocket universe at Jonathan's house, away from everything. She was my backup as Conduit."

"Still am, sugar," Whitney said. This time, her voice came out of the radio, which was only about half as weird as when it was coming out of the male Djinn. "And I'm just about the only damn help you've got, so be grateful. I can't believe you stuck me with this job."

"Not intentionally," David said, and winced as I prodded his wounded side. "Believe me, I'd rather have my powers back."

Neither of us mentioned the big, stinky elephant in the car, which was Kevin, sitting in the backseat, looking shaken and deeply disturbed. Kevin, who had somehow acquired powers he shouldn't have had.

Like Cherise.

Surprisingly, it was Kevin who interrupted the pregnant pause. "I don't want it," he blurted. He looked green, and I wondered if he was about to get sick all over us. He swallowed twice, and finally seemed to get himself together. "I want to give it back to you. Whatever the hell that is."

"Don't think it works that way," Whitney's voice said, briefly snowed by static midway through. The tuner slid to another station, and she came through more clearly. "If it wasn't you, it'd be somebody else. Maybe somebody not as ready."

"What are you talking about? And where are you taking us?"

"If I told you, you wouldn't believe me," Whitney said. "Told you, you were going to regret making me do this, boss man."

"Whitney, just—" David made a frustrated little gesture. "Get on with it. I'm bleeding."

"Bet *that's* new for you," she said, about as sympathetic as a shark. Talk about your steel magnolias. "Making you just a little irritable?"

"Whitney, I'm going to climb through that radio and kick your ass," I snapped. "He's not the one you ought to be worried about."

She laughed, a rich, whiskey-dark sort of sound. The least likely Djinn I'd ever met, and I'd met some doozies. I guessed that was why she'd made such an impression on David in the first place. Choosing Whitney for his backup as Conduit had been unorthodox, to say the least, and (I suspected) not exactly popular with the few thousand others who probably felt they had a better shot.

But she had qualities; I'd give her that. For one thing,

none of the other Djinn would ever be able to get the better of her, because none of them could understand her. There was such a thing as being too human, and Whitney was the poster child.

"You are just full of it, Joanne," she purred. "Nice to know some things just never change. Now, what were we talking about?"

"You said if it wasn't Kevin . . ."

"Of course. Ain't that obvious? If it isn't Kevin, it's whoever's standing closest to you two. You didn't really think the law of averages worked that way, that the two people you picked to tag along just *happened* to end up with your lost powers?"

When she put it like that, I had to admit, it *did* seem unlikely. There had been lots of people on board the ship, and any one of them could have received the power that had been ripped out of us in the formation of the black corner. . . . So why had it been the two people closest to us now?

"It's not them," I said slowly, working my way through it. "It's us."

"You're not nearly as silly as you look," Whitney said. "Fact is, whatever happened to you out there, it blew you apart and put you back together again, but somehow your power got left out. It's like a ghost, trailing you around. It'll settle into anybody you spend time with, including those two."

David straightened up, which probably wasn't smart; more blood darkened his shirt, and he pressed a hand to the wound. "Then we can get it back."

"Can't get it back," Whitney said crisply. "Not like you are. You're all locked off, and I have to tell you, you ain't looking too good. Never mind that hole in your side. . . . You're drying up like a water hole in the Sahara, running out of power. Won't make it all that much farther, you know."

I looked over at David in alarm. His face was set and pale, giving away nothing, but I knew it was true. Whitney wasn't known for her tact, but she wouldn't lie, not about that. "Nothing I can do about it," he said. "If I can't get my powers back . . ."

"Not on your own. But that's why I'm taking you to someplace you can get some help."

"Whitney, *you* can do it," I said. "You've got the Conduit to the Earth now. You could fix this."

"Could," she agreed blandly. "But my orders were to stay right here, in this cozy little house with the roaring fire where nobody can get at me. And I like it here. You seen what's going on out there? It's messy."

She was hiding out in Jonathan's house, a peculiar little bubble of the aetheric that seemed to float apart from everything else. Time and space didn't really exist there—or at least, they existed only as Jonathan had first created them to be. Which wasn't like anywhere else. The advantage was that anything in that house was protected from the chaos here on Earth.

The downside was that the protection was very specific. Humans couldn't reach the refuge, only Djinn, and only Djinn who were allowed in. David and I were completely out of luck.

"You have to come *here*," I repeated. "Whitney, he's . . ." *Dying.* I couldn't really say it. Saying it would make it terrifyingly real. "Please come."

Her radio-wave voice gentled, turned warm and compassionate. "I know," she said. "I know how scared you are. But if I leave here, I'm gone, and you know it. Every Djinn out there is *hers* now, no thoughts, no personality. They're just lashing out at whatever hurts her. You don't want me out there. I wouldn't help, and I'd be just as lost as the rest of them."

Except, curiously, for the Djinn driving the car. I

frowned, staring at him. He turned his head and stared back, not bothering to watch the blurring road. Djinn—they're really not like us. And sometimes it's really, really creepy.

"He's empty," Whitney said. "Something bad happened to him, a long time ago, poor thing. Mother Earth can't lay a finger on him."

"But you can."

"Well, yeah." Whitney sounded surprised. "You got to know how to do it, that's all."

I decided I really didn't want to know. I was tired, beaten up, filthy, and David was . . . was really in need of help. "Where are you taking us?"

I must have sounded so miserable that even Whitney was moved, very slightly, toward pity. "Someplace safe," she said. "You rest, now."

I didn't want to, but the Djinn reached out and past me, putting a hand over David's shoulder. David let out a sigh and slumped against the car door. The bleeding from his side slowed, and I saw his color start to return to normal. Whitney, working her magic through her supernatural surrogate.

The Djinn let go and reached for me. I knocked his hand away. "No," I said sharply. "I'll stay awake."

"Suit yourself," Whitney said, back to her old bad attitude. "Want me to pinch you if you drop off?"

"Bite me, Whit."

The Djinn made an unsettling teeth-snapping noise, and I looked sideways at him, scooting a couple of inches closer to David. When I was sure I was safe-ish, I looked back at Kevin and Cherise.

"You two okay?" I left it an open-ended question, and it was up to them whether that applied to injuries, mental instability, shock, or just plain hating the world.

"I don't want this," Kevin said, again. "I didn't ask for this. It feels—wrong." He licked his lips, his eyes haunted under the emo flop of hair. "It hurts when it comes out. I don't think it's safe."

That made sense. In fact, I thought it was a credit to Kevin's strength that it only hurt, because using the power of a Djinn Conduit would probably have torn apart most normal people. Even many Wardens. I wasn't sure what it had done to him, but Kevin didn't scare easily, and I felt for him.

"Sorry," I told him, and reached over to touch his arm. He jerked away. "We'll find a way to do this. I swear."

"Well, I don't mind," Cherise said. "Because controlling the weather is *awesome*. I want to do more."

"Well, you're not going to," I said, which sounded sternly authoritative but was a wet paper sack, so far as enforcement might go. "Cher, you need to stay away from it as much as possible. It may not seem like it's hurting you, but it probably is. I don't want anything to happen to you."

She normally would have smiled in response to that, but instead she just looked away out the window. "You say that until you need me. Then it's all 'bring it.'" That didn't sound much like Cher, and it bothered me.

"Hey." I tried to catch her eyes, but she kept looking away. "Cher, you know I care about you. You know I don't want you hurt."

This time she did look at me, squarely and calmly. "I know," she said. "Until you don't have a choice, and then you'll do anything you have to do. It's what I always like about you, Jo. That ruthless streak under all the girly polish."

We had that in common, I realized. Cherise was sweet and compassionate, funny and talented . . . but she was also, deep down, a survivor, with a broad streak of ambition and a little bit of larceny baked right in. In another age, she might have been a charming criminal, holding up coaches at midnight on deserted roads and kissing all the pretty young men.

"We do what we've gotta do," she said. "Right?"

"Right," I said softly. "But until we've got to do it, *don't*. Please."

That won a smile, finally. "Sure," she said. "Have all the fun yourself, then. Now—" She yawned broadly and bundled herself more comfortably against Kevin. "Now I need some beauty sleep. And a shower. But I'll settle for sleep."

The experience must have been overpowering, I realized, because both she *and* Kevin dropped off in under a minute, dragged down by exhaustion. Made sense. Their bodies weren't made to take that kind of strain. I remembered how it had felt in the beginning, when my powers first began to surface—it was like hormones on crack. I'd been hungry and tired and bitchy all the time, prone to mood swings and fits of pouting, complaining about how *hard* everything was when I wasn't griping about how nobody ever trusted me enough to do things myself.

Cherise had a lot to handle. Kevin, even more.

I checked David's side. His wound was healed, but still red and inflamed; bruises were forming, and evidently Whitney had decided that bruises weren't anything requiring first aid. He was sleeping peacefully. Ahead of us, the road unspooled, lit by furious stabs of lightning and the glow of the headlights. The Djinn kept a machinelike precise grip on the wheel and a foot on the pedal.

And before I knew it, I'd joined the rest of them in sleep.

Chapter Five

I woke up with the sun on my face, which felt nice, but the good feeling faded fast as I blinked and looked around, out the car's windows.

We were still on the road—not a surprise—and I supposed with a Djinn at the wheel we didn't need to stop for gas. Cherise and Kevin were still deeply asleep. David, however, was awake, and as I moved my head off his shoulder, he reached out for my hand. That felt nice.

What wasn't nice was the world outside our speeding car.

We were traveling close to the coastline—I could see the gray smudge of the ocean through occasional hills—but what was most noticeable to me was the thick, gray pall of smoke that hung in the air. I could smell it, thick even through the filter of the car's vents. It gave everything outside an unreal, unfocused look. "It's snowing?" I said as flakes brushed across the windshield.

"No," David said quietly. "It's ash."

I swallowed. "Can you see the fire?"

"Not yet. But it's got to be huge to produce this kind of effect."

The radio suddenly slid channels. I expected more homespun passive-aggressive advice from Whitney, for which I really was *not* in the mood, but instead it landed on a news station. Even before I started getting the sense of what they were talking about, I could hear the tension in the broadcaster's voice.

". . . continues with major flare-ups to the west of I-95, including the Cumberland State Forest area, the Amelia Wildlife Management Area, Masons Corner, Flat Rock, and Skinquarter. There are unconfirmed reports of a major explosion and uncontrolled burn near Chesterfield Court House and the Pocahontas State Park. If you are anywhere in this area, immediate evacuations are under way. Do not remain in your homes; this is an extremely dangerous situation that is overwhelming emergency services. It is only one of several emerging situations that are splitting the resources of our fire, medical, and police throughout the area. Reports are also coming in of significant damage in the Midwest due to torrential rains and flooding, as well as seismic activity along critical fault lines. The Red Cross is—"

Without warning, the voice dissolved into blank, white static. I waited. It didn't come back.

I reached out and switched off the radio. I couldn't help it; the feeling of doom was overwhelming. I could hear the suppressed panic in the reporter's voice; I could feel my own heart pounding uselessly, trying to trigger some kind of survival response.

There was nowhere to run. Not anymore. I was certain that if the broadcast had continued, we would have heard more. A lot more, from all over the country. It was starting in the rural areas, but moving toward the cities, and when it got there . . .

"Faster," I said aloud, to the Djinn. "Whitney, if you can hear me, for the love of God—"

The radio clicked back on. "You brought this on yourselves," she said. "Don't go dragging God into it. You were warned a million times that if humanity got to be too much of a threat, it would get dealt with. Day of reckoning, Joanne. It's here. Should have spent more time listening to those preacher-men—not that any of that would have headed it off, I suppose."

She sounded annoyed, verging on pissed off, and I shut up. She was, indeed, the only real help I imagined we had in the bullpen, and it wasn't a very smart strategy to alienate her.

Satisfied by my silence, apparently, Whitney edged more speed out of the howling engine, and we fled into a dim, surreal day.

Judgment Day.

About an hour later, my phone pinged. It hadn't rung, but I supposed the connections were bad and getting worse as more and more panicked callers took to the cell phone skies to find their loved ones.

It wasn't a call; it was a text, from Lewis. It said LOST PARTS OF WASHINGTON STATE—WILDFIRES OUT OF CONTROL. LARGE LOSS OF LIFE.

I swallowed. He wasn't telling me to ask me to do anything; I knew that. He just had to tell *someone*. Lewis was, right now, the man at the top, listening to all the litany of horror. It had to go somewhere. I supposed it might as well come to me as bleed-off. We were all going to need counseling before this was over, provided there were any of us left, and of course provided there were any mental health professionals left standing.

The next text said, HEADING FOR SEATTLE. LAST STAND FOR FIRE WARDENS IN THE AREA. WILL UPDATE.

I stared at it for a long, silent moment, then texted back, UNDERSTOOD.

I did understand. I knew why he was texting me, what he wasn't saying to me, all those fragile and silent things that both of us knew would never be acceptable in the light of day. My fingers hovered over the keys, and I almost added, LOVE YOU, because I did, desperately, like the brother and friend he had been to me these past few years. But I knew what he felt was different, and stronger, and I didn't want to give him false hope and wrong impressions.

So instead I said, BE CAREFUL, and sent the message.

David, watching me, said, "It's bad."

"Lewis and the Wardens are trying to save Seattle," I said. "It's not good." I realized that the pixels on that phone screen might be the last thing I had to remember Lewis by, and a lump formed in my throat. I swallowed it, blinked away stinging in my eyes, and thought, *No, it isn't. We'll get through this. We always find a way.*

Looming up out of the misty haze in the distance was a tangle of metal. Some kind of crash, leaking black smoke, but no visible flames.

It was a bus, flipped on its side. It had collided head-on with a car—I think it had once been a car, anyway. Nothing was moving in either vehicle.

"Slow down!" I said. The Djinn ignored me. "Stop! You have to—"

We flashed by the wreck at the speed of light as the Djinn expertly drifted around the debris and found open road. Not enough time for me to get all the details, but enough, and it felt like my stomach was trying to crawl out through my throat.

"No survivors," the Djinn said, in that eerie chorus-like voice. "No stops."

Cherise and Kevin were wide awake now in the back,

but neither of them said anything. When I looked back, they were clutching hands and avoiding looking anywhere. David said nothing, either. His face was disturbingly blank.

"But—" I couldn't let it go.

David touched my cheek. "He's right. Wherever we're going, we have to get there. We can't stop. Not for anything. I know you can't accept that, so I'll take the responsibility, all right? We don't stop, not even if you scream and hate me."

I gulped. "I wouldn't—"

"Yes, Jo, you would. What if that had been a school bus? What if you'd seen crying children?"

I couldn't answer him. I knew he was right about me, and I knew he was right about *everything*, and it hurt. Badly.

"Whitney," I said. "Can you hear me?"

Her voice came out of the Djinn's mouth this time. "Unfortunately," she said.

"Put me back to sleep," I said. "I don't want to see this. I don't want to see any of it until I can *do* something."

David put his arm around me and pulled me close. I let my head fall against his chest.

I was just dropping off when I saw an old man stagger out of his car, which was half off the road, and fall on his side. We passed him by in a flash. *Did I see that? Yes, I did. I know I did.*

"Stop," I said. The Djinn once again ignored me. "Whitney, I'm not telling you again. *Stop this car!*"

"What for?" she asked, bored and resentful. "So you can go play Low-Rent Nightingale? You said we need to get to the Oracle. I'm doing my best."

"Please," I said. "Please stop the car. I'm begging you."

Whitney was silent for a second, then I felt the Djinn braking the vehicle, whipping it around in a tight turn, and heading back. "You need to know when to let it go, Joanne. You really do." Thirty seconds later, he pulled the Mustang to a stop. The old man was feebly moving, trying to pick himself up, but he wasn't able to do much. I bailed out and ran to his side. He was in his seventies, maybe into his eighties, with a tight cap of silver/gray curls over a face of great dignity—a patriarch, for sure. African American, and he'd probably been tall and broad in his younger days, but now he was lighter and more stooped, and I was able to help him up to a sitting position. More car doors slammed. The others were joining me.

"Hi," I said. "My name's Joanne. You looked like you needed some help."

He nodded breathlessly. He was wheezing, and his hands trembled badly. "I saw the devil," he said. "Back there on the road. It was killing people."

I exchanged a look with David, and knew he was thinking exactly what I was—Djinn.

"I'm not supposed to be driving, but I had to get Mindy out of there. The whole place was going crazy. I just started feeling sick. My chest hurts." His face was taking on an ominous gray color, and he made a pained expression and grabbed for his arm. "Damn."

He was having a heart attack.

"Sir, what's your name?" I asked. "Sir?"

"George," he finally panted. "George Templin Bassey."

"Nice to meet you, George. I'm going to help you lie down, okay? You take slow, deep breaths. That's right, slow, deep breaths." I sat back on my heels and looked at Kevin, then Cherise. "One of you is going to have to try to help him."

"How?" Cherise asked. She looked scared, and I didn't blame her. This was a fairly significant amount of responsibility to be dumping on someone.

"If you've got my powers, you've also got Earth Warden powers," I said. "That means healing. George here needs your help. I'll walk you through it, okay? Kevin, he said something about Mindy. See if there's anybody else in the car."

Kevin opened the car door and peered in, and almost got his face chewed off by a squat, ferocious English bulldog, who lunged off the floorboard at him with furious, deep-chested barks. Kevin slammed the door again. The bulldog continued to glare and bark. "Uh, yeah, found Mindy, I guess. She's a charmer. Looks okay, if you like fangs."

Under other circumstances, I'd have laughed. Kevin had been fine with fighting toe to toe with a particularly dangerous Djinn, but give him an angry dog, and he was just like anybody else. That was refreshing.

I pushed away that momentary pulse of amusement and focused back on Cherise, who was staring at George with wide eyes.

"Okay, ready?" I asked. She shook her head. "Yes, you are. Give me your hand."

I thought for a second Cherise was going to revert to a second-grader and hold her hands against her chest, but finally she stretched one arm out, and I took hold and guided her to place her palm on George's forehead. He was moaning softly, and he really didn't look good. "I need you to feel the ground under us," I said. "It's full of energy. It feels like honey, or syrup—something slow and golden, okay? Can you feel that?"

Cherise squeezed her eyes shut, and finally nodded. "It's not very strong," she said doubtfully. She was right. It was my weakest specialty, generally. "What do I do?"

"Imagine pulling that up into your body. Once you get it started, it'll just flow on its own." God, I realized I *hated* being a teacher. So much easier to do it than to say it. Words were so clumsy for this kind of thing. If I could just *show* her . . .

The frown deepened on her face, then cleared. "Oh. Oh, right, I get it. That feels weird. Good, but weird."

"Weirder than getting hit by lightning?"

"That felt *great*!"

We were wandering off topic, and poor George was looking more than a little spooked. "Well, this will, too. Now, I want you to just let that power move into your hand, your fingers, your palm. Then let it flow from you to George. Don't try to direct it. Just let it flow."

I remembered learning this, in fast, terse lessons from other Wardens who hadn't had the time to teach me all the proper techniques. Being a late bloomer meant I'd missed all the classical education, but I had a good working knowledge of down-and-dirty first aid. One of the key things Lewis had taught me was that if you don't know how to do fine control with Earth power, don't try. There's a certain instinct to it that pulls the power to where it's needed most. Bodies want to heal. All we have to do is help them.

"It's going in," Cherise said. I couldn't see a thing, but Kevin was watching in fascination, eyes gone wide and unfocused as he followed along in the aetheric. "I think it's working. I can see it in his blood. It's moving— there's some kind of a block. I think I can—"

"No!" both David and I said at the same time. I kept going. "No, I told you, let the power work. Don't try to direct it!"

From the look on her face, she was trying, but she'd already made the mistake, and I could see it in George's choked gasps. Wielding Earth power is like working with nanotechnology—you have to be able to make controlled, very slight adjustments at a microscopic level. It's not brute force.

Cherise cried out, and George arched his back. His

eyes rolled back in his head. "I tore it!" she yelled frantically. "I tore something, it's all bleeding out—"

Kevin reached out and added his hand on top of Cher's, and even as magically blinded as I was, I felt the power flooding out of him. His eyes sparked and changed, and George's labored breathing suddenly and dramatically eased.

"Oh," Cherise said, in a very small voice. "Like that. I see."

Kevin sat back, staring at her with those glittering, powerful eyes, and he said, "Do you? Because you almost killed this guy because you were stupid. She *told* you not to do that. You blew out an artery, for God's sake!"

Cherise went white, clearly horrified and shocked as Kevin turned on her. It wasn't him, I realized; it was the fact that with David's power, he was seeing way too much. He saw Cherise's secret delight in having power, *finally*—something that as a Warden he'd probably never have picked up, but it reminded him of someone else.

It reminded him of his stepmother, I realized. Yvette. He'd seen her turn into a predatory monster, driven by that same kind of excitement and ambition. What he saw in Cherise was the opposite of Yvette Prentiss . . . a woman without any of that power, without any desire to have it or use it.

He was hating her right now, and she could tell.

"Hey," I said, and put my hands on their shoulders. "Good work. He seems better. George, are you feeling better?"

He nodded, but he looked scared. Well, I'd have been right there with him, if I'd had two amateur psychic surgeons rummaging around in my innards. "Who the hell are you people? You with the government?" He *was* feeling better, because I heard suspicion kick in.

"In a way," I said. "Kevin, how's the patch? Solid?"

"It'll hold," he said. "He had a blocked artery. It's clear now. He'll be okay."

"Kev—," Cher said anxiously. He stood up and walked away, head down, hands in his pockets. "I'm sorry! I didn't mean to do it!"

"Give him a minute," I said. "Cher, he's used to the other you. The one without powers. He's never trusted other Wardens, not any of us, not deep down. He hates feeling that way about you, too. Understand?"

She didn't, really, but she blinked back tears and acted like she did. We got Mr. Bassey on his feet, had him walk around a little, and then put him back in his car. Mindy was extremely excited by this, and obviously protective; she stood with her stubby little legs on his and growled at us through the window.

"Do you have someplace safe to go?" I asked George, as he started up his car. He looked at me like I might have been completely insane.

"I'm going to the church," he said. "Devil's walking the streets, and I don't know what you people are. Church is the only place I'll feel safe."

I nodded. "Be safe."

He put aside his suspicion long enough to say, "God bless you all."

Mindy barked.

As his car pulled away, I heard Whitney's pained voice on the radio say, "*Now* can we leave? Sweet Mother Moses, you people are more sentimental than my grandmother into her third bottle of sipping whiskey!"

"Where does she come up with this stuff?" I asked David.

He shrugged. "I don't even know why she's a Djinn," he said. "It's part of her charm."

The excitement of having saved one life—well, two, if you counted Mindy's—made me feel pretty good about things for a while, but my impulse to do-gooding was very firmly brought under control by Whitney, who informed us in cold, final tones that we *would not* stop until we got where we were going.

The next time I tried to get her to stop for a roadside rescue, she put me out like the proverbial light, and I had just enough time to think, *You Southern-fried bitch . . .* and I was gone.

For a long time.

"Jo?"

Then somebody was shaking me. I fought my way up out of what felt like the deepest, most dreamless rest I'd ever had, and for a long second after opening my eyes I felt . . . good. Happy, even. At peace, because the face I was looking into was David's.

He shook me harder. "Jo, wake up!" The urgency in his voice made me blink and scramble for a better grasp of things around me.

We were no longer in the Mustang. I didn't even *see* the Mustang anywhere. I was propped against a brick wall, sitting on a sidewalk, facing a street. It was eerily quiet here—one might even say dead, because I didn't see a single sign of life. Not a bird flitting overhead, not an insect moving, not a single person in a car, window, or park. I looked up and down. It was a Norman Rockwell kind of street, clean and neat—a business district, with quaint little shops and cafes.

All deserted.

Overhead, the sky was gray, a kind of thick, featureless gray that seemed wrong even for an overcast. As I stared at it, I realized that it looked like smoke behind glass.

"We're in Seacasket," I said. "Home of the Fire Oracle."

"There's nothing here still alive," David said. "We don't know why. We haven't found any bodies—not even of insects. Nothing. They're just . . . gone."

That was unsettling. The Fire Oracle wasn't exactly my BFF, but he'd been a lot less antagonistic than the Air Oracle the times I had met him. Not anywhere close to human, but willing to acknowledge us. Seacasket was an unnaturally perfect sort of town, always had been; I thought it was some kind of side effect of the presence of the Oracle. Things had just always seemed a little too much in their place.

"Where's Cherise? Kevin?" I looked around; I couldn't see them, either. "Is the Djinn still with us?"

"He went with them," David said. "I stayed with you."

Which didn't answer my question. I grabbed his hand and pulled myself up to my feet. I still felt sticky, hot, caked with sweat and coated in powdered concrete dust from our mall adventure. My hair was lank around my face, and if I could have wished for paradise, it would have been a spa whirlpool tub, and a skin treatment.

Later.

"Where did they go?"

For answer, he nodded down the street. I looked and saw nothing, but I headed in that direction while David quickly caught up. It felt good to walk; my legs had been out of practice, with all the driving. And suddenly, I felt another need, a really practical one. I stopped, feeling stupid, and said, "Bathroom?"

"There's a gas station up here," David said. "Nobody in it, but the bathroom is open. We used it earlier."

"We" meaning everybody but me, I assumed. It seemed like a mile to the corner, where the banners for the gas station hung limp in the still, perfectly neutral air. It was like strolling through a movie set, deserted but ready for the cameras to arrive.

The bathroom was sparkling, except for the presence of a few paper towels in the trash can, which I presumed came from my traveling companions. After taking care of the obvious and pressing need, I took the opportunity to splash water on my face, scrub off the worst of the grubbiness. Nothing I could do for the clothes, which would need to find an incinerator to throw themselves into at some point, but they'd do for now. Although I would have sold a body part—possibly a major one—for fresh underwear.

I took a deep breath and looked at myself hard in the mirror. My eyes were shadowed, raccooned with dark rings. I looked anxious, drawn, and haunted.

Nice to know I was at my best. I tried to summon up the old confidence, and saw a glimmer or two of it in the smile, the cock of my head.

Well, I thought. *If I'm going to go down, I'm going to go down fighting. I don't have to be ashamed of that.*

David knocked on the door. "Are you all right?"

All these years, and he hadn't learned how women linger in a bathroom? "Fine," I said, sighed, and ran my fingers through my hair again—not that it helped. Then I put that confident smile back on and opened the door. "Let's go scare up an Oracle."

The Fire Oracle's official public entrance—well, public to the Djinn, not to us measly humans—existed in a cemetery. Like the town of Seacasket, it was a little too perfect—a carefully manufactured setting that gets nominated for set design at award shows. It was the very definition of historical and peaceful, what with all the green grass and lovely statues and well-tended gravestones and mausoleums.

Not a single person visible. Not a bird cheeped. Not a blade of grass stirred.

David and I both stood outside the gates for a moment, looking in; I think we were both feeling a dread we couldn't consciously explain. Bad things had happened in this cemetery to me before, and I couldn't help but feel a crawling sense of foreboding.

The air was just so *still*.

"Jo." David was looking down at the neatly raked gravel path that wound through the picturesque landscape. "Footprints."

Two sets of them. One matched Kevin's giant, battered kicks; the others were Cherise's, judging from the small size. "Where's the Djinn?" I asked.

"Floating," David said. "Djinn do that."

It had been a dumb-ass question, and I'd known it as soon as I'd opened my mouth. Many of the Djinn didn't bother to manifest themselves physically all the way; I remembered the one who'd started out guarding Lewis's old house. He hadn't bothered with anything below the knees.

David, for whatever reason, had always taken care to do the whole human body. I'd always loved that about him.

Imara, our half-Djinn child, had always done that, too. I had a sudden, visceral flash of her standing here in this exact place with me, smiling, and it took my breath away, shock followed by grief. Imara wasn't gone. I knew that, but I'd had her for such a brief time, and then . . .

David took my hand. "You're thinking about Imara."

"Stop reading my mind. It's creepy that you can do that even when you're not a Djinn."

"I'm thinking of her, too," he said, and I heard the sadness in his voice, too. "I'm thinking that if we can't do this, we're going to lose her completely."

"That isn't going to happen." *Come on, confidence—get it in gear!* "And we're wasting time. You want to leave this up to Kevin and Cherise?"

He winced. "Definitely not."

"Then let's go."

We walked together, hands clasped, down the gravel path. Except for the crunch of our shoes, it was like moving through a dream, full of color and light but nothing else. The essential *life* of the place was gone, or at least hidden.

The door to the mausoleum we wanted was standing wide open. Darkness was a thick, black square in the doorway, like a hole in the world, and I hesitated, glancing at David. "Well?" I asked.

He nodded, shut his eyes, and walked forward into it, still holding my hand tightly in his. The darkness slipped over him like water, not shadow—it had a thickness to it, and its own surface tension. I watched him disappear into it, staring at our linked fingers until his were gone and mine touched the dark.

It was cold. Very cold.

Like David, I took a deep breath and went in anyway.

The trip through the cold felt as if it took forever, an eternity of freezing to the bone, and when it stopped, when I finally was able to move again, I found myself shaking violently, almost unable to stand. The darkness was gone, at least, and the air felt warm.

No. The air felt *hot*.

I pulled in my first breath, and it scorched my lungs. David was already coughing, and as my eyes adjusted to the sudden dazzle of light, I realized we were standing not three feet away from a blazing inferno of red, gold, and white flames that seemed to have no upward limit. The fire just dissolved into a haze of lurid glow at the top.

We were in a small rock chamber, round and rough-hewn. It was basically a big chimney, much taller than it was wide, with an opening in the center through which the fire blazed. It was *not* a safe place to be standing, but there were no doors, no windows, not even a handy alcove in which to try to hide. To make it even worse, I was still violently shivering from the passage through the cold, even while my skin was registering burning pain. I smelled the distinct, bitter odor of hair crisping.

Someone came at us from the other side of the brilliant blaze, and suddenly I felt the pressure of the heat ease back. It didn't leave completely, but I wasn't in danger of becoming baked goods.

Kevin. He looked singed and breathless and wild around the edges. His movements were fast and jerky, fueled by way too much adrenaline. "We have to get out of here!" he yelled. "It's trying to kill us!"

He'd extended some kind of fire protection over me and David, which was damn nice of him, considering. I wondered if Cherise had smacked the back of his head to make him think of it. "If it had wanted to kill us, we'd be dead!" I yelled back, over the roar of the flames. "Has it said anything?"

Kevin gave me a blank look. "It's a *fire*."

"Trust me. It talks!" Even with Kevin's power canceling out the fire—and this went well beyond the kind of power that Kevin the Fire Warden could have summoned up; it was more on the scale of a Djinn, which fit with the flickers of poison green in Kevin's eyes—the air pressed boiling hot against my skin, and I could feel it hungering for me. Not that it had anything against me, personally; it just devoured. That was the nature of fire.

My body tried to sweat, to protect me, but that was like spitting in a volcano. Wisps of steam rose off my skin, but it didn't cool at all.

Kevin stared at me in utter confusion, working through what I'd told him, and then turned to face the fire. "Hello?" he said. It would have been cute if it hadn't been so dire. "Uh—hi? Anybody home?"

Cherise staggered around the far curve of the room and headed for us. She looked like I expected I would have in her place, if I'd stumbled in here with a haphazard set of borrowed powers I didn't know how to use, only to find myself in a killing trap.

In other words, not happy.

"What are you doing?" she yelled at Kevin. He gave her a harassed glance. "We have to get *out*!"

Before I could stop her, she turned to the rock wall and slapped her palm against it.

As she did, she let loose a furious burst of Earth power—uncontrolled, instinctual, driven by her panic and fury. What was it I'd said? *She's like a baby with a nuclear bomb and a shiny red button.*

She'd just pushed the button.

"No!" The scream tore itself out of my throat, but I was too late; she'd used enough power that a sharp crack formed in the rock where her hand had slammed down. Encouraged, she did it again. She would have done it a third time, but David got to her first, grabbed her from behind, and pinned her arms behind her; even human, he had a lot of strength in those muscles, and as small as Cherise was ...

She used Earth power, which, dammit, *I'd* taught her how to pull, and threw him off, almost into the fire. I grabbed him around the waist and tackled him down, landing both of us on the hard rocky floor only a few inches from the blaze. I felt my hair cook, and rolled us both as far from danger as possible.

Cherise hit the rock wall a third time.

There was a mystical significance in threes for the Djinn. Ask a bound Djinn any question three times, and they're forced to answer—maybe not the way you wanted, but they have to take action.

Cherise triggered the Rule of Three in a much more active way.

The Oracle's fire formed into a huge, white-hot ball, and flew at her. Cherise screamed and ducked, but it was so large that even hitting the floor like me and David, several feet away, wouldn't have saved her.

Kevin saved her.

He stepped into its way, eyes flaring with an unholy Djinn light. He didn't try to put up his hands or fight it, or even stop it. He just *stood there*.

It was very likely one of the bravest things I'd ever seen. And it was *Kevin*. Surely, one of the primary signs of the End Times.

The fireball slowed, and coasted to a halt, flicking little hissing tongues of flames at his face from a distance of no more than inches. He didn't blink. He didn't back up. It drifted closer. I knew, instinctively, that if it touched him, he'd go up like an oil-soaked rag, and dread clenched my stomach into a trembling knot.

The ball lengthened to the vague shape of a man— red as lava on the surface, and clothed in fire, but with that same white-hot core shining from its center. It chose the same height and build as Kevin.

And it didn't back off.

Something like a mouth formed in its blind, masklike head, and some kind of sound came out of it, but it was like nothing I could recognize as speech. I thought it was what it would sound like as the marrow boiled in your bones. Threatening and fatal.

Kevin bared his teeth and kept on staring back. "Do it," he said. "But you go through me first."

The sound from the Oracle stopped abruptly, and the mouth disappeared.

It turned—well, no, that was how my purely human senses wanted to interpret it. Actually, it just reversed its body, putting its head on the other way, and walked the few steps back to the center of the pit where the pillar of flame had been.

Then it sat down in midair, floating, legs crossed in a lotus position, hands turned palms up.

Kevin blinked, and some of the insane Djinn shine drained out of him. "Uh—what's he doing?"

"You're asking *me*?" I asked. "No idea!"

"He's listening," David said. "Talk." He offered me a hand up as he rolled to his feet. He was favoring his side again, and I hoped that wasn't fresh blood. "Say something."

"Me?" I asked.

"No, he can't hear us," David said. "Either of us. It's as if—human voices don't register within the range of his ears. That's the best I can explain it."

"But he can hear me?" Kevin asked. He was helping Cherise to her feet. She was dusting herself off, shaken but not hurt. Behind her, that dark crack promised escape—to her mind—and she kept looking toward it. "What about Cher?"

"Maybe," David said. "I don't know. Jo could be heard, but she was a special case. I'm not sure about Cherise."

"Guess that makes you our spokesmodel, Boy Wonder," Cher said. "Go on. Get us *out*."

"Uh, I think we came for a reason first."

"Screw that. We need to *go*." For the first time since I'd met her, Cherise sounded like a petulant child, sulky and stubborn and used to having her own way. "*Now*, Kev!"

Kevin frowned at her, like he was having the same thoughts I was. "Chill, we're fine. Look, it's not even that hot in here anymore."

"Compared to what, the inside of a nuclear furnace?"

Kevin looked at me and David, clearly wondering when, as the supposed authority figures in the room, we'd step in. David held up his hands. "She already tried to kill me," he said. "You're on your own."

I sighed, walked over to Cherise, and put my arm

around her. She jerked in surprise but let me do it. "You really need to calm down, Cher," I said. She gave me a furious look, and I saw that the panic and instability in her was reaching critical levels. "Cher. Deep breaths."

"I need *out*!" she wailed, and tried to turn toward the wall.

I wasn't about to let her get us all killed, and I didn't think. I just dropped my arm from her shoulders, pulled my fist back, and hit her with a perfect right hook to the jaw.

She went down like a bowling pin. I caught her before she hit the ground and eased her flat. "Kev," I said. "Put her out. Now." Because I'd hit like a girl, just dazed her plenty, and she wasn't going to be at all thrilled when she shook it off. Kevin wasn't an Earth Warden, but he had David's power, and that meant he had everything he needed to do as I asked.

If he could access it.

Kevin crouched down and put his hand tentatively on her forehead. Cherise tried fitfully to bat it away. "Sorry," he said, and I saw a spark of fire catch green in his eyes as he channeled power. It probably was spectacular on the aetheric level, but here, with my human eyes, I could only see the faintest glow around his fingers.

Cherise went limp, breathing heavily. I checked her pulse—strong and steady—and gave a solid thumbs-up to Kevin, who looked deeply relieved. "Don't make me do that again," he said. "It feels *really* weird. What if I get it wrong? What if I put her into a coma or something?"

"She'd still be alive," David said. "She won't be if she unleashes more power in here. The Oracle won't let it happen again. He'll just destroy her."

Kevin swallowed hard, looking at the serene, floating figure, wreathed in flames. "Yeah? What about me?"

"He sees you as Djinn. He expects it from you."

"I—" Kevin stared at David now, with the same kind of alarm he'd given to the figure of the Oracle. "What?"

David tried again, with strained patience. He was leaning against the wall now, and the hand holding his side was subtly trembling. I stepped up next to him to take some of his weight. Also subtly. Or not. "You're the only one here who can talk to him, using the powers that I used to have. So do it. Explain it to him. Oracles see everything, but their context can be far different from ours. He needs to understand what all of it means to us. To humanity." David had never put himself on that side of the *us* before, except in relation to me. I stared at him in involuntary reaction. He shrugged. "I am one of you, for however long it lasts. It's—weirdly restful."

"You're in *pain*!"

"Yes, but it's a different kind of pain than I'm used to enduring. That's something."

That made about as little sense to me as talking with the Oracle would have, so I shut up. Kevin didn't need side chatter. He was looking sweaty and scared and well aware of the stakes at play here, in this burning furnace of a room.

"Hi," he said to the Oracle. "Okay, I have no idea how to do this, but I'll try. . . ."

"Power," David said. "Use it."

Kevin closed his eyes and took a deep breath. When he opened them, I saw a faint green shimmer in his eyes. Sort of like the Hulk, getting a little bit angry. "Hello," he said in a stronger voice. "Can you hear me?"

The Oracle didn't make any sign he did. More serene, though extremely fierce, hovering ensued, and the green glare in Kevin's eyes brightened steadily, like someone was turning up a dimmer switch in the back of his head. Eerie.

"Hear me," he said, when his eyes were utterly Djinn. It wasn't loud, but it was . . . profoundly powerful.

The Oracle still hovered, but now features manifested on its face. Eyes opened, and they were the same green as Kevin's.

"I hear," the Oracle said. "Speak."

But that was the last thing Kevin said, at least that I could plainly hear; his lips didn't move, but the intense stare between the two of them continued.

It occurred to me, after a few long seconds, that it felt just a little hotter in the room.

No, I was wrong. It felt like it was getting *steadily* hotter, fast. Like a blower had come on, venting heat back into the room.

"Not good," David said. "Get low."

"Why?"

"Cool air sinks?"

Oh. I'd forgotten even the most basic physics now, thanks to the extreme state of death I was expecting to happen any second. I helped him down to his knees, then got face-first on the floor along with him.

Kevin was still standing. And now, flames were whipping around the floating lotus-position Oracle, flaring up and twisting in a miniature whirlwind—but never blocking the connection between his stare and Kevin's. As I watched, the flames stretched out, circling around Kevin.

Binding the two of them together.

Kevin took a step closer. Then another one.

"Kevin, don't touch him!" I yelled. "You can't—he'll kill you!" Because at his core, Kevin was still human. Still a Warden. And we didn't belong here.

Kevin stopped inches away. The fire was now blazing so hot around them that it was white-hot, like a curtain of flaming diamonds. Even with my face pressed low against the hot stone floor, every breath I gasped in was torturous and searing.

And then, with a tremendous burst of heat and light

that seemed to char the entire world, Kevin collapsed. He did it in stages: knees went first, then he folded backward and caught himself with one outstretched arm. The arm failed, and he hit the floor, faceup.

The heat in the room suddenly dialed itself down. *Way* down, until it felt icy. That probably only meant that it was down to survivable temperature, but the relief was overwhelming enough to make me sob. I felt David shiver from the sudden chill, next to me.

When I tried to get up he said, "No, don't move." His voice was hoarse. "Stay down. This isn't yours to do. Trust me."

I had no idea what he was talking about. He stood up, swaying on his feet, his face a dirty, pale color that didn't look at all right.

"David!" I started to get up to join him, but he didn't pause.

He walked into the center of the room, where the Oracle had turned into a blazing white-hot ball, and before I could stop him . . .

. . . He plunged *into* the fire.

Chapter Six

I screamed. I couldn't help it—the shock and enormity of it was horrifying.

I saw the man I loved most in the world burn.

It took place in a matter of a second, no more than a flash of light against my retinas, but there it was, frozen in horrible detail.

His skin flaring into black and red lace as it burned away.

His muscles shriveling, revealing white bone beneath.

A single X-ray flash of his entire skeleton coming free of its disappearing flesh.

A faint drift of ash falling to the floor.

Gone.

No.

That was my world, breaking apart into tiny, hazy fragments too small to notice. Too small to matter.

Like all of us.

Like humanity itself.

I heard that horrible, rending screaming of the Djinn on the ship. I saw Imara, falling on the steps of the chapel in Sedona with the life leaving her eyes. I saw my old friend Paul getting in the way of a burst of power from my hand. Destroyed. Murdered, by me.

I saw all the lives, the thousands and *millions* of lives, which were going out right now, like sparks drowning in darkness.

No more. No more. No more!

I realized that I was still screaming, only now it had turned to words. "What did you do? *What did you do?*"

The Oracle floated there, wrapped in a ball of blinding white fire, as uncaring as the sun.

My scream turned into a shriek of utter rage, and I stumbled to my feet, lungs burning under the pressure of the fury that was boiling out of me, and I lunged for the Oracle. He could damn well take me, too, the uncaring son of a—

David manifested himself out of the air and caught me in strong, solid arms before I could finish my suicidal dash. Not the same David who'd just disappeared in that horrible flash. This David was different, and achingly familiar. Pure, smooth skin with faintly metallic burnishing. A little more perfect than human. Copper flames dancing in his eyes.

This was the Djinn David.

"Easy," he said, and his voice was the same, gentle and low and strong. I melted against him, weak with relief, breathless. "Easy, Jo. I'm here."

I couldn't speak. All I could do was shake and hold on. His fingers combed through my hair, and I felt the sweaty tangles relax, felt my filth and disarray swept away in a tingling tide. His way of showing his love and concern for me. It always had been.

"Jo? Were you about to throw yourself into the Oracle after me?"

I swallowed hard and tried to laugh it off, because his tone seemed so baffled and concerned.

"Of course not," I said. "It was getting cold out here. Needed to warm up."

"Sorry," he said, and kissed me, and that was the same warm depth of emotion and love and promise as always. "I had to move fast, once I realized what he'd done."

"The Oracle?" I looked over his shoulder at the silent, glowing orb.

"He separated out the powers from Kevin and contained them, but it was only temporary. Lightning in a bottle. If I didn't take it back right away, it would have been too late."

"So you decided to commit suicide, on the off chance it would all work out. Nice. Thanks for giving me a vote." I was trying to sound unconcerned. It wasn't working, not at all. There was an edge to my voice, a raw hurt, and he pressed a kiss against my forehead with such gentleness my breath caught in my chest.

"I was dying either way," he told me. "I never would have left this place alive as a human. I didn't have the strength. It was the only chance I had."

"Did it—" I couldn't ask that question, not directly. "Did you feel it?"

David's face shut down, but his eyes remained warm and loving, focused on my face. The Djinn fires burned a little brighter.

"We always feel death," he said. "It's that memory that makes us different from the Old Djinn. We remember what it feels like to lose ourselves to the dark."

The Oracle pulsed light, just once, and David turned back to it. As Kevin had done, David had silent communion with the power that lived in this place. Unlike Kevin, it took a long time, and at the end of it, David didn't fall down. He just took a step back, looking thoughtful. Was that a frown? Yes, I was pretty sure he was frowning. He was staring down at the ground, so I couldn't be sure. One thing I *was* sure of, the place was heating up again, temperature climbing one steady degree every few seconds. In no time at all, the oven would be set to broil again.

"Uh, honey?" I finally said. "What about me? My powers?"

He looked up and shook his head. "Not from him. He could take them out of Cherise and hold them for a few moments, but he can't put them into your human body. You'd have to be reborn as a Djinn, and those powers are designed for a human form, not one like mine. It wouldn't work. You'd never survive. I'm not sure Cherise would, either."

My day just kept becoming more awesome. "So what are we going to do?"

"For a start, get out of here," David said. "To protect himself, the Oracle has put up barriers against the influence of the Mother; it's one of the most difficult things he's ever done, and he's very upset. When he's upset . . ."

". . . It gets hot," I said. "Yeah. Got that part."

"I could survive, but the three of you won't. I need to get you out of here before the temperature rises too far."

"What were you thinking about?" I asked.

"What?" He had his back to me now, conveniently examining the walls.

"You were thinking about something after you cut it off with the Oracle. What did he say?"

"Oh, you know Oracles," David said, and ran fingertips over the crack Cherise had put into the rock. He shook his head, and under his hand the crack bonded itself and disappeared. "Not that way."

"That wasn't an answer."

"You're right," he said.

"What did the Oracle say?"

"Jo, don't—"

I put my hand on his shoulder, and felt the heat radiating from the skin beneath his shirt. "What did the Oracle say?"

His muscles tensed under my touch, and I saw the color in his eyes flicker, less copper, more red. He didn't like it when I used the Rule of Three on him—which was why I rarely did.

"The Oracle said the Mother is waking up," he said. "And there's no way to stop her. If he tries, he'll just be consumed along with the rest of the Djinn. He's trying to remain separate as long as he can."

"He has to at least try to talk to her, tell her our side!"

"No. He doesn't." David moved steadily around the circular room, avoiding Cherise's sleeping form and Kevin's unconscious body, both lying close together. "He's not the guardian of humanity. His connection runs between the Djinn and the Mother. That's all. He owes you nothing."

That was direct, and painfully true. "But—"

David stopped, hands hovering over one part of the wall. "Get Cherise," he said. "When this opens, I need you to drag her through, then come back for Kevin. I'll have to hold it open."

"Then how are you going to get out?"

He gave me a fast glance. "I can go anywhere now. You can't."

Oh. Right. That made sense.

I grabbed Cherise under the arms and dragged her to where David was standing. She mumbled a little—waking up, which wasn't a good thing at the moment. "Hurry," I told him. He didn't bother to nod; his full attention was fixed on the wall in front of him. As I watched, it wavered, then fell into dust, revealing that black, oily surface like what we'd pierced to get here in the first place. Once that was done, David remained where he was, unmoving, staring.

"Go," he said, just the one word. I wondered how much strength this was taking. A lot, I assumed.

I towed Cherise backward through the cold, clinging liquid, fell for a thousand years, and landed with a jolt as I tripped over a tombstone and went sprawling. Cherise was with me, lying in the bright green grass. I picked myself up, dusted myself off, and charged back through the barrier. Falling, cold, et cetera . . . it was almost routine now. I grabbed Kevin and did a rinse-and-repeat, only this time I sidestepped the tombstone as I got thrown out of the barrier.

The black liquid shadow vanished with a pop. Gone. I left Kevin and Cherise tumbled up together and went to look inside the mausoleum. Just a plain old jumbo-sized family crypt, with marble benches and plaques on the wall. Sunlight filtered in graceful Tiffany patterns through the far rose window, bathing the room in brilliant, soothing color.

"David?"

My voice echoed on the cold stone. There was no answer.

As I turned around I ran into him. He was standing right behind me. I smacked a fist into his chest, but not too hard. "Don't *do* that!" I yelped, and he smiled. In the sun, he looked chillingly beautiful. I'd kind of gotten used to his slightly rough human looks. This was all that, only distilled into perfection.

I wondered how he saw me now, with his Djinn sight. Not the Warden I'd been. No power. No real value in the world. It hit me with a jolt that David was seeing me as just any other human, and for a moment I felt true, horrified panic and loss. He'd loved me for what I was. Did he love me for what I was *now*?

He touched me gently under the chin and bent to kiss me. It was a thoroughly sexual kiss, all heat and heart, and the warmth spread through my body like liquid, gathering somewhere around my womb. It felt ... wonderful. He didn't break the kiss until we both heard the mumbling from Cherise break into actual words.

"...hot, have to get out..." She sat up suddenly enough to dump Kevin's head off her lap, and he groaned and rolled over, facedown. "We have to get out—oh. Wow. Did I get us out of there? If I did, I'm awesome and *oh God* my jaw hurts! Ow, what the hell!" Cherise had a bruise forming there where I'd clocked her—red right now, but it'd be a spectacular sunset before it was done, I'd bet. "Little help?"

I smiled at David, stepped back, and went to offer her a hand.

She hauled herself up, looked down at her clothes, and groaned. "I look like a bag lady who got dressed out of an incinerator *after* it was burning. How come you look so good? And I stink like a mule, too. Ugh. Did we get anything out of that at all? Because if we didn't, I'm totes billing the Wardens for ..."

I glanced over at David. He had his arms folded, watching us quietly. Waiting for Cherise's monologue to end, I presumed. Which, eventually, it did, and she ended up staring at him as her voice trailed off.

"Oh," she said. "Is he back? All magic-y again?"

"Yes," he said, without an ounce of amusement. "I'm back."

She cocked an eyebrow, almost back to the old, sunny Cherise. "Nice paint job. Very plush." She stopped short of asking for a ride, which was, considering it was Cherise, tactful restraint. "So you got us out."

"With your help," David said, very generously. "Yours, and Kevin's."

Kevin, for answer, rolled over on his back, stared up

at the sun, and groaned again. "I hurt all over," he said. "Did I lose at mixed martial arts? Maybe with a ninja?"

"Have you ever even tried mixed martial arts?" Cherise asked, and held out a hand to him to pull him to a sitting position, then to his feet. "Because you should. Those guys are smoking hot. In a bad-guy sort of way."

Cherise wasn't this shallow, but she could give a really good impersonation of it when she wanted. Right now, she was (literally) whistling past this graveyard, which, no matter how picturesque and perfect, was a less than ideal place for us to enjoy our continued survival.

Kevin knew all that, which surprised me. He folded Cher in an embrace, bent and whispered something in her ear, and then took her hand. They started walking down the gravel path toward the road.

At the gates of the graveyard, I saw the gleaming shape of the Boss pull up, idling with an intimidating growl. Our anonymous Djinn chauffeur was behind the wheel. I'd just started wondering where he'd gotten himself off to, but I supposed Whitney had pulled him well out of danger. She wasn't the type to sacrifice important assets unless it was absolutely necessary. I think she trademarked the phrase *You're on your own*.

That chain of thought linked, fast as the speed of light, back to David, and I suddenly rounded on him, fists clenched. "Wait!" I said. "Why are you still you?"

The only thing, as far as I knew, that had protected David from becoming subject to the whims and will of the Earth had been the fact that his powers had been taken from him. Once restored, he should have been dragged into the collective hive mind with the rest of the Djinn.

I hadn't surprised him with my question. He sighed and stopped walking before he could run into me, but he didn't answer. Not at first. Finally, he looked up at the smoke-gray, unnaturally smooth sky. "She can't reach me," he said. "Not here. The Fire Oracle has an excellent shield up. It may not last, but it's kept him safe this far. When I leave here, I won't have that protection."

"You knew this could happen," I said. "You knew, and you did it anyway."

"I didn't have a choice," he said. "I still don't. My options are very limited, Jo. I wish it weren't the case, but it is, and we have to accept that."

"What *options*?"

"I could stay here with the Oracle. If I go outside the borders of Seacasket he can't help me anymore." David shook his head. "Staying here isn't really an option. I can't do much here to help you, and I can't protect you."

"You can protect yourself."

"Not really my focus."

"There's nothing wrong with—"

"Second," he interrupted, "I could leave with you and try to resist the Mother's call. It's possible I could, for a while; I have before. But that was when she was only partially aware. You heard what the Oracle said: she's waking up. I won't be able to stay apart from her for long. She'll be much, much stronger."

I swallowed, throat tight, and waited for the other shoe to drop. Presuming there were three shoes.

"Last, I can go directly from here to the aetheric, to Jonathan's house. It's kept Whitney safe and uncompromised. It'll do the same for me. I can do you some good there, as long as the avatar stays with you."

"But—" It was hard to get the words out. "But you won't be with me."

"Staying with you was never a choice," he said. "That's what I meant. My options are limited, and all of them take me away from you. If I'd stayed human, I'd have died in the cavern. If I stay with you, I'll turn against you. If I leave, I won't be able to be with you, to—" Djinn or not, David was distraught. He was just handling it much better than I was. "But I'll always do what I can. Always. It may not be enough, Jo. I may fail you."

He sounded so unhappy about that, and it broke my heart. "You've never failed me," I said. "Never. And you never will, because this isn't a pass/fail kind of score, David. I love you. I want you to be safe. That's all."

I meant it, though my knees had started trembling at the thought of leaving this place without his presence at my side. It wasn't even so much the power he could bring to bear on our behalf—it was the sheer comfort of him. I needed him.

And I was going to have to do this without him, or lose everything. David on the opposite side of this was a death warrant for all of us. He was just too powerful.

I smiled. It actually felt warm, and real, and confident, even if I truly was scared to death deep down. "I'll be fine," I said. "We'll be fine. Walk me to the car before you go, okay?"

He took my hand, and for a moment we just stood together, drinking in each other's warmth, the reality of our bodies standing in the same space, the same time.

He kissed me. It felt so warm, so sweet, so *real* that I felt tears burning in my eyes. It was so perfect with him, and we never had *time*.

He kissed away my tears, put his hands on my shoulders, and leaned his forehead against mine for a long, lovely moment, and then, without a word, we walked together to the waiting Mustang. David handed me into the passenger seat. He lifted my hand to his lips and kissed it, and I felt his lips against my skin like the warmest summer sun.

"We'll be okay," I told him again. He nodded, shut the door, and as the Djinn behind the wheel gunned the motor and sent the car hurtling down the deserted, silent street, I turned to watch David.

He disappeared into a mist. Gone.

"Wait," Kevin said, and twisted around to look. "Where is he? Where did he go?"

"He's not coming," I said.

"But—"

"We'll be okay," I said again, firmly.

I was, I realized, a damn good liar. I could make everybody believe it, except me.

Chapter Seven

Leaving Seacasket was like living in a jump cut in a movie. One second, the world was still and hushed and silent and perfectly ordered, as if someone had pressed a giant pause button. . . . The next, we were in chaos.

By chaos, I mean it was worse than when we'd arrived. *Much* worse. The gray vanished, and suddenly the skies were crowded with black, bloated clouds that bloomed constantly with greenish lightning. Wind lashed the car hard and shoved it from one lane to the other, even with the Djinn's uncanny reaction time. The sides of the road were littered with wrecks, shattered trees, downed power lines. I couldn't see any electric lights at all in the houses and buildings that blurred past us. I could see occasional smaller lights—flashlights and candles—moving inside, and I wondered how terrified those people must be. All they could do was wait.

All we could do was keep moving.

Cherise reached over the seat to try the radio, but no matter where she dialed there was just pure static, or one of those emergency alert broadcasts telling people to stay in their homes and wait for more information.

I imagined Twitter had probably exploded from the strain, if the internet had survived thus far. Not to mention Facebook.

"Where are we going?" Cherise asked.

The radio hissed, and the slider took over on its own like a transistorized version of a Ouija board. I expected to hear Whitney's dulcet Southern tones.

I heard David's.

"Jo," he said. "All right?"

"Yeah, we're fine," I said, which was a brave interpretation, given the outside world. "Where are you?"

"Jonathan's house, with Whitney."

The station changed, lightning fast. "We are *not* going to be good roomies," Whitney cooed. "I already want to kick his pretty ass across the room. I wonder if I can."

David regained control of the radio. "From here, we'll do what we can to lessen the dangers around you as you go. Whitney's going to continue to pilot the Djinn who's driving you."

"None of which answers the vital question of *where are we going!*" Cherise said, hanging half over the seat.

"You're heading for Sedona," he said. "But be warned—that entire area is under siege. It's not going to be easy."

It never was. "We're going to need to stop," I said. "We can't keep going like this. Rest and food, water and bathrooms. Very important."

"We'll find you shelter," David promised. "Try to rest for now."

Easier said than done, as the thunder crashed and the lightning struck with the regularity of a strobe light to the eyes, as the Djinn driving swerved to avoid first one unseen obstacle, then another. It was like being back at sea again in a full-force gale.

But eventually, inevitably, even that couldn't keep me from sliding away into dark, dreamless sleep. Cars have that effect, even dodging, swerving ones, if you get used to it. Weirdly soothing. If the Djinn had been on its own, it could have blipped easily from one spot to another by taking a shortcut through the aetheric planes . . . but with humans it was tricky at best. Even the Djinn who had the most experience and ability at taking humans through the aetheric in physical form, not just spiritual, had a less-than-confidence-building success rate. Say, fifty percent.

So we traveled the old-fashioned way, miles passing under wheels. It was a lot of miles, because we were moving very fast despite the dangerous and unpredictable conditions. I woke up periodically, prodded by anxiety or bad dreams, hunger or thirst, or the more basic bodily functions. Food and drink turned out to be no challenge at all; shops were deserted, and many had already been looted. I didn't mind drinking store-brand cola if it was all that was left. I tried not to see what it all meant, what all this widespread smoking devastation and desperation meant for civilization as a whole.

Things were falling apart. There were people in small groups, and they ran when we roared by.

The internet on Cher's mobile phone had gone down in a haze of 404 Not Found errors. Then her mobile had failed, too. And mine. And Kevin's.

We all had different network providers. I assumed that, too, was not a good sign.

We were just heading into the St. Louis area, from the Missouri side—a long and exhausting ride, with as few stops as possible in places that were only marginally dangerous. I'd hoped that maybe the calmer center of the country might still be holding its own.

I was wrong.

You could see the dull red-orange glow of flames

coming from St. Louis a long way off against the cold night sky, and low-hanging, constantly rumbling clouds.

"I hate this," Cherise said, fidgeting anxiously. She'd been fidgeting a long time, nervous with the crackle of power in her blood and the fear of actually letting it loose. I'd managed to get *that* through her head, finally, and we'd done long hours of power exercises, with Kevin as her spotter, to teach her how to use the aetheric properly, how to center her power and ground it, how to use it in more delicate ways than sledge-hammering every problem into smithereens, along with everything that *wasn't* a problem.

She was actually not sucking at it. I couldn't help but feel that maybe this was a little bit due to my excellence as a teacher, but it probably wasn't.

Over the radio, David's voice said, "I need to prepare you for what's coming." That was ominous, because he'd never said that before, and we'd already been through some rough patches on the way. He sounded very sober. "You're going to come up on some problems in the next ten miles. I'll direct you on the blockage in the road, but we may have to take detours as things get worse."

"That's it? Roadblocks?" I felt a little surge of irritation. "Not exactly news, David."

"It's not cars," he said. "It's people. They're desperate, and they're terrified, and they're angry. They'll attack the car if it gets too close. They think they can run to safety, but there is none."

That was very different, and we all knew it. Cherise asked, in a small voice, "How many people?"

"Right now, there are three main groups," he said. "Two of them are fighting each other for food and transportation. All together, they number about fifty thousand."

"Fifty—" Words failed me. I couldn't even echo the number. I glanced in the back and saw that Cherise was staring fiercely at the radio, tears welling in her eyes. "Fifty thousand people. Refugees."

"That would imply they have some kind of refuge to flee toward," David said bleakly. "They don't. If they try to leave, they'll get picked off by the storms, the fires, the sinkholes. Animal attacks. And there's no safe harbor for them, not anymore."

"The Wardens—," Kevin began.

"They already killed the Wardens who were trying to help them," David said flatly. "Mob mentality. Just don't get close. If you don't share their beliefs, they'll kill you, too."

"What beliefs?"

Kevin didn't need to ask the question, because we topped the next hill and saw the first of the crowds that David was talking about. They were filthy, ragged, wild-eyed, and armed with rifles, axes, sharp sticks—I didn't see a single person who didn't have some kind of weapon, even if it was just a stone to throw. A few were carrying badly painted signs that looked like they might have been written in dried blood.

REPENT OR DIE.

Oh man.

"You want to know the biggest joke?" Whitney's voice said, echoing through the silence in the car. "These are the Episcopalians. You don't even want to run into the hard-shell Baptists right now, brothers and sisters."

Kevin crossed himself. He did it in a rush, like it came from someplace deep within him, and I wondered how he'd been brought up, in his early days. Catholic, probably. Cherise and I had both been churchgoing girls, too, until recently; I wasn't what I could call committed, but I had always honored God. Wardens never doubted the presence of higher powers. Heck, we had a direct line to *something*, even if it wasn't the Head Bearded Guy.

But this . . . this was people clutching at straws, using religion as an excuse for murder and destruction. And it made me sad and angry.

"We avoid them," I said. Some of the crowd had already caught sight of us and were streaming in our direction. "If we can't stop them, we have to stay out of their way."

"But they're just *people*," Cherise said. "The same people who'd help you out if you had a flat tire. What *happens* to them? What happens to *us*?"

"Survival," I said softly. "It's selfish, and it's dark, and we've always been a species willing to do anything to satisfy our needs. Individuals have morals. Mobs have appetites."

The Djinn had taken a sharp left turn down a side road and rocketed along it at insane speed, dodging falling tree branches, a wrecked and still smoldering SUV, and some things in the road that it took me long-delayed seconds to realize were actually dead bodies. I started to ask, but then I realized that I didn't want to know how bad this was, how far it had gone. I just wanted to *stop it*.

And I didn't see any way to do that.

Misery crept up on me, and I swallowed hard against an ache in my throat and stomach. I wanted David. I wanted his arms around me, his strength beside me.

"Jo," his voice said, and I closed my eyes and pretended he was here, physically here. It was easier than I'd thought. Maybe I was going crazy. "This has happened before. It's happened in other countries, to other people; it's even happened here, in some areas. Riots, purges, wars, genocide. There's never a moment on Earth when someone isn't suffering and dying at the hands of others. You know that. Human nature isn't your fault."

"I know," I whispered. "But it feels like it is."

Maybe he would have tried to offer me more therapy, I don't know, but right then, Cherise screamed and yelled, "Stop the car!"

David must have been the one in control, because there was no debate about it. The Djinn braked the Boss to a stop on the damp pavement in a noisy slide.

"Uh, Cher, that mob is still heading this way," Kevin said, sensibly checking out the rearview mirror. "Might take them a few minutes, but—"

Cherise wasn't listening. She bailed out of the car and darted out into the glow of the headlights, and I saw her scramble over debris toward the side of the road. "Dammit," I said. "Kevin. Go with her. Hurry."

He was already on his way, and shot me an irritated look. "Like I wasn't going to anyway," he said. "Thanks, *Mom.*"

I was *so* glad he wasn't my kid. It felt like cowardice, but I stayed behind. I was nothing but a liability right now, and at least one of us needed to stay with the car. Kevin didn't seem to mind that decision in the least. In fact, he grinned fiercely as he passed through the headlights, plunging after Cherise to the side of the road.

It seemed to take forever. I watched anxiously through the back window. The mob was coming, and I could hear them screaming. It was a deep, animal roar, and I imagined this was how those soldiers throughout history had felt, holding their ground and waiting while the enemy charged.

It wasn't good.

I got so focused on the approach of the crowd that it surprised me (complete with yelp) when Cherise yanked open the back door and climbed in with something bundled in her arms in a dirty blanket. It squirmed. Kevin piled in after, looking grim, and yelled, "Go go go!"

Off we went, leaving the swiftest of the mob to clutch at a spray of gravel and dust.

The bundle in Cherise's arms wailed. It wasn't the cry of a hungry or tired baby; this was more—aware. A toddler, maybe two or three years old. Cherise unwrapped the blanket, and I saw a small, round face capped by shiny, thick black hair. The child looked as miserable as I felt.

"Cher," I said. "We can't—"

Kevin leaned forward, cutting me off. "There was a whole family back there," he said. "Mom, dad, two other kids. This one's the only one still breathing. So shut up, okay?"

I swallowed. "What happened to them?"

"What do you *think* happened? They had something. Somebody else wanted it. Probably a car; they didn't look like they'd been walking, and they didn't have any bags."

Kevin was right. I couldn't say no to helping this kid. Maybe I should have; maybe Lewis would have. Maybe he would have said something about the greater good and saving the most number of lives.

All I could say, looking at that little face, was, "Okay."

Whatever David thought, he kept it to himself. The Djinn proxy driver guided us through a winding set of back roads, turning left, then right at intersections until we arrived back at a main highway again. I didn't know where we were, and I wasn't sure maps had much relevance anymore. Cherise and Kevin had something to do now; they had found some crackers and juice boxes in their stash of snacks, and were now arguing over whether a kid that age wore a diaper. I didn't add any insights. They both seemed very earnest about the whole thing, which was a little endearing.

The night passed quietly enough. We'd outrun the worst of the storms, for the moment; no wildfires chased us through the silent trees. It almost looked normal. I rolled down the window, and night air fluttered over my face like a damp veil. I breathed it in and felt, for a moment, a little calmed. *This still exists. There's still hope.*

David said, "We should have good travel for the next few hundred miles. This part of the country's still relatively unaffected."

"Yeah, why is that?" Kevin asked.

I already knew the answer to that. "It's rural," I said. "And the trouble is focusing on centers of population first. That doesn't mean it won't spread fast, but for now, people out here are as safe as they can be."

"It's more than that," David said. "There's a black corner near here—a small one. It's been here for a thousand years or more. But it tends to keep the Djinn and the Wardens well away."

I blinked, because I hadn't known *that.* It made sense, though—black corners were places that canceled out supernatural forces, all kinds of supernatural forces. It was wasting energy to go near one.

Which made them *perfect* for hiding people who didn't, and couldn't, tell the difference.

"Pull over," I ordered.

"It's better if we—"

"David, pull the car over *now*!"

He did. There was no use trying for Google Maps or GPS; I went at it old-school, rifling the glove compartment for maps. There was a road atlas, years out of date but good enough. I flipped through it until I found a map of the entire continental USA.

"Show me on the map where the black corners are," I said. Small black areas painted themselves out. There weren't many, but they were there . . . and they were scattered from coast to coast, north to south. Almost . . . deliberately. "Okay, looking good. David, you're talking through the radio."

There was a long pause, and then David said, in the tone of someone who really didn't understand why I was stating the obvious, "Yes . . . ?"

"Is that just to us, or can you do it anywhere?"

"Define anywhere."

"All radios in specific areas."

Another pause, and then he said, slowly, "Yes. Yes, I can."

"Awesome. You are the new Djinn Emergency Broadcast System." I got out of the car and spread the atlas out on the hood of the idling car. Cherise and Kevin got out with me; Kevin was holding the toddler, who had fallen charmingly asleep in his arms. "I need dimensions on these black corners. Specifically, how many people they can hold, whether there's any food and water, shelter, that kind of thing. Get me all the information you can."

"Uh—how?" Cherise asked blankly. She held out her phone. It still said NO SERVICE. "Internet go boom."

"The aetheric's still there," I said. "You and Kevin get up there, find me these two black corners; they're the largest ones. Tell me whatever you can. Do it fast."

Kevin handed me the baby, which was a smart move. I wasn't sure he wouldn't drop the kid on his head at the best of times, but being out of his body wouldn't help him be Best Surrogate Dad Ever. The child was surprisingly heavy and warm, and settled against me with a sleepy murmur. I smoothed dark hair, balanced him (her?) on my hip, and stared down at the map as Cherise and Kevin stood, immobile and vacant next to me. Both of the areas I'd indicated to them were remote; whatever had happened there to damage the planet's awareness had been significant, but it had also probably happened a very long time ago. Maybe even before humans began building their first mud huts. Maybe they'd been even larger, and the Earth was slowly, steadily healing in those areas.

But what was important to me was that if I put people inside those borders, they'd be safe from supernatural forces. As safe as I could make them, anyway.

Cherise came back first, staggering as her spirit reunited with her body and catching herself with both hands against the car's fender. She snatched her palms off it immediately. "Ow!" she said. "Damn. Hot. And I'm not talking about myself, you know." I didn't need to put her back on track. She took in a deep breath and continued. "It's pretty large, but it's wild out there. Overgrown. No shelter or structures I could see. There's a stream, though, so fresh water. You'd have to arrange for the food."

"Roads?"

"There's a kind of road—damn, that map's too small. Guess you can't zoom in."

"It's *paper*, Cher."

"Kidding. Anyway, yeah, there's a way in, you could probably drive it. Not sure how tough it would be, though."

"How many people could it hold?"

"It's about as big as half of Manhattan, so you figure it out. Of course, unless they're living in trees, you can only put them on the ground floor."

It was better than nothing. Not a lot better, but still.

Kevin returned a few minutes later. He had better news, from the western black corner—which was large, empty, and easy to reach. Only problem was, it was barren. *Really* barren. No source of fresh water running through it, or even near it. It was also hotter than hell there, and even with tents and temporary shelters it might be fatal conditions for many.

But we didn't have a choice. I ordered everybody back into the car. Kevin took the kid back from me; the baby woke up and started fretting. Kevin bounced him in his arms, waking a surprisingly cheerful set of giggles, and the kid put its chubby arms around his neck.

"Boy or girl?" I asked. Kevin gave me a long-suffering, disgusted look.

"Boy, obviously," he said. "Wow. I thought you were all up on the birds and the bees."

I tried again. "What's his name?"

"How am I supposed to know? The kid was lying underneath his dead mom. He didn't come with *papers*." Kevin's eyes glittered in the white backwash of the headlights, but not with Djinn power, not anymore. Those were real, human tears. "They left him there to starve or get eaten. So maybe his name ought to be Lucky; what do you think?"

"Kevin," I said, gently. "Deep breaths."

"Fuck you," he snapped, and got in the car. I ached for him, because nobody—not even Kevin—should feel the kind of agony I could hear in his voice. He hated this as much as I did, as much as Cher did. I could feel that pain and panic burrowing inside me like a carnivorous small animal. *Make it stop. I don't want to do this anymore. Make it all go away.*

For a few seconds, it was so overwhelming that I wanted to scream. I forced myself to take deep, steady breaths, and stared at the map until my eyes blurred. I blinked, and tears slid cold down my cheeks, but I wiped them away impatiently. *I have no time for this crap*, I told myself. *Sack up, Jo. Right now.*

I wanted to be strong, but it seemed like the solid rock I'd always felt to be inside me had turned to slippery, clinging mud, and I wasn't sure I had any emotional footing anymore.

"Jo?" That was David's voice, coming from the car. I grabbed the atlas and got back inside. The second I slammed the door, we got moving again at Djinn speed, turning the night into a shadowy blur beyond the windows.

Except for the cold white moon, almost full, that floated up overhead like a balloon. Its glow almost eclipsed the stars. Out here in the dark, there were so many of those, thick as spilled sacks of gems in the heavens. Easy to feel small.

Easy to feel a sense of the ice-cold infinite out there, too, for whom the death struggles on this planet were of merely academic interest.

Perversely, that made me feel better.

"David," I said, and was glad that my voice sounded steady now. "I need you to send messages to all the Wardens you can reach. Tell them we've identified two main areas where they can send refugees, and give them coordinates and the details. Give them the coordinates of the other black corners, too. Even if some will only hold a few people, it's something. We should use it."

"I'm on it," he said, and oddly enough, he laughed.

"What?"

"Coordinating. Isn't that what Lewis tried to sentence us to from the start?"

The radio turned itself off.

I leaned back in the seat, which no longer felt remotely comfy after the long, long hours, and glanced over at the Djinn driver. "So," I said. "How you doing?"

I didn't really expect an answer, and I didn't get one.

It was a long drive to the next major town.

We never quite reached it.

The sun was just coming up, and we still had six hours or so to go to the next town big enough to merit the name, when I finally put my foot down and said that we needed beds, showers, food, and restrooms. That wasn't as tough as it sounded to achieve; two curves of the road later, we spotted a roadside motel, the no-name-brand kind made of bravely painted cinder blocks that doesn't have to go into double digits on room numbers. Technically, it was a motor court. I wasn't sure what the difference was, except that "motor court" sounded slightly more upscale than "no-tell motel."

It wasn't.

The office was locked, but somebody had already done yeoman work breaking in the door, which swung wide open. The cash register was on the floor, cracked and empty. There was a TV missing from a stand in the corner, cable connections left dangling. Looters always take the TVs. And it always seems insane, but never more than now.

There were keys hanging on hooks behind the counters. I grabbed three and tossed one each to Kevin and Cherise. "Be careful," I said. "Could be anybody out there. Make sure you lock the doors once you're inside."

Kevin cast a significant look at the busted office door. "Yeah," he said. "That'll help. What do they make these things out of, cardboard? An arthritic eighty-year-old on a walker could kick these things down."

"Your body odor could knock it down faster," Cherise said crisply. "I cannot *wait* for a shower. They want to go all *Psycho* on me, fine. At least I'll die clean."

She held out her arms, and Kevin passed her the toddler, who was awake, alert, and watching me with shining black eyes. He was drooling on himself. I didn't take it as a compliment. "Come on, Herbert."

"You are *not* calling him Herbert," Kevin said, as Cherise got the boy situated on her hip.

"Okay, how about Ronald? I'm trying to go with a dead president theme, here."

"He's too good looking. Go with Thomas."

"Tommy," Cherise said immediately. "Jefferson. Yeah, okay. How's that, Tommy? You like that, big man?" She made nonsense sounds to him, and Tommy laughed and clapped his hands. "Tommy it is. Awesome. Tommy and I are going to get clean."

"Enjoy," I said. I was going to be in hot pursuit of that shower, but first I wanted to go through the office. The looters had probably taken everything of value, but I wasn't looking for things to pawn or spend.

Kevin hesitated at the door. "You going to be okay?"

I flipped a hand at him without looking up from the contents of a drawer. He shrugged and went away.

The drawer seemed heavy, although there wasn't much in it. I frowned playing with it, and realized that it had a false bottom. I pressed on the back, and the front popped up.

Underneath that lay a big, black semiautomatic pistol, with two full clips and a box of bullets . . . and a sawed-off shotgun, and shells.

"Sweet," I said, and stuffed it all into a recyclable shopping bag that was lying on the floor. Small-business owners. Like Boy Scouts, always prepared.

I also found a private stash of alcohol, which I left, except for one bottle I planned to use for first aid. Or morale emergencies, whichever came first. There was also a pretty significant first aid kit, well stocked, and some shelf-stable cookies, power bars, and chips that I put into another bag.

I was feeling pretty good by the time I locked the flimsy door on my motel room. The room was clean and empty, and as far as I could tell, nobody had bothered to loot it. The bathroom still had soap and shampoo. With the power off, it was dark as a cave, but I'd brought a flashlight from the office, and set it up to shine on the shower area. I dumped my filthy clothes in the sink to soak. The water was lukewarm, but that was better than nothing.

The shower started out lukewarm, then turned cold, but I didn't care; feeling clean again was an intense relief. I could have hope again. Hope that if I had to die, at least I would do it with shiny, bouncy hair.

Something flashed across the glow from the flashlight. I gasped, got soap in my eyes, and rinsed as fast as I could. *It's a moth*, I told myself. *A moth flying around in front of the light. You'd have heard somebody come in.*

I listened. The falling water drowned out any sound of an intruder.

"It's a moth," I breathed, willing myself to believe it. Okay, I was in a creepy deserted motel with no lights. Okay, I was in a horror movie cliché, naked in a shower in a creepy deserted motel with no lights.

But dammit, I wasn't going to be some horror movie damsel who got *killed* naked in a shower in a creepy deserted motel. With no lights.

I shut off the water with a firm twist of the knobs, grabbed the thin shower curtain, and rattled it back. Water trickled ice-cold down my back from my wet hair and brought up chill bumps all over my skin.

Nobody there.

I grabbed a towel, dried off, and wrapped it spa-style around my body, then used the second one to do the turban thing. This wasn't the kind of place that provided free plush robes, or even paper-thin ones. I stood on the cold tile, picked up the flashlight, and angled it around in every corner of the small room.

Nothing.

"Moth," I said, triumphantly, and propped up the light to help me see what I was doing as I scrubbed my clothes with bath soap. I refilled the sink several times, finished by wringing it all out, and hanging it up on the side of the tub and the shower rod.

Then I walked out into the main room, which was

flooded with light from the opened curtains, and saw the Djinn sitting on my bed waiting for me.

And not just any Djinn.

Rahel.

Rahel was back to her old self—beautiful, sharp-edged, dressed in a neon yellow tailored pantsuit with a plunging neckline white shirt. Cornrowed hair, with amber and gold beads woven throughout. Her long pointed fingernails matched her outfit, and her eyes were a pure, luminous white.

I stopped in the doorway and braced myself with one hand. Rahel didn't move. She didn't speak. She didn't seem to even know I was there.

I licked my lips and said, "Rahel?"

For a moment, nothing happened, and then her head tilted, very slowly, to one side. Beads clicked together with a dry-bones rattle like the warning of a rattlesnake in slow motion.

I stood there waiting for it, but she didn't move again. I took a tentative step forward, then another one. No reaction. I made it to the rickety side chair that came with the "office table" and its cheap lamp, and sat down because I wasn't sure if my legs would hold me for too long. She didn't feel like Rahel. She *looked* the part, but Rahel would already have fired off some snarky, lazy insult or threat, clicked her fingernails, tried to kill me, laughed . . . *something*.

What was wearing Rahel right now was very far from the Djinn I knew.

"Who are you?" I whispered. Those white eyes stared at me, unblinking, but blind. I just happened to be the direction in which they stared; it didn't feel like *focus*. "Is this—are you—"

I couldn't exactly come out with it, but I understood, on a very primal level, who was looking out through that blank gaze. An intelligence so vast that it couldn't possibly understand me. So huge that it was trying to make sense of something impossibly tiny to it.....As if by staring unaided at the surface of the table, I could see the molecules that made it up. She was *trying* to understand. But I didn't think she did. Or could. And that was ... alarming.

"Can you let me talk to Rahel?" I asked, in the softest, most respectful voice I could manage. "I just—she can translate for you. Help you understand." Although how that was going to get across I couldn't imagine. It was like an ant trying to communicate with me by the pheromones and scents that made up its language. I couldn't detect it, much less understand it.

So much easier to squash the bug, especially when the hive was so, so large.

I was screwed.

Rahel stared through me for what seemed like an hour, but couldn't have been more than a couple of minutes, and then suddenly her head snapped back upright, and she surged up to her feet, took two steps forward, and her hand went around my throat. I yelped, trying to press backward; the chair tipped against the wall, pinning me in place. I kicked at her, for all the good it did. It was like kicking bare toes into solid rock. I felt the sharp, biting sting as her fingernails pressed in, and I had a grim, graphic vision of how it would look when she flexed her hand and drove those nails into soft flesh and ripped my throat out in a spray of blood....

But that didn't happen. Rahel froze, our faces inches away. This close, the white glow in her eyes broke up into a coruscating brilliance—every color, all colors, flickering by at such speed that only the constant white glow was left. I was looking into something that humans should never see, and I felt parts of my mind giving up, shutting down, refusing to hold the information flooding into them. I could hear that awful shrieking again, just as I had on board the ship, and I couldn't shut it out.

And then, just like that, it was over. She let go, I over-balanced and fell to the floor on my hands and knees, and Rahel turned and stalked toward the door.

It blew outward in a spray of splinters—wood mist, really—and the untouched lock and knob fell with a clatter to the concrete outside. She didn't pause on her way out. I heard one of the other doors slam open, and heard Kevin yell.

"Kevin, no!" I screamed, and scrambled to get to my feet. "Leave her alone!" I wasn't at all afraid he could hurt Rahel, only that he was going to actually get her attention.

I made it to the door too late. Kevin had a fireball in his hand, and before I could shout again, he was throwing it at Rahel's back.

Sometimes, the ant stings.

And there's really only one response to that, isn't there?

I threw myself backward and to the side as Rahel spun, braids flying, and backhanded the ball of fire out of the air, sending it rocketing at blurry speed for the proverbial bleachers. Before that had even happened, she was launching a counterattack at Kevin, a wave of force that hit the building and blew it apart in a cascade of shattered concrete, rebar, and splintered wood.

I was on the floor, hugging cheap carpet. I'd lost my towel, but that was completely meaningless at the moment. As things came apart around me I grabbed the mattress on the bed and yanked it off the frame. It slid across, tilted down, and formed a small sheltered space as I curled up into a protective ball.

I heard screaming. Could have been Cherise, or the toddler. Tommy. Could even have been Kevin. I hated myself for hiding, but my body wouldn't move, wouldn't obey my orders to get up and help.

Nothing you can do, part of my mind said. *You're not a Warden. Rahel can't even see you. You're just collateral damage. Keep your head down.*

What had I told Cherise, once upon a time? Mere humans were part of this, too. They were the reason the Wardens kept fighting.

And I had to fight for myself, too. No matter the odds.

Another stunning blow hit the building, and the roof overhead ripped off and went flying. The front window shattered, and a piece of glass plunged all the way through the mattress to emerge two inches from my face in a lethally sharp exclamation point. I choked on concrete dust as the cinder-block front wall collapsed in. Some of the blocks—not all, thankfully—slammed down on top of the mattress, pressing it down on me, and I burrowed in toward the bed frame to gasp in more air.

And then it got quiet.

I went very still, listening, and over the faint groan of debris that was still succumbing to gravity, I heard slow, deliberate footsteps. They weren't heading away.

Rahel was going to finish the job.

I huddled there, heart pounding. All the will to get up and fight had bled right out of me at the sound of those footsteps; there was something terrifying about them.

The sound of death.

I closed my eyes as the crunch of shoes on debris stopped nearby.

The mattress covering me suddenly flipped up and off, flying into the air like some startled bird. I gasped as its comforting weight disappeared. I'd never felt so exposed, naked, and helpless in my life.

I forced myself to open my eyes, and saw Rahel standing over me, staring down with those eerie white eyes. I remembered the first time I'd met her—how she'd just appeared in my car, nearly sending me off the road in surprise. How she'd casually tormented me, but helped me, too. I'd seen Rahel do amazing things, and terrible things, but it had always been *her*.

This wasn't her. And suddenly, that made me angry.

"All right, *Mom*," I said, and climbed up to my bare feet. I'd lost my towels, not sure where or how; my cold, damp hair straggled down my back and over my shoulders, and I was unevenly coated in concrete dust like I had a serious case of mange. "You want me? Here I am!" I had a black rage boiling inside me, fueled by sheer terror, and I wasn't the type to go down without a fight. I bent and scooped up a bent piece of iron rebar. It felt gritty and cold in my hands as I took up a batting stance.

Rahel reached for me. I swung, connected with her shoulder, and the rebar *snapped in half*, sending a piece flying away to clatter against the rubble of the far side of the destroyed room. I wasn't done. I jabbed at her with the broken end, hoping to bury it in her guts, but she just batted it easily away. When I tried it again, she took hold of the rebar and ripped it out of my hand.

She flung it contemptuously after the other half.

I thought desperately of David—not as a savior, not as someone to come running in and sweep me off my feet. I thought how desperately I was going to miss him, and how much this would hurt him, and how sorry I was not to be able to tell him—tell him . . .

As Rahel swiped a hand full of razor-sharp talons toward my neck, I knew I was going to die. I'd heard other people talk about coming to some kind of peace, acceptance, whatever. Not me. I wanted to howl out my defiance and fury.

Instead, I ducked.

The claws missed my throat, my face, and tangled in my hair. She instantly grabbed a fistful, yanking me off balance toward her. I fought, scratched, punched, did everything I could—a wild animal, fighting for my life.

I heard a distant, wild screaming somewhere at the very limits of hearing, a banshee kind of sound that dopplered closer in seconds. A freight train full of demented shriekers, all of it hurtling straight for me.

Maybe that was death. Rahel's claws flashed, and I managed to get my arm up to defend my throat. I didn't feel the cuts, but I saw the skin part like tearing silk, weirdly beautiful. Even the spray of blood looked beautiful—brilliantly colored, every misty drop frozen in crystal clarity.

Then the screaming freight train hit me, full force, and my world went dark. Agony rolled through my body, as if every cell was being ripped apart, rolled in acid, and set aflame . . . but somehow, impossibly, I was still alive.

I heard myself shrieking, just like that sound I'd heard, and then fire exploded out of the ground to engulf me.

No, not fire.

Power.

Thick golden streams of power, flooding up my body, wreathing me in glorious streamers, whipping around and around and then plunging *in* to waken an explosion that should have ripped me apart.

It should have ripped the world apart.

But instead, I opened my eyes and saw the haze of the aetheric, overlaying the drab, gray destruction. I saw the swirling, unsettled energies, the anger, the stain of all the past in this place.

And I saw the Mother, looking out of a Djinn's eyes in blind, unthinking fury.

I knocked Rahel's arm aside and slammed my palm

down flat against her chest, directly between her breasts. Force rippled out and down my arm, and blew explosively in a tight-focused blast from me to her.

I knocked the Djinn into the air, over a pile of fallen concrete blocks, and out into the relatively clear area of the parking lot.

I looked down at myself. I was covered in cuts, concrete dust, and blood—so much so that I might as well have been wearing a really skin-tight outfit. But everything was still working, at least while the adrenaline was pumping.

Good enough.

I walked over the broken concrete and glass, heedless of more cuts, and followed Rahel out to where she'd fallen. Not surprisingly, she was already back on her feet, and her sharp teeth glittered as she snarled.

I kept walking toward her, but as I did, I reached for power, and it came, welling up out of the ground, descending from the skies, crackling and bleeding out of every electrical impulse around me. I formed it into a ball of luminescent poison green and threw it like a fastball, straight for her face.

She tried to bat it aside, but it dodged, even quicker than a Djinn, and detonated against her torso in a hot flare that knocked her completely down. I reached up into the troubled skies and rubbed water and air molecules together, gathering static into a massive potential energy that turned the clouds black and green.

Then I flipped the polarization of the molecules in the ground, then the air above her, clicking over the changes faster and faster until the circuit was open . . .

. . . And lightning struck in a thick, burning column, pinning her down. Rahel's body convulsed and dissolved into mist. Not dead—you can't kill a Djinn like that—but seriously inconvenienced. Even a Djinn has a safety overload, and I'd just burned it right out with those three consecutive strikes.

She'd be back, but not for a while.

I looked around and remembered the power I'd gathered overhead as the sky snarled and rumbled. I reached up and bled the energy back out, slowly, distributing it in a soft, gentle rain that sluiced the blood and dust from my skin. I was still full of power—stuffed with it—but I knew how to let it slowly sink back down into the waiting, silent ground.

A final sigh, and I opened my eyes.

And collapsed.

Ow.

The concrete wasn't a soft landing, and I realized that my body had simply failed after conducting that much power, energy, and adrenaline. I was shaking now as the tide of hormones receded in my bloodstream and left me feeling human, and vulnerable, again.

I was also hurting. A lot. I looked down at my arm, which was bleeding from deep cuts, and thought, *I need to do something about that.* It took me a long minute to remember the first aid kit that I'd salvaged from the office. It, and the guns, had been in a bag in my motel room.

I rolled up to my knees, then to my feet, cut off the rain and dried myself off with another burst of power—not so much eliminating the moisture from my skin and hair as moving it somewhere else. Balance. Ma'at.

The sight of the motel was appalling. It was a ruin, barely recognizable as the cheap building we'd arrived at just an hour ago. My room, at least, still had a partial wall standing, though the roof had been yanked off and tossed twenty feet away in a jumble of broken wood and shingles.

Cherise's and Kevin's rooms were worse.

Cherise and Kevin. The kid.

It came to me in a physical shock. In the press of adrenaline, fighting for my own life, I'd forgotten about them, but now it came dreadfully clear.

I had my powers back.

Cherise had been harboring my powers, and there was only one reason for those powers to pull away from her and go in search of someone else—if Cherise was no longer a living vessel for them. And I was the only one left standing.

Oh God, no.

I forgot all about the wound on my arm and ran to the mass of broken blocks that was where I remembered Cherise's room to be. "Cher!" I screamed, and started throwing rubble aside, searching. "Cherise!"

I heard something soft, like a kitten, and stopped to listen. Far corner, under yet another mound of debris— but under the debris was a mattress. She'd done as I had; she'd grabbed the mattress and ducked under it for cover. *Yes. Yes, it was going to be okay. . . .*

I cleared the rubble off the filthy, broken mattress and pitched it away, heaving with all my strength.

Under it, Cherise lay motionless, with her body half covering the toddler she'd rescued. Tommy. He was the one making the mewling sounds, and when light hit him and he saw me, he let out a full-throated howl of panic and pain. I turned Cherise over enough to pull him out, and checked him with trembling hands. He was bruised, but I couldn't find any broken bones. She'd protected him.

She'd protected him with her body, and her life.

"Cher," I whispered, and smoothed her bloodied hair back from her face. "Oh, no, sweetie. No, no, no. You can't do this to me. You can't."

She'd been badly battered by the falling wall, even with the mattress for protection, and I saw the unnatural shape of her legs where they'd been broken and twisted.

Her face was oddly unmarked, except for a spot or two of blood. I could almost hear her laughing and saying, *I always knew I'd die pretty.*

"No," I said flatly. "You're not dying on me, bitch. Not happening."

I saw a flicker inside of her, a golden tongue of fire that hadn't yet gone out. She wasn't dead ... but she was dying. No breath, no heartbeat, and her cells were burning up the last of their energy and shutting down.

I put Tommy down, dragged Cherise flat, and began CPR. I imbued every pump of my hands on her chest, every breath I blew into her slack mouth, with Earth power, giving her body an artificial jump-start of energy for those starving cells until I could get the rest going again. It was exhausting, sweaty work, but I wasn't going to give up. She was *there.* Cherise was still alive, buried under the broken rubble of her own body, and she needed me.

The Earth power saturating her body formed a link to me, reporting back on all that it found wrong inside my friend. It wasn't good. It was going to take a lot to bring her back, and even more to restore her to anything like health.

I needed someone like Lewis, someone who had the gift, the fine and delicate touch of healing. But all I had was me, and I would have to be enough.

I started with the worst of it—ruptured spleen, damaged liver, torn internal blood vessels that were flooding her with blood and compressing her lungs. A depressed skull fracture that had driven splinters of bone into fragile tissue.

Each of those took time, and massive concentration and energy. The skull fracture was the worst and most delicate, and when I'd finally coaxed out the bone splinters and dissolved them, and repaired the damage, I had very few reserves of power left.

But I couldn't stop. Her legs needed healing fast, or she'd lose them. I moved down her body and made sure she was kept unconscious as I moved the broken pieces, aligned them, and started binding them together in golden strips of power, spiraling up the structure and holding it together. The power sank slowly into the bone and fused it together—not strong, yet, but set.

Then I let her come up from the dark, leading her slowly and gently back to the light.

Cherise opened her eyes with a choking gasp, coughed, and stared blindly up at the sky for a few seconds before her pupils contracted and focused on my face.

"Tommy?" she asked. I pulled the toddler over. He was still whimpering, but at the sight of Cherise's smile he waved his hands and smiled back.

"He's fine," I said. "Cher, don't try to get up. Stay down, let your body adjust, okay? I have to put some braces on your legs."

"My legs?" She looked confused, then alarmed. "Oh my God, what happened to my legs?"

"They were broken," I said. "I fixed them, but you're going to have to watch it for a while. The braces are just to keep you from banging into things, twisting, that kind of thing." I tried to get up, but my body wouldn't do it. It just—refused. Okay, sitting was good. I was all right with a little rest, I supposed. I reached out and pulled over a couple of broken pieces of wood, wrapped each one in sheets from the bed, and wrapped the whole thing around her right leg, then repeated my construction project for the left.

Cherise said, in a very small voice, "I don't feel good anymore. Not like I did."

"I know." That energy, humming and snapping through my body, was something that I'd never known I had, really, until it was gone. I could understand how Cherise felt, to have been given that gift, and then to lose it.

"You've got it."

"Yep."

"Because I died," she said, which made me stop what I was doing and look at her in mute concern. "What? It's true, right? I died, and I lost the power, and it moved on to the next person it could reach. Had to be you, or . . ." Her eyes widened, and we both said it at the same time. "Kevin."

I hadn't spared a thought for him, not a single second. If I had, Cherise wouldn't have made it. But she wouldn't see it that way, and I wouldn't blame her a bit. It was a callous thing to do, not to at least try to find him. Problem was, now that I had the time, I didn't have the energy. No way could I find him, or heal him if I did.

"David," I said, and closed my eyes. The cord that bound us together was back in place now, strong and vital, but stretched very thin. Still, I knew he could hear me. I knew he *would*. "David, I need you to find Kevin."

"David can't do anything; he's in Djinn Disneyland," Cherise said, and batted at me weakly. "You have to go! Go find him!"

"I can't, Cher." I said it softly, but I thought she could feel the absolute truth of it. "I just can't right now."

Her eyes filled with tears, and she tried to push herself up. I held her down. She yelled at me, cursed, called me names that would have stung if I hadn't been so tired and drained.

Then she went quiet, and I looked over my shoulder to see the Djinn who'd been driving our car walking through the rubble toward us.

Draped in his arms was Kevin's lank, limp body.

Cherise let out a sound—not a scream, not a cry, but some awful mixture of the two. It was raw and unthought, and scraped at me like fingernails on a burn. *Oh, sweetie, I'm so sorry*, I thought wearily. We'd all said we understood the risks, but this was different.

We never really understood until it came down to this.

The Djinn knelt down and put Kevin on the carpet next to Cherise. There wasn't a mark on Kevin, nothing at all.

He was just . . . gone. The life had been taken right out of him. All the working pieces were still there, in a body that could have still lived on, but some great, overwhelming force had commanded it to be still.

And I knew, as I touched his hand, that there was no way I could bring him back. Kevin—all that had made up the complicated, fragile, angry, vindictive, sometimes brave boy I'd known—all that was gone, blown away like a puffball on the wind.

His eyes were open wide, pupils expanded to drink in the light. He looked very, very young. His hair still gleamed in the dim, cloudy light—wet from his shower, or from the rain I'd brought down. He'd been strong, and sometimes he'd been good, and losing him shouldn't have hurt so very badly.

I put my hand on his forehead, one last and gentle benediction from someone who should have liked him more, helped him more, done better for him. He'd been torn apart as a child, made into a monster, and he'd *tried*, dammit. He'd tried so hard to be different.

He would have been a good man eventually. I knew it.

I wanted to cry, but the tears wouldn't come. They choked me deep inside but refused to rise. Maybe I needed them. Maybe it wasn't time to mourn.

"Jo." It was David's voice, coming from the Djinn's mouth. "There's nothing—"

"I know!" I snarled at him, suddenly and irrationally furious with *David*, of all people. "Just leave me the hell alone, okay? I know there's nothing I could have done!"

He rose to his feet, staring down at me, and then nodded. "I'll get the car," he said. "Let me know if you want to bury him before we go."

Now Cherise was screaming at him. I didn't think David minded. He was staying quietly neutral, aware that we had to deal with this in our own ways. He moved the Djinn back, out of our view.

Cherise finally stopped spitting out accusations, and gathered up the wailing, frightened toddler in her arms, hugging him close. I'd never pegged her as the motherly type, but watching her, I could see it. She put on a smile for the boy, soothed him, and when that was done, I could see that she'd reached some fragile acceptance inside.

"We're not just leaving him here like this, like road-kill," she told me. "Promise me."

"I promise," I said. "I'll make sure he's taken care of."

I meant it, of course, and she could tell that. She didn't make any objection as I gestured for the Djinn to come back and scoop Kevin up in his arms. I knew it was David on the inside of the avatar, but somehow I couldn't make myself reach out for him. It wasn't *really* David. Just a flicker of will. A phantom. A shadow.

I pulled myself up to my feet without any help from him, looked down at myself, and said, "I need to find my clothes." It was a measure of how insane things were that nobody else seemed to have noticed I was naked. Cherise, in fact, looked surprised. "I left them in the bathroom."

For answer, the Djinn nodded toward a spot on the carpet—a relatively clean one. A pile of clothing materialized there—white shirt, sturdy pants that looked suspiciously like I remembered the drapes to be. My own shoes, recovered and cleaned. Plain white bra and panties and socks.

Djinn couldn't create out of thin air, but they could

recycle. He'd used the raw material of extra sheets, the curtains, towels, whatever textile was around, and he'd managed to produce a decent attempt at a wardrobe. Clean and dry, if not stylish.

I struggled into it fast. It fit, of course. Djinn tailoring always fit. I tied my hair back with a stray scrap of fabric blowing in the dirt and started to follow the Djinn out of the rubble.

"Jo?" Cherise called. I looked back. She was sitting up, cradling the fretful boy in her lap. She looked huge-eyed and emotionally shattered, but at least she was physically okay. For now. "I want to go with you."

"No. If you put any weight on those legs right now, they could break again. They need at least an hour to finish building the seal in the break. That's as fast as I can do it."

"Okay." She swallowed, but didn't look away. "I want to see him buried. Please. Take me with you."

I hesitated, then nodded. "I'll send the Djinn back for you," I said. "Wait here, okay? I promise, it'll only be a few minutes."

She didn't like it, but I think she saw that there was no way I could carry her myself, physically or with any kind of magical power. If I pulled power from the world around me again, it'd be a case of diminishing returns and a harder crash once it was over. I couldn't afford it.

Not knowing that this was far from the end.

I found the Djinn easily enough; he'd left a lighted trail of orange light through the trees. He hadn't gone too far in, but far enough that I lost sight of the road and the wrecked motel. In here, among the pines, things were hushed. The air smelled sweet and heavy, crisp with the smell of the needles.

Untouched.

The Djinn had dug a grave—six feet deep, wider than needed—beneath a particularly impressive branching tree. Kevin's body lay wrapped in a simple white sheet from the motel, and he no longer looked like the boy I'd known, or the man I'd wished he'd had a chance to become. He looked . . . empty, rendered pale and sexless by the shroud. I wasn't sure I wanted Cherise to see him like this, but I'd promised.

"I'll get him in," I said. "Go get Cherise and the kid. Don't let her walk yet."

The Djinn nodded and misted away. I stood there looking at Kevin for a moment, then hopped down into the damp hole in the earth, reached up, and rippled the ground to move him toward me and onto a hardened cushion of air. I floated him down into my arms, and lowered him the last bit on my own. He still felt heavy. Somehow, I'd expected him to be lighter now.

I leaned over and kissed his lips gently. "I'm so sorry," I said. "Find peace, Kevin. I've never known anybody who needed it more, and deserved it more."

That didn't seem to be enough, but I couldn't think of anything else to say.

I levitated myself up on a heated column of rising air and stepped off at ground level, just in time to see the Djinn arrive back at a run with Cherise and the boy in his arms. They looked like toys, the casual way he balanced them, but I knew he wouldn't drop them. No chance.

He looked around, then formed a plain wooden chair that was the same color and texture as the trees around us. Fallen wood, probably, reshaped for the purpose. He lowered her into it and came to stand next to me.

"He did a lot of things he probably regretted," David said. "But he tried to do good. That counts."

"He died trying to save us," I said. "That counts for everything."

We linked hands. It didn't feel like David, but that didn't matter right now. I just wanted to feel a touch, anyone's touch, to remind me I wasn't all alone in this. I felt a breath of relief pass over me that made me feel a little weak. *I wish you were with me*, I whispered, deep inside.

And I heard his whisper back, along that golden cord that bound us on the aetheric plane. *I am with you*, he said. *Always.*

Together, we filled in the hole. Apart from the singing of birds in the trees, the busy rustle of animals carrying on their lives, there wasn't any sound. When I looked at Cherise, she was silently crying. The boy was staring at us in confusion, about to break into wails of disapproval for all this craziness, but not sure if he should.

We smoothed the dirt on top of Kevin's grave, and I sent a pulse through the Earth, bidding the seeds to grow. Grass and flowers, pushing up green and fresh.

"You deserved better, Kevin," I said. "You always deserved better than what you got, and I'm sorry."

The Djinn said something, after that—something in warm, liquid syllables, lyrical and lovely that rose and fell in emotional arcs of poetry. When he was done, he bowed his head.

"That was beautiful," Cherise said, even though I knew she hadn't understood it any more than I had.

"It's our prayer for the dead," said David's voice. "Given to those who fall in battle."

When he said *our*, I sensed that he didn't mean the Djinn. He meant the human he'd once been, living in that long-ago time.

I squeezed his hand. "It is beautiful," I said. "Promise me you'll use it for me if it comes to that."

"No," he said. "I won't. Because I won't be here to do it if you're gone."

We stayed a while longer, but the air was getting cool, and we had miles to go.

The Djinn carried Cherise back to the waiting Mustang, which had only suffered a few scratches and dings out in the parking lot during the general destruction. Good. I'd destroyed way too many automotive works of art in my time. I didn't want to leave the Boss behind, too.

I looked back at the place where Kevin Prentiss had died until it fell away in the rear window, just another wide spot in the road. Nothing special.

It was special now. It always would be, for me.

I waited for the tears, but they stayed where they were, simmering, angry, *hungry*.

"Floor it," I said to the Djinn, and to David through him. "I want to see our daughter."

He didn't respond, but the Mustang leaped up to a whole new level of fast.

Chapter Eight

Weirdly enough, nothing else was happening in Missouri, or in Oklahoma as we dropped down toward our Arizona destination. Open roads, lots of traffic. Some towns still had power and some sense of normalcy, including—improbably—Oklahoma City.

People were actually *going to work*.

I supposed that was a good sign; life had to go on, until it became impossible. It was just . . . strange.

I rose up into the aetheric and found a powerful bunch of Wardens at work—Earth, Fire, and Weather all locked in a tight-knit unit, constantly repelling attacks on any number of levels. They were stretched thin, but coping. I soared up higher into the spirit world, looking at the patterns of lights and color, shadows and twisted representations of the physical world.

Lewis had figured it out. He'd teamed up his people in those triangular bases of power, positioning them at strategic locations. I looked back toward the east, where the chaos had been the worst, and it was dying down.

For now, the Wardens were handling it, even against all the odds.

It wasn't a battle we could win, but we could fight to a standstill—for a while.

I spotted Lewis on the aetheric. I'd expected him to be in Seattle, but he was a brilliant, incandescent blaze of power located in Nevada right now. I couldn't imagine what had drawn him there, but it was unmistakably him. And he was still moving, though not as quickly as I was, given the jet-powered chariot skills of the Mustang.

He was going wherever the battle was the fiercest, I thought. As he should.

I cut my grip on the aetheric and dropped back into my body with that familiar, faintly disorienting jolt, then pulled out my cell phone and checked it. The grid was back up, and I speed-dialed Lewis.

No answer. I wanted to tell him about Kevin, but this wasn't something that would be good for voice mail. I'd wait until I could tell him on the phone, or face to face. The news wasn't going to get worse, or better, with time.

I was just hanging up when the phone rang, startling me into a frantic juggling act. When I'd renewed my grip on it, I accepted the call and held the phone to my ear.

Piercing shrieks of static. I yanked the phone away again, no doubt making one of those pained faces, and then carefully eased it back as the feedback diminished into a thick net of noise. The screen said PRIVATE CALLER. I had no idea who it was.

And then I did.

It was me. My voice. And it said, "You need to stop. Stop now."

I took the phone away and looked at it again. Yep, there was a call. Private Caller. And it was my voice.

Saying, again, "Are you listening to me? Don't come here!"

"Excuse me, who am I talking to?" I asked, which was a pretty reasonable question at the moment, if a bit existential. This took *talking to myself* to a whole new level of weird. Then, belatedly, I got it. *"Imara?"* My Djinn daughter had been a virtual clone, down to the voice, although she'd always somehow sounded more sassy to me. Maybe because I wasn't used to being on the receiving end of the sass. "Imara, is that you?"

The answer drowned in static, and then my—her?—voice came back strong, again. "—have to stay away, Mom, do you understand?"

There was a particularly violent shriek of feedback, and the connection cut off. I was surprised there wasn't smoke curling up out of the receiver, as loud as that had been. I waited, but the phone didn't ring again.

The Djinn behind the wheel—still driving top speed on very treacherous roads—was staring straight at me, not at the road. "Jo?" David's voice, out of the radio. "Jo, was it Imara?"

"Yes. Can you reach her? Is she okay?"

"I can't see her. Like the Fire Oracle, I think she's hidden herself. I'll try to get through."

"Hurry," I said, and chewed my lip nervously. "I think she could be in trouble."

"We're all in trouble," David said, which wasn't the most inspirational speech he'd ever delivered. The radio shut down. The Djinn turned back toward the road.

I turned around to look in the backseat. Cherise was asleep, cuddled up with Tommy in a camouflage-patterned sleeping bag. We'd stopped in at a sports outfitter in Oklahoma City—Muzak still playing over the speakers, although shoppers were noticeably rattled and tense, and buying survival gear instead of lawn games—and stocked up on things like insulating blankets, sturdy boots and clothes, portable shelters, water and survival foods. Next best thing to Army surplus. And a lot more expensive, since it catered to the weekend wannabe warrior market.

It had felt deeply surreal to be signing a credit card slip while the world was in the throes of chaos, but I supposed one way or another, I'd be paying off my debts.

Cherise looked tired and pale, and from the way she was whimpering in her sleep, she had bad dreams. I reached back and smoothed her hair until the whimpering went away. Baby Tommy seemed to have adapted much more easily; he'd taken to Cherise quickly, and he was a happy kid, smiling and burbling most of the time. From the way he filled his diapers, he was healthy enough. I would have felt better having him checked out by an honest-to-goodness Earth Warden or, at the very least, a pediatrician, but for now, we were all doing okay. Cherise was out of the braces. Her legs had healed straight, and although she continued to be weak and tired, she was recovering remarkably well from having just about died. The jury was still out on how she was going to deal with Kevin's death, long term.

If we had any long term, of course.

Up ahead, traffic was snarled, again. As we got into more civilized areas, it was perversely harder to get around these days, what with people frantically trying to get to their survivalist mountain hideouts, or to their relatives, or just to the store to stock up on emergency batteries. We were coming into Amarillo—not exactly a major metropolitan area, but busier than the deserted Texas Panhandle highway had been. The air was dry and stable overhead, and the landscape was mostly flat and scrubby, with tough vegetation. Very different from the trees where we'd left Kevin.

I hoped I wouldn't end up dying somewhere without trees. I liked trees.

Even the Djinn's prodigious driving skills couldn't cope with the jam of traffic, and pretty soon we were cooling our engine at an idle, watching brake lights. Funny; this type of backup on the East Coast would have been a howling chorus of impatient horns sounding. Not here in the Southwest. People just . . . waited, listening to their music or talk radio, poking at their hair, arguing with whoever was in the car along with them. Or with themselves, apparently. I didn't hear a single angry honk.

"This is restful," I said, to nobody in particular. The Djinn wasn't exactly chatty company. Cherise was asleep. The radio stayed quiet, not falling for my opening gambit. "David? Do you think we should stop?"

"You all need rest," he said. "I'll find you a place to stay for a few hours, and someplace to eat."

That sounded heavenly. Not that I couldn't sleep in the car and eat bagged food, but stretching out on real sheets was better than sex right now. The mere thought of fresh food made me salivate.

"We should probably push on," I said, being the brave little toaster. "It's only about another ten hours to Sedona, and that's not counting the bat out of hell multiplier."

"You'd get there exhausted," he said. "It's been hard, and it's going to get worse, I think. You need to rest while you can." He spoke with authority, and I remembered that in his brief human life he'd been a soldier. He'd been used to exhaustion, to snatching what little rest and relief he could in between fighting for his life.

I gave in. Truthfully, it had been a token protest anyway, and Imara's inexplicable warning had made me worried. My daughter, like David, had a much wider view of things than I ever could. What if we were making things worse instead of better? What if we were actually forcing the battle instead of preventing it?

I couldn't think straight anymore. I'd been holding back emotions for a while now, but there's one thing about emotions: they never really go away if they're strong. You can bury them, but like a vampire they keep lurching back up. I knew that I was still numb about the loss of Kevin, but it was going to come out, and probably soon. I'd rather suffer through that in private, lying in a bed and hugging a pillow. It wouldn't help Cherise to see me lose it.

I'd put him in the ground myself. I'd felt the unmistakable absence in him, the void where his life had been.

No, I didn't want to remember how it had felt to hold his empty shell, or how he'd looked so pale, bound up in that cheap motel sheet—but the image wouldn't go away.

With a shocking intensity, that mental picture suddenly shifted, and it was *Lewis's* face pale and still, it was *Lewis* lying in my arms as I abandoned him to the dirt— alone, cold, unmarked. I almost gasped out loud with the emotion that brought rolling through me, and rested my burning forehead against the glass as I squeezed my eyes shut. *No. No, that's not going to happen.*

David and I had our powers back. Cherise had survived. We'd saved some lives along the way. We were *winning*, dammit. I couldn't get spooked now. I couldn't lose focus. That was another good reason to recharge. When I was in the throes of exhaustion, it was far too easy to let things overwhelm me, even the unlikely threats. I lost all ability to filter.

While I was thinking, David had been acting, and I felt the Mustang suddenly leap forward. I looked up and saw we were hurtling straight for the back of a stopped eighteen-wheel truck . . . and then the car lurched sideways with a scream of tires, jumped over a curb, and bumped down on the other side, onto an off ramp. Free of the traffic block, we rocketed down the access road toward a nice, neat-looking, moderately priced hotel/ motel.

We passed it. I looked back as it receded into the distance and said, "Uh, that one would have been okay—"

"No, it wouldn't have been, sugar." Whitney's accent never failed to make me want to roll my eyes. She could *not* have been more annoying about how thick she laid it on. "You're going to have company coming soon. Won't do to put you up someplace that's going to just come down on you. Again." She sounded utterly certain of herself, and casual about the threat, too. Lovely.

"What kind of company?"

"The kind you don't want to stand up to, not that you could. You remember little Venna."

Ouch. Venna was the very last Djinn I'd want to have on my tail right now—even worse than Rahel. Venna was impossibly strong, and she was clever, too. Great friend, awesomely bad enemy. I thought about that little girl, the image of innocence, with those ghostly white eyes like I'd seen in Rahel.

I shuddered. "Where can we go?"

"I'm working on that," Whitney said. "I'm taking over the car now."

We blurred past a *lot* of inviting-looking roadside inns, took some turns, and ended up on the northeast side of town, as best I could tell. Businesses of any kind thinned out and stopped.

Wherever she was taking us, it wasn't going to be the Hilton.

The car slowed and stopped in the middle of nowhere. I could see a faint smudge on the horizon off the blacktop to the right, but I couldn't tell what it was.

"Uh, Whitney? Hello?"

Nothing. No answer from her, or from David. I tried poking the Djinn, but it just sat there, inert and hot to the touch. It was like poking a bag of especially firm rubber.

Cherise yawned and sat up, rubbing her eyes. Tommy

woke up with a grouchy grumble, turned his face toward her neck as she lifted him up, and promptly fell asleep again draped all over her. She patted his back, smiled a little, and then looked at me. "What's going on?"

"Nothing."

"Well, obviously nothing, because we're just sitting here. Why are we just sitting here?"

"Because David and Whitney are arguing about it," I said. I just knew that was the case, and I knew that it indicated a potentially major problem. "Whitney says Venna is headed this way. Maybe it's a coincidence, but maybe she's on our trail, too. Either way, it's not good news."

Cherise shuddered. "Ouch. Okay, got it—crisis imminent. Again—we're sitting. Why are we sitting?"

"Because running off without a plan is an even worse idea," David's voice said, coming from the radio.

Whitney's voice, at the same time, came from the Djinn. "You're not thinking straight about this, boss man. You try to run them, she'll catch up. You try to hide them in the middle of all those people, she'll just mow down everybody in her way. This is your only real shot at keeping them alive, and you know it."

"This is the *opposite* of keeping them alive!" David snapped back.

"I hate it when Mommy and Daddy fight," Cher said, with just enough sarcasm to cut through. "We're not just pieces getting pushed around on a board, you know. Tell us what's going on."

David got there first. "She wants to take you to a nuclear weapons assembly plant."

I think Cherise and I both said it at the same time. *"What?"* I think we were both pretty restrained about it, really.

"That's it up ahead," David said. "It's not a good idea. It's so easy for Venna to destroy not just that place but everybody in this part of the state, given all that raw material to work with."

"I know that," Whitney snapped. "But it's also one of the only places we can lock off against her, not just with wards and shields, but with lead-lined concrete and bunkers designed to withstand nuclear attacks. Best possible place to hide them, especially if we can erase their traces on the aetheric."

Wow, Whit must have been upset, because she'd lost most of her *Gone with the Wind* accent. And she used bigger words.

"It's too dangerous," David said flatly. "No. We go on. I'm sorry, Jo, but if we keep moving we can stay ahead of Venna."

"Venna can materialize any place she wants, and you know it," I said. "How exactly do we stay ahead of her?"

"We're shielding you. She can't know exactly where you are."

"But she can narrow the area. And like Whitney said, anybody standing around us is collateral damage."

He fell silent, which indicated that my logic was, sadly, unassailable. I deeply wanted that little oasis of a working roadside inn, a meal with cooked food and actual silverware, but I understood the risks, and they were far too high—not for the three of us, but for everybody who had nothing to do with it.

"Is she really looking for us?"

"We think so," Whitney said. David said nothing, which I took for unwilling assent. "She's not the only one. There are at least four Djinn quartering the country. She just happens to be the one in this area. They're looking for signs, and ignoring the other Wardens."

Mother Earth must have really been pissed about me kicking Rahel's ass. Not good news.

"How about the other Wardens?" I asked. "Anybody close?"

"The three teamed up to cover this area are together in Albuquerque. Not close, but we could try making for their location. Strength in numbers."

"Not against Venna," Whitney said, which was probably true. "Not unless you're throwing an oiled-up Lewis into this cluster."

"Oiled-up . . ." David sounded utterly mystified, which was probably a good thing, because the image that flashed through my brain was exactly what Whitney intended. Thanks, Whit, you button-pushing bitch. David elected to go with a more literal interpretation. "He's still in Nevada. Too far."

"So it sounds like we don't have a lot of options," Cherise said. "Is this nuclear place safe for kids?"

"No," I said, "and it isn't safe for us, either. But I think Whitney may be right. There isn't any safe place just now. Maybe it's the closest we can get. David—can you get us in?"

"Security's tight, but I think so. The plant's closed now and under lockdown. Once you're inside the security perimeter you won't be seen."

"Surveillance," I reminded him. "Heat sensors. Motion detectors. Doesn't have to be an actual person to bust us for breaking and entering."

"Nothing electronic is going to pick you up," Whitney said. "I guarantee that."

Well, that was about the best I could ask for, in terms of reassurances. Go back, or go into the bunker?

Cherise, oddly enough, asked the logical question I hadn't bothered to think about. "How long are we staying there?"

"Until we can get Warden tactical support," I said. "Until we know whether we should go on to Sedona. If Imara really doesn't want us there, then we're making a mistake. We need to understand where we're needed, at this point." My whole goal, I realized, had been retrieving David's powers, and my own. Mission accomplished. Now what? We still had a major, and very difficult, war going on that we were unlikely to win. Restoring David had saved his life but placed him squarely on the sidelines, trapped except for what he could channel through our strange Djinn chauffeur.

Restoring me shifted the balance a little, but only a little. I had to choose where, and how, to apply the strength I could bring. Instinct cried out for me to keep running to Sedona, to see my daughter, to defend her with every breath I had and every power at my command. But Imara wasn't a helpless child; she was an Oracle, more powerful than her father and me combined, most likely. Instinct could be leading me the wrong way.

I needed to think. And I needed a safe place to do that.

"The plant is our best bet," I said finally. "If we have to make a stand, it's got our best chance of survival."

"I'm not dying in some *nuclear warehouse*," Cher said. "Look, enough already. I love you, Jo, but I can't take little Tommy in there. It's wrong. It's full of radiation and crap."

She was right; it wasn't any place to take a small boy. No matter how carefully this place conducted its business, it was an inherently dangerous environment for adults, never mind kids.

And I realized that at this moment, our roads were taking different turns. That made me sad, but it also relieved me, just a little. Cherise was warm, and funny, and a true and constant friend, and I loved her.

I didn't want to leave her in a cold, unmarked grave somewhere, like Kevin. I *couldn't*.

"You're right," I said softly, and reached over the seat to take her hand. "Cher, it's not safe for you or for him. I know you feel responsible for him. I can't ask you to just drop him off somewhere, and I can't let you, or him, come in there with me. I can control any radiation exposure I get. You're too vulnerable, and I can't—I can't let you get hurt. Not again. Not for me."

She looked confused for a second, then sad and a little angry—not at me, at herself, because I was sure what she was feeling inside was more relief than frustration. "So that's it? You're just going to turf me, after all we've been through?"

"No," I said. "I'm going to give you a mission to keep yourself and Tommy safe, and to get a message through to Lewis letting him know where I am, and that I'm back up to full power. Can you do that?"

"Don't bullshit me, Jo. It's not a mission; it's called shuffling the stupid bikini girl out of the way." Her eyes filled with tears, and they broke free in silver trails down her face. "Damn you. And thank you."

"Sweetie—" I didn't know what to say. I finally just reached over and hugged her, and Tommy as well. I kissed them both. "You're brilliant."

"You're a jerk," Cherise said. "And I adore you, by the way."

"Ditto."

"Ditto? Wow. Feel the love!"

"Now? I thought we'd get a room and do it up right." I blew her a kiss, and she blew me a raspberry. Smiling through her tears. "I'll be okay, Cher. You know I will. But I have to know *you'll* be okay."

"Yeah," she said softly. "I will. So—how does this work? Do I walk, or . . ."

"No. *I* walk. David, Whitney, whoever's driving, take her back to town and find someplace safe she can stay. Without me, she won't be a target. I'll head toward the plant. You can come back for me."

There was radio silence, which I figured indicated yet another behind-the-scenes Djinn smackdown, and then

David said, "I'll make sure they're safe. Don't try anything before I bring the car back."

"Aye aye, Captain." I reached in the back and grabbed one stuffed duffel bag loaded with water, food, insulating blankets, a flashlight, batteries, guns, ammo . . . everything a girl needs on vacation, except tanning oil and makeup. We'd packed them in individual bags, in case we had to grab and got separated. Good thinking on our part, and it paid off now, because with one final smile at Cherise, and a wink, I stepped out of the car, shouldered the duffel bag, and started jogging up the deserted road toward the distant shimmer of buildings. Before I'd taken two strides, the Mustang's engine fired up, and I heard tires screech as it did a one-eighty, heading back toward Amarillo.

Damn, that thing was fast.

My jog settled into a walk after a while. The day was bright, but not too hot, mercifully. I could sense that the land was troubled around me, restless, and I began to extend my awareness out. There were living things around me, lots of them, mostly small, but all universally pissed off, thanks to the influence of the Mother. I was more worried about a snake coming after me than a lightning bolt. I'd have a lot more warning from the lightning bolt.

My watch clocked in fifteen minutes before I had the perimeter of the building fully in sight. I slowed down and stopped, because there wasn't a lot of cover, and I was fairly certain that even *thinking* about strolling up to the gates was strongly discouraged. I sat down and had some water. Four separate colonies of fire ants were making tracks in my direction, streaming with grim purpose over rocks and dirt. Next to full-fledged army ants, fire ants were one of the creepiest warrior insects out there, in terms of their dedication to a cause. I formed a barrier that fended them off, respectfully keeping a good twenty-foot distance between them and me. Piles of ants started forming, trying to scale the invisible wall. They'd keep doing that, forming ladders and chains out of their own bodies, climbing and climbing, until they found a way over, or gravity toppled them.

Like I said. Committed.

My cell phone rang. The cheerful tones sounded even more out of place here than they normally did, and I slapped at my pockets quickly, trying to muffle it. I was too far away for the perimeter guards to hear anything that small, but it still spooked me.

I turned off the ringer and looked at the screen.

It was Lewis.

"I talked to Cherise," he said. "She told me about Kevin."

Oh, God. I hadn't thought— Of course she had. Of course she would. I heard the anguish in his voice. "He—he was trying to protect us," I said. "I'm so sorry. He was—" Was what? A good kid? He hadn't been, really. But he'd tried. "He was brave." Yes. He was that.

He cleared his throat. "Okay," he agreed, and sounded grateful. "Cherise tells me you're back on the playing field, Jo. You and David."

"David's more cheerleader right now than suited up to play, but that's better than nothing." I swallowed and clutched the phone tighter. "We almost didn't make it, Lewis. I thought I was going to lose him."

"I'm pretty sure he thought the same about you. But I knew you'd come through. You always do." He let a second pass, then changed the subject. "I need you to do something for us."

"Ready." I already knew it wouldn't be picking flowers, or even something easy that a lower-level Warden would do. He saved the worst jobs for his best people.

"I need you to distract the attention of the Djinn. I need something big, spectacular, and damaging that they'll have to deal with directly. Do you think you can do that?"

My mouth went dry, and I sipped more water before I could answer. "What are we talking about, Lewis?"

"We need to hit her back," he said. "We're playing defense, Jo, and we're getting slaughtered. Get her attention, pull her to your location, and the Djinn will follow. We'll head toward you as fast as we possibly can. You won't be alone."

Actually, I would be, and he knew it. The Wardens could only travel so fast, and the Djinn could be anywhere they wanted, when they wanted. Not even close to a race.

He was asking me to do something that would make a significant sting to the Earth, and then he was asking me to stand still while the Djinn came to destroy me.

There was a name for that: suicide bomber. And me, sitting here next to a plant chock full of plutonium, uranium, and nuclear weapons. I could do the math, and the math divided by zero.

"Lewis," I said slowly. "You understand what you're asking me to do?"

"Yes," he replied. "Believe me, I do understand. But they're targeting our Warden network, and it's folding. Once that's broken, things will get worse again, very fast, and there'll be nothing we can do to stop it. We've got only about another day, Jo, before they destroy every Warden on the planet. After that, it won't even be a week before humanity is purged down to almost nothing. It's extinction. This is the best move we have."

"And better me than you," I said. "I don't mean that in a cruel way. The Wardens need a leader, and you've got us this far. I understand that you need to go on." I gulped in an unsteady breath. "I don't. I get it."

"Jo . . ." There was so much torment in that one whisper, so much horror and frustration, that I wanted to reach through the phone and hold him, this man who was sending me to my death. "Only somebody of your quality could do this in the first place, and minimize loss of life. You're my only choice. I wish it was—" His voice failed, broken, and all I heard was harsh, uneven breathing as he tried to get hold of himself again.

I felt a wave of resentment pass over me. *How many times? How many times do I have to be the one who gives?* It was a valid question. I'd worked my ass off for the Wardens, I'd saved them time and time again. Why did it have to be me, again?

One thing about waves: they pass. The emotion peaked, then receded, and in its wake I felt . . . calm. Oddly centered.

"I'll get them here," I said. "I'll hold them here as long as I can. Lewis?"

"Yeah?" His voice was low and husky, choked with what he couldn't say.

"Make it worth it."

"No pressure." There—some of his usual dark humor was back in place, armor against the world. I laughed.

"No pressure," I assured him, and just before I pressed the END CALL button, I whispered, "I always loved you, just a little bit. Bye."

I cut the signal before I could hear his response, if he could have managed to make one. I didn't think David would have objected to me saying that. It was true, and it was the last chance I'd have to make that particular statement count.

Silence. I listened to the wind, which was blowing in from the north, bringing the bitter taste of sand out of Oklahoma. Red dust, filming the horizon. The sun was a fierce, hard ball in the sky, heading west, dropping on its predetermined course without any thought at all for whatever happened here on this complicated little oasis of life. I'd always wondered if other planets had some kind of vast awareness, too; maybe Earth got into neighborhood scraps with Venus and Mars, or yelling matches with big bully Jupiter. Maybe the sun had its own voice, its own life. Maybe the entire *universe* was alive with life, in forms we couldn't recognize because we were too limited in our sight.

I finished my water, closed my eyes, and thought about God. My mother was a church-going woman, and I had grown up in Sunday school and after-school programs. It hadn't damaged me, but it hadn't altogether satisfied me, either. I wanted to know answers, and religion expected me to have faith.

Maybe religion had been right, and the answers were too vast, too complex, and too hard for me to begin to grasp, but that didn't mean I wanted to stop trying.

"Please," I whispered. "Please understand who we are, what we've achieved. How far we've come. How far we have to go. Please tell her to stop. Please listen to your children."

If God didn't stop her, I didn't think the Wardens could, but I had to give them a fighting chance. Even if it meant doing something terrible. Something that I would never do under different circumstances.

I heard the car coming up the road—I'd know that throaty growl anywhere. I stood up, hoisted my pack, and looked around at the barricade.

The fire ants were swarming in a thick, unsettling sheet over the invisible shield, grimly determined to find something soft to kill. I also saw rattlesnakes, and somewhere beyond, a coyote paced, watching me with ravenous eyes. Overhead, birds circled, and as I looked up, a thermal-riding red-tailed hawk spilled air from its wings and began a smooth attack glide, clawed feet ready to slice.

I didn't want to see him crash into the barrier; it would probably kill him at that speed. Instead, I heated a column of air and he flew right into it, lost control of his glide, and had to swing out and flap to regain altitude. Confused, he climbed again.

If only it was that easy all the time.

The Mustang pulled to a halt on the road, and the Djinn opened the passenger side with a wave of his hand. I took a second to think and ready myself, then dropped the barriers.

I *felt* the anger, then, the furious and baffled rage of the Earth. The ants collapsed in a wave as the barrier fell, and swarmed toward me from all sides. I didn't hesitate. I pulled power out of the ground and jumped from a standing position to an area outside the swarms, and hit the ground running.

Behind me, I heard the coyote howl, and heard his jaws snap on air. *Damn*, he was close. I could outrun the ants and snakes, but that coyote . . .

His teeth sank into my calf. It felt like I'd been stabbed and squeezed in a vise at the same time, and I yelped and went down as his weight dragged me off balance. He was snarling, teeth locked into muscle, and shook his head to try to cause maximum damage. I reached for Earth power and flung a raw handful at him; it hit him like pepper spray, and he let go with a startled yelp, dancing backward as I lurched to my feet.

Ten more feet to the car.

A rattlesnake struck at me without any noisy warning. He was concealed in the shadow between the blacktop and the dirt, and there was no way I could be fast enough to dodge; by the time I spotted his movement, he was already there, sinking his fangs into my arm. *Jesus*, that hurt. I grabbed the snake and pulled him off, flinging him as far as panic would allow, and kicked back at the coyote as he tried another grab for my calf. I got him far enough away that I dove forward, landed belly down on the seat, and scrambled to shut the door behind me.

The coyote got his head and shoulders in the way and lunged, snarling. I smacked him with my fist on the nose, and he backed up, shocked and hurt, just enough for me to get the door shut.

David's voice was coming out of the radio, but it was just noise right now.

"Go!" I yelled. The Djinn floored it, and we left the angry delegation from *Animal Planet* behind.

I immediately turned my attention to the snakebite, which was going to be much worse than the coyote's damage to my leg. Neither attack had hit any blood vessels, at least. The snake's venom hadn't found its way into my circulatory system yet, but it would soon if I didn't slow it down—now. I kept the arm down, below heart level. The pain of the bite was bad, but it was definitely going to get worse; the area around the fang marks was already swelling and discoloring in shades of angry red and mottled white. In terms of bite intensity, probably a three or a four. I didn't think it was quite bad enough to be classed as a five, which would have put my odds way, way down.

I knew enough about snakebites to know that ice wouldn't work, and neither would the old Western cliché of cutting open the wound and sucking out the poison. What *would* work was antivenin. Which I didn't have.

Well, the good news was that this bite probably wouldn't kill me. It would just make me very, very sick. And I could lose the arm. I licked my lips, hoping that there wouldn't be any major symptoms, such as tingling, just yet. There weren't. That was a good sign, I thought.

We were closing the distance fast to the perimeter, and I realized that this was, in fact, *perfect.* "David," I panted, finally settling down enough to put something into words. "Don't try to hide us. Take me right to the main gate, dump me off, drive away."

"I can't do that! Dammit, Jo, stay still. I'm turning the car around and taking you to a hospital."

"No. You can stabilize me for now, right? I don't need to be healed. Just do enough to make me functional."

I was wrong about the lip-tingling. It started, and increased, and it felt like someone was sticking pins in my mouth. *Very* unpleasant. I felt dizzy, too.

The Djinn's hand flashed out and closed around the arm with the bite, and I screamed at the flash of agony that ripped through the nerves . . . but then it calmed to a dull, fiery ache, and I could breathe again. Tears stung my eyes from the intensity of the discomfort, but the torturous prickling of my lips and mouth receded, and the dizziness steadied. "Keep the swelling," I panted. "I need proof. Just get me ambulatory."

"This is insane!"

"No, this is a plan," I said. "I'm a snakebite victim. They have to take me inside for medical treatment. I need you to take down their external communication systems, so they can't call out an ambulance. They'll have antivenin in stock, in a place like this. I'll be fine."

I didn't feel fine, not at all. David didn't like my brilliant plan, but then again, he didn't know the extent of it, either. He *really* wouldn't like the rest of it, and I wasn't planning on enlightening him. Not yet.

"Once I'm in, you can bring the car in however you can manage it," I said. "Including blipping it in there. I'll find you." I wouldn't need the car, because of course the plan was that probably I would never leave. But it would be nice to have the option, in case things changed somehow for the better. Not that I had a single hope they would, but you know hope: it springs eternal.

And having David close—even *virtual* David, talking through a radio—would make me feel braver. I hoped I'd get to tell him, before the end, why I was doing this. I hoped I'd get to say good-bye.

"I don't like this," David's voice said, coming now out of the Djinn's mouth. We were coming up fast on the turnoff to the plant, which was protected by a guard-house and pretty serious fencing. The compound—I didn't know what else to call it—stretched on in a sprawl within the fence boundaries. The guardhouse was manned by two men, both armed, and there were more armed men in sight, watching with pointed vigilance as the Mustang coasted to a stop just beyond the guardhouse. Both guards stepped out, hands on their sidearms, watching us with cold, professional intensity.

"You're sure you want to do this?" David said.

"I'm sure," I said, and then, impulsively, "I love you, sweetheart."

I opened the door before he could respond, and bailed out in a heap. It wasn't hard, with the torn calf and the venom coursing through me. I felt generally pretty wretched.

The Mustang backed up in a shriek of tires, and the passenger-side door slammed shut as he braked, did a perfect sliding turn, and accelerated off down the road in a blur of dust and smoke. That was probably Whitney. David wouldn't have been as prompt in executing the hell-out-of-Dodge part of the plan.

The guards were shouting, and one of them ducked back into the shack. I heard alarms sounding, and thudding boots. Nobody touched me, so I slowly flipped myself over on my side. My head was pounding, I was too dizzy to sit up, and, with a sudden spasm, I threw up. Mostly the water that I'd been drinking, but disgustingly convincing that I wasn't faking anything. The swelling on my arm was bad, and getting worse.

They patted me down for explosives, yelled for medical assistance, and finally, one of them leaned down and barked, "Name!"

"Jo," I whispered. "Joanne Baldwin. Security clearance. Check—check with—military." I wasn't lying. Wardens had security clearances. Mine was as good as his, I'd be willing to bet. I hadn't endured all those questions and poking around in my personal life to fail to cash in my chips now. "Rattlesnake."

"I can see that," he said. Some of the ferocity left his voice. "Stay still. Help's on the way."

The other man, I was sure, would be running my name back through channels. That was fine. I was fairly sure that nobody would turn away the help of a Warden, even an injured one, at a sensitive installation—not in times like these. Hell, I was *security*.

I felt filthy, doing it, but they were making their own logical assumptions. I wasn't lying to them, not one bit. I lay there on the pavement, retching helplessly, feeling miserable and in severe pain, but David had done as I asked—I wasn't getting worse. Not yet, anyway.

There were conversations, hurried and clipped ones, with people who I assumed were higher up in the organization. Phones were used. Pictures were taken. A medical team arrived with a gurney, evaluated me, not surprisingly came up with a diagnosis of snakebite and some kind of animal attack, and loaded me up with a pile of hospital-approved blankets on top.

The gates parted, and I was wheeled inside the compound, past neatly lettered signs that warned of criminal prosecution to the fullest extent of the law for any violations of security protocols. More guards accompanied the medical team. I supposed I would have been handcuffed to the gurney, except for the snakebite, which made that impossible.

The first building we came to was obviously some kind of administration complex—big, blocky, heavily secure. Lots of locks, key cards, biometric scans just to get me into a hallway. A security officer was there, and he clipped a badge on my shirt, neon red, that proclaimed I was a supervised visitor. I didn't feel like a visitor. I felt like a prisoner. It probably had tracking devices built in, so I could be found and caught in seconds if I managed to totter up off the bed.

I didn't think I was going to bump the terror alert level any, given how I felt right now.

A doctor took over, clearly the Head Medical Cheese, and he did some unsympathetic probing of the snake-bite wound. "It's genuine," he said to a guard standing next to him. "Probably a stage four bite. She's very sick, and she needs antivenin urgently." He bent over to look into my pale, sweating face. "What's your name?"

"Joanne Baldwin."

"How'd you get here, Joanne?"

"I was walking," I said. "Snake bit me. Car picked me up but he dropped me here."

All completely true. The doctor frowned, clearly not thinking much of someone who'd dump me and drive away, but he shook it off. "Looks like a prairie rattler bite," he said. "Let's get some CroFab in her, stat."

In a gratifyingly short time—although every heart-beat felt like it lasted a year, thanks to the unbelievable and escalating pain—a nurse hustled back in with a vial and a hypodermic. He checked the label—thorough, I liked that in a doctor—and filled the hypo with the straw-colored liquid. I hadn't really noticed, but some-one had already put in a central line—and they must have been good at it, because I didn't like IVs, not at all. The doctor added the antivenin to the flow, then reached for another vial. There were six on the table. I wondered if that was some kind of a record.

"Okay, this is going to take about an hour to get into your system," the doctor said, after emptying the last vial. "If you start having trouble breathing, let us know immediately. Anaphylaxis is a possibility with this anti-venin, but it isn't common. You're not allergic to sheep, are you?"

I gave him a blank look. "Sheep? Really?"

"Really."

"How the hell would I know?"

"Good point," he said, and grinned. "Lie back and relax. Keep your heart rate down. I know it's miserable, but the antivenin will help, trust me. I'm going to take a look at the bite on your leg."

In the great scheme of things, I'd almost forgotten the coyote bite; truthfully, it hardly registered, on the scale of *Ow That Hurts* right now. But when he started probing the wound, I found myself gasping and guarding, and he shook his head. "Let's irrigate, get some antibiotics on board, and I'll need to lay in some stitches. You are some lucky girl."

I'd have given him the finger if I'd felt up to it.

Someone arrived and handed him a packet of notes, which he speed-read, and as the nurse worked on cleaning the bite, he leaned casually on the gurney and flipped pages. I wasn't fooled.

"So," he said. "You're a Warden."

"Yes."

"Not an Earth Warden?"

This was the tricky part, because I was going to have to lie to answer, or explain more than I wanted. "Earth Wardens can't heal themselves," I said. "Not easily. It's a drawback."

He nodded. "So it is. Is it as bad out there as we've heard? Storms, fires, earthquakes? Some people are calling it the end of the world."

"It's not," I said. "But it could be the end of us."

That sobered him up. He closed the file and tucked it under his arm, looking down at me. Doctors always looked similar to me; there was some kind of posture they had, upright and ever so slightly arrogant, but with good reason. This particular doctor's name badge read REID, HOWARD. He didn't look like a Howard to me; he had thick dark hair, a long, thin nose, and smile lines around his mouth. An angular, mobile kind of face. Eyes of indeterminate color, maybe a dark blue. Not kind, though. Assessing and guarded.

"Is that your professional opinion?" he asked. "Since that's your job, isn't it?"

"Yes," I said.

"How serious is it?"

"I wouldn't go buying any long-term investments." I coughed, because talking was making me feel sick again. A nurse got me water and a sippy straw.

Dr. Reid stared at me for a few long seconds, and whatever calculations were going on, I couldn't follow them.

I shut my eyes as he got around to the stitches.

Dr. Reid wasn't the only person on the base who knew what a Warden was; I could tell from the steady stream of gawkers who found a reason to drop into the infirmary over the next hour. Among them was a tall man wearing casual clothes but with a straight-up military bearing. No rank visible on the badges, but I was willing to bet, from the way people gave him room, that this man was high up.

"Hello," he said to me immediately, with the assurance of somebody who doesn't often meet equals, much less superiors. "How are you feeling?"

I wasn't feeling well at all, and was starting to think that this snakebite ploy was a Very Bad Idea, but I forced a smile. "I'll live," I said, and cleared my throat. "Joanne Baldwin."

He nodded. "I had you checked out. Roland Miles. I'm the director of the plant. I had to give special authorization to get you inside the gates." By the look he gave me, I'd better humbly appreciate the sacrifice. Oh, and I did. Really. "I've given instructions that you're not to leave this bed for any reason, and that as soon as you're stable, you're going in an ambulance to a hospital."

"I'm a prisoner."

"If you were a prisoner, you'd be handcuffed to the rail," he pointed out pleasantly. "We're just taking all necessary precautions for your health."

"Including not letting me out of bed. What if I have to go to the bathroom?"

"Bedpan," he said, and I didn't think he was kidding. "I take my responsibilities here extremely seriously, Miss Baldwin, and what I see about you in my classified files doesn't inspire confidence. You seem to have a running feud with the Wardens, and a shooting war going with authority. Now, why are you really here?"

He settled himself in a chair next to my bed, and that put our eyes level. I didn't like it. I didn't like the very perceptive aura I was reading off of the guy—he was just plain human, but he was nobody to underestimate, clearly. They wouldn't have put him in charge of what had to be a major terrorist target if he hadn't been utterly capable.

"Wait," I said, and gestured urgently to a nurse. She handed me a kidney-shaped bowl, and I retched up what little I still had in my stomach. It wasn't theater, it was truly that bad, and after I was done I fell back against the pillows, feeling shaky and still in sharp, cutting pain. "So just to be clear, you think I got myself snakebit as part of a clever plot?"

"Maybe," he said, unmoved by my clearly unhappy condition. "I'm not taking any chances with you in my facility. You do have security clearances sufficient to gain entry under normal circumstances, so I'll let you stay until Dr. Reid says you can be moved, but the second that happens, you are out of here. With my best wishes, of course."

"Of course," I said, and swallowed hard. "Water?"

He was kind enough to fetch the cup and sippy straw, and I drained it in a rush.

"I know what's happening out there," he said, once I was done. He refilled the glass, which was a considerate thing to do, and set it within easy reach. "I know how bad it is. And I can't think it's any accident somebody like you just happens to show up on our doorstep, snakebite or not. You want to level with me, Joanne?"

"Well, I'd *like* to, but I don't think your security clearance is high enough," I said. "And I'm not in a share-y mood right now, what with all the venom and throwing up and you being a giant prick."

He laughed. It was a real laugh, genuinely amused. Nice to know I was entertaining, even now. "Now that's the Joanne Baldwin people told me about. You'd be a smart-ass to Death himself, wouldn't you?"

I had been before. But that probably wasn't something to share except on a need-to-know basis. "If you want to know what's going on, stick your head outside," I said. "Humanity's sitting on a bomb, and the timer's clicking down. That's what's happening. Forget global climate change; we won't be around to see the last of the polar bears drown. *That's* why I'm here, Roland. I'm on bailing duty on the *Titanic*."

He didn't like that answer, not at all, and it didn't spark any kind of laughter this time. He was a smart man; he could identify truth when he heard it. "And why come here?" he asked.

"I *didn't*! I was dumped out by the idiot who picked me up. I think he could have been running drugs." In this part of the country, that was an extremely plausible scenario. Carloads of Mexican Brown were caught all the time, zipping their way up through the Southwest. They weren't fighting a major drug war in Mexico for nothing.

That was my first real lie; only it was actually speculation. I hadn't stated it as a fact, only a perception. I waited, and watched Roland Miles's aura up on the aetheric. It was tougher to read regular people than Wardens, but there was no mistaking the troubled colors that surrounded him. The man was under a lot of stress, and he was wary. I didn't blame him. He certainly had every right.

Wary he remained, but I didn't get the sense that he detected any hint of a lie in what I'd said. That was good. It wasn't that I couldn't tackle the defenses he could probably bring to bear, but it would be very, very messy. Lives would be lost, and there was a decent chance that I'd end up having to do what I'd planned without evacuating the plant first. I didn't want that on my conscience. Especially as the last act of my life.

Dr. Reid buzzed in the infirmary door, trailed by another nurse, this one carrying a tray full of the antivenin bottles. He nodded pleasantly to Director Miles, who stood up and moved his chair away from the bed to make room as Reid bent over me, taking my pulse, probing the badly swollen arm, and generally being a nuisance before he nodded. "Second round," he said, and began loading the antivenin into the IV drip. "I didn't figure that one dose would do you. That was a nasty bite. How's the pain?"

"Intense," I said.

"On a scale of—"

"Ten." And I wasn't kidding, it really was. As an Earth Warden I was all too aware of the damage the venom was wreaking on my tissues, and it scared me. There was definitely going to be scarring from this, if I survived the day. In a weird way, it was comforting to think that I didn't have much of a chance of that, anyway.

Six vials of antivenin later, Dr. Reid gave me some kind of additional shot. I didn't see him do it in time to countermand, but I knew I was in trouble the second the warm, weighty feeling of pain relief began to spread through my body. Oh *crap*. I couldn't fall asleep. That would ruin *everything*.

"No!" I gasped. He'd only emptied about half a syringe into the central line, and now he looked up, frowning. "No narcotics, please."

"You're in pain."

"I don't want it."

He shook his head, but it was, after all, a patient's right to refuse medication. So I got enough to dull the raging, chewing pain, but not enough to get rid of it, or to lull me into dreamland.

Best of both worlds, really.

Miles tried to ask me something else, but Reid cut him off. I closed my eyes and went up into the aetheric—a struggle, considering my physical condition—and watched Miles leave the room. Lucky thing about the plant—the buildings had always been built for pure industrial use, and there weren't a lot of emotions soaked into the place. Where they existed, they were centered mostly on the area where I was currently resting—injured and scared people had been brought here over the years, and that lingered. But outside, the aetheric shape of the place was orderly, almost sterile. This was an administration building; as I expanded my view I saw activity in several other locations, in some areas going down deep into the ground.

That was where I needed to focus my efforts. Deep in the ground. But not yet, not until I was capable of moving on my own.

It took another forty minutes, but the swelling began to go down, to the pleased murmurs of the medical staff. The venom slowed its progress, and the antivenin began to break it down into harmless chemical strings that were swept away in my body's efficient housecleaning system.

I didn't feel *good*, but I felt better. Clearer. I drank a lot of water, and one of the nurses, on Dr. Reid's approval, provided me with some kind of high-protein bar. I was able to keep it down, which was great.

By the time the second sixty minutes had passed, my arm was only a little swollen and red. Reid bandaged up the wound, after antibiotic shots, and gave me detailed instructions on what to tell the doctor at the hospital when I arrived.

"Dr. Reid," I said. He stopped his medical lecture and looked at me, frowning. "I need you to listen to me."

"I'm listening."

"I can't leave," I said. "I need to be here. And you need to help me get everybody out of this compound before it's too late."

"Too late for what?"

"I'm going to do something to help us survive what's happening outside, but it's going to be very messy. I don't want your deaths on my hands when I do it. So I need you all to leave the compound, do you understand me?" I held his gaze, and I put all of my Earth Warden powers of persuasion into it. "Isn't there some medical protocol for evacuation?"

"In the event of a major radiation leak," he said. "Yes. But—"

"Trust me, there'll be one by the time you call the alert. How long to get everyone out of here?"

He looked around, blinked, and said, "We're on skeleton crew, so probably no more than fifteen minutes once the alarm sounds. That's to load everyone into the vehicles and evacuate to the secondary rally point."

I loved a place that had their drills down cold. It meant people might actually survive this. Not *me*, of course. But these people, in specific.

"You know about the Djinn, right?" He nodded. I'd figured that since he knew about Wardens, he'd be up on the current information out there on Djinn as well. "The Djinn aren't under the control of the Wardens anymore. They're under the control of the Earth, and the Earth is very, very angry. Understand? The Djinn are going to come here, and they're going to destroy everything. So you need to be sure you get this done, doc. If you don't, it's going to be very, very deadly to your colleagues."

"I've got to talk to Director Miles."

"If you want my advice, don't," I said. "Director Miles will have an apparently sensible solution that will mean a short-term gain for you here, and long-term disaster for the human race. Let me do this. I'm a Warden. I wouldn't take this risk if there was any alternative, believe me." I hesitated, then said, "I don't plan on walking away from it, if that helps."

"You're not talking sense," Reid said. "We can defend this place. That's the whole point."

"You can't defend shit against the Djinn, not when they're like this," I said. "Trust me. I've been up against them, and it's not a war you can win. It's not even a *war*. It's more like an extermination."

He knew enough about Djinn to understand I wasn't overselling it, and he shut up, watching me.

"Look," I said, more gently. "Doc, I know you wouldn't be working here if you didn't have the highest ethical standards. If you weren't completely trustworthy. But the thing is, I'm not some agent of another government or cause. The organization I'm part of transcends borders, and governments, and causes, and religions. We're here to save the most lives we can, just like you. You *have* to help me. I know it seems wrong, but—"

With no warning at all, guards flooded into the room, boots and helmets and hard expressions. Oh, and large weapons, which all ended up aimed at me.

Director Miles walked in. Dr. Reid cast a guilty look

around, then stepped away from my bedside as Miles advanced toward me.

"Did you really think I wouldn't have you monitored?" he asked.

I smiled. "Actually," I said, "I was pretty sure you would. That was the whole point. Now that I have your undivided attention, let's talk about how this is going to go."

"Oh, I already know how it's going to go," he said. "With you, handcuffed to your gurney, heading to the nearest FBI holding cell. Probably the medical wing, of course. We're not lacking in compassion."

"Only in sense," I snapped back. "I could bring down this place around you, you know. And I will, if I have to. But I'm offering you the chance, one time only, to save your peoples' lives. I suggest you take it, Miles."

"Tell you what. The doctor here is going to trank you up six ways from Sunday, and you can tell the FBI all about it." He nodded to Reid, who stepped up to my IV with another syringe.

I yanked the line out, clamped down on the immediate bleeding, and used a sudden, localized increase in air pressure around the syringe Dr. Reid was holding to crush it, spilling liquid sleep all over the floor. "Good luck with that," I said. "You're going to have to kill me."

Miles hesitated, then nodded. Regretfully. "I suppose so," he said, and addressed the guards surrounding me. "Shoot her if she moves a muscle. Or opens her mouth again. Lisa, get her handcuffed to the gurney, now."

"Wait!" Reid said. "Let me bandage that first." He meant the leaking hole in my arm where the IV had been. Miles didn't like it, but he nodded. Reid was efficient with the pressure bandage and cloth tape, and stepped back as the guards moved in to slap the cuffs on. I winced as they closed around my still-swollen wrist, but they were fairly gentle about it. Didn't matter, anyway. Clearly, Director Miles had never tried to jail an Earth Warden, even a relatively inexperienced one like me. Handcuffs were a nuisance, but a completely insignificant one.

Since the orders had been pretty clear to the guys with itchy trigger fingers, I kept still and quiet, and reached down deep into the ground for power. It came slowly; this wasn't a place that was rooted deep in natural forces, but no matter how industrial it was, no man-made structure could keep out the flow of power to a Warden.

Instead of using it in an attack, I let it gather inside of me in a thick, still pool, filling me until I felt like an overflowing tub. Seductive and slow, that power; not like the energy I pulled for weather, or for fire. Instead of trying any dramatic gestures, I began to hum, very softly. It was Brahms's "Lullaby," and with the power imbuing every gentle note, it began to affect everyone in the room almost immediately. I was careful—I didn't want them falling over, just drowsy and slow. I even got Director Miles, finally.

The only one I excluded was Dr. Reid.

I deepened the humming, and the power, and the guards one by one slid into a very gentle sleep. They didn't fall, exactly—just folded up against whatever wall was closest and slid down to curl up in an utterly blissful rest.

I was kind of proud. That was subtle stuff, and not something I'd been able to do very often. But it almost emptied out my power reserve, and I didn't have time to replenish it now. I expended a little more energy zapping the handcuffs, which fell away with a soft little *click*, and then swung my legs out of bed.

Dr. Reid was clearly trying to decide whether to tackle me, shoot me, or help me. He must have come down on the side of helping, because as my balance wavered dangerously, he moved to me and got me steady again. "This is crazy," he said. "They'll kill you."

"Eventually," I said. "Really not an issue right now, though. I didn't hurt them. They're just sleeping. What I need you to do is to declare a medical evacuation, *now*. Miles can't stop you. I assume you're pretty much the authority now?"

He nodded. His face was taking on new lines and stress, and I was sorry for that. "How do I know you're telling me the truth, about what you're going to do? What if you're just here to steal warheads?"

"If I was going to steal warheads, I could get a Djinn to do it," I said. "I'm not stealing anything, and I promise you, nothing is leaving here except your people. Deal?"

"Deal," he agreed, but he didn't look happy about it. "Only because I'm pretty sure that if I don't agree, you'll just put me out, too, and find some other way."

"That's true. But I'd rather not. Doing this kind of thing takes power, and I need to preserve mine right now. Understand?"

"No." He checked my pulse, and frowned. "How's your pain level?"

"Manageable. I'll be okay." Relatively speaking, anyway. "Do your thing, Doc. Get them out of here."

"Where are you going?"

"Where I need to go." I reached out and took Director Miles's badge from his jacket, and replaced my bright red visitor's ID with his. "This will get me in the doors?"

"No. Biometric scanners. You won't match."

I could handle those, but it would mean expending more power. "I'll make it work," I said. "Get moving. You haven't got long before this place isn't safe anymore."

I left it deliberately vague as to whether I was going to make it unsafe, or the Djinn would. To be fair, it was probably going to be a team effort.

Reid didn't like it, not at all, but I could see that he'd been doing some checking on who I was and what the situation out there in the rest of the world might be. He was convinced, but like all good humans, he was still in denial.

I didn't really have time for his stages of grief. "One other thing," I said. "I need your coat."

"My coat?" He looked down at it. "Why?"

"Because people ignore other people in uniform in a place like this, and it's easier to get on over my arm than one of their uniforms," I said. "Coat, please. You can keep the badge."

He stripped it off, no doubt rationalizing that if he didn't, I'd just knock him out and take it anyway. Which I would have, probably. I took it and very carefully threaded my wounded arm through the sleeve, hissing a little as the not-very-flexible fabric scraped over sensitive, burning skin. Once I had it on, though, I felt better. I buttoned it up, grabbed a gun from one of the snoozing guards, stepped over another one, and went to the far door. When I swiped Miles's card through the reader, the door buzzed open.

Reid was still watching me, and I could see the struggle in him—shoot me? Stop me? Wish me luck?

In the end, he didn't say or do anything at all. And that was okay.

I slung the semiautomatic rifle over my neck and used Oversight to get a good look at where I was going. The good news was that given the relatively mild aetheric energy of this place, I could fairly easily spot approaching people and avoid them. Nothing special about the building—hallways, doors, offices, desks, filing cabinets. It was very clean. As Reid had said, there was only a skeleton crew here, so I made it from the infirmary to the door I'd identified as being closest to my goal in record time.

Outside, the wind was turning cool, rattling loose bits

of gravel and sending an occasional tumbleweed rolling around. I hugged the exterior of the building for a second, looking for guards; there were several, and at least one had a high vantage point and a rifle. That wasn't so great.

I'd have to have faith in the lab coat.

I set off across open ground, walking with a purpose and trying not to show off the fact that I had a giant *weapon* with me. I tried to walk like a doctor on her way to a patient. Calm, but focused.

It must have worked, because I made it across a hundred yards of open space, under the eyes of at least four heavily armed men, to the entrance to what was, at the aetheric level, a maelstrom of black energy.

Weapons, built for maximum damage. Even dormant, even stored, that energy swirled and eddied around them, restless and hungry. Disturbing. I swallowed hard, stood at the door, and swiped my card. There were all kinds of warning signs telling me that I had to follow strict security and safety protocols while inside this facility. Yeah, I was going to absolutely do that, first chance I got.

The biometric scanner lit up, requesting me to put my hand on the glass. I did, and while it was reading, I reached deep inside the works and blew it apart. Easier than it sounds, with high technology. When your security depends on soldered connections, you are screwed if an Earth Warden wants in.

The security designers were good, but not quite good enough. I managed to intercept the signal that zipped over to the door to tell it to lock down and sound the alarm, and converted the energy into the all-clear electronic pulse.

The door popped open, and I stepped into a sterile little anteroom, with another, identical scanning system at the far end. Protective gear was neatly stored, and I put on a suit, more for blending in than for what it would offer me. Second door, same verse, and then I was inside a hallway. There, a large, colorful map indicated that I was in a blue section. Blue section was the least dangerous, I gathered.

There were a few workers in this part of the plant, but a confident walk, a wave, and a badge seemed to do the job nicely. Nobody was doing much at the moment; operations were at an idle, and boredom had set in. I followed the color-coded maps to the elevators at the far end. More biometrics, which was a pain in the ass; I hoped they hadn't security-locked the bathrooms, too.

Finally, after the third biometric I had to destroy, I decided to take an end run around the problem. Fire codes said that all security doors had to open in the event of a fire emergency.

I created one. Not a big one; I didn't want to bake anybody, or even give them smoke inhalation, but I pulled some jittery power from the electronics and built myself an impressive-sized fire in a nest of empty boxes in a storeroom. Fire suppression kicked in, but with a little concentration, I was able to keep the fire blazing despite the countermeasures.

Thirty seconds later, the biometric scanners began flashing FIRE EMERGENCY, and I heard the clicks as secured doors began to unlock. The elevators stopped working, but I could get around that; it was a simple mechanism, and I needed to go all the way to the bottom anyway.

I stepped inside just as three people in protective gear—one with an automatic weapon slung over it—entered the corridor and looked straight at me. He had fast reactions, and I couldn't jam his gun and keep the fire going at the same time. Too many balls in the air.

He got off five shots, aiming straight for my chest.

Chapter Nine

I don't remember getting hit; my entire concentration was on slamming shut the elevator door, cutting the cables, overriding the friction brakes, and letting the car drop in a free fall. At first I felt sick and dizzy, and figured that was an effect of the falling, but then I smelled blood. I looked down and saw two separate wounds in my side, ragged holes puncturing my protective white suit. I unzipped it and stepped out. There wasn't any pain yet, or a lot of bleeding, though red rings were steadily forming on my lab coat around the bullet holes.

"Fantastic," I said. "That's just great."

Gravity was definitely a harsh mistress, and never more than at a time like this. I watched in Oversight, gauging how far I'd fallen, how much farther still remained, and trying to do complicated math in my head. I was approaching seriously terminal velocity, and I was going to have to start slowing my descent.

"Jo!" David's voice, blasting unexpectedly from the speaker in the elevator. I jerked, and my concentration shattered. Pain began an insidious drumbeat in my side, dammit, *too soon.* . . . I pushed it, and David, aside and concentrated harder. I was sweating now. Shaking. And there was a growing pool of blood forming around my shoes, how had that happened? Didn't seem right.

I dropped to my knees, then pitched forward flat on my stomach. I screamed at the impact, because *damn* that hurt, but it was important to try to distribute impact force over as wide an area as possible.

I reached out for power in the air around me, found it, and began building a thick, cold cushion of air beneath the falling elevator. I increased its density, and felt a significant decrease in the speed at which I was falling.

But I was still falling.

David was saying something, but I couldn't pay attention, not anymore. I needed more power, more braking, and I needed it *now.*

I couldn't get it. When I reached out for power, it slid through my grasp like oil. I felt weak, clumsy, and wet—oh yeah. I was wet because I was lying in a pool of blood.

David was almost screaming at me now. I couldn't spare a second of concentration; I had to maintain what I'd already done, keep slowing down, try to make this crash survivable. I was running out of elevator shaft.

I threw one last, ultimate effort into it and eased the car to a sliding, jerking stop.

The button dinged, and the doors opened.

For some reason, I couldn't get to my feet. Maybe because the blood was slippery. I was a mess, and I needed a bath, a nice warm bath to let all of this float away. . . . That sounded good.

But I forced myself up, bracing myself with both bloody hands on the doors of the elevator. My vision was spotty, with circles of darkness swallowing the glare of white lights. Everything seemed to be moving except me.

Walk, I told myself sternly. *You have to do this. Now.* Because deep down inside, I knew that I wasn't going to have the strength to wait and do it in a more orderly fashion.

I didn't make it very far, but then I didn't have to—this whole area was hot and live with the kind of thing I needed. This was a storage area, deep underground, and the doors were massive affairs on hydraulics. There were six doors. I fell at the first one, flailed around on the floor for a while, and left a hell of a bloody mess trying to get up. The control pad was way the hell up there. That seemed wrong. Why didn't they build them closer to the floor, for convenience?

Oh, the hell with subtlety.

I blew the door off its hinges in a massive burst of superheated air. It flew over my head, slammed into the far wall with an impact hard enough to be felt in Switzerland, and embedded itself in the concrete to a depth of at least a foot.

Inside that storage locker, about the size of a medium-sized residential home, were stacked row upon row of containers marked with vivid red radiation warning stickers. All very neat and orderly. The aetheric here seethed black, and my own distress didn't help much.

One more thing to do.

I triggered a reaction.

It wasn't really all that hard; destruction never is. All I had to do was put some chemical chains together, add heat, pour in energy, stir to a rolling boil.

I didn't have enough left in me to set up any kind of protective shielding—not that I thought it would have worked in any case. I hoped that the evacuation had worked. I hoped that Dr. Reid and his people were safely outside the facility.

Right now, though, that was a very moot point.

I rolled over on my back, staring up, and my last conscious thought was of David. How much I wished I could die in his arms, if I couldn't live in them.

I heard his scream echoing through the hallways a second before the brilliant flash of light, and then it took all the power I had left to hold the explosion *in*, point it *down*, driving it like a spike deep into the skin of the Mother.

Then there was just . . . light.

And dark.

I didn't expect to ever open my eyes again—who would, really? After exploding a stockpile of nuclear material? Who the hell survives that?

Me. I'm just lucky like that.

I opened my eyes and found myself floating in a sheer bubble surrounded by flames and destruction. I was still bleeding. There was a pretty significant amount of red pooled at the bottom of the bubble, and my clothes were soaked. My heart was struggling to keep on pumping what little remained.

So, I wasn't going to go out in a blaze of glory. I'd just bleed to death, lying here inside of this protective cocoon that I swore I hadn't constructed, and wasn't maintaining. I couldn't have, because there was almost nothing left inside me to use.

Someone had saved me. Sort of. And I hated them for it.

Something moved, out there in the fire, in the rubble, in the chaos of smoke. I breathed slowly, steadily, listening to my laboring heart, and watched the figure come clear.

It was the Djinn Venna, in her *Alice in Wonderland* blue pinafore. Her pale, long hair shone in a shimmering curtain around her shoulders. Her hands were clasped in front of her small body.

Her eyes blazed milk-white.

"I kept you alive," she said. "Don't you want to thank me?"

"Not really," I said, and coughed. That hurt, as if I was tearing pieces of myself loose with every movement. I ended up sobbing, and tried to stop. "Let me go."

"No," Venna said, and watched me with icy focus. "You hurt her. We all felt it. The others will all come here to hurt you in return. I have to keep you alive for them."

This was the part that Lewis and I hadn't discussed, because it was a terrible thing to even think about. He'd hoped, as I had, that I'd be dead, obliterated in the destruction.

Survival was one hell of a lot worse as an outcome. I wished I could *will* myself to death, but there are some things I just couldn't manage, and my heart refused to do anything but keep beating, beating, beating.

"Venna," I said. "Venna, you have to help me. Please help me."

"No," she said. It was a flat, inhuman sound, and there wasn't even any anger behind it. There was *nothing*. "You stay alive."

I should have been dead already, I realized; from the amount of blood I'd lost, and the fact that the flow had slowed to a leak from the wounds, I'd *already* bled out. Whatever my heart was pumping, with such great effort, through my veins was not my blood.

I was an animated corpse, living at Venna's whim.

I remembered David's screams, and I wondered if he knew. I wondered if he could see, from that distant, cold vantage point of Jonathan's picture window, helpless to stop this, helpless to do anything but grieve. If he left, if he tried to rescue me, he'd be lost himself. *Don't do anything crazy*, I begged him silently, through the cord that still, even now, was holding us together. *Let me go. Let them do whatever they want, so long as they come here and leave the Wardens alone. I'll hold out as long as I can.*

It sounded brave. I didn't feel brave, not at all. I felt sick, weak, and dying, and more than anything, I didn't want to hurt anymore.

Venna was joined by more figures, moving out of the aetheric shadows and into the real world. Some of them I recognized—there was Rahel, glowering at me with real hatred. Ashan, the leader of the Old Djinn—he, at least, didn't need any incentive to loathe me. He'd gotten a jump-start, early on. I saw plenty of Djinn I'd clashed with before, only a handful of whose names I'd ever learned.

So many Djinn, all with those eerie pearl-white eyes. All stalking me like tigers. Talk about overkill.

I floated in my blood-soaked bubble, waiting for the end.

Venna was the one to make the first move. She reached through the force bubble and ripped a hole in it, gutting it from within. It made a sighing sound, and disappeared, and my blood fell in a sudden rain to the smashed concrete and steel. Followed by my body. I screamed as I hit, although I'd sort of promised myself I'd keep my dignity and not give them the satisfaction. Yeah, that hadn't even lasted until they actually touched me.

Venna leaned over me as I struggled to right myself. She reached out with her little-girl hand and touched my cheek in a curiously gentle way, cocked her head to one side, and then—with no warning at all—she walloped me so hard that I flew ten feet into a broken wedge of folded steel. It had once been a door, I supposed. If I could have bled more, I would have. It didn't seem at all fair that I could hang here in this state, on the edge of death, and that my nerves hadn't shut themselves off yet. It would be okay if I couldn't *feel* this. But that was the whole point: they wanted me to feel it.

Every last bloody second of it.

I coughed and clawed my way out of the rubble. I got to my feet and stood there, trembling but erect. I lifted my chin and said, "That's all you've got? You hit like a girl, Venna."

She bared her teeth and became a feral animal, rushing at me with clawed fingers and snapping teeth, and I knew this wasn't going to go well, not at all.

But I'd signed up for the whole ride, hadn't I? I'd known what I was getting into, and in that split second before Venna actually reached me, I gave up all hope of living through any of it. That was a black kind of peace, perversely comforting.

Something hit Venna before she reached me—a pale blur, something big and muscular. Venna was knocked off course, into a pile of rubble. Her screams of rage pulverized a few of the concrete blocks into beach sand, and I blinked, amazed that I was still standing.

There was another Djinn standing in front of me—facing away from me, toward the others.

Oh.

It was the nameless Djinn who'd been chauffeuring us around the country. The vessel. The avatar.

And now, it said, with my own voice, "Stay away from my mother, you bastards!"

Imara. My daughter, the Earth Oracle. Like David, she couldn't leave her own personal stronghold, where she was holding out against the madness of the Djinn ... but she'd found a way to remote-pilot the avatar, the same way David and Whitney had done.

"Imara?" I blurted. "What are you *doing*?"

"Saving your life, I think. Honestly, do you ever stop doing insane things? What were you *thinking*?" The Djinn glanced over his shoulder, and in his expression I saw my daughter's harassed shadow. "You shouldn't be here. I can't believe you walked into this with your eyes open."

"Would you feel better if I'd blundered into it stupidly?"

"Maybe I would." Imara snapped the Djinn's head back around as Ashan walked forward, and I felt the energy change, grow darker. Ashan had killed my daughter, in her original Djinn form. She hadn't forgotten that, not at all. "Back off."

He didn't seem to even hear her, or care that there was any kind of obstacle standing in his way. When he got within reach of the Djinn, Ashan simply reached out and pushed, and the Djinn went flying, off balance and overmatched. The only comfort I took was that Imara herself wasn't being hurt. She was safe, somewhere else.

Ashan was looking every bit the vicious, smooth businessman he'd always appeared to me. He'd always been partial to well-tailored suits, and this one was gray, matched to an off-white shirt and sky-blue tie. His physical form had no more personality to it than a store mannequin.

He reached me, not seeming to hurry at all, and grabbed me around the throat. He did that alien head-tilt thing, just like Venna, as if trying to decide exactly what type of pond scum I might be, and—still holding my throat—turned and dragged me toward the others. Venna had gotten up and was engaged in mortal combat with the Djinn avatar, who was doing his—her?—level best to keep the kid away from my back.

But my dangers were also right in front of me, and there were a lot of them.

Ashan pulled me into the middle of the Djinn, then turned and stared right into my eyes.

"Tell us why," he said. "Why you did this."

"I needed to get your attention," I wheezed, around his iron grip. "I think I have it now."

"You do." Ashan's smile was as artificial and cold as the rest of him, and just as assured. "You will regret it."

"Oh, sweetie, *so* ahead of you on that one. Let me go or I'll bleed all over you."

"Promise?" His smile widened. "Maybe soon we'll let you die. Would you like that?"

I had my hands free, so I shot him a finger. "Not as much as I'd like to watch *you* try it." It was getting harder to talk around his kung-fu grip, and I wasn't sure that last smart-ass remark came out as anything but garbled chokes. Ashan liked to play with his food. I thought that as long as I was giving back, he wouldn't move on to the next phase of agony.

Maybe.

The avatar had lost his battle with Venna. That didn't surprise me much, but it did alarm me. It meant that Imara was playing hurt, or handicapped. Normally, she could have wiped the floor with any Djinn who got in her way, but now the avatar was down, battered and hurt, and Venna was stepping calmly over the body to get to me.

The beaten Djinn avatar rolled over and up to its feet, but it wasn't in any shape to come at Venna again on my behalf.

The Djinn looked past Venna, at me, and I saw my daughter's torment in those strange eyes. "Mom," she said softly. "Get ready. He's coming."

Ashan's hand gripped tighter, bending cartilage in my throat, and what little air I was gasping in cut off. I flailed at him, and it made no difference. None at all.

It never occurred to me to wonder who *he* was, until

a shadow formed in the corner of my eye, and David walked out of it, carrying a . . . box?

I was clearly hallucinating. Oxygen deprivation.

David put the box down, lunged forward, and grabbed Ashan's arm.

And *broke* it.

Ashan yelled in surprise and let go of me as he stared down at the dangling odd angle of his forearm, then caught hold of it with his left and snapped it back into a straight line, reconstructing the damage—but it gave David time to grab me and pull me away from Ashan.

David's eyes were molten bronze, blazing so hot I could feel the feverish intensity behind them. He glanced at me once, a frantic, horrified look, and then put his attention on Venna, who was shrieking toward us like something out of a first-rate horror movie.

He slammed her back, into the Djinn avatar, who in turn slung her hard into a wall and pinned her there.

"No time," David gasped. He was trembling now, and I could feel the fear in him. "Jo, in the box. You know what to do. I—"

He cried out, fell to his knees, and I watched the David I knew disappear. He fought it, oh God he fought it with everything in him, but he was a Djinn, and a Conduit, and he couldn't hold back.

I watched his eyes turn pale, then white.

Panic drove me to follow his orders. I could lose myself; I could stand that. I couldn't see him reduced to a puppet, something used to hurt me. He wouldn't survive that. God, why had he done this? He'd been safe!

I ripped back the top of the box and found . . . bottles. Lots of bottles, all with corks in the tops.

It came to me in a blinding rush what he wanted me to do.

I grabbed the first one I could reach, popped the cork

with my thumb, and focused on David as the Mother took possession of him.

"Be thou bound to my service!" I yelled, and didn't dare stop for a breath. "Be thou bound to my service! Be thou bound to my service!" As incantations go, it wasn't much—I spit the words out so fast that they were almost incomprehensible, and for a terrible second I thought I'd rushed *too* much . . . that it wouldn't work at all.

It felt like the entire Djinn world took in a collective breath, and I knew I had only a few seconds to live. They wouldn't be playing with me anymore now. Not anymore.

David screamed—an inhuman scream, torment and fury—and dissolved into mist.

Venna, behind me, broke free of the avatar and lunged for me. If she could force me to break the bottle before I corked it, he'd go free.

I hung on to the slippery glass like grim death, and corked it. I hadn't waited for the mist to flow inside, but I hadn't really needed to; it was the corking that mattered, and suddenly I felt a complex network of power snap into place between me and David, overlaying the bonds we already had.

Now all I had to do was release him.

Venna hit me like a freight train just as I thumbed out the cork, and I was smashed against the floor. Somehow, I managed to cradle the bottle against breakage, and I curled in on myself, holding it, keeping it safe.

The Djinn piled on me, and I knew, as I felt unnaturally hot, strong hands take hold of parts of my body, that I'd be ripped to pieces.

David reformed in the middle of the Djinn and fought them off. That sounds simple. It wasn't. His eyes blazed bronze again, and I could see the focus and fear on his face as he stood over me and wreaked damage on his fellow Djinn. It allowed me the space to crawl away, inching along over broken concrete and steel to where he'd left the box.

The avatar was there, holding bottles with the corks already out. He passed me one, and I focused on Venna, who was ripping at David like a wild animal. She'd kill him, and me, if she wasn't stopped. "Be thou bound to my service. Be thou bound to my service. Be thou bound to my service."

I got all three iterations out before Venna reached me, and she shrieked and disappeared. I hadn't been at all sure that it would work on the Old Djinn; I'd suspected it wouldn't. But maybe, somewhere out there, somebody liked me after all, despite the evidence to the contrary.

I corked the bottle and slotted it back into the box. The avatar, in turn, threw me the next empty. This time, I targeted Ashan.

Ashan snarled and misted away before I could complete the incantation. Coward.

Rahel didn't run. She leaped like a spider out of the shadows as I turned my concentration on her, and sent me, and the bottle, flying before I could stammer out more than half the incantation. The avatar dropped what he was doing and grabbed her, wrestling her to a halt before she could rip my head off, and I finished gasping the last iteration out: "—bound to my service."

Screams. Mist. A cork in the bottle, which went back in the box.

But the rest of the Djinn weren't going to let me continue this; most of them had been corked before, and even if they hadn't been under the Earth's control they'd have come after me in earnest. They'd killed Wardens for far, far less.

David broke free of a knot of them and backed up to stand over me. He dragged me to my feet and said, "Get us help."

He meant Rahel and Venna, locked in the bottles. According to the rules that governed bottled Djinn, neither he nor any Djinn could touch the containers once they'd been filled. I had to open them myself.

One of the other Djinn thought faster than I could move. She couldn't touch the bottles, but she *could* touch the box they were stored in, and she overturned it, sending dozens of bottles—all corked, all identical—skittering over the debris. Two of them were full. I just had to find those two.

It wasn't quite a needle in a haystack, but hanging as I was on the edge of death, it was close enough.

"Keep them off me!" I shouted to David and the avatar—whether Imara or Whitney was piloting it now, I couldn't tell—and lunged for the first bottle. I uncorked it. Nothing. I dropped it where it lay and went to the next. Nothing, again.

One of the bottles was smashed. I hoped that wasn't one of the two I was looking for, but I didn't see either Rahel and Venna coming to wreak unholy vengeance on me, so probably not.

A Djinn grabbed my ankle as I reached for the next bottle, and yanked me toward him. I managed to close my fingers around it as I was dragged backward, and as I felt him take hold of the other leg, I knew he was going to wishbone me—just rip me in half with one pull.

I uncorked the bottle, and felt that rush of power and control settle in.

Venna formed, blue eyes calm and utterly in control. She looked down at me, nodded, and grabbed hold of the Djinn who was about to subdivide me. Venna didn't mess around. She couldn't kill him, but she could—and did—rip enough out of his physical form that he had to mist away and recover.

Then she turned to me and helped me up. I was now holding *two* open bottles, hers and David's, and it occurred to me that balancing another one was going to be problematic—but I needed to throw Rahel in on their side. There were far too many possessed Djinn, not enough defenders, and already David had bloody cuts on him that weren't healing. It was a sign of how much power he was expending.

Plus, I needed healing, and I needed it fast, so that I could funnel power to my Djinn before it was too late.

Under normal circumstances, David could have healed me, and I could have replenished his power after I was feeling better—but these circumstances were far from normal. We were in a smoking, radioactive hole in the ground, fighting for our lives against an enemy that could, at any time, destroy us all.

I went up into the aetheric, looking desperately for something, anything to help ... and found it, heading our way at a very fast clip. Two bright, shimmering spots that radiated power.

Wardens.

They were still minutes away, but they were coming, and they were powerful. It would help. With two more Wardens to anchor the bottled Djinn, and capture others ...

But first I had to make it until they arrived.

Venna and David suddenly left their individual fights, heading for the same spot at the same time, which looked like a recipe for disaster. I should have known better. One of the Djinn had picked up a massive section of concrete, and was pitching it out of the shadows and smoke at me. It would have flattened me like a cartoon if it had landed.

David and Venna caught it and threw it back into the Djinn, bowling a few of them over. But David staggered, and I saw his wounds start to bleed more heavily. Venna also was looking less than steady.

Because I was losing ground, too. Adrenaline had

sustained me for a while, but now I could feel my body starting to lose its way. Having the additional drain of the Djinn didn't help, either.

I didn't think I was going to make it until help arrived. That might have been a character flaw, but I could feel the resignation growing inside of me, the willingness to finally, ultimately just . . . let go.

David looked at me, and I saw the emotion in his face, the knowledge. He understood what I was feeling, and thinking, and he couldn't bear it. He couldn't.

He exchanged a look with Venna and backed up next to me, took me in his arms, and poured energy into me, healing me in a hot, burning rush that made my body arch against him in a parody of love. I heard myself screaming, I heard him whispering to me, frantic and desperate.

"No!" Venna said sharply, and grabbed David and pulled him off me. She shoved him away, at the oncoming group of three Djinn who were coming at us. "Stop them!" He let out an anguished yell and hit them head-on.

Venna grabbed my hands and took up what David had started. She poured power into me in a burning wave, forcing my body together and sealing it with more power than I'd ever felt. It hurt, oh God, it felt like being boiled alive, and I knew I was screaming but I couldn't stop.

She wasn't just healing me, she was undoing what she'd done to me before—and that was some serious magic. Whatever she'd done to suspend me at the edge of death, it had been significantly more powerful than I'd thought.

Venna drained herself dry. I saw the blaze in her blue eyes die down, go dim, and then go out. She released my hands and started to disappear—but not into mist. Into sharp-edged shadows, angles, an alien and terrifying geometry that I recognized instantly.

She had just given up so much of herself, so fast, that she was becoming a creature made up of hunger. She was losing herself, but not to the Mother; she was losing herself to desperation.

Her eyes turned black, all black.

Ifrit.

I think that some part of Venna was still aware, because instead of battening on the closest possible Djinn—David—she bypassed him, grabbed hold of one of the three he was fighting, and hooked her oddly angled, blackened limbs around the other Djinn. Ifrits fed by ripping away aetheric energy, draining their victims as they voraciously and endlessly fed, to sate a hunger that couldn't really be stopped, not by any power short of an Oracle's.

Venna had brought all her primitive fury and power to it, and within a matter of seconds, she'd reduced the screaming Djinn she was holding to ashes. *Ashes.*

She'd destroyed him utterly.

The stronger the Djinn, the more viciously predatory the Ifrit could become—and Venna was, without question, the most fearsome Ifrit I could dare to imagine. She went after another victim, who prudently misted away and left the fight.

I was still shaking and sweating, on my hands and knees. I felt better, and much worse, at the same time; light-speed healing will do that to a human body. I'd be dealing with the aftereffects for days. For now, though, I needed to overrule my body's shock, and just get *on with it.*

David helped me stand. He was watching Venna's rampage, lips parted as if he literally couldn't believe it. I wasn't sure I could, either.

Venna shifted and made for a Djinn I knew slightly— she was exotically beautiful, with white hair and eyes that normally glowed a brilliant yellow. She tried to mist away, but Venna was quicker, and sank her claws into the Djinn, who howled in rage and pain.

"We have to stop her," David said. "She'll kill everyone. Everyone."

I scrambled for Venna's bottle and said, firmly, "Venna. Back in the bottle. Back in the bottle. *Back in the bottle!*" I almost added, *Dammit*, because she wasn't listening to me. . . . But then, inevitably, the compulsion set in to obey, and she was dragged away from her victim in a mist of shifting black that oozed slowly back into the glass container.

I jammed the cork in.

There were still ten or so Djinn facing us—no small number, and Ashan could decide to pop back in at any minute. But Venna had bought us just enough time. The Wardens were here.

And they were Earth Wardens, which was good; the radiation in here would fry Weather or Fire Wardens. Two Earth Wardens would be a lot of use.

I wasn't prepared for who they'd be, and it took me a few seconds to recognize the man scrambling down the maze of broken concrete toward us. He—or they—had cleared a tunnel along the way, so I could see faint glimmers of daylight, far above. He was Hispanic, good looking in a tough-guy kind of way, with muscled arms that rippled with flame tattoos. Like most Earth Wardens, he favored jeans and hiking boots, which served him well here.

Following him was a tall, thin, pale woman with hair as white as the Djinn on whom Venna had just been munching. She had skin to match, coloring that missed albino only by the shade of her eyes, which were an unmistakable shade of green. They weren't a Djinn's eyes, not anymore, but they once had been.

That was Cassiel, the Djinn who'd been locked into human form. And her partner, Luis Rocha.

"Sorry we're late," Rocha said, and jumped down the rest of the way to land with a solid thump next to me. "*Madre*, you don't go halfway when you blow shit up, do you? There's enough rads burning in here to barbecue lead. We can't stay here long."

"We have to," I said. "How'd you get here?"

"We were close, and Cassiel's hell on wheels with moving fast. Hey, Cass, you remember Joanne?"

Cassiel inclined her head, just a little. She didn't smile, or look at all excited to see me again.

That took a turn for the worse as she looked at her fellow Djinn. "They're hers," Cassiel said. "They won't stop coming for you. They know you hurt her."

"I know that," I snapped. "It was kind of the plan. Here. Rocha, take this. Try to bind one of them."

"Try to *what*?" He looked shocked, as I pressed a bottle into his hand. "What the hell are you talking about?"

Two Djinn came for us before I could answer. David took one and got body-slammed into a pile of broken rock and bent rebar, and I felt suddenly sick at the damage he was taking, for me. I raised up wind and began whipping it around the chamber, vicious eddies and currents that pulled at the Djinn and flowed through them. Unless they commit completely to human form, Djinn often wear shells—bodies that aren't quite completely stable.

Wind is their enemy, and I shredded several of them apart into vapor. They tried to reform. I kept hitting them with blasts of air.

The ones who'd taken on entirely physical forms came at us in a rush, and I realized, belatedly, that the one who'd been heading for me had disappeared. He'd veered off course, and was lunging for Cassiel, who had grabbed the bottle from Luis's hands.

"Be thou bound to my service," she shouted, and had

just enough time to repeat it two times before his fist slammed into her chest. She staggered under the blow, but it was nowhere near as deadly as it could have been, because the Djinn was dissolving into mist when he'd made contact. He siphoned into the bottle, and she corked it and tossed it to Rocha. Then she took a deep breath and grabbed another bottle.

He stared at her with utter disbelief as she bound another Djinn. She shoved that bottle into a pocket and grabbed yet another empty—only that one turned out to already be occupied. Rahel misted out of it—the Rahel I knew—and took a look around at the chaos. Then she flashed me a reckless, shark-toothed grin and threw herself into the fight.

Cassiel raised an eyebrow and put that bottle in another pocket, and kept on binding Djinn in a terse, methodical way until the only one left was the one David was fighting.

Luis finally decided to join in, and bound that one.

Silence.

I dropped to my knees again, shaking and sweaty, coated in my own drying blood, and I realized the enormity of what we'd just done. We'd enslaved the most powerful of the Djinn, and if anything was going to make the rest of them come screaming after us, that was it. Well, Lewis had wanted me to be bait. I didn't think he'd expected me to achieve it on this level of success.

"What did we just do?" Luis asked nobody in particular. "*Fuck.*"

"We did what we had to do, to survive," Cassiel said, in her cool, uninflected way. "But we won't survive long if we don't leave this place. The radiation is too high even for Earth Wardens."

I nodded, and climbed painfully to my feet. I needn't have bothered; David swept me up in a carry position, and I reflexively threw my arms around his neck for balance. "You're hurt," I said. "Let me walk."

"I'm not the one wearing the entire contents of my veins as body makeup," he said grimly. "Shut up, Jo. Let me help you."

Feeling him against me was better than morphine, and I couldn't find it in myself to argue with him, not now. *God*, I didn't realize how much I'd missed him when he'd been gone. A voice on the radio, a presence in an avatar—those things weren't David. *This* was David.

"Don't *ever* do anything this stupid again," he told me, as Cassiel led the way up the treacherous rocky tunnel. I rested my head on his shoulder and sighed.

"If I had a nickel for every time somebody said that . . ."

"Jo, I'm serious. I'm not letting you die for them. Let *him* die for the Wardens for a change." By *him* he meant Lewis. There was more than a bite of anger and jealousy in there. Although he and Lewis had always been friends, they were also always rivals. Frenemies? "This is out of control. I'm sorry I had to do that."

"Do what?"

"Bring the bottles." He looked at me bleakly. "The last thing I wanted was to enslave my people, again."

"Starting with yourself."

"It was the only way I could come here and protect you. If you hadn't claimed me, I'd have been one of them. I'd have come after you, and you know I couldn't live with that. Not if I—" He didn't want to say it. We climbed in silence. It was a brutal angle, and uneven footing, and I was pretty sure that I'd never have been able to manage it on my own after all. Even David slipped from time to time, and Cassiel and Rocha were helping each other along.

I looked back over my shoulder, but there was no sign

of the Djinn following along, other than Rahel, standing at the bottom of the tunnel. "Rahel?" I called.

She shook her head. "I'm not walking," she called up, and clicked her long fingernails together. "See you on top."

She misted away.

Man, I wished I could do that—although I felt the burn inside me as she pulled power from me, just as David had to do to continue this grueling climb. He probably would have preferred to blip out, too, but he couldn't take me with him, and I could tell he wasn't about to leave me on my own, even with two other Wardens to help.

We didn't speak the rest of the way, but I took huge comfort in just being with him. For now, at least.

We arrived at the top, and Luis Rocha collapsed toward the ground in a fluid crouch when he got there, breathing hard. Cassiel, who was only lightly winded— the bitch—settled down next to him. "Damn," Rocha wheezed. "Next time remind me to angle my tunnels better."

"You were in a hurry," Cassiel said, as if all this was the most normal thing in the world. She began taking bottles out of her pockets and setting them out in front of her. Luis added his, and I gave up all of mine except for the one that contained Venna. There was no way I was risking her getting out, not until we had some way to control her.

I looked around. The buildings were toast, shattered and leveled, and black smoke still poured out of some of the holes that were left. I'd done a good job of directing the initial damage from the blast; pretty much the entire compound was gone, but only inside the fence. Even the guard towers seemed to still be okay, although I wouldn't go climbing them without good reason. A gleaming Harley-Davidson motorcycle was parked just outside of the fence, as was the Boss, which no longer gleamed; it was covered in layers of grit and grime. As dusty as it was, it could have been there for years.

I saw no signs of anyone else. I guessed that Dr. Reid had finally come down on my side, and hustled the skeleton crew off the base and into total evac mode. Good. I would have shouldered the burden, but I was so, so glad I didn't have to do it.

"We're not the only ones who were headed this way," Rocha said, and accepted a bottle of water from Cassiel out of the pack she was carrying. I hadn't noticed before, but she was dressed in white motorcycle leathers. They were immaculate, even after all the scrambling around down and up the tunnel. She passed me water as well, and took the last bottle for herself.

It wasn't until the liquid hit my tongue that I realized how incredibly parched I was, and I sucked down the bottle so fast that the plastic crackled in protest. I drained the whole thing in a rush, then had to sit down as it filled my stomach. Right, that was too fast. I kept it down, but it was a struggle.

Once the discomfort faded, I looked down at myself. Ugh. *Not* pretty. My body was mostly healed, but there was no helping the filthy coating of blood and dirt I was wearing, or the ragged clothes. The lab coat had helped, but it was shredded and so bloodstained I might have been an extra in a chain saw massacre movie. A dead one.

It occurred to me, belatedly, what Rocha was telling us. "Who else is on the way?"

"Cops, fire, every federal agency still in business, probably. Maybe the military. This wasn't some small-time target, you know. It's going to get a lot of attention."

Well, that's what I'd intended—just not from the human world. "So I suppose the smart thing to do is . . ."

"Seal up the tunnel, contain the radiation, and get the hell out of Dodge? Yeah. That'd be it." Rocha was taking his time with his water, which I wished I'd done, but he was almost finished. He tipped it back and drained the last mouthful, then tossed it down the tunnel.

"Bad recycler," I said, and tossed mine in with it.

"Jo, you brought down the whole fucking complex. I don't think water bottles really count at this point."

He held out his hand to Cassiel as he stood, and she rose to match him. Their hands linked, and I felt the low hum of power start to build.

"We should help," I said to David. He shook his head.

"No, you need to rest. So do I. Let other people do the work for a while."

Not really my style, but I could see his point. While they were filling in the tunnel—I could feel the rumble under my feet—I rooted around in Cassiel's pack and found another bottle of water. Probably wasteful, but I stripped off the lab coat and then my shirt underneath, which wasn't quite as filthy. I used it as a washcloth to swipe blood and dirt off my face, arms, and hands. Short of calling up a gully-washing rain, there wasn't much I could do to get any cleaner until we reached civilization. Or at least a bathroom.

Dust plumed out of the collapsing tunnel, but we were out of line of the blast, luckily. I felt the long burn of the radiation through the soil, but even that was dialing back to a low background hum as Rocha and Cassiel put their blocks in place. It took about five minutes, and I heard the distant call of sirens in the distance before they were finished.

Funny, I'd have thought it was later—it seemed like days had gone by—but the sun was just now slipping toward the horizon, turning the whole landscape a fierce blood red.

I used the lab coat to wrap up the Djinn bottles, and stuffed them into Cassiel's pack. "Try not to fall on that," I said. "That would be bad."

She looked at me with those odd green eyes, and cocked an eyebrow. Very Mr. Spock, it seemed to me, although she probably didn't even know what that would mean. As Djinn went, she was very much out of the pop culture loop.

"Do you imagine I like enslaving my own?" she asked. "Having done it, do you think I would like for them to win their freedom and come after me?"

I hadn't really considered it, but Cassiel was a Djinn through and through, in every way except her physiology, which was stone-cold human . . . except that she couldn't survive without a Warden partner to replenish her energy stores. She'd never liked people, and she *really* had never liked Wardens. So this had been a dramatic step for her to take, and one that indicated how human she was really becoming.

Right now I was pretty sure that she loathed it.

I inclined my head to her without another word, and after a long stare, she looked away, toward the horizon where there was a distant glitter of fast-moving vehicles. "We need to go," she said. "Now. The Djinn will be back on us soon, and we don't need the entanglements with humans."

I thought—but didn't say—that we were actually in a much stronger position now, with all the bottled Djinn at our command. Some of them would be royally pissed, and would do everything in their power to sabotage us, but I thought most of them would understand why we'd done it, and how vital it was for them to put aside their personal issues until we could put Mother Earth back to a sound, restful sleep.

Then they could—and probably would—kill us just for the principle of the thing. The absolute last thing the Djinn wanted was Wardens getting their hands on bottles again. The cooperation the Djinn had originally given, thousands of years ago, had come back to bite them in a big, big way; many of them, David included, had suffered through centuries (or even millennia) of harsh servitude at the hands of Warden masters.

They'd kill to prevent it from happening again, and now Cassiel, Luis and I were a big risk to them.

"One problem at a time," I said. "Let's get the hell out. Any ideas where to go?"

Rocha shrugged. "It's all pretty much apocalyptic, so take your pick. We were going to head to Sedona."

Fate seemed to want me to go there, but Imara had very clearly said *don't*. I couldn't understand why, but I was willing to take it on faith; my daughter had risked a lot to come help me here, even for a few minutes. I didn't want to put her in even more danger.

"David?" I looked at him for a suggestion, and he smiled a little.

"Trouble finds us," he said. "Let's head for where the Wardens are gathering. That's where they can use us, and the Djinn you claimed."

He was hiding it well, but I could tell that he hated the whole claiming thing even more than Cassiel. He was angry with himself, because he'd been the one to think of it. The one to find the bottles and deliver them.

He could rationalize it, but he'd never be able to excuse it. I knew David way too well. Like me, he took on too much and felt too much. His predecessor as Conduit for the Djinn, Jonathan, would have been able to shrug it off as necessary, and that would have been the end of the story. Not David.

I ached for him, but in this, I agreed with my imaginary Jonathan: it was necessary. We'd release them as soon as we could, but for now, it was the only way to keep any balance to this fight.

Cassiel picked up her backpack, and we ran for the vehicles. The ground was pitted and treacherous from the blast, but we made good time and got to the fence just as David blew it open for us. David and I piled into the car, and found—to neither of our surprise—the Djinn avatar sitting at the wheel, ready to go. Cassiel and Luis mounted the motorcycle; interestingly, she was the one driving. I wondered how *that* negotiation had gone.

"Drive," David told the Djinn, and no sooner had he spoken than the engine fired up and the car leaped forward, spitting sand as it dug in and raced for the road. We hit asphalt a few seconds later, and when I looked back I saw the motorcycle turning in behind us. "Whitney!"

"You rang, boss?" She sounded just the same as before, amused and none too concerned with our lives. "That was a rock-stupid thing to do, you know. And now I'm stuck back being the damn Conduit, because you went and got yourself claimed. Again."

"It was that or end up on the Mother's chain," David said. "I'll take a slightly limited version of freedom."

"You'd better *hope* it's slightly limited." Whitney's voice cooled, and all of a sudden her rich Southern accent dropped completely away. "Let me make it clear, both of you: I'm not standing for Djinn being stuck in bottles. I know why you did it, but it's filthy betrayal and I'm going to see you burn for it. Understand?"

"Of course," David said. "I need you keeping a lookout for Djinn coming in for us."

"Maybe," Whitney said. "And maybe I'll just think about it, boss man."

That didn't sound good. Whitney was crazy but consistent, and if she meant what she said, we had a fifty-fifty chance of her just washing her hands of us and letting the Djinn in without a fight.

Granted, we had resources, but I didn't like losing

Whitney's support. We were in enough trouble as it was.

"Please," I said. "It's my responsibility, Whit. Take it out on me if you have to."

Whitney made a sound that I found particularly irritating. "Oh, I will," she said, and the Southern accent crept back into her voice. "Believe me."

"Whitney," David said. "Hide us. Now."

"Oh, all right." I felt something pass over us, like a shimmer of heat, and I knew that she'd done as he asked. From now on, we were traveling unseen by anyone without Warden powers—and probably by most who actually had them. It wouldn't fool someone of Lewis's quality, but it would serve to get us past any roadblocks, helicopters, and sharp-eyed patrols.

We zoomed past a road five miles out where several shining military-style vehicles were parked in neat lines. I got a flash of Dr. Reid's face as he spoke to a group of people. He'd done it. He'd evacuated the compound.

That made me feel better, and also, oddly, very tired. Maybe the anxiety had been keeping me alert, but now I felt like I was dropping fast toward exhaustion. Not too surprising. It had been a big afternoon, what with nuclear explosions and getting shot and bleeding out.

I must have yawned, because David smiled and pulled me close. He felt better than one of those memory foam mattresses.

"Do you want to sleep somewhere more comfortable?" he asked, and touched his lips gently to the skin just beneath my ear. I couldn't work up much in the way of sexual excitement, but I shivered a little and gave him a weary smile of my own.

"I'm going to dream about hotels. Fancy ones, with the nice fluffy bathrobes and slippers and expensive soaps. None of this window-unit air conditioner crap."

I stopped and thought about it for a second. "Does that sound self-absorbed, given the ending of the world and all?"

"Maybe a little," he said. "But I understand. And I wish I could give it to you. The best I can do is the back-seat, for now."

I sighed. "That'll do."

And truthfully, a fabulous hotel would have been wasted on me, because after I'd climbed over the seat and pulled David's warm, long coat over me, I was asleep before a mile passed under the fast-turning wheels.

I'd like to say I didn't dream, but I did. It was vivid, and shocking, and it felt, well, *real.*

It felt like I'd stepped out of a dark place and into a bright, harsh sun, and I raised my hand to block out the glare. Only it wasn't the sun at all.

It was a giant, vaguely man-shaped form stalking toward me, and everything it touched in its way—rock, trees, fleeing animals, a car full of people—burst into instant and immediate conflagration. It was the Fire Oracle, but pulled out of his hidden sanctuary and made subject to the will of the Mother.

It was burning *everything.*

I watched from my frozen, helpless spot as it stalked toward a town in the tree-lined valley below me. That was when I got a sense of scale, and realized that this glowing, terrifying creature was towering hundreds of feet in the air, taller than any building in the modest downtown. I could hear the screaming coming up out of the town, like birds sounding an alert. I could see tiny forms of people running, but there was nowhere to hide. The Oracle walked, and everything, *everything* turned to slag and ashes. It left behind nothing alive. *This* was what the Djinn and the Wardens had feared for so many thousands of years.

The extinction, without mercy, of the entire human race, done systematically and thoroughly.

I was watching tens of thousands of lives end, and I knew it would happen over and over and over, and it was so *neat*, so *clean*. Nothing left to bury. The charred land would heal itself, as it so often did; nature would take over the abandoned ground. Animals would return, free from being hunted out of existence by humans.

I felt a hand on my shoulder, and turned to face ... myself. No, it was my daughter, Imara. She looked haunted, the way her father did. The way my own face appeared now, seeing this horror unfolding in front of me.

Imara's face was mine, but her eyes were different, more like David's. She was dressed as she was when I'd seen her in Sedona, in a dress made of shifting red sand. It flowed around her, constantly in motion, and flashes of her bare skin showed through. It might have seemed somehow flirtatious, but instead, it was stunningly beautiful. There was a peace and power that radiated from her the same way that heat radiated from the Fire Oracle, or menace from the Air Oracle.

She silently put her arms around me, and I felt the sand move around both of us, whispering secrets.

"Baby," I said, and felt the hot pressure of tears. "Oh, sweetheart. Thank you. I wanted to see you."

"I know. I wanted to see you, too."

I looked back over my shoulder. The town was still dissolving in flames and screams, and my entire body ached with the intensity of the horror I felt. Imara's arms tightened around me.

"No, Mom, don't try. You can't stop it. You can't help it. This is why it's so important for me to stay where I am, and not let anybody close. I know you didn't mean to do it, but you breached the Fire Oracle's barrier when you broke out of there. You weakened it. And once you did, the Mother's influence got through to him. He lost himself. That's why I need you to stay away from Sedona, and I'm so sorry—I know that sounds terrible, and I wish—I wish—" Imara took in a deep breath. "I wish I could keep you safe with me. But I can't."

"Is all this happening now?" I asked. The smoke and flame and screams kept rising, and now I started dreading the moment when the screaming would stop. "Is this a dream, or is this really happening?"

"Mom—"

"Tell me."

Imara looked at me with pity in her eyes, and said, "It's why the Wardens needed you to distract those of the Djinn you could. And you did; you took out some key players. But it's not going to be enough."

My fists clenched, and my nails dug in deep enough to burn and cut. "The Wardens have to *do something*!"

"They are. But this isn't something Wardens can fight. It isn't even something the Djinn can fight, although if you command them, they'll try. Elemental powers are walking the planet now, and there's no reasoning with them. No clever tricks or last-minute reprieves. The game's over. Humans have lost." She said it so gently, and with so much compassion; I knew she'd lost her humanity when Ashan had killed her, but I liked to think that through me, she retained some memory of it. Some sense of the magnitude of what was happening right in front of us.

But what I saw in her was a distance that I couldn't cross anymore. She was part of the Earth, and the Earth had rejected my species as flawed and failed. So no matter how much Imara still felt for me, she couldn't bring herself to feel it for all those suffering and dying below us.

I swallowed a hard lump in my throat and managed to ask, "Then why are you here?"

"Because I can help you, Mom," my daughter said. "I can help you become something else."

"A Djinn? Been there, done that, not doing it again. I'm human. I *like* being human."

"But you'll be alone. The only human left. I can keep you safe, but *only* you. No one else. Is that what you want?"

"No," I said, and then said it more loudly, because the screaming down there was drilling into my head like a vicious power drill. "No! Dammit, Imara, you have to *help us*!"

"I'd like to," she said, and it sounded genuine. "I wish I could. But I don't have any way to do that, and even if I did, maybe it's for the best, Mom. Maybe this is what needs to happen, so things can start over. Cleanly."

"I don't believe that." I backed away from her and stood several feet away, fists clenched. "I will *never* believe that."

"When things die, you have to let them go," Imara whispered, and I saw eternity in her eyes. "You let me go, didn't you? You accepted it. You have to accept this, too."

I couldn't even speak. My mouth had gone dry, my throat tight, and all I could manage was a violent shake of my head.

Imara sighed and folded her hands together. "I'm sorry," she said. "Now I have to go."

"You *saved my life*! You can save theirs, too!"

"I did," she said. "But life isn't a permanent condition. You know that."

And the sand hissed up over her, whipped into a blinding ball, and then it blew apart in all directions, stinging my skin as it landed.

Imara was gone.

I looked down at the valley. The Oracle was reaching the far edge of what remained of the town. There was a large building there. I could just make out the word HOSPITAL in lights at the top before the power failed.

I grabbed hold of a tree that fluttered its leaves in the hot wind, and watched with dry, aching eyes as the building melted and burned. I thought about the patients in their beds, the babies in their cribs, the doctors and nurses staying at their posts despite the destruction coming at them.

Then I held up my arms and summoned storms. Not the carefully constructed sort that Wardens are supposed to wield, oh no. I slammed together air and water with careless disregard for the balance, the consequences, for anything that I'd ever been taught. I needed rain, a lot of rain, and I needed it fast.

I put together one mother of a hurricane, and I did it in under ten minutes. The clouds were thick and black and stuffed with death, and I unleashed it right over the Fire Oracle as it reached the borders of the town. Water poured down with a vengeance, and I saw steam rising from the Oracle's body. The destruction of the town cooled, but the Oracle kept burning, and burning, and burning, no matter how much rain I threw at him.

Then the Oracle turned and looked at me, really *saw me*, and I woke up as suddenly as if someone had slapped me across the face. I jerked upright, and realized I wasn't standing halfway across the country watching that terrible march; I was in the backseat of the Mustang. I was sweaty, hot, fevered, and scared, and fumbled for some of the supplies that Cherise and I had bought what seemed liked ages ago. Water. I needed water.

David said nothing. He didn't even ask me what I'd been dreaming about. Maybe he knew.

I choked on the lukewarm liquid, but got it down, and gasped, "It's true, isn't it? The Fire Oracle. He's walking."

David slowly nodded.

"Can't you stop him?"

"No," he said, and I heard the infinite regret in his

voice. For the first time, I also heard resignation. "Oracles can't be stopped—not by you, not by us. Once they've been unleashed, they won't stop until the Mother tells them to stop."

"There has to be something we can do. David, I *saw it*. I saw a town—I saw people—I saw—"

He grabbed me and held me as the Mustang plunged on into the night. Stars overhead, cold and precise and uncaring. David didn't try to tell me it would be all right, and he didn't try to promise me that we'd find a way to survive. He didn't promise anything at all.

I sensed desperation in the way he was holding me. He didn't believe that we could make it.

"No," I said shakily, and swiped at my eyes with my hands. "No, we'll make it. We're going to find a way to stop this. We have to. We can't give up."

"It's not about giving up; it's about facing facts," David said. "You think we can fight the Mother. We can't. She's judged, she's made up her mind, and there's no changing it."

I couldn't accept that, I just couldn't. It didn't make any sense to me that we couldn't somehow fix this, make the Earth understand and see humanity as her own.

I pushed it aside, because there wasn't any point in arguing with David about it. "Where are we?" There was a glow on the horizon, a big one, and since it was due west of us, I didn't think it was sunrise.

"Las Vegas," he said. "Lewis brought the unassigned Wardens here. They've been working with the Ma'at to fortify the town."

Vegas would be a prime target, I realized, purely for the fact that it existed in such defiance of the natural order in the desert. So many people, so much artificial water, so much energy being consumed.

I remembered the town I'd seen destroyed, and multiplied that times the huge population of Vegas, and felt shaky all over again. "All right," I said. "It's as good a place as any to make a stand. Plus, we might get in a Cirque show and some time at the roulette tables."

"I didn't think they let Wardens play roulette. Or slot machines."

The casinos in the know certainly didn't. An Earth or Weather Warden could jinx a roulette wheel as easy as snapping fingers, and put a Fire Warden near a slot machine and forget about it. "Look, if the world is going to end, I'm going to win all the money I can. Just because. They say you can't take it with you, but really, has anybody *tried*?"

Vegas sounded good to me for another reason—accommodations, and shopping. I desperately needed a shower and new clothes, and even though I could ask David to magically clean me up, it wasn't the same thing at all as sinking into velvety hot water, scented with lilacs, and floating. . . .

I was fantasizing about a peaceful afternoon and a hot bath the way perverts fantasize about porn.

Hell, maybe I'd throw in some shopping. I'd always loved the clothing stores in the big casinos. Nothing like hitting couture when you're depressed, and if you're going to certain death, why not go out wearing Valentino or Prada?

Even the best fantasies have to end, and mine didn't last long. I went up into Oversight and got the lay of the land. It was unnaturally still, locked down on all fronts. I could see the restless fury of the land and the air, but the Wardens were keeping tight controls on everything, for now. With the amount of energy building, though, it was going to be impossible to hold it off forever.

I checked the rearview and found that Cassiel and Luis Rocha were still behind us, keeping a steady, patient distance. I supposed they'd also received their orders to join up with the other Wardens, or else they had business of their own, though what could possibly be more important than the end of humanity was impossible for me to guess. I supposed it was a matter of perspective.

Suddenly, the Mustang gave a surprised little cough and sputter, and the engine ... died. We had just crested a hill and gotten a view of the incredible display of Vegas lights shimmering below, like some opium dream about living jewels.

"Please tell me that we threw a rod or something," I said as the Djinn glided the car off to the side. I heard the harsh blatting of Cassiel's motorcycle catching up to us, and then it, too, cut off without warning. She coasted the bike to a halt behind us and set the kickstand, and she and Rocha jumped off and got ready for trouble.

The Djinn behind the wheel said, in Whitney's voice, "Oh, *hell*, I should have known this wouldn't go so easy." She sounded deeply annoyed. "Everybody out of the car, right now. Get whatever you want to keep."

I bailed out, and David followed me; we each grabbed a bag full of supplies, and I unzipped one bag and found the shotgun and pistol that I'd liberated from the motel where we'd lost Kevin. I loaded the shotgun with shells and tossed it to David without looking; he caught it the same way. "What are we shooting?" he asked, quite reasonably.

I loaded up my pockets with ammunition for the shotgun and the pistol, checked the clip, and shook my head. "No idea," I said. "But I hate to be underdressed in the event of an attack—"

I didn't have time to finish, because a silent missile dropped down out of the dark sky and sliced razor-sharp claws at my face. I'd been extending my Oversight *out*, not *up*, and the only warning I had of the huge bird's approach was the sudden cool breeze on my face as it backwinged to slow itself. It shrieked as I fell backward, and I rolled, trying to avoid its next dive.

David turned on a lantern, and I saw the biggest damn bird I'd ever seen gliding low over our heads, angling for another strike. It was a freaking *bald eagle*, and it was utterly magnificent. I'd have been transported with its beauty if it hadn't just taken a swipe at my eyes. The wingspan was enormous, probably at least six feet, and it was an expert hunter.

Cassiel suddenly stepped into the circle of light, lifted her arm, and made a sharp, whistling sound.

The eagle glided in, and for a second it looked as if it was going to land tamely on her leather-clad arm—not that the leather would be any kind of defense against those incredible claws. They'd punch through even the toughest hide like it was rice paper. Cassiel's pale green eyes were watchful, totally focused on the bird as it made its approach.

She barely had time to dodge out of the way as it spilled air from its wings at the last second, altering its trajectory, and let out an ear-piercing shriek as it thrust its claws forward. It raked her leather jacket from neck to waist, shredding it, and with mighty flaps of its wings, it gained altitude again and disappeared into the sky.

"I can't hold it," Cassiel said. "And there are others coming. Many others."

"Birds?"

"Large birds," she confirmed. "Owls, eagles, hawks. And on land, other things. Bears, wolves, mountain lions. They will catch us. We have to run."

I lifted the gun. She smiled a little.

"Do you think you have enough bullets for the world?" she asked. "Don't be a fool. You can't make a stand here."

Cassiel was right, but we were still far out from the relative safety of the lights of Vegas. Out here, there wasn't much—but down the hill about two miles there was some kind of hotel, clearly shut down, all lights off. "Down there!" I said, and grabbed up the bag I'd dropped. "Come on, let's move!"

"Wait," said Whitney's voice from the car radio. "I can't start this thing, but I can push it. Get in. Might as well ride."

Cassiel shook her head. "I will take my motorcycle. I can coast it down the hill after you."

"Not a great plan, Cass; that bird isn't going to give you a pass just because you used to be a Djinn."

"I know," she said, not bothered at all. "But I'm not leaving the motorcycle. I like the motorcycle."

"Well, *I'm* taking the car. Have fun," Rocha said, and got in with me and David. Cassiel shrugged and strad-dled the bike, kicking up the stand, and pushed off. She must have had damn good balance, because the heavy machine hardly wavered at all.

Whitney's push-method for the car worked just as well; it started slow, but picked up speed on the downhill grade, and we ate up the distance fast enough.

As we got closer I saw *why* the hotel was closed. Some kind of fire; the six-story pink stucco exterior was blackened around the windows and doors, and its plastic exterior wall-mounted sign was half melted. There were one or two cars, but they looked like derelicts and had signs of fire damage. The giant parking lot was deserted except for tumbleweeds and trash.

The road grade was evening out, and the car was slowing down. I made a command decision and said, "Whitney, how far can you push us?"

"All the way to where you want to go," she said. "If you insist."

"Get us to the Vegas strip. This doesn't look like a very safe—"

Our tires blew out—at least two, from the separate bangs I heard, and the lurch of the frame first right, then left. Oh *perfect.* Somebody really didn't want us getting to the other Wardens.

"I amend my earlier statement," Whitney said.

"Can you fix the tires?"

"Sure," Whitney said, "if I was *there*, sugar. I'm not."

"I can," David said quietly. "But it's going to take some power. Are you up to it?"

I nodded, not sure I was, but willing to give it a shot. David closed his eyes and concentrated, and I felt the car lurch again as the tires melded themselves back together and reinflated.

They immediately blew out again. David flinched in surprise. "There's something working against me," he said. "Feel it?" I did. It was big, and inimical, and I didn't like it at all. Whitney stopped the car. "Whitney, keep moving. We can run on rims." No response. "Whitney?"

The radio stayed dead. The avatar just sat, staring blankly ahead, like a doll whose batteries had run down.

Suddenly, David looked sharply to his right, into the dark, and said, "We have to get out of here. Now."

"We were doing that," I said.

Luis Rocha didn't waste time arguing; he popped open the door. "I'll push," he said. "Better than hanging around with a big target around our necks."

The avatar wasn't steering, though; he was just sitting, inactive, and David finally dragged him out from the wheel and shoved him into the backseat, then installed me as the driver. Ah, that felt strangely good, even with busted wheels. Rocha and David got behind the car and pushed. I thought it was odd that David didn't do it himself, and odder still that they were working so hard at it. . . .

And then David stumbled and went to one knee. Rocha let loose of the car bumper and stopped to help him, and I instinctively hit the brakes in alarm.

That was our undoing.

The wheels sank into asphalt that suddenly felt like mud—thick, clinging mud. The front tipped down, and I realized that someone, something was softening the road underneath me. Miring the car in a modern-day tar pit.

"Out!" It was a white shadow at the window—Cassiel—and she didn't wait for my agreement, just reached through the open window and dragged me unceremoniously through. She was sinking into the road, too, and slung me through the air to the side. She was stuck, but she pulled herself free with a wrenching effort and jumped for the safety of the gravel at the freeway's shoulder. Luis Rocha, already there, caught her as she landed.

David was off the road, but down, and I scrambled to get to him. He was panting, eyes wide and blind, pupils very large.

"What is it?" I asked, and ran frantic hands over him looking for injuries. "David, what's wrong? What's happening?" Because I couldn't see it in Oversight. I couldn't see anything. . . .

Anything at all.

It was as if the aetheric had gone completely dark.

The breath went out of me, and I felt utterly, completely alone in a way that I hadn't since I'd been stripped of my powers. I still had them—I could feel them inside me—but I was blind, in a magical sense. I heard a surprised sound from Cassiel, and a curse from Luis. It wasn't just me, then. We were all stricken with this supernatural blindness.

And something was very, very wrong with David.

He managed to focus on my face, and said, very faintly, "Kill him."

I looked over at Luis Rocha, who held up his hands in defense. "Not me, man. I'm not doing it!"

But who did that leave? Not Cassiel, not me ...

The avatar.

I looked over my shoulder at the car, which was still sinking—it was up to the door level now, embedded in the road's soft surface. It was as if the road was *eating* it. Digesting its metal and rubber, plastic and glass. There was a constant crackling sound, and a fizzing, that was faintly sickening, especially considering how much I *loved* that car.

But the avatar wasn't inside it anymore.

"It's the Djinn," I said to Luis and Cassiel. "Watch out. He's not channeling Whitney anymore."

"Who *is* he channeling? Satan?" Rocha asked. " 'Cause this doesn't feel so great, and I can't see a thing on the aetheric. Cass?"

"No," she said tersely. "I hear the bird. It may be coming in for us again."

If she could hear the whisper of feathers in the wind, I couldn't. But she was right, because a second later I saw the blur of feathers, and the bald eagle dive-bombed Luis. He wasn't fast enough, and the claws ripped bloody furrows in his upraised right arm. I felt the force of the wind from the eagle's furious wing beats as it hovered, snapping its hooked beak at his face.

Cassiel was faster. She reached out and grabbed the eagle's body below the widespread wings, and as the bird shrieked in alarm and battered at her, she summoned up power, and I felt myself sway with weariness.

The bird went quiet. Not dead, just stunned and sleeping. "Hush, child of the sky, I won't hurt you," she told it, and I saw a kind of tenderness in her that was ... unexpected. She'd always struck me as pretty damn pragmatic, but maybe that was only when dealing with humans. She took off her jacket and wrapped the bird securely, with its head sticking out. It made an effective straitjacket. "We need shelter. There were more on the way."

She'd also said something about bears, and wolves, and mountain lions. I didn't want to deal with that out in the open, either, especially since the normal Earth Warden defenses weren't working.

Cassiel's motorcycle, which had been parked on the side of the road, suddenly tipped over and began sinking into the black tar. She let out a curse that I was pretty sure she'd learned from Rocha and ran to muscle it away from the asphalt and onto the sand—not that that was going to help, I wanted to tell her. There was no safe ground, not really.

But I'd feel better with a roof over our heads and something like walls giving us some defensive shelter.

"Right, the hotel," I said. "David, can you get up?"

He nodded, but his face had gone pale under its metallic luster, and I didn't know how much he could do on his own. Rocha and I each took a side and helped David stumble across the long parking lot, heading for the doors. They were blocked off with DO NOT ENTER yellow tape and plywood across what had once been a glass entry. I burned the padlock into slag and unlocked the hasp, left David leaning on Rocha, and stepped inside the ruined casino and hotel with the battery-powered lantern upraised.

The light couldn't reach far, but it looked like a typical Vegas sort of lobby—ornate carpet (stained by black smoke and loads of footprints), marble counters that still looked intact, some kind of fancy ceiling overhead but probably not as nice as one of the name-brand casinos, like the Bellagio or the Venetian. This was where your grandmother's bingo club, not the high rollers, stayed when they went to Vegas. Whatever guest rooms still remained were probably no better than an anonymous chain hotel on the cheap.

The fire had consumed most of the casino, it looked like; the damage got worse, and the smell of burnt wood and plastic was chokingly strong, still, even though there was no hint of embers around. This place was a total loss. I imagined they were waiting on insurance before demolition, but in the current dire circumstances every insurance company in the world was probably out of business already, no matter how well funded. This place had just seen the Reaper early, that was all.

But it was still standing, and it would do.

"Right," I said. "Looks like this part of the building is the least damaged. Follow me."

It was horror-movie spooky as we moved in our own little island of light through the silent, dark, cavernous lobby. Carpeting squished in places under my feet—still not completely dried from the hundreds of gallons of water that had been dumped in here to finish off the fire, I presumed. The smell of mold overtook the stench of smoke as we went farther in, and I saw black swathes of the stuff on baseboards and in corners. Yeah, this place was finished, even in less apocalyptic circumstances. In Las Vegas it was always considered easier to demo and rebuild than renovate.

At the far end of the lobby was a long marble concierge's desk, and behind it was an almost undamaged door that said STAFF ONLY. I felt like breaking rules. I opened it a couple of inches and peered inside, and saw a big lounge area with nice chairs and sofas, a big-screen TV (dead, of course), and coffeemakers with glass carafes full of molding brew. Snack machines, phones, even an internet portal in the corner. And beyond that . . . showers and lockers.

It looked perfect, and I led them all inside.

"Oh," I sighed. I couldn't help it; the sight of those gleaming bathroom fixtures was just about more than I could take. I forced myself to check for security. It being a casino hotel, there weren't any large windows, only slits up near the ceiling too narrow to crawl through.

There was an emergency exit at the back, but it was secure. I summoned up more power in the form of fire and used it to hard-seal the metal door to its frame. If I had to undo it, it might slow us by critical seconds, but better to be safe. I didn't like having easy access at our backs.

"Clear," I said, and came back with the light. Cassiel and Rocha were easing David down into a chair. "I think the coffee's past its sell-by date, but there's shelf-stable food, water, and sodas. And showers." I put the lantern on a coffee table and knelt down next to David to take his hand. "Talk to me. What's happening?"

"Darkness," he said. "Can't see anything. Feel—drained. Like there's something trying to pull my power away from me."

That wasn't good news, not at all. And the fact that Whitney had so precipitously deserted us wasn't good, either.

"He's right," said a new voice from behind me. I whirled around, ready to blast something with a fireball, but then I held up as the speaker walked into the light. Rahel, back to her old golden-eyed self, but subdued. She seemed as uncertain as David. "I was following on the aetheric. I hit—something. A block. I had to take physical form to get this far. I don't think I can reach much of my power. It's like—"

"Like a black corner," David said. "But only at half strength. It feels artificial. Imposed."

Rahel walked over to a candy machine, smashed a hand through the glass, pulled the whole thing out in a spray of fragments, and contemplated the selection. She chose a Three Musketeers bar, which I found weirdly amusing, and I watched as she peeled it and bit. I didn't think I'd ever seen Rahel eat before.

She chewed for a few seconds before swallowing and saying, "It's coming from the avatar. You know this?"

"David told me," I said. "But I don't know how to find him. Do you?"

"No need to find him. He'll come to you, soon enough." She nibbled her chocolate bar and selected other things from the machine—M&M candies, a Twix bar, some kind of cookies. She tossed those to each of us. Weirdly, I'd been craving M&M's, and the smack of that yellow packet in my hand felt like manna from heaven. I ripped it open, popped two peanut candies in my mouth, and chewed. The rush of sweet/salty grounded me a little more, made me feel just a touch better.

"So we wait?"

"Yes," Rahel said. "I'll keep watch. Perhaps you should shower." She emphasized that with a sniff and a pained expression. "If I'm trapped here with you, sistah, you can at least not reek of blood and sweat."

I almost, almost smiled, but I didn't think I had that particular expression in me at the moment. Rahel didn't wait for a response. She walked past us to lean against the doorway to the lobby, peering out with infinite patience as she nibbled down the candy bar.

I looked at David. "You going to be all right for a few minutes?"

He nodded. "Be careful."

"Trust me, nothing is going to stand between me and that shower right now. I'd shoot Gandhi and Mother Teresa both to get to it. That's literal. Because I have a gun."

I kissed him and felt him respond, just a little. He wasn't *that* bad off. "Be *careful*," he said again.

I stood up. Luis and Cassiel were huddled together, talking in low voices, but they looked up when I cleared my throat. "Shower," I said. "See ya."

Selfish, I know, but at least Rahel had reinforced my obsession with getting clean. I ducked into the staff shower area. Lockers were mostly empty, although a few employees had left behind bath products and—in some cases—magazines of questionable taste. I grabbed a selection of shampoos and conditioners, and a still-clean towel, and I dumped my filthy clothes into the sink to soak with some liquid soap on board. Even the rough wash I'd given my shirt back at the nuclear plant hadn't held up well.

The water was on, but—no surprise—cold. I yelped in surprise when the icy drops hit me, but the sensation of water around me was so breathtakingly good that I ignored the temporary discomfort. I used a little candle flame of power to heat the water locally, and that was even better. It took three shampoos of my hair to get all the dried blood and grit out of it, but by the time I'd finished I felt, once again, clean and whole. I shut off the water, dried myself, and went back to where I'd left my clothes in the sink.

They weren't there. The sink was empty and dry.

I wasn't alone in here.

"You should burn those," said a voice from the shadows, outside of the reach of the thin light trickling in the door from the other room. "They really don't suit you."

Ashan. I pulled in a breath to yell, but my vocal cords seemed to be paralyzed. I couldn't even get out a squeak. I saw him now, materializing out of the shadows, perfectly manicured, with that faintly contemptuous expression that never seemed to leave his face. He looked like every terrible boss I'd ever had, and every bad boyfriend, too.

Except for the white eyes. Those weren't like anybody I'd ever known at all.

"It's over," he said. "And you owe me pain, Joanne Baldwin."

I needed to scream. I needed to move, but my whole body seemed to be frozen now, and all I could do was watch as he paced forward, confident and steady as a panther.

He was in no hurry, and it seemed to take forever before he was standing in front of me. I realized that there was someone else in the shadows—the avatar, left abandoned like a defective toy. His eyes, too, had gone white.

Ashan closed his hand around my arm, and my towel disappeared in a flash of heat around me. For a second I thought he wanted me naked—and that was particularly sickening—but no, he just wanted me clothed. I'll say this for Ashan: the bastard is cold and brutal, but he does understand fashion. The clothes that settled on my skin were tailored, understated, and more or less what I would have picked, if I'd been able.

"Don't thank me," he said, as if he'd read my mind. "I just don't want you to imagine I have any use at all for your flesh. Humanity serves no purpose to me except as . . . fertilizer." He smiled, a thin razor-cut of his lips. "There'll be a rich growing season for years to come, in the silence that follows this day. And we have *you* to thank for it. You and my imposter brother."

I wasn't sure which I hated more—the sad, resigned distance of my daughter about the loss of the human race, or the lip-smacking delight of Ashan. No, I was sure; Ashan, for the win.

I'm going to kill you, I thought, and I hoped he really could read minds after all. *I'm going to smash you until there aren't two aetheric particles sticking together with your name on them. I'm going to stop you.*

It was about as effective as a rabbit's scream in the jaws of a wolf, but I was going to have attitude to the end. What else did I have?

I had power.

His blackout of the aetheric had distracted me, and so had his special guest appearance in my shower, but I could still pull power. I *had* to pull power, even though the whole area seemed resistant to it.

I filled myself with Earth power, and reached out for

the metal pole behind him. With one swift pull, I yanked it out of the tiled floor, bent it, and slammed it into his back. There was no pointy end. I wanted it to *hurt*.

He jerked and looked down at the hollow metal pole—about three inches in diameter—sticking out of his chest. A human would have bled, but Ashan never bothered with genuine human flesh and blood, so it was really more of a shell—a particularly convincing plastic doll. It probably hadn't hurt him, but it had really fucked up the line of his expensively tailored suit, which did my heart good.

I pulled the pole out of him before he could get a grip on it, remove it, and beat me dead with it.

It obviously hadn't hurt him much, but that was okay, because the pole was a distraction, and I hit him with my *second* attack, which was a vicious piledriver of wind that focused on that hole I'd made in Ashan, from front to back. The wind forced itself into him, and I increased the pressure to insane levels. Ashan's white eyes widened. I suddenly found myself back in possession of my voice.

"Bye now," I said, and with a brutal burst of Weather powers, I blew him to pieces. His scream was short-lived, but very satisfying, and then he was a misty afterimage on the air, and I blew *that* back to hell where it belonged.

I hadn't killed him, but I'd definitely hurt him that time. The fact that he didn't re-form and come after me was proof of that.

David hit the door at a run and skidded to a halt, staring at me.

"One second," I said. "I have something to do."

I walked out to the other room and began yanking open cabinets until I found a bottle of some kind of coffee flavoring. I dumped its contents out and walked back to the shower area. By then, David had oriented on the remaining threat: the avatar, who was still standing frozen in the shadows.

"Sorry," I said to him, "but we can't let you run around loose. You're too much of a wild card." I held out the open bottle. "Be thou bound to my service. Be thou bound to my service. Be thou bound to my service."

Nothing happened. I frowned at him, then at the bottle. Yep, it was empty, and open. I shook it, which was a stupid thing to do, but to no effect. I tried again, reciting the words thrice.

The damn thing just *stood there*.

"It won't work," David said. "There's nothing in him to capture. He has no soul. He's just a vessel—his body is already an empty bottle, in a way." He sounded ragged, but sure of what he was saying.

"So what do we *do* with him?"

"Kill him," he said, very softly. "The avatar is physical. It can die."

There was something really unpleasant about that idea, and I didn't care to examine it too closely. "Can't we—I don't know, evict Mommie Dearest from the avatar?"

"No. We either leave it here, where it can strike at us any time she wants, or we kill it. But there's no other choice, Jo."

It felt vile, somehow, and I couldn't shake it off. But he was right, I'd be destroying a shell, not a person.

Not a person who'd driven me halfway across the country. Who'd saved my life.

I couldn't stand to think about it any longer. I picked up the gun from where I'd left it sitting next to the sink, cocked it, and aimed at the avatar's head.

David put his hand on my shoulder—not to stop me, but to steady me.

And I fired.

It was the worst thing I had ever done.

Chapter Ten

The aetheric blindness was gone immediately, and David's powers came flooding back, restoring him. Everybody was happy.

Everybody but me. I kept reliving the kick of the gun in my hand, and the sight of the avatar's head—

"Jo." That was David, sitting down next to me on the couch. I had been silent for a long while, and they'd been sensible enough to let me be, but David clearly thought I'd brooded enough.

"Leave me alone," I said.

"You did the right thing."

"I know that. Just leave me alone."

He sighed and kissed my temple, very gently. "I would have done it for you."

"You think I'd have felt better watching you kill one of your own?" I swallowed a bitter mouthful of stomach acid and wondered vaguely where I'd left the M&M candies. I thought I could have used one right now to get the terrible, bloody taste out of my mouth. "No thanks. I'll handle my guilt like a big girl."

David hesitated, then put his arm around me. I opened my eyes and saw that Luis Rocha was slumped in a chair, snoring (somehow, adorably), and Cassiel was pacing, looking like a caged beast with claustrophobia. I didn't think she would have hesitated to pop a cap in an avatar, but then again, I didn't really want to be her, either.

She bugged me.

"I should tell you who he was, once," David said, and that made me turn and look at him in surprise. His brows went up. "You thought he'd always been an empty shell?"

"Well—yeah. Kind of."

"He was Old Djinn, once—but not like Ashan. More like Venna. He was curious about humans, and liked to help them. He was caught in a convergence of forces, very rare, while trying to save humans from an earthquake. It destroyed the Djinn he had been, and left the shell behind. Since then, he's been wandering. Empty. Jonathan thought about destroying him, but he said— he said—" David stopped, thinking, and then continued more slowly. "He said that we'd need him someday."

"Oh *Jesus*, David!" I found myself covering my mouth with both hands, appalled. Jonathan had demonstrated a turn for prophecy, more than once. "Why didn't you stop me?"

"Because I think what Jonathan saw was how much *you* were going to need him. I think he did what he was—designed to do." He shook his head. "That sounds wrong. That's not what I meant. But I feel that his destiny was already over."

Again, that didn't make me feel better. I wasn't sure anything right now could make me feel better because *Jesus Christ* I'd just pulled the trigger and killed someone, even if it hadn't been a person, a real person, or even a real Djinn.

My body still replayed it, over and over. And it hurt.

"You need to rest," David told me, in that tone that husbands get sometimes. He meant it, and when I opened my mouth to protest, he covered it with one hand. "Stretch out. Come on. All the way. Legs up. There you go."

I still felt miserable, but I had to admit that being down felt a whole lot better than sitting up. Cassiel had gotten adventurous and raided a linen closet, and found bags of clean sheets, towels, and blankets. They weren't the kind of high-thread-count stuff you'd get at the tonier hotels, but they felt good on my skin.

Like the clothes Ashan had gifted me with. Bastard. Well, at least he hadn't dressed me in knockoffs. Could have been worse.

I flinched again as the sound of the shot rang in my ears, and David's warmth settled in behind me, holding me close. His hand stroked my forehead, then glided down my neck, over my shoulder, down my arm. . . . It wasn't erotic, but damn, it really was. Just being touched relaxed something in my body that seemed to have been permanently knotted up, fused into a hard mass.

I let out a slow breath, and with it went some of my grief, my anger, my disappointment. I remembered the first night that I'd insanely decided to sleep with David; I hadn't known his name then, or that he was a Djinn, or that he was going to alter the trajectory of my life on a course up, toward the stars. He'd been so kind to me then. And he'd touched me exactly the same way, and despite all my best efforts at seduction, he hadn't touched me any other way. Not then.

It occurred to me now that I should have valued that more. I should have realized right then that he was something . . . special.

But at least I'd been smart enough to hang on to him once I *did* realize what I had.

"Why are we waiting?" I asked. "The avatar's gone. We can go now."

"We will," David said, and his mouth was so close to my ear that his lips brushed teasingly over its curves. "You need to rest. You picked up a big dose of radiation outside of Amarillo, and I can't heal you properly if you're awake. So sleep. Once morning comes, we'll move on."

Cassiel paused in her pacing to look at us in a guilty sort of way, as if she just realized she was probably being annoying, and settled into a chair close to where Luis was sawing logs. Rahel stood at the door, a silent statue, watching and waiting.

I don't think I intended to fall asleep, but between the seductive warmth of David's hands and the exhaustion buried deep in my bones, I really didn't have a choice.

I woke up to David's hands, again, but this time they were shaking me, and when I started to speak he put a finger to my mouth. Unmistakable warning. I went still, fighting my way back toward some kind of alertness, and saw that Luis Rocha and Cassiel were already up and on their feet, hands clasped. Rahel was closing the door with calm, competent motions, locking it, and waiting with her entire body radiating tense expectancy.

We were all very, very quiet. I don't know why, but I felt that primitive kind of terror, the kind our ancestors probably felt hiding in caves and hoping the lions and tigers passed them by.

Something slammed into the locked door with a shocking roar, and the wood jumped and bowed inward.

The being quiet strategy hadn't done much, clearly. I got up, and David unfolded himself from the couch as well, both of us laser focused on the door, which wasn't going to hold. I threw Earth power into it, along with Rocha and Cassiel, and that helped, but whatever was on the other side of it had Earth power as well, and man, was it *pissed*.

Rahel, with a negligent wave of her hand, ripped the heavy serving bar loose from the left-hand wall and slammed it against the failing door like the world's largest burglar bar. "I think it's time to go," she said. "Back door?"

Oh yeah, I'd sealed it. Good planning. But then, it was probably good that I'd done it, because I was no more than halfway through undoing my melted metal seal when another pissed-off, very large thing slammed into that door as well. If I'd undone it faster, it probably would have sliced me open on its way to destroy everyone else.

"Not that way," I said. "What the hell is out there?"

"I don't think you want to know," Rahel said, as if it was amusing to her—and it probably was. "Go up, not out. Nothing out there strikes me as good at climbing."

David nodded, looked up, and ripped open a significant hole in the roof, which spilled in predawn light of an uncertain gray color. He flexed his knees and fired his body up, landed easily fifteen feet above us outside the hole, and did a little scouting before nodding down at us.

"Damn," Luis said. "Forgot my jet pack. Knew I should have packed that."

Cassiel let out a sound that was too frustrated to be a sigh, and offered him a cradle of her linked fingers for his foot. He raised both eyebrows. "Are you kidding, *chica*?"

"Do I seem to be?" she snapped. "Hurry."

He put his booted foot in her hands, and she tossed him straight up, letting out a yell of fury that sounded like it was ripped out of her spine. It was an impressive demonstration of how strong she was when using her

Earth powers, and even as solidly built as Rocha was, she got him up high enough that he grabbed the hand David reached down to him. David pulled him up without any effort at all.

"Rahel," David said. "Bring Cassiel. Joanne can make her own way." I loved that about him—he knew I wouldn't want to be evacuated ahead of the others. Besides, he wasn't wrong. I was a Weather Warden. Lifting myself up wasn't a challenge.

Rahel looked at Cassiel, and Cassiel looked back. I felt sparks fly, not the romantic kind, and I wondered what kind of unpleasant history there was between these two. Knowing Cassiel's nature, it didn't surprise me that she'd clashed with Rahel. It only surprised me that Rahel had survived it.

Rahel looked like she *really* didn't want to touch Cassiel, and Cassiel looked pretty much the same.

"Do you want me to make it an order?" I asked Rahel. She gave me an *are you kidding?* sort of look, and then I remembered that Cassiel actually held the bottles, all of them except Venna's, which was buried in my own bag. So technically, I couldn't order Rahel to do squat. Not and have her listen.

"No need," she said. "And no time. I'll take my shower later."

Mee-*yow*, that was harsh. Cassiel might have scratched back, but Rahel grabbed her around the waist and leaped up, dragging Cassiel with her. She let go as soon as they reached the roof, not even bothering to steady Cassiel, who went sprawling.

Rahel grinned.

"Play nice," I said, and formed an air cushion under me, then heated it. Low pressure above me, high below, and zap, Bernoulli's principle was my friend. Up I went, on my invisible elevator pad, and stepped lightly off just as the back door below gave with a metallic shriek.

David and Rahel replaced the roof, rapidly duplicating existing materials over the hole. With any luck, it'd buy us time.

Above us the rest of the hotel rose up in a central column. The pink stucco was, in the light, smudged mostly black, and the windows were all boarded up. In the daylight, the place looked even more derelict than at night.

But what drew my attention were the things pacing at ground level below us. My mouth went dry, and I suddenly wanted to retch. That was just *wrong*.

"What the hell is that?" Rocha was asking, sounding just as shaken as I felt.

"Chimera," Cassiel said. She'd rolled to her feet and was studiously ignoring Rahel, although I had the feeling that she wasn't going to forgive, or forget for the next several millennia. "It's a forced merger of several animal forms. Bear, mountain lion, scorpion."

That was what creeped me out the worst, I decided. The bear with the mountain lion's head I could handle, but the giant curving arthropod stinger that twitched and curled and dripped with venom . . . no, that was just too much. This thing was a killing machine, and there were *several* of them.

Not only were the chimeras awaiting us, but there were wolf packs, too, thin and half starved and snarling up at us. They made running starts and leaped up the wall, trying vainly to claw themselves up. I knew something about wolves, and that wasn't normal. Not in the least.

"Above us!" Rocha yelled, and I yanked my attention skyward. There was a small battalion of birds up there, big ones. I didn't see any more bald eagles, but there were a couple of gigantic hawks, and several smaller ones. One or two turkey vultures were riding the thermals, evidently waiting for the inevitable mop-up operation. "We need a shield!"

I got one up just in time, and I curved it as much as I could, so that as the birds stooped and fell toward us they wouldn't hit quite so harshly. Even so, at least half of them collided with such hard smacks I knew they'd broken their necks. Blood ran down the sides of the shield, sickeningly bright in the rising sun. The surviving birds took wing again, circling, and I knew they'd make another run. I hated it, and I reached out, trying to find them on the aetheric, trying to turn them aside.

No use. They were being completely controlled by a force far, far more ruthless and powerful than me.

David yelled a warning and ripped a large satellite dish clean off its moorings. He threw it as if it were a discus toward the edge of the roof, where one of the bear/lion/scorpion things was clawing its way over the edge. The satellite dish hit it squarely and tipped it backward, off balance. I saw the scorpion legs underneath the fur, and once again felt the urge to retch.

The things *could* climb. Great. That was just *perfect*.

"We're in trouble, guys," I said. "I'm going to have to take drastic measures."

"By all means," Rahel said. "I always find that entertaining."

I shot her a dirty look and readied a fireball. When the next chimera crawled creepily onto the roof and scuttled toward us, roaring out a mountain lion's snarl with a bear's boom, I let it fly. The temperature was well into the thousands of degrees, and the bear's fur burst into flame. The chimera writhed and shrieked, and I pushed it, still burning, off the roof.

When I looked over, the dying chimera was being torn apart by its kin. Ugh. I just love nature.

"There's more coming," Rahel said quietly. She had dropped all hint of being amused now, though to her all this was still a highly academic exercise. "I would suggest you find a way out."

My car was roof-deep in the road out there, and I didn't think it was ever coming out, or that it would be in any way drivable if somehow it did. It was for damn sure that three of us wouldn't fit on the motorcycle, and even two wouldn't survive these things—these chimeras—which would rip anyone apart in seconds once they were at ground level. Even Cassiel. Two Djinn couldn't carry three of us to safety without taking us through the aetheric, which would likely kill us anyway.

"Right," I said. "Rahel, take Rocha. David, take Cassiel. Get them out of here. Take them all the way to Vegas if you have to. David, you can come back for me. I can hold out." I was the logical one to remain; my combination of powers was something that outclassed Luis Rocha's not inconsiderable talents, and even Cassiel's, which was limited by her connection to him. I could pull Earth, Fire, and Weather to defend myself, and now that I knew these things were killable, I felt confident I could hold out.

David looked as if he wanted very, very badly to say no, several times, loudly, but he knew I was right. Luis and Cassiel were vulnerable here, and they'd saved our lives before. They deserved our help now.

He gave me a furious look, and I saw the sparks of fire and gold blaze up in his eyes. Truly a Djinn, in that moment, with his skin shading to metallic bronze. "Don't die," he said flatly. "Promise me."

"I promise," I said. "Get out of here. I'll wait."

He kissed me, and it was a hungry, desperate kind of kiss that left my whole body tingling and alive, my lips sunburned with the force of his emotion. My husband. I touched his cheek and said, "I will always love you, David."

He kissed my palm. "There is no force in creation that will keep me away. You know that."

"I know."

"Then wait for me."

He turned, fury in his movements, and threw his arms around Cassiel.

Then he launched himself up off the roof, into the air, and began to fly.

Rahel watched him go, then turned her attention to me. "Until later, my sistah." She blew me a kiss, put her arms around Luis, and purred, "Well, this is certainly an upgrade from my last passenger." I had to laugh at the discomfort on his face, and then she flexed her knees and they were gone, too.

Another monster scrambled over the edge of the roof.

Time to go to work.

David didn't come back.

Neither did Rahel.

I paced myself, there on that smoke-stained roof, under the glare of the Vegas sun. I had my pack, and in it was food and water, which I gulped down as the chimeras kept coming, and coming, and coming. Mother Earth must have run out of bears and mountain lions, because around noon, a new breed came scuttling over the horizon and attacked the building.

And these used to be human.

I couldn't believe what I was seeing at first, because my brain refused to process the information. It was too disturbing, too sickening. I had to face it once the first of them scaled the wall, *way* too quickly, and used its human hands to pull itself up over the lip and its scorpion's feet to race toward me. The human face on the thing had rolling eyes and a lolling, foaming mouth, but being driven mad clearly hadn't affected its razor-sharp reflexes. I dropped the juice box I was sucking on and pulled down lightning—overkill, but this thing was completely disturbing, and my skin crawled with the idea it could even exist in the same time and space with me.

I zapped it into a blackened mess when it was still fifteen feet away. My ears rang with the blast, and I felt singed and disoriented, but oddly better for ridding the world of it.

That was before I heard the clattering, and realized that there were a *lot* of these monsters, and they were climbing in steady, relentless streams. As I watched, stomach dropping, I saw that two more had already cleared the ledge on one side, and at least three on the other. At least the damn bear/lion creatures had been *slower.*

The roof wasn't going to work any longer.

I started fires around the roof line to give myself a little time as I stuffed things back into my bag. The fire should have slowed them down, and maybe it did, for all of fifteen seconds or so, but then they ran shrieking— *human* shrieks—through the walls of flame and came straight for me with those deadly stingers upraised and ready.

No time for anything fancy. I had to evacuate.

I levitated myself up on a strong updraft, and— apprehensively—over the flames and the struggling, snapping chimeras that were swarming up the building. This wasn't something even most hard-core Weather Wardens were good at doing; short bursts of this kind of thing were fine, but if I faded now, I'd be dropping myself into a boiling mass of these things at the base of the wall. I had to keep going. I had to hope that it would take them time to realize I was gone and to find me.

Personal levitation is exhausting, sweaty work, and my pack quickly felt like it increased in weight from ten pounds to fifty, to a hundred. I breathed in ragged, gasping breaths, holding diamond-hard focus on keeping the forces in delicate balance as I sped along, skimming over the desert at the speed of maybe thirty miles per hour.

Not exactly fast, but I didn't dare push faster. Every bit
of forward motion I added made it harder to compen-
sate on all the other, constantly shifting energies. I'd
never done this for longer than a minute, at best.

I held it for almost fifteen minutes before my concentration snapped, and I tumbled out of the sky toward
a razor-sharp stand of brush cactus. At the last second,
I altered course and landed in sand instead, and hit
the ground running. It was good I did, because when I
looked back I saw that my footprints were filling up with
something dark.

Fire ants. My very touch on the ground was bringing
them boiling to the surface.

Not just fire ants, either. The desert's defenses were
on high alert, and I had to dodge swarms of smaller, non-
chimeraed scorpions as well as some tarantulas crawling
out of their holes ahead of me. Running was not my best
sport, and broken-field running even less so, but I didn't
have a choice. When I reached out with Earth powers
to try to clear my way, it only made things worse, as if
the entire wildlife was sensitized to the presence of a
Warden in their midst.

My breath was burning in my lungs, and I knew I'd
have to stop soon, or at least slow down. But I wasn't
sure how I could, considering the fierce antibody reaction to my passage. Not only that, but as I looked back
over my shoulder I saw movement about a thousand
feet behind me. Chimeras, and they were catching up.

Las Vegas was a long, long way off. It looked drab
and overbuilt in the desert shimmer. I realized that no
planes were flying in or out, and although there was a
road up ahead, about a half a mile out, there were no
cars on it. It was eerily quiet.

No sound except for the overhead shriek of hunting
birds, which made me realize how vulnerable I was to attack from that avenue. I didn't want to have to kill more

birds. I didn't want to kill *anything*, except maybe those awful chimeras, but I didn't think I was going to have a choice. Mother Earth had declared war, and I was going to have to fight back, hard.

Except that I wasn't sure anything I had would really keep me alive for long.

I put on a burst of speed, pulled from Earth power, and outpaced the scuttling pursuers, heading for the road. Not that the road was safe, given that it had already *eaten my damn car*, but it was flat and clear of fire ant burrows, at least.

What it *wasn't* clear of were hornets. They boiled up out of nowhere from the side of the road, a bomber squadron of inch-long furious insects, and headed straight for me as soon as my feet hit the asphalt. I gasped and instinctively swatted at them with a blast of air, driving them back as I kicked my run into even higher gear. I was dripping with sweat now, gasping like a fish out of water, but I couldn't slow down. I could hear the relentless buzz of the insects zipping closer.

I came to a sudden halt, closed my eyes, and formed a hard shell of air around my body. The bugs hit the windshield with vicious force, leaving gruesome splatters, and those that didn't die immediately jabbed their stingers into the barrier, over and over, trying to get to me with their last breath. A few, warier than the others, backed off and circled, looking for an opening.

I couldn't wait forever.

I dropped the shell and ran for it, and the remaining hornets dashed in pursuit. The first one came close enough to smash with another gust of air that sent it tumbling, stunned or dead, to the gravel shoulder of the road. My legs felt like lead now, and my muscles were starting to wobble uncertainly as the stress and lack of oxygen took their toll.

The first hornet got me, and it felt like being hit with

a bullet. A bullet dipped in acid. I yelped, slapped a hand down on my arm, and felt the insect's body squash under the slap. The sting hurt, and then began to burn. I gritted my teeth and stopped again, pulling down my windshield. Three more hornets met their gooey death, leaving only two who were smarter than that, or slower.

The running battle of attrition went on for another half mile. I smashed one more hornet, but the other two harassed me, flying in with vicious darting motions. I crushed another one when it landed on me, luckily before it drove home its stinger.

The sole survivor dive-bombed me relentlessly, and score two more stings before I finally managed to kill him, too.

I windmilled to a gasping, gagging stop on the hot asphalt, barely able to keep upright. My left arm, where the first sting had landed, felt hot and swollen; so did the back of my neck and my leg, where the others had scored hits. But I wasn't going to die of that.

No sign of the chimeras behind me.

No new threat racing up out of the desert to confront me.

There was even a cool breeze ruffling my hair, and I lifted my chin, grateful for anything that lessened the misery I was in . . . and then my eyes snapped open, and I saw the dust devil dancing out there in the desert, a sinuous rope shape made visible with all of the sand it was sucking up. It was mesmerizing to watch as it twisted, bent, and got darker.

I dropped down into a crouch, hardened the air again, and covered my head with my hands as the dust devil— no, dust *tornado*—raced toward me with the fury of a freight train. It hissed at first, and then, once it was on me, the hiss rose to a blinding roar. I could feel the sand scouring over the shell that protected me, and the heat increased. I couldn't stay in the shell long without making it gas-permeable, but that meant opening myself to the dust storm. I'd suffocate, one way or the other. My only hope was to disrupt the dust devil's delicate, powerful structure.

And I probably would have done that fairly easily, if it hadn't been for the fact that a chimera slammed into the shell around me, and when I opened my eyes I found myself face to face with the lolling, foaming mouth and rolling eyes of a madman. His hands scrabbled at the surface, and I saw that the sand was ripping at him viciously. I'd seen a man stripped of skin once, in a storm like this, and as I saw the first raw patches appear on his body, I felt my stomach clench in nausea.

I couldn't help him, whoever he'd once been. He was gone. And this thing that wanted to take a piece out of me wasn't in any way human.

The scorpion tail drove down, hit the hard shell around me, and snapped its stinger off. The chimera howled and lost its footing. The dust devil blew it away into a maelstrom of sand and debris, and I concentrated on Oversight, examining the structure of the twister hovering over me. It was a perfect little engine of destruction—colder air whipping down and heating itself as it moved faster and faster in its spiral, then the hot air blasting up like a furnace through the center of the devil to the sky, where it cooled and spiraled back down. A perfect marvel of physics.

But this one—this one was no accident of nature. This one was being held together by an iron will, and when I tried to break it, it was like hitting a bank vault door with a toy hammer. Someone wanted to kill me, badly.

And I thought I knew who it was.

I kept the shield in place and straightened up. I started at a walk, well aware that I was going to exhaust the oxygen content of the air in this shell in less than a minute once I started running.

The dust devil stayed on top of me, blinding me, slamming me with debris and scouring sand that whipped at killing speeds. I broke into a jog. It paced me.

I kicked it to a run, lungs burning from more than effort now. I could feel my energy dropping, and the danger was that as I used up my available air I was going to start losing focus. Losing focus meant losing the protection of the windshield, and that meant I'd die.

No. There had to be a way. There had to be.

I realized that I was breathing too hard, and getting too little. That hadn't taken long. A headache was already starting to form, and my legs were informing me that any step now might be the last I was going to take.

I dropped the shield, sucked in a dust-laden breath, closed my eyes, and dropped flat on the hot pavement. The dust devil screamed as it closed over me, clearly sensing triumph, and I tried not to scream as it battered me with raw fury.

When I'd hyperventilated enough, I put the shield back in place and ran on. I'd only gotten a few steps when the dizziness started. I couldn't keep this up.

I crouched down again, grabbed my pack and opened it, groped inside, and found the one Djinn bottle I'd kept with me.

I thumbed off the cork.

A rush of black mist, and hidden in it I saw sharp angles and edges and alien geometries. Venna, in the form of an Ifrit. I'd never understood how much Ifrits really comprehended—not much, in all probability—but this was one moment when her needs and mine aligned perfectly.

"Ashan," I gasped, and spat out a mouthful of sticky dirt. "He's out there. Go get him."

I couldn't tell if she knew what I was saying, or if she sensed his presence, but she let out a shriek that vibrated at the very limits of my hearing, and disappeared.

Seconds later the dust devil collapsed in a confusion of sand and clattering license plates, barbed wire, and pieces of broken brush. Its demise left drifts of brown sand and chips of red sandstone littering the road in concentric circles around me.

I dropped the shield and spent the next several seconds just *breathing*. My whole body was shaking with effort, and sitting down seemed to be the only thing to do, really.

Down the road, about a hundred yards away, Ashan was screaming. Venna had battened on him, and sunk sharp, angular spikes into his pseudobody. When he tried to mist away, she only consumed faster.

I coughed and tasted blood. The bottle was in my hand, and the cork was dangling, ready to be slammed back in place. All I had to do was recall Venna before it was too late.

Ashan screamed, and screamed, and screamed, and I didn't call Venna back to the bottle until his pale, shrieking face had dissolved into bloody mist, and had been absorbed into her twisted, nightmarish alien form.

It broke up into mist, too—black, greasy mist that turned gray, then white, and reformed around the body of a small girl in a pinafore dress, crumpled on the pavement.

"Venna!" I could barely stand, but somehow I managed to run to her side. Her eyes were open and blank. I touched her face, and she felt cold. "Venna, can you hear me?" I wasn't sure that she would be stable in this form; sometimes Ifrits used up their energy and reverted to the primitive form.

But not Venna. She lay there, broken and defenseless, and when I saw her finally blink it brought tears to my eyes.

She didn't get up. I pulled her into my lap and held her, and she felt like a child, like any child. Her arms slowly rose and went around me, and I felt her body start to shake.

I realized after a few more seconds that she was speaking, very softly. Her voice was a thin, anxious thread. "I didn't want this. He was my brother; I didn't want this. . . ."

Ashan was dead, killed in one of the only ways possible for a Djinn. She'd ripped away his life energy to save herself, and—as a byproduct—me. I couldn't feel nearly as bad about that as she did, but I didn't have to gloat, and I didn't. I just held her and rocked her gently. Even Djinn need help, from time to time, and I was glad to give it.

Until I looked back, and saw more chimeras coming.

"Ven," I said then, and nudged her head off my shoulder. "*Venna.*"

Her eyes cleared a little, and she regained some of the distance and poise that I was used to seeing in her. "Joanne," she said. "You put me in a bottle." That was a dangerous thing for her to be realizing right now.

"I had to," I said. "You were Ifrit. You could have killed David."

She nodded slowly, processing the information, and then turned her head to look at the oncoming group of chimeras scuttling up the road toward us. She frowned. "Those aren't right," she said, and extended her hand. One by one, the creatures blew up in gouts of blood and some kind of pale fluid. It was nauseating, but effective. In seconds, not one of them remained.

Venna turned her gaze back on me. "You put me in a bottle." I didn't repeat my answer; she already knew what I had to say. The only question was whether she'd actually accept it. I knew I could blow up just as gruesomely, and as easily, as those chimeras littering the road out there, and I knew better than to think Venna wouldn't do it, if she thought it was the right thing to do.

She stared at me with Djinn-fired blue eyes, and finally said, "His powers came to me. I'm the Conduit for the Old Djinn."

I should have seen that coming, but somehow, I didn't. I blinked at her, and bit back an automatic, and utterly suicidal, *congratulations*. "I'm sorry," I said instead. "I had to do something."

"Yes," she said, and looked moodily out at the land around us. "Yes, I can see that. She's trying to reach me, but she can't as long as you have me anchored in the bottle. My power flows through you."

"Venna—"

She made some kind of decision, and stood up. I waited as she dusted off her dress—not that it would ever get dirty. She could just be moving away so that she wouldn't be splashed with my gore when she exploded me.

Yeah, I try to look on the bright side.

"Are you going to sit there?" she said. "Or do you want to see Lewis?"

"I want to know what happened to David," I said. "Something must have. He would have come back for me."

"Yes," she agreed. "That's in his nature. Come." She extended her small hand, and pulled me to my feet with such ease she might as well have been a linebacker. When I started to drop the grip, she held on.

"We're going through the aetheric," she said.

"Wait, that's not—"

"Trust me."

And then everything was a rush of color, light, a feeling of being destroyed to a cellular level, *pain*, and then, suddenly, I was facedown on the carpet of a casino floor, gasping for breath.

Slot machines were ringing, just like the world was still normal. Just like everything that I'd been through had been a terrible, passing nightmare.

I felt like a sack of overcooked spaghetti, and I wasn't sure I could get to my feet at all, but Venna tugged me back upright. She gave me a long, level look and said, "You should put me back in the bottle now. The longer I'm out, the more of your energy I burn. You can't afford it now."

I cleared my throat and nodded. "Thank you."

"There will be a price," she said coolly.

That was positively chilling, but I tried not to let her see how much that got to me as I said the words, she misted away, and I capped the bottle firmly. She was right. The second the cork slotted in place, I felt better, stronger, and almost capable of standing on my own. But, since there was a handy wall to lean on, no sense in pushing it.

I heard the metallic rattle of guns being readied, and peered around to see a line of men and women facing me with serious weaponry, and even more serious expressions. Most of them were wearing the tailored blazers of security for the Luxor hotel.

All of them were Ma'at, and I could feel the shields being readied against anything I might try to throw at them.

I was too tired for this crap. I held out my fingers in a peace sign—which was one more finger than I was inclined to show them—and said, "Take me to Lewis."

Venna hadn't answered me about what had happened to David, but Djinn were like that.

Lewis would answer, or I'd beat it the hell out of him with my bare hands.

Chapter Eleven

They took me out of the casino area—most of the dedicated players hadn't paid a bit of attention to the sudden show of firepower—and hustled me through a maze of corridors to a *salon privé* on the second floor. It had the hushed, elegant vibe of a place where only the highest of high rollers was hosted.

The Ma'at guards opened the door—some kind of biometrics—and pushed me inside before closing it after me. It was a large room, and under normal circumstances it would have been exquisitely appointed, but the Wardens had no time for that nonsense, clearly. Expensive antiques had been shoved like driftwood into corners. A round mahogany table that would have caused those *Antiques Roadshow* guys to weep had been unceremoniously loaded down with files, computers, and satellite phones. There were folding tables set up with coffee and food, and cots—mostly full of sleeping people—crammed in at every angle possible. The clear space that was left was where the Wardens were working.

I saw Luis and Cassiel, and made straight for them. "What the *hell* happened to David?" I yelled. That got almost everyone's attention in the room, even the sleeping ones. I shoved cots out of my way, creating a logjam effect, and scrambled over people to land in front of Cassiel. "He was with you! Where is he?"

She said nothing, but she looked sideways at a tall man pushing his way through the crowd. I didn't even have to look at him to know who it was—the subdued tingle of his powers was unmistakable against mine.

Lewis.

He grabbed me and hugged me fiercely, which would have normally been nice, but right now I wasn't interested in anyone comforting me. I wanted *answers*.

The words died in my throat when I focused on his face. He looked terrible, worse than I'd ever seen him. Ages older than he'd been when we'd parted back in Miami.

He was tearing himself apart.

From the look on his face, I wasn't in much better shape. I pushed all that aside, grabbed him by the collar of his rumpled, days-old shirt, and said, "*Where is he?*"

Lewis closed his long fingers over mine, but he didn't try to take my hands off him. "He's all right," he said. "Jo, I'm sorry. I couldn't let him leave again. I couldn't take the risk. Ashan is out there—"

"Not anymore," I said. "Ashan's gone. Venna's the Conduit now."

That made him pause, but only for a second. "How— Never mind. It's good that he's gone. He was poisoning her view of us. Maybe Venna can—"

"I can't let her go," I interrupted. "Lewis, if I do, she'll be as bad as the others. She's probably more powerful than Ashan, and if she gets thrown at us again . . ." I couldn't think of words to describe how bad that would be. Ashan had been bad enough, but having Venna bent on destroying us . . .

He gazed down at me for a long while, and then said, "Come with me."

I let go of his collar. There was something in the quiet, almost miserable way he said it that made me gulp; I didn't want to see Lewis feel beaten. He'd always been the one who just didn't give up. He cheated, he schemed, he lied, he manipulated—but he didn't give up.

If he did now, I didn't think I could bear it at all.

He took my hand and led me past the silent Wardens. There were only thirty or so in the room, and half of those were wounded, some badly. I stopped to touch a few hands. Nobody had anything to say. I saw the same beaten weariness in every face. Well, maybe not Cassiel's, but she was always the exception. That would require she actually gave a crap.

Lewis led me into a side room—probably some fancy sitting room where countries were bought and sold, never mind companies. It was empty and still. The air conditioning blew on my face and reminded me of the hot stinging spots that remained on my neck, arm, and leg. *Ow.*

He shut the door and turned to face me.

"You left me to die," I said. "Didn't you?"

"Jo, I couldn't risk it. We need David here, and there were no guarantees that we wouldn't lose you both. Rahel told me how bad it was out there, and I put him back in the bottle."

That raised the hair on the back of my neck, and I knew my posture shifted into something that was a hairbreadth short of attack. "You put *David* back in the bottle. You stopped him from coming to me."

"Yes. I got it from Cassiel. Don't blame her. I didn't give her a choice, and she didn't know why I was asking."

Screw that. Cassiel had known. Deep down, *I* had known, too. I'd felt it, I just hadn't wanted to admit it.

Lewis was still talking. I struggled to hear him over the angry buzz in my ears. "Jo, I trusted you. I believed you'd find a way, and you did."

"No," I said. "You left me to die, and you didn't *see* that out there, Lewis. You didn't see what was going to tear me apart!"

He didn't answer that. I understood the misery, now. He really had stood there at that table and made the cold-blooded decision to pull my rescue party, and consolidate his resources.

And leave me trapped and alone.

"Enough," I said. "*Enough.* If this is what it takes to win, fuck it, I don't want to win anymore. Give me David's bottle."

"What are you going to do with it?"

"I won't break it, if that's what you're worrying about," I snapped. I felt that I hardly knew this man anymore, even though I'd spent half of my life thinking of him, loving him just enough to be able to not let go. "I want my husband, and I want to leave."

"And go where? Do what? Jo, this is the *end*! There's nowhere to run! She's hunting us down, all the Wardens, everywhere. Most of us are already gone, for God's sake. Did you see them out there? *We're dying!* And when we're gone, everyone else dies. Maybe it'll take a few more days, maybe a week, but in the end, she won't let a single human stay alive. I know that. I *feel* that!" Tears suddenly welled in Lewis's eyes and spilled down his face, and he just—folded up, as if I'd gut-punched him. No, as if a Djinn had gut-punched him. I realized how tired he was, how shaky, as he sank to his knees on that fine Aubusson carpet. Funny how the wine red color looked like blood, as if he had—like me, back in the plant in Amarillo—already spilled every drop he had to give. "I've tried everything. Everything. And they keep coming, killing, destroying. Imara won't let us near her. The Air Oracle is destroying entire *islands* out there. The Fire Oracle—"

I knew about the Fire Oracle; I'd seen it in my dream. As angry as I was, his horror and grief struck me, and I sank down to a crouch across from him. He was weeping uncontrollably, the tears of a man stretched too far, asked for too much.

"Listen to me," I said, and reached out to tilt his chin up. He swiped at his face, angry with himself but still unable to stop. He was one step from a complete breakdown, and I could see it in him. "Listen. I know it seems hopeless. I know you think there's nothing more we can do. But we *can*. We *must*. What's our choice, to sit here and die when the hammer comes down? Screw that, Lewis. I didn't fight my way through what I have to give up."

Consistent, I wasn't. A few minutes ago my only thought had been to grab David's bottle and get the hell away from Lewis, from the Wardens, from all this crushing, endless responsibility. But seeing Lewis break . . . That reminded me of something.

It reminded me that no matter what I did, how hard I tried, I could never really be free of the Wardens. I *was* a Warden, and always would be, until the day I died.

"Give every Warden a bottle," I said, "starting with the most powerful first. It's time for the Djinn to be on our side. We already broke the rules; let's make it count. And dammit, *give me David*!"

"If you'll give me Venna," he said, and tried for a smile. I nodded agreement. He gulped in a deep breath, and seemed to steady himself. "All right. We've got Djinn. We've got the Wardens I've been able to pull together. We've got the Ma'at, not that they're up to a fight of this magnitude. What else?"

"We've got Imara."

He was already shaking his head before I finished the short sentence. "Nobody's got Imara, and she wants to keep it that way. I told you, I tried. She won't come, and she won't talk to us. She won't give us sanctuary. She's locked inside her own world, and she's letting live or die on our own."

I pulled Venna's bottle out of my backpack and held it out to him. "Give me David. Give me David, and I will bring Imara in on our side."

"How?"

"Just give me the bottle."

He had it in his pocket. As he passed it over, I felt heat emanating from the glass. David was really, truly pissed off, and I knew that the second I released him I was going to have a very hard time keeping him from breaking Lewis's neck.

Lewis uncorked Venna's bottle, and the child stepped out of thin air to stand at his side, hands folded. She looked up at him, innocence itself, and said, "If you give me stupid commands, I'll kill you."

"I expected that," Lewis told her. "For now, help Joanne keep David from killing me. Which he's about to try to do."

Venna raised her eyebrows, but it wasn't in surprise. I was pretty sure that was amusement. Other than that, she gave him absolutely no assurances.

I took a deep breath, cradled the bottle in my left hand, and pulled the cork with my right.

A storm exploded out of the bottle, and the pressure of the room changed so abruptly my ears popped. David materialized in midstride, long coat swirling like smoke, and lunged for Lewis's throat.

Venna caught his hand about an inch from its target with no apparent effort, and said, "Maybe you should greet your wife first."

David whirled around, and I saw the look that Lewis had just faced. I'd never imagined David could seem that angry, or that deadly, but his beauty had taken on cold, unmerciful edges, and the glitter in his eyes was the color of blood.

He blinked, and it went away. "Jo?" He didn't wait for me to answer. In one step I was crushed against him and held tight, so tight I thought he'd accidentally break my back. After a few breathless seconds he eased off and looked down into my face. His eyes widened, and I knew he was seeing what I'd just been through. Hard to hide things from a Djinn, especially one who knew as much about me as he did.

That triggered the rage again. I knew what he was thinking—he'd seen my horror and desperation, seen how close I'd come to being killed out there, and he was blaming it on Lewis. Well, rightly so, but there wasn't time for it. Before he could lash out again, I grabbed him by the chin and held him still. "No," I said. "I'm all right. And we need him as much as he needs us."

The fact that I was so baldly logical about it helped clear the anger out of him, at least for now. He shuddered as it passed, and nodded to me, and I let go. "We'll talk about this later," he said. "Right?"

"Absolutely," I said. "Although I plan on three days of spa treatments, with mud baths and all-day massages. So probably after that."

It got a twitch of a smile out of him before he looked at Lewis, and Venna standing so small and delicate beside him. He said, "Ashan?"

Venna looked down. "Gone," she said. "I grieve that it was necessary, but he was mad with power. He twisted nature. It can't be done, no matter his motives."

Venna had described Ashan as her brother, and from the pain that I saw in her, I believed it. What she'd done would be a long time healing, I thought, if it ever did.

"You're the Conduit."

"Yes," she said, just as quietly. "Not by my choice. But I am the logical replacement."

"Can you reach her?" David asked. I knew by *her* he meant Mother Earth. Venna slowly shook her head.

"Not while I am bound," she said. "And once I am free, I become hers. Maybe without Ashan's anger driving her she will be calmer, but the damage has been done. We have to find a way to speak to her before it's too late."

"We'll do it," I said. "David and I will go to Imara. She'll let us in; she has to. And once we're in, we can reach the Mother through her."

Venna studied me with eerily calm eyes. "That will kill you, you know. You're not strong enough."

"I've done it before."

"When she was sleeping. She's not sleeping anymore." The matter-of-fact way she said it made me pause. "You die, and David becomes hers. It's what will happen. Imara knows. That's why she kept you away."

Venna had a turn for prophecy, too, and that chilled me deep. "But she'll let us in."

"Yes," she said. "She's your child. She'll let you in."

"Then we have to try it." I turned to David, but he didn't look nearly as convinced. He was looking past me, at Venna.

No . . . not at Venna after all.

At *Lewis.*

Lewis wouldn't return the stare; he looked at the floor, deliberately avoiding any kind of contact. I wondered why, until Venna turned to Lewis, adding her stare to David's. "She will talk to you," Venna said.

"Lewis?" I blurted. "Why?"

Lewis let out a sigh, and now he did look up, troubled and very tired. "Because I'm the first triple-threat Warden born with that configuration in generations, and I may be the most powerful one since Jonathan walked the Earth." He was right. A triple-threat Warden—one who could wield all three powers with equal strength—was extremely rare. So rare, in fact, that the Wardens themselves had tried to capture and study him, in hopes of figuring out how to artificially create the condition in others. Lewis had spent his time as a lab rat, and as a fugitive; he'd been a thief, a con man, a hero, a leader, and a ruthless general.

"Before you go," David said slowly, "you should know the truth about Jonathan."

That came out of left field. Jonathan had been the leader of the Djinn for countless ages, and he'd been David's friend and brother in arms—maybe more, for all I knew. I had only met the Big Grand Poobah a few times, and he'd spooked me, in general, more than Venna. I knew Jonathan had been born human, and Warden; he'd become a warrior general, and died in battle, with David, on a field full of slaughter. His death had sparked the Mother to create the first of the New Djinn: Jonathan, formed out of the death of so many.

David had been brought with him, because Jonathan had refused to let him go.

What else could there be to know?

Venna suddenly glanced away from all of us, as if listening to a sound that didn't register to me at all. "We'll discuss it later," she said. "Time to fight now."

Lewis jerked upright and hit the door running into the main room. Venna blipped out and probably materialized ahead of him.

I looked wordlessly at David, and he took my hands and held them.

"I hate him," he said. "I hate that he left you out there alone. Whatever comes, I'll never forgive him for that."

"Amen," I said. "But let's live through this first, okay?"

He gave me a smile and kissed me, and we went to join the fight.

At first glance, it looked like nothing was happening. Lewis was standing at the table that I assumed doubled as the Warden War Room. Venna snatched up Cassiel's bag (without permission) and began flitting from Warden to Warden—literally, buzzing in and out of reality faster than a hummingbird—and opening the bag so they could take the Djinn bottles inside. Seeing that Venna herself couldn't touch them, that was a pretty good compromise. She ran out of bottles after twelve people, but I could see at a glance in Oversight that her evaluation of who were the most powerful was dead-on.

"Be careful," I said in a voice pitched to carry. "Those Djinn may or may not want to follow your orders. Some of them may turn on you, but it's the best shot we have."

"They won't," Venna and David said, as one, and exchanged a look. Venna continued, "We'll make sure they don't. There's no time for politics now."

Wow. That was quite a statement, coming from the new head of the Old Djinn. Ashan had been *all* about the politics, and—of course—the superiority and general hatred. But there was a new sheriff in town, tiny as she might be, and I rather enjoyed the idea.

One by one, the Wardens uncorked their bottles. Most looked damned nervous, and I didn't blame them, but as the Djinn misted into evidence around us, none of them made aggressive movements. They stood, silently waiting, just as Lewis was.

Lewis said, in a faraway kind of voice that told me he'd gone far out on the aetheric, "It's coming. Get ready."

I went up with him—not as far up, because I'm not Lewis, and he could, as always, take things further than any other living Warden. I'd never really understood his limitations, but I understood that he had them, and he was more than likely pushing them now.

I didn't need to soar quite as high as he did, because what was coming for us was perfectly evident, in vivid reds and deadly blacks, poison greens and rotting yellows. It was a tsunami of power rolling through the desert like a wave, sweeping everything ahead of it, and although I didn't know exactly what it *was*, there was no question of what it *did*.

That was the Four Horsemen. That was the Grim Reaper.

That was Death, and it was coming to wipe Las Vegas off the face of the Earth.

I had no idea what our powers could do against it, but I looked at David and said, "Can the Djinn stop it?"

"No," he said. "Not even the Djinn can do that. But we can hold it back, for a time."

"Do it," I said.

He nodded and vanished, and around the room, other Djinn did the same. I went up on the aetheric to watch, and I saw the wave sweep toward the glittering, insane tangle of lights and colors that was Las Vegas—and stop, frozen in its tracks. The Djinn had taken up positions all the way around the perimeter, and as I watched, I saw that while the wave was still seething, bubbling, it was at a standstill.

David misted back in, along with Venna. "It's not going to hold," Venna said. "You have less than a day, probably only hours. There are millions here. Once the Djinn fall, there's nothing to stop it, and they will die. All of them."

I looked around at the room, at the Wardens in their shell-shocked state. I remembered those insane gamblers still stuck at the slot machines out there in the face of the end of the world as we knew it.

I thought about Cherise, who might already be lost, but would be soon if we didn't find a way to stop this.

"There's no more time," Venna said. "If you want to live, we must go now."

"It'll take hours to get to Sedona," I said. Venna gave me an exasperated look.

"No, it won't," she said, and reached out to take my hand, and Lewis's. "Hold on. I will take you."

"Wait!" I said, "Imara has a barrier in place! You can't get through it!"

"She knows we're coming," Venna said. "She doesn't like it, but she knows. It's her choice whether she destroys us to protect her own existence."

"You're gambling on her allowing us entrance."

Venna smiled. "It's not a gamble. She's your daughter."

She seized our hands, and I had just enough time to anticipate how bad this was going to be. . . .

And then it was much, much worse.

Venna dragged us through the aetheric planes, and my *God* it hurt, like being towed through coils of barbed wire. It seemed that the aetheric itself was burning, aflame with all the growing and intensifying fury and determination, pain and panic. More and more people were realizing that there was no escape, and the pressure was building to fatal levels.

Somehow, we made it through to the other end without losing our lives. Even with Venna, traveling through the aetheric was more of a crap shoot than I liked, and Lewis in particular seemed badly affected by the whole trip. He staggered and sat down, hard, on dry red dirt.

We were in canyons of sandstone, as crimson as the surface of Mars, and overhead the sky was a cool, featureless, unnatural blue.

We were inside Imara's bubble. As it had been in the Fire Oracle's area of influence, the world seemed to have been frozen here—I couldn't see a single living thing moving. No birds, no insects. Not a breath of air. It was eerily silent.

Venna said, "I told you she'd let us in."

"Don't get cocky," Lewis said. "She doesn't have to let us get any closer."

The floor of the canyon was sand covering a hard-pan surface of bedrock. Whatever river had carved this particular bend was long vanished, and rain was something rarely seen here. The canyons towered the height of four-story buildings over us, built out of layer on layer of reds, oranges, and browns. The ground was like a tree—you could read its history by the rings and layers of its life. The life of this land was long, and hard, and austerely beautiful.

Overhead, the sun was black in the center, rays blazing out in intense bursts from the edges. It was frightening and strange, and I wasn't sure what I was seeing at first, until Lewis said, hoarsely, "Eclipse."

"It's not an eclipse out there," David said. "Not one scheduled in this part of the world for years to come."

It didn't matter. This was Imara's domain, and she could do anything she wished here. If she wanted to blot out the sun, she could.

I looked up. At the top of the cliffs above us was a harsh glitter of glass windows built into the structure of the rocks. "She's up there," I said. "We're on the wrong side. The stairs are behind it."

The Chapel of the Holy Cross was built by man, but it had been laid on the template of something that had been there for ages, maybe since the beginning of time. Standing here, I could see through this world and into the next, with Oversight, and the chapel took on huge, shadowy dimensions, filled with power and significance, pain and endurance.

"No time for the stairs," Venna said, and tried to take

our hands. Lewis and I both stepped back. She raised her eyebrows. "What?"

"No more of that," Lewis said. "We've pushed the odds too far already. You'd lose one of us this time."

"You say you need to go up there," she pointed out. "What would you like us to do?"

"Carry us," I said. "Get us to the top, but not through the aetheric. Can you do that?"

She considered it for a few seconds, locking eyes with David in silent communication, and then they both nodded.

"She's going to try to stop us," David said. "Whatever you do, don't let go."

He put his arms around me, holding me tight against him. I looked over at Lewis and Venna, and burst out laughing. It was ridiculous. He towered over her on approximately the same scale as the cliffs towering over all of us. What was she going to do, hug his knees?

Venna looked vexed, then she simply changed her body, growing, filling out into the size of an adult woman. She kept the pinafore and the blond hair, but when she'd finished, she was Lewis's height. "There," she said. "That should do."

"Talk about *one pill makes you larger . . . ,*" Lewis said, which even now, at the end of the world, made me smile.

Venna wasn't as amused. "Turn around."

David and I were face to face, but evidently Venna didn't feel that close to Lewis. He turned his back to her. She stepped up and fastened her arms around his waist, and without even a pause, she launched herself, and him, into the air. David followed. The shock of being airborne, without any real means of support or propulsion, made the less rational parts of my brain scream in panic, but David and Venna kept rising, steady and controlled, as the cliff's multicolored shadings flickered by in front of us.

"All right?" David asked me. My hair was blowing in the wind created by our passage, and I pulled it out of my face to nod. He looked grim and focused, probably anticipating the conversation we were about to have with our child. "Almost there."

Almost being, of course, not quite good enough. I'd noticed the height of the cliffs before we'd taken to the air, and we should have already been to the top. They weren't *that* tall. But now the cliffs seemed to be stretching themselves taller, and taller, and taller, and we kept rising on and on, racing to get to a point that continued to outpace us.

"Imara!" I yelled. "Imara, stop! Let us in, *please*!"

For a long few seconds, it seemed that she'd keep playing this game until the Djinn ran out of power and plummeted back to the canyon floor, miles below now . . . but she wasn't cruel, our daughter. Just pissed.

The cliffs stopped rising, and in a matter of seconds we were on the rocks. I tried not to look back at where we'd been. We were far, far too high for comfort.

There were no trails on this side of the chapel, so we had to scramble over ancient ledges and boulders to get to the peak, which rose up in a defiant jut of glass and a simple, elegant cross that buried itself into the rocks.

There was a kind of a path on the downslope that intersected with the stairs, and I led the way down it to the concrete steps.

This was how I'd always come here, up these steps.

This was where I'd seen my daughter die, and the memory still burned, both here and on the aetheric. My heart pounded harder as we ascended, heading for the entrance to the chapel at the top.

Venna stopped. "I have to wait here," she said. "I can feel it. You three have to go on."

I cast an uncertain look at David, who was holding

my hand. He nodded. "She's right," he said. "We have to go alone."

As we climbed the steps, Lewis said, "There was something you were going to tell me, back at the Luxor. Something about Jonathan."

"It's about how he died," David said. "I told you he died in battle, and that's true. What I didn't tell you is that we were losing. Our forces were being slaughtered; the plains were heaped with our dead and dying. Jonathan and his guards—I was one—were the only ones left."

We reached the top landing. The unnaturally occluded sun seemed to cast a shadow over all of us. Below, Venna stood watching with her glimmering blue eyes, and I realized she'd stopped in exactly the place where Imara's body had come to rest, broken, when she'd died.

"Jonathan reached out to the Mother," David said. "In fury, and rage, and desperation. He woke her up. That's why so many more died. He wanted to destroy everything, including himself. But instead, she . . . took him. Made him Djinn. That's how he died. I was already wounded, probably dying. He held on to me and dragged me through with him. But she consumed him, Lewis. Body and soul. She can't do anything else when she's drawn to a human. If you do this—"

Lewis was very still, listening to this, and I wished I understood what he was thinking. He was usually much easier to read, but now . . . now I didn't know. My skin was cold, and even though the air was still, I felt phantom winds blowing in this place. The aetheric was unsettled, on the verge of explosion.

"Before we go in," said Lewis, "I want to say something to both of you."

David cast a quick glance at me, frowning. "What is it?"

Lewis smiled. "I wanted to tell you that the best man won," he said. "I would have loved her, but you adore her. You make her better. You protect her, and honor her, and that makes me glad, David. Jealous as hell, but glad."

David said nothing. I didn't think he really knew what to say to that.

Lewis shifted his attention to me. "You were the only woman who ever really touched me," he said. "But I wouldn't have been good for you. And now we can leave all that behind."

It was good-bye, and it was final, and I felt the changes in him, in me, even in David.

David silently offered his hand. Lewis took it and shook. I stepped forward, and he kissed my cheek. With his lips close to my ear, he whispered, "You're pregnant, Jo. Tell me that doesn't make you happy."

I gasped and pulled back, staring into his face, suddenly overcome with shock. "I would know—," I said, and stopped, because I *did* know. I did. I felt it now, that tiny seed of life, still just a cluster of undifferentiated cells. David's baby, conceived on the ship. *Our* baby.

I looked at David, and I saw the knowledge in his face, too. The wonder. And a little bit of fear. I reached for his hand, and he almost broke mine with the force and fierceness of his grip.

I felt shaky and on the verge of tears, and I didn't even know why, really, except that there was a sense to all of this of endings. Maybe endings without new beginnings.

"Are we done?" I finally said, and forced a cocky smile. "Because there's world-saving to be done."

"Right," Lewis said. "There always is, isn't there? That part never changes. Hey, if it's a boy, name him after me, will you?"

"You don't have to do this," I said. "I could try—"

"No. There comes a time when you have to realize

that you can't save the world alone, Jo. You have to let someone else take a shot. And it's my turn."

I took a deep breath, forced a smile, took one last look at the blackened sun in the red sky, and opened the door of the chapel. We got on with it.

Chapter Twelve

Imara was standing at the front of the chapel, silhou-
etted by the giant sweep of windows that displayed the
eclipsed sun, the red sky, the dramatic drop of the canyons. It was the kind of view that would make anyone
religious, I'd always thought, but right now, all I could
see was my daughter, standing motionless in front of all
that glory, with sand whipping around her like a tornado.
Her black hair was lifting on an invisible wind, and her
eyes were just as dark, lid to lid, like a night sky flecked
with exploding stars. She was . . . terrifying.

And angry.

"Imara," David said, and walked down the aisle
toward her. "I'm sorry, but we had to come. You know
this place won't last much longer. You'll fall, and when
you do, you'll destroy. We can stop it, if you'll help us."

She laughed. It was a wretched, despairing sound,
and it lashed at our faces like slaps. I winced and wanted
to turn away; I hated seeing her like this, so alien and far
from the child I'd known. *All grown up*, some part of my

brain contributed helpfully. *Parents never do understand their children.*

"You're fools," she said. "I tried to stop you. I tried to tell you, it's *useless.* I don't want to see you hurt, don't you understand? I can't protect you!"

"We're not asking you to, sweetheart," I said. "Please. I know you can hear her. Open yourself up, and let us talk through you. I'm begging you, for the sake of the half of you that was once like me. *Please.*"

"Mom, it won't *help*, don't you get it? You think she doesn't know about humanity? About what it is, what it's done? This is the reckoning. We all told you it would come." Imara was crying, black tears like oil that marred her perfect, pale face. "If I open the connection, I can't shut it off. I'll be lost. We'll all be lost."

Out there, canyons trembled, and rocks shifted, and I saw part of the cliff face opposite shear away and fall to the rocks below. Her perfect sanctuary couldn't hold. *She* couldn't hold.

None of us could.

"Please," Lewis said, and stepped forward. Imara's black eyes focused on him, and I saw him falter, just a little, before he continued moving toward her. "Please let her see me."

"She'll destroy you," Imara said. "Don't you know that?"

"Yes," he said. "I know. It's the only chance we have. I'm willing to take that risk."

"It's not a risk. It's a certainty."

I took in a sharp breath, and David's grip on my hand tightened, warning me not to interfere. We'd done what we could, and now, Lewis had shouldered the burden.

As I'd known he would, from the beginning. This was what Lewis had been saving himself for all along—not his survival, but to be sure that his death counted for something important.

I'd thought, more than once, that he was a cold, manipulative bastard, and that was all true ... but *this* was true, too. He'd sacrificed others, but he'd done it because he knew, eventually, that he'd stand here, in this place, and be the only one who could change the world.

My heart was breaking to pieces, but I understood.

Imara took in a deep breath and closed her eyes. Behind her, the eclipsed sun exploded back into fiery, full life, burning brighter, brighter, until I had to shut my eyes and turn away from it.

When the light receded, I looked back, and met the eyes of Mother Earth.

They weren't white. They were all the colors of the sea swirling together, deep blue and warm turquoise and milky jade green. They were so beautiful. So peaceful.

So utterly merciless.

Her gaze held me, and I felt drowned in a vast, astonishing warmth. But it wasn't acceptance. Everything in me was being emptied out, examined, and found wanting.

The warmth abruptly cut off, and I sank down to my knees, sobbing with longing to feel that again, *be* that again. I thought I'd touched her consciousness before, but it had been nothing like this, this—*power.* I'd never felt anything like it, and I knew that, like the screams of the Djinn, I'd never be able to *not* feel it, on some level. She had taken me, marked me, and discarded me.

Next to me, David slowly, gracefully, bent one knee, and I saw him stare fearlessly into her eyes. Imara's face took on a hint of a smile, and I felt the echoes of the warmth that cascaded into him, through him, waves of ecstasy that burned even as removed as I was from the experience. Only a Djinn could have withstood that, and even David finally bowed his head, trembling and shaking.

She fastened that deadly, warm, perfect gaze on Lewis,

and I heard him let out a sound that was something between a sigh and a moan. His body went rigid, head
thrown back, and light streamed from him in golden
flickers and flows, cascading into Imara.

Into the Earth.

"No," he said hoarsely, and with a huge effort, he
stopped. He denied her.

I couldn't imagine how that was possible, but he *did
it*. He advanced toward her, until they were no more
than a foot apart, and Lewis said, "You can't have me.
Not like this. Not if you destroy my people."

The sea-blue eyes slowly blinked. "Your people chose
this," she said, and her voice was vast and bell-like, and
the windows behind Imara shattered in a hail of glittering shards that fell away into the canyon. Wind whipped
in, and I saw storms forming, black and furious. More of
the canyon cliffs opposite fell away as the land rocked
and shifted. The wooden pews in the chapel burst into
white-hot flame and burned to ashes in seconds. "They
were warned."

Lewis was shaking now, and he fell to his knees in
front of her, but his fists were clenched. "No," he gritted
out. "Let them live. Let us live. You owe me this."

She laughed, and it was the harsh, ripping sound of
claws, the whisper of feathers, the roar of lions. I was
terrified, and so small, so very small before the power
in this room.

The power that Lewis still resisted.

"I owe you *nothing*," the Mother said. "You owe me
everything. And I will have it in payment for pain."

"That's what you want!" Lewis shouted, and somehow his voice rang louder here, in this place, than hers.
"But I know what you need!"

I had no idea how he could be doing this, *talking* to
her—Imara was the only one who could have made that
connection, amplified his voice to a level where it could

be heard and understood by something as enormous as Mother Earth. Only Imara could have enough humanity left in her to bridge that gap. The other Oracles couldn't; even the Djinn couldn't, without being destroyed.

My daughter's birth, her death, her raising as an Oracle—all of it was a plan. A plan so vast, so complex and I could only now see glimmers of it, and the beauty and tragedy of it choked me with tears. This wasn't the Mother's plan.

This was something greater, and more astonishing, and just for a moment, I glimpsed the hand of God.

"Then what do I need?" the Mother hissed, and I heard a multitude of snakes, felt the burn of venom in my arm again.

Lewis didn't hesitate, and I have no idea how much courage it took, how much fear he had to overcome.

He stepped *into* her, kissing-close, and said, "You need me."

For the first time, I felt Lewis unleash the full range of his Earth powers, and my *God*, it was like nothing I'd ever felt before, from any Warden. It was pure, animal seduction, and it came from a place in him that I'd never known existed. He wasn't surrendering to her. He was *seducing* her. I felt the overwhelming heat of it wash over me as a reflection, an echo, and I swayed on my knees and almost went down.

This was what made Lewis unique among Wardens. This was why he'd been born in this age, so that he could stand here at this time, and do something no other human on Earth could do.

Remind the Earth that nature was more than tooth and claw, death and pain.

"Hear me," Lewis said, his lips hovering just a fraction above hers, his body radiating that passion. "We are part of you. Part of everything. Hear me."

He was swaying a little, side to side, and she swayed

with him. It was a slow, hypnotic dance, and the sand whirling around my daughter's body slowed its angry rotation, slipping and falling in a red rain to pool around her bare feet.

"I hear you," she said, and it was Imara's voice, my voice, the Mother's voice, the echo of millions. And there was a kind of drugged wonder in it. "*I hear you.*"

"Then feel me," Lewis said, and kissed her.

The light that exploded from them should have burned us alive, it was so purely white. Even with my eyes shut, my arms blocking the glare, I could see the two of them standing there together, swaying, merging, dancing.

David let out a sharp cry and got to his feet—not a cry of alarm, but one of triumph, of joy, of absolute *relief.* And all around him formed Djinn, the Djinn I had known, the ones I had never known, the ones who'd been my mortal enemies. Venna came, and Rahel, dozens more, and more, and more until the chapel was full. Their eyes were burning not with white, but with a pure gold.

The light slowly died at the front of the chapel, and Imara and Lewis collapsed to the floor. She lay in a pale heap, hair covering her face, and as I watched the sand slip back over her in a whispering blanket, I knew she was still alive. Still an Oracle.

She opened her eyes, and sat up, staring down at herself—and at Lewis.

He wasn't moving.

I saw the grief move over her face, and she reached down and put her fingers on his cheek, very gently. She looked up at me, and I knew instantly that Lewis . . . Lewis was gone. The flesh that lay there was empty, the soul taken.

"No," I whispered, and all the barriers inside me broke. I'd witnessed something that had never been seen by any human before—none who'd ever lived—and it had been shocking and moving and terrifying, but in the end, all I could feel was that I'd lost him. I'd lost Lewis.

Imara straightened his body, folded his arms, and stood over him. She looked out at the Djinn and said, "You're here to bear witness. Say his name."

"Lewis," said a thunderous chorus of Djinn voices. "Lewis. Lewis."

And a shining being misted into existence, more beautiful than anything I'd ever imagined. Angels would weep to see him now, and it wasn't for several long heartbeats that I recognized his face, his body. It was Lewis, perfected, the way David had been perfected.

But Djinn Lewis shone with so much power that it couldn't be contained in him. The aetheric caught fire around him, and it was a white blaze of joy.

Every single Djinn—New Djinn, Old—all of them went to their knees.

I went, too, more because I didn't want to be the only one standing. David's face was blank, his eyes very bright, as he said, "He's the Conduit. All of us, together again. One people, not two."

Lewis had replaced Jonathan, in ways that David and Ashan could not.

I slowly stood up again, and Lewis's attention fixed on me. His smile hadn't changed at all, really.

"Hey," I said. "So—about humanity—"

"Through me, she understands," Lewis told me. His voice made me shiver, because it was like him and yet somehow . . . not. The seductive power he'd unleashed was still putting raw edges on him. "The human race will survive. Better get your act together, though. It's a limited time offer."

I nodded, not sure what to say to him anymore. David stood up next to me, and slowly, one by one, the Djinn rose.

"Right," Lewis said. "The Djinn will help clear the damages, heal the sick and injured, rebuild alongside you. We're partners now. The way we should have been."

I cleared my throat. "And the Wardens?"

"Going to take a lot of work to bring them back," Lewis said. His smile grew brighter. "I can't think of anyone I trust more to make that happen, Jo. You, and your son."

Son. I put a hand over my stomach as my lips parted.

Lewis waved his hand, and the glass windows of the chapel filled in again. The Djinn had to shuffle around as wooden pews replaced piles of ashes. Creation, at the snap of his fingers.

"Is she still awake?" I asked.

"For now," he said. "She'll sleep soon. But I think you'll find things much easier now."

The Djinn were disappearing now, heading off to their newly appointed tasks. Outside the window, the sky was a pure, perfect blue, with a few light clouds drifting high. A bald eagle swooped low, so close its wings almost brushed the glass, and I wondered if it was the same one we'd left wrapped in Cassiel's coat in Las Vegas.

I watched it soar away. When I looked back down, Djinn Lewis was gone, and his silent, empty shell was all that was left.

David took my hand. "Time to go," he said.

I took in a deep breath. "What about—"

Imara gave me a smile, and looked down. Lewis's body sank into the floor, into the stone beneath. I saw the fading whisper of it moving deep, deep into the Earth.

Gone.

"Good journey, Mom," Imara said, and whispered into shadows and sand.

Behind us, the door of the chapel opened, and the priest blinked at us in surprise. "Oh, hello," he said. "The chapel isn't officially open yet, but if you'd like to come back—"

"Yes," David said. "We'll come back. But we have things to do."

We walked out, into bright sunlight, and descended the steps. I had no idea what we'd do when we got to the bottom—no car, no transportation of any kind. I didn't really feel like taking a bus.

"Things to do," I repeated. "We'll go get the rebuilding started, round up the Wardens, recover the Djinn bottles and smash them. After that, though, it's three days of spa, mud baths, and all-day massages. Anything I'm forgetting?"

"Shopping," David said, straight-faced. "And a bedroom with a locked door."

"Mmmm, I said. Joy gurgled up in me like bubbles, and I found I was poised on the edge of giggles. "Can we move that to first on the list?"

"Probably not." He smiled, and stopped on the steps to kiss me with all the passion and sweetness I could ever want. "That's an installment."

"I'd like to give you something on credit, too, but it's a public space. And a church."

He laughed, and we skipped down the rest of the steps to the parking lot.

Sitting in the middle of the lot was a black 1970 Mustang Boss 429, gleaming like new. I stopped and threw David a questioning look. He tossed me the keys.

Next stop, Las Vegas.

And the world, beyond.

Epilogue

"Mo-o-om!"

I was in the middle of a pile of paperwork and a simultaneous conference call with Warden HQ, which had already gone on for two hours and was likely to go on for two more. I counted to ten, silently, and hit the mute button on my phone just as someone, of course, asked me for my opinion. Ah well. I always told them family came first. "What is it?" I called, with extreme patience.

"I need you!"

"Do you need me *right now*?"

"Well—yeah, kind of!"

That was when I smelled something burning, and the smoke alarms went off at the back of the house. I jumped up, scattering papers in a summertime paper blizzard as I dashed toward my son.

He was standing in the doorway saying, "Mom, I didn't mean to; it wasn't my fault. . . ."

"Lewis Kevin Prince, get *out of my way*!"

He knew that tone, at least, and, head down, shuffled aside so I could see the *freaking bonfire* that was raging in the corner of his room. Those curtains were *toast*.

Again.

I called up my mad Fire skills and snuffed it out with only a little puff of smoke. It was worse than I'd thought—carpet melted into a toxic cesspool in the corner, the paint done for, the aforementioned curtains gone from white to charred rags. It could have been worse. At least this time, he'd kept it away from the closet, the computer, the game system, and his huge rack of books.

Our son was eight years old, and nobody in the entire history of the Wardens had shown this kind of crazy potential at this age. Potential for destruction, sure, but not with such an impressive amount of firepower. Literally.

I looked at the damage, sighed, and said, "Lewis, I'm going to have to get your dad for this."

He looked so gleeful for a second that I wondered if that had been his plan all along. Dad, home, with us. If it was, he was smart enough to look immediately angelic. Not hard for him—he was a gorgeous kid, with floppy straight dark hair and big blue eyes. He had his father's features, though. In the pictures I had hanging up around the house, there was no doubt at all as to his parentage.

I really don't know where he got the stubbornness from, though. And the wild streak.

The front door slammed open, and a cheery voice yelled out, "Get some clothes on, you, you hippies!" Cherise. Good thing I'd put the conference call on mute. Yikes, that would have greatly enhanced my standing in the Warden executive offices. "Hey, are you burning a roast again? You really suck at this housekeeping thing, you know. Good thing I brought pizza and Bellinis."

Only in Cherise's world did that combination make sense. I loved Cherise's world.

"Aunt Cher!" Lewis quickly abandoned the disaster of his bedroom and pelted out toward the living room. "Did you bring it? Did you?"

I followed him, because standing there in contemplation of the wreckage was just not helping. Cherise wasn't alone; holding the pizza box was Tommy, whose shy smile always delighted me—like Lewis, he'd grown up to be a beautiful boy, and with far better manners (from Cherise! Who knew?). Lewis ran up to him and took the pizza, which made Tommy frown a little in anxiety and trail him toward the kitchen. "Don't eat any yet!" I heard Tommy say sternly. "We need to wait for our moms!"

I could just imagine what Lewis would say to that. "Lewis, listen to Tommy!"

Yeah, right. Poor Tommy.

Cherise put her purse down—Prada, very nice—and added her designer sunglasses to the pile. She looked summer-hot, and life was definitely being good to her these days. She'd started up a personal stylist business, and was now all the rage among the Miami elite, with a rising number of Hollywood clients as well. "So," she said. "I'm assuming the fire's out?"

"Don't worry, you won't smudge anything."

"Damn straight." She flopped on the couch, put her sandaled feet up on the coffee table, and folded her hands over her trim stomach, which the sundress left bare. "You're not bailing on us, are you?"

I flopped down next to her and stretched out my legs. Mine were longer and better toned, thanks to running around after my hyperactive hamster of a son. Cherise's had a better tan. "I have a conference call."

"When?"

I gestured vaguely toward the open door of the office, where people were still mumbling on the phone line without me. "Forever, apparently."

"Come on, it's a holiday! You work every holiday. Be a do-bee, not a don't-bee."

"I've got beer in the fridge, don't I?"

"You could be drinking that beer *at the beach*. Followed by a really swell dinner with your friends. I'm here to make sure you go."

I sighed. It was Memorial Day, and Memorial Day had a special meaning now for the Wardens. We didn't officially have ceremonies—hadn't since the first year—but all of us thought of Memorial Day as the day we honored our fallen friends and comrades. And we gathered, wherever we were, to break bread together and just . . . be glad we were still alive.

Over the past eight years, a lot had changed. The destruction wrought during Mother Earth's brief, angry wakening had changed the face of a lot of communities around the world . . . and utterly obliterated a few. From the ashes, people rebuilt, and they rebuilt well. The remaining Wardens had helped, too. Finally, eight years out, the trauma was starting to lessen, but it would never really fade. Not for any of us.

I made a decision, and popped my head in the kitchen. As usual, Lewis had persuaded Tommy that they didn't *really* need to wait for permission to start on the pizza. I shook my head and said, "Go ahead, boys. Eat up. It just means you can't go swimming for thirty minutes."

"Mom!" Lewis promptly said, and looked very disappointed. "That's not even true. It doesn't matter if you eat."

"It's true today, buster, because you've had half the pizza in about five minutes and you need to stop. Now go get your beach stuff."

He and Tommy dashed off toward Lewis's bedroom,

still clutching their last pieces of pizza. I sighed and closed up the box and put it away in the fridge, retrieved a six-pack of bottled beer, and added it to my always-ready beach bag.

Then I went into the office, unmuted the call, and said, "Ladies and gentlemen, can I have your attention?"

The voices fell silent. Twenty Wardens, all waiting for me to say something profound.

"Go enjoy your holiday," I said. "We'll pick this back up tomorrow. It can wait."

Nobody argued. There was noticeably more good cheer in their voices as they signed off.

Cherise had brought her car—a sedan, *not* a Mommy-van; even if she eventually had a dozen kids, I didn't think she'd ever go to that extreme. It was a brand-new Ergani, the sleek electric one, and she seemed to like it. I missed the feel of the engine, but I had to admit that hers was more planet-friendly.

We spent a few blissful hours at the beach, sipping our beer and watching our kids play. As the sun began to sink toward the western horizon, we packed up, whistled for Lewis and Tommy to drop whatever arcane thing they were doing with shells and sticks, and piled back into the car, tired and happy.

Cherise drove us to the restaurant where we always seemed to congregate for these types of events: Fuego. It was full to capacity in the dining room, with benches of people sitting outside admiring the sunset and waiting for tables, but Cherise strolled right up to the desk and said, "Warden party."

"Right this way," said the flawlessly decked-out greeter, and led us past all the mildly resentful people to a private dining room along the side of the building.

It was already full, which confused me—I'd just been on a long-distance conference call with most of these people, and yet here they were, in Miami. Marion Bearheart in particular looked smug. She was sitting near the end of the table in her gleaming wheelchair, resplendent in black leather and Navajo turquoise. She inclined her silver and black head toward me—more silver than black, these days—and smiled a warm welcome at all of us.

Other friends were at the table, too. Peter, the new head of Weather operations; Anjali, who was over Fire; Carl, fresh from getting his hands dirty with Earth powers; a few others, too.

"How . . . ?"

"We had help," Marion said, and nodded farther down the table, where a very small blond girl sat kicking her feet in a chair too big for her. Venna inclined her head gravely. On the other side of the table, so did Rahel, with an absolutely enigmatic smile that still managed to be terrifying.

And at the end of the table, standing, was David.

Lewis ran to him immediately, and David whirled him around and picked him up in a close embrace, then immediately let him slide down when Lewis started to wiggle. I didn't go to him immediately; I loved seeing the two of them together.

Cherise shoved me from behind, pointedly. "Well, go on, jump the hottie, or I'm all over *that*!"

"Mom!" Tommy protested. "That's disgusting."

"I know, kiddo." She kissed the top of his head and shooed him off to join Lewis in picking out seats where they could cause the most mayhem possible. David reseated them next to him, which was very smart.

I walked over to my husband, no longer leader of the Djinn, and stepped into his warm, sweet embrace. I rested my head against his neck, touched my lips to his ear, and whispered, "Thank you."

"You're welcome," he said. "Lewis says hello. He's

renovating Jonathan's house. I think he likes the challenge."

I had to laugh. Lewis *would* like trying to knock out walls in an eternal structure. Maybe he'd manage to put some paint down, though.

"Hungry?" he asked me.

"Starving," I whispered back. "Let's go home and do something about that. A whole lot."

"Later," he laughed, and did terribly provocative things just by drawing his fingers lazily up my back. I shivered in total delight. "I promise you, you'll get your fill."

"And you?"

"Never," he said, and tipped my chin up so I could meet his eyes. "You know that. Now stop flirting and sit."

As if it had been *my* fault. Hardly.

The servers were already circulating, putting out trays of appetizers and pouring wine and other drinks, and we were all sitting down together, human and Djinn. It hadn't seemed possible, just a few years ago; some of the Djinn had wanted me dead for bringing back the ability of humans to claim them.

Lewis had simply broken the ability. No more claiming. And now, no more reason for us to hate—other than the normal reasons people always seemed to come up with.

Sitting down to a meal with them still felt . . . groundbreaking, somehow.

I kicked it off by picking up the glass the server filled up with red next to me, lifted it, and said, "To Lewis."

Everyone looked up, and one by one, they lifted their glasses in response, and drank.

"To humans," Venna said, when I was about to sit down. I looked up, startled, to find her smiling. "You may learn something yet."

With my hand in David's, I looked around, and I couldn't help but think we already had.

There was always tomorrow to worry about, but for now, I was focusing on tonight. And so I lifted my glass, inclined my head, and toasted the human race—flawed, fallible, crazy, and wrongheaded as it usually was.

We all did. Just this once.

Sound Track

Songs and inspiration and stuff! Please support the artists by buying the music—otherwise, they might have to stop making it. And we don't want that.

"The A.B.C. of L.O.V.E" .... Pravda
"Life Changes" .... Rose Smith
"Angel of Desire" .... Autumn
"The World" .... Earlimart
"Weathervane" .... Shannon McNally
"Awaken" .... Bulletproof Messenger
"Step Into the Future" Scott Fisher and 1 a.m. approach
"Addicted2Me" .... Anjulie
"See Line Woman" .... Ollabelle
"Magic Tree" .... Kirsten Price
"Driving Down Alvarado" .... Annie McCue
"Gone Away" .... Funky Nashville
"On Fire" .... JJ Grey & Mofro
"I'm Good, I'm Gone" .... Lykke Li
"Disappearing" .... Simon Collins
"Lonely Ghosts" .... O+S
"Mama Told Me (Not to Come)" .... Three Dog Night
"2080" .... Yeasayer
"Ain't No Rest for the Wicked" .... Cage the Elephant
"Nothing Left to Lose" .... Deepfield
"Heads Will Roll" .... Yeah Yeah Yeahs
"The Great Divide" .... Wolfkin
"Red Red Rain" .... Javelinas
"Uprising" .... Muse
"The Cut" .... Nathan Hamilton

"April Fools and Eggmen"...................... Fair to Midland
"I Know What I Am" .... Band of Skulls
"Change in Weather" .... Aimee Allen
"Clubbed to Death" .... Rob Duggan
"Remains" ....Maurissa Tancharoen & Jed Whedon
"The Grey Robe of the Rain"...........The Stone Coyotes
"Bad Romance"...Lady GaGa
"On the Corner" .... Sarah Borges
"Will It Go Round in Circles"..................... Billy Preston
"Hotblack".. Oceanship
"Torn Asunder"...................................The Stone Coyotes
"This Is War" ....30 Seconds to Mars
"New Fang" ....Them Crooked Vultures
"The High Road"...Broken Bells
"Burning Hell"...Joe Bonamassa
"Feels Like the End"..............................Shane Alexander

The brand-new series from

RACHEL CAINE

THE OUTCAST SEASON NOVELS

Undone

Once she was Cassiel, a Djinn of limitless power. Now, she has been reshaped in human flesh as punishment for defying her master—and must live among the Weather Wardens, whose power she must tap into regularly or she will die. And as she copes with the emotions and frailties of her human condition, a malevolent entity threatens her new existence...

Unknown

Living among mortals, the djinn Cassiel has developed a reluctant affection for them—especially for Warden Luis Rocha. As the mystery deepens around the kidnapping of innocent Warden children, Cassiel and Luis are the only ones who can investigate both the human and djinn realms. But the trail will lead them to a traitor who may be more powerful than they can handle.

Available wherever books are sold or at penguin.com

R0044

Welcome to Morganville, Texas.
Just don't stay out after dark.

The *New York Times* bestselling Morganville Vampires series
by Rachel Caine

College freshman Claire Danvers has her share of challenges—like being a genius in a school that favors beauty over brains, battling homicidal girls in her dorm, and finding out that her college town is overrun with the living dead.

Glass Houses
The Dead Girls' Dance
Midnight Alley
Feast of Fools
Lord of Misrule
Carpe Corpus
Fade Out
Kiss of Death

rachelcaine.com

Available wherever books are sold or at
penguin.com

THE ULTIMATE IN
SCIENCE FICTION AND FANTASY!

From magical tales of distant worlds to stories of
technological advances beyond the grasp of man, Penguin has
everything you need to stretch your imagination to its limits.

penguin.com

ACE
Get the latest information on favorites like
William Gibson, T.A. Barron, Brian Jacques,
Ursula K. Le Guin, Sharon Shinn, Charlaine Harris,
Patricia Briggs, and Marjorie M. Liu,
as well as updates on the best new authors.

ROC
Escape with Jim Butcher, Harry Turtledove, Anne Bishop,
S.M. Stirling, Simon R. Green, E.E. Knight, Kat Richardson,
Rachel Caine, and many others—plus news on the
latest and hottest in science fiction and fantasy.

DAW
Patrick Rothfuss, Mercedes Lackey, Kristen Britain,
Tanya Huff, Tad Williams, C.J. Cherryh, and many more—
DAW has something to satisfy the cravings of any
science fiction and fantasy lover.
Also visit dawbooks.com.

*Get the best of science fiction and fantasy
at your fingertips!*